MW00650492

ASHES

A DARK ASYLUM ROMANCE

THE BOYS OF CHAPEL CREST

K.G. REUSS

BOOK TWO

Books From Beyond

Cover Design: Moonstruck Cover Design & Photography, moonstruckcoverdesign.com

To all my screamers.

FOREWORD

Dear Reader

Please be aware Church: The Boys of Chapel Crest is book one in this series and must be read before Ashes. For an even better experience, I recommend reading it in this order:

Church

Bells

Ashes

Stitches

Sinful

Shadow

Asylum

Please know this series is loaded with triggers. Read responsibly. Triggers can be found in the pinned section in my group on Facebook: K.G. Reuss's Renegade Readers.

Happy screaming

-K

PROLOGUE

ASYLUM

I watched as she walked across the commons, her black braid hanging to her waist, her eyes downcast. Her skirt was shorter than I'd like because it made all the creeps stare. I didn't like people looking at her.

Beautiful. Perfect. Rinny. Our Rinny. Look at me. FUCKING LOOK AT ME.

I gave my head a slight shake and breathed out, hoping to quiet the noise inside.

When the sounds lessened, I stepped out of the shadows and followed her, taking note of every motherfucker looking at her. Cataloging their names. Their expressions. The words falling from their lips they didn't think I could make out. I didn't need to hear the words to know what they were saying about her.

But I was good like that. Knowing things no one else did. I called it my superpower, if monsters like me possessed such things.

She rounded the science building, unaware I was following her. I was always following her. To classes. To her dorm. To the fucking watchers' house. I made it my business to invade every facet of her life, whether she knew it or not. I was sure I still haunted her dreams even after all these years.

She was supposed to be dead. Safe. Far away from any fucker who could harm her. She was our Rinny. My forever girl. My everything. I was supposed to meet her in the afterlife after I'd killed all the wicked. We were meant to kiss and make love and dance on moonbeams together. Forever.

It was strange how I'd become what I hunted.

Life had been going well for me. Then she came back from the dead.

To torment me with my sins.

She stopped walking to wait for Bryce Andrews. Her face was expressionless to those who didn't know her, but I knew her. I knew everything about my forever girl.

She cared for Bryce. It was in her eyes. Always her pretty eyes. It was where she hid her secrets. I always knew to look at her eyes if I wanted the truth from her without her saying a word.

It was there the day I'd tried to lead her to heaven.

She'd loved me too. She'd also feared me.

Ah, fear. More powerful than love it would seem because now my forever girl only lived in fear because of me.

I didn't like that.

But I also loved it.

I watched as Bryce grinned at her. Spoke to her. Touched her.

I breathed in and out slowly, watching.

She never saw me unless I wanted her to see me.

Even when she slumbered, and I stood over her bed in the darkness.

Dante Church was making my life difficult though. He also watched her. I had to be careful because he was just as good as me.

Fucking watcher.

I knew her demons though. They played with mine. A game we'd been part of since our souls had collided all those long years ago.

Our Rinny.

My greatest failure.

My greatest weakness.

My greatest love.

I didn't follow her this time. I had work to do. Someone touched my forever girl. Someone she didn't want to touch her.

Danny Linley.

And Danny Linley needed to pay.

†

I DIDN'T TYPICALLY ENJOY KILLING.

The kill wasn't where my triumph lay. Not even close. In fact, I found the entire act of death to be bittersweet and sad. Disappointing, really.

It was in the torture and fear where my pleasure was. In the screams. Because there were worse things than death. Carving out an eye. Tearing fingernails from fingers, one by one. Forcing them to watch as I sliced deep into their flesh.

Their fear. Fuck, I loved the fear.

Ah, fuck. Glorious.

Screams. Screams were the cherry on top of a big fucking sundae of agony.

And Danny Linley could scream.

"P-please. P-p-please. I-I'm s-s-sorry," he choked out as I cocked my head and stared down at him on his bathroom floor, which was covered in blood and piss. His hands and feet were bound. For a large guy, he was easy enough to subdue.

"What are you sorry for?" I tilted my head in the other direction as I surveyed him.

He knows what he's sorry for.

I know.

Don't let him lie. Don't kill him either.

I'll let her see her trophy. She needs to see my love. I have so much to prove to her. To our Rinny. My firefly. She needs to know.

"F-for t-t-touching S-S-Sire—"

"Ah, ah, ah," I tsked, running my blade along his tear soaked cheek. "What did I say she is?"

"F-forever girl. Y-your f-f-fore-ever g-girl."

"And what does that mean?" I pressed, my knife traveling gently down his neck.

His Adam's apple bobbed in his throat.

"I-I don't d-don't k-know." He wept.

I sighed, kneeling beside him. "It means, she belongs to me. She's mine. Forever. Simple really. Right?"

He nodded, snot dripping from his nose.

I raked my gaze over him.

"A-are y-you going to k-kill me?"

"Should I? I don't like to kill people, Danny. I really don't." I pulled my knife away from him and sat back onto my ass to watch him.

He trembled on the cold tile. He was still black and blue from Stitches beating the shit out of him.

Truth be told, I'd enjoyed watching that. Stitches was truly glorious when he let go.

"I don't w-wanna die."

"Hmm." I nodded. "Interesting since you signed your own death warrant with our Rinny."

"I-I didn't know. I lost c-control. I s-swear. I'm so s-s-sorry, Asylum. I-I'll d-do what-whatever you want me to do. J-just please. Let me g-go."

"Well, that's the problem. You can't touch my forever girl and then think you won't be punished for it."

"A-Andrews touches her. The w-watchers touch her—"

"She wants them to, though," I snapped, hating the truth, but knowing it nonetheless. I'd seen. I knew.

Danny sobbed softly on the floor.

"I won't kill you," I said, coming to a decision.

He looked at me with hopeful eyes.

"No." I moved and straddled his body. "I'm just going to make you hurt really, really bad. Then you won't forget the rules. And what are the rules?"

"I-I don't touch your fore-forever g-girl."

"Correct. What else?"

He stared up at me with wild eyes.

I sighed. "The answer is you promise to scream even though no one can hear you. You fucking promise to remember who you're fucking with. The rules are you don't forget who the fuck I am or my mercy. That part is important." I leaned in to whisper in his ear. "I am merciful."

He struggled weakly beneath me and opened his mouth to scream. I was fast though and stuffed his wadded-up sock into his mouth before I began to hum our song, my knife carving all sorts of pretty, intricate, deep lines into his quaking body like my blade had a mind of its own.

But we all knew who was in control.

Me. Always me.

And Danny Linley wouldn't soon forget it.

It was amazing what I was willing to do all in the name of love.

And obsession.

But my forever girl deserved it all, and I'd make sure she got it.

Starting with Danny-fucking-Linley.

ASHES

My chest ached. My head pounded.

"Relax," Stitches said thickly, his leg bouncing as he sat next to me in the waiting room of the medical wing. "She's OK. Angel is OK. She's OK," he whispered on repeat, his head in his hands.

I knew his words were more for his benefit than mine.

She wasn't OK. We all knew she wasn't.

The image of pulling her limp body out of that cement tomb inside the mausoleum would haunt me until my dying day.

And her voice as she had screamed for Church on repeat. Him, hauling her into his arms, rocking her, weeping as he had tried to calm her trembling body.

But she was gone. Wild. Unhinged.

My heart had broken as her screams for Church had turned into a soft, shaky hum of a song I hadn't recognized.

Church's words as he had held her in his arms. *"He broke her. He broke my specter. Fuck, baby. Come back to me."*

I'd never seen Church cry before. Not even when his mom had died.

We all had realized she was too far gone. She'd gone stiff and silent after that. Like a pretty stone statue as Church had begged her to look at him.

Nothing. There had been nothing left inside her.

Seth Cain had won.

But what did he win when she was just a shell now?

Seth had fallen to his knees in front of Church, whispering frantically to her. Clinging to her hand. Trying to take her from Church before Stitches had snapped out of his heartache and had punched him in the face over and over.

It had taken me coming to in order to stop Stitches from killing him.

We'd brought her straight here to the medical wing. And that was where we'd been for the last three hours.

Church was inside with her. Sin was nowhere to be found. He still wasn't answering calls or texts. I was beginning to worry about him too.

I didn't know where the hell Seth was. I didn't give a shit either. As long as he was far away from me was all that mattered now. I was barely keeping myself together.

"What's going on?" I immediately got to my feet as Church came toward us.

Stitches looked up with bloodshot eyes.

"They've called her family. They're on the way." He breathed out, his body shaking. "It's not good. She's. . . not here right now. Her mind. The doctor thinks she's catatonic. They have her in bed and medicated. They're doing some other shit to her. Testing and whatever. S-she won't even look at me. Her eyes. . ." His voice cracked.

"Fuck," Stitches choked out, tugging at his hair as he rocked in his seat. "Fuck!"

I closed my eyes briefly. *This couldn't be happening! We'd just gotten everything sorted with her. She was getting better. Fucking Seth Cain. . .*

"Headmaster Sully has Asylum here," Church said, drawing in a calming breath, as if reading my mind. "I told them about how we found them locked together in that fucking coffin. He questioned him, and they're keeping him here for observation tonight. Fucking prick is going to pay."

"He won," Stitches said softly. "She screamed for him."

Church's body vibrated with rage. "She screamed for *me*."

I didn't want to argue about it right now. If she didn't get better, it wouldn't fucking matter who she'd screamed for.

"We need to find Sin, and Stitches needs to sleep," I said, taking in my friend as he continued to rock.

He was barely holding on. We couldn't let him spiral. He'd only just gotten better.

"I don't want to leave her," Church said, his voice rough.

"We need to sleep. They know to contact us," I said, knowing damn well everyone needed to rest. We were running on fumes. When Church couldn't find her tonight, we'd rushed around, searching for her for hours.

Even Bryce got punched in the face when Church lost it after a two-hour search for her had ended in nothing.

And fucking Sin wasn't answering his phone.

"I'm not leaving. I already told Sully. I told the fucking staff. I'm staying. Take care of Stitches and get some rest. I'll let you guys know if anything changes."

He didn't wait for an answer. He pivoted and stormed back the way he'd come.

Sighing, I looked at Stitches. He rubbed his eyes.

"You need to rest. You haven't taken your meds."

"Fuck the meds. They won't fix what's wrong," he said, his voice hoarse.

"We don't need anything else shitty happening. We need to be strong for her right now. When she comes back to us, she'll need us to be ready. OK?"

He didn't move from his seat. I thought I was going to have to get physical with him, but he finally rose and pushed past me without a word.

I followed him out, my guts tight and worry thrumming through my veins.

†

SLEEP EVADED ME. I lay in bed staring at my ceiling, Sirena on my mind. A tear worked its way out, and I hastily swiped it away. I wasn't sure what went down in that mausoleum, but I wouldn't rest until I found out. There was no way she'd go with Seth willingly. Her fear over him was evident. I'd seen it.

When the sun rose, I got up and showered then went downstairs to check on Stitches. He was shirtless and sprawled out in his bed, sleeping soundly. Judging by the state of his twisted sheets, I'd say he'd struggled to get to that point.

Quietly, I closed his door and went to the kitchen to make something to eat, deciding I'd try Sin again since I knew he wasn't home because his shoes weren't at the door where he always left them.

My thumb was just over his name when the front door opened, and he trudged in, looking like he'd been drinking.

"Where were you?" I demanded.

He shuffled past me without a word and sank onto the couch.

"The fuck, man? We've been trying to reach you since last night. Where the hell were you?" I glared down at him.

"Drunk. High." He scrubbed his hand over his face.

"Sirena was hurt."

He nodded wordlessly.

"She's in the medical ward. We found her and Asylum locked together in the mausoleum. Stitches almost killed Asylum last night. And Church... isn't fucking well."

Again, Sin nodded wordlessly.

"Don't you have anything to fucking say?"

He breathed out. "Is...is she OK?"

I unclenched my fists and pulled my lighter out. I sat down and flicked it opened and closed five times as I tried to control my emotions.

Sin peered over at me as I breathed in and out.

"She's not OK," I finally said.

"What's wrong with her?" his voice was soft.

"She's lost her mind," I whispered, flicking the lighter opened and closed five more times. Stop. Again. Five times. Faster. Fuck, I was going nuts thinking about her terrified in that box.

"What do you mean?"

I glared at a fixed point on the wall. "She screamed for Church. It's how we found her. She screamed and screamed. It was the last place we looked for her. It took us forever to get inside because the door was locked. By the time we got the lid off and Church pulled her out, she was. . . gone. She was humming. Then she went stiff and hasn't reacted since." The words were hard to choke out.

"Seth won?" Sin asked softly.

I nodded.

"Where's Church?"

"He won't leave her side. He held her. I watched him beg her to come back to him. He fucking cried." I turned to Sin finally. "Church never begs or cries. If she doesn't come back, we're going to lose him and Stitches."

Sin's Adam's apple bobbed in his throat as he swallowed. "It doesn't matter. She's Seth's problem now."

I scowled at him. "You're a real prick."

He nodded. "I know."

"You know what. We needed you last night. I don't know why you ran off or what the fuck you were really doing, but fuck you, Sinclair. You know what she means to us—"

"And I fucking told you assholes not to get attached!" he bellowed, getting up. "*I fucking told you.* No one wanted to listen! Now look! I said it was dangerous getting close to her. I said she'd fucking break us, and I was right! Seth won. Let. It. Fucking. *Go*, Asher. Please. Let her go."

"She'd break *you*." I snarled, rising and facing him down, pissed off he refused to feel anything. "You're so fucking scared of getting hurt that you're hurting your own damn feelings. If anyone is going to break us apart, it's you!"

He glared at me, a muscle popping along his jaw.

"What the hell is going on?" Stitches demanded, staggering into the room, his shirt off and his sweatpants hanging low.

The long scar along his torso seemed more prominent today. Redder. Angrier.

"This prick came home," I snapped.

"Where were you?" Stitches demanded, shoving him.

Sin staggered back and caught himself on the edge of the couch.

"I said, where the fuck were you, Sinclair?" Stitches pushed him in the chest again.

Sin shoved back, fury on his face. "I was fucking out. Past that, it's none of your goddamn business, Malachi."

"We needed you. *Angel* needed you. You fucking bailed on us."

"I'm not doing this. I already told Ashes you guys were looking for trouble with her. This is what I was talking about. Walk the fuck away from her. It's over. Ashes said she screamed for Seth. She's his. Not yours. Not Ashes's. Not fucking Church's. We aren't good for her. She's not good for us. Game over." He smacked Stitches in the chest, sending him backward before he bulldozed past us and stormed to his bedroom, slamming the door behind him.

"Piece of shit." Stitches growled, glaring at Sin's door.

"He's hurting too," I murmured. "You know he is."

"Fuck him." Stitches pulled his phone from his pocket and hit send on a number. A moment later, he spoke, "Sin's home… He's a prick… Yeah. He's been drinking. I could smell it on him like cheap perfume… Yeah. He's in his bedroom." He nodded as he listened to what had to be Church. "I-is she awake? Is sh-she OK?"

I watched, my breath held, as Stitches closed his eyes, his body trembling.

Fuck.

"OK. Yeah. Bye." He hung up. A moment later, he heaved his phone across the room. It slammed against the fireplace and bounced to the hardwood floor.

"She's not OK," I whispered, more as a statement than as a question.

"She's not," he choked out. "But I want fucking answers. I won't stop until I know what went down. And then, someone is going to pay."

He went back to his room, leaving me alone in the living room, standing there feeling lost.

But he was onto something. I wouldn't stop either. I wanted answers too. I'd do whatever I had to just to get them.

No one fucked with my heaven and got away with it.

No one.

CHURCH

She breathed in and out evenly, her dark lashes resting on her porcelain cheeks. I held one of her hands, our fingers entwined. She hadn't moved an inch in hours. The doctor on call had shot her up with meds which had knocked her out before he took off for shift change.

I wasn't the praying sort. *After all, who answered a demon's prayers?* So I pleaded softly with whatever entity could hear to bring her back to me. To us. Because fuck, I'd lose more than her if she didn't snap out of this. I'd seen the way Stitches rocked. I'd seen Ashes's face. And Sin. . . well, I knew I'd break his nose whenever I saw him next for disappearing on us when we'd needed him. Something about his vanishing act didn't sit right with me.

"Mr. Church, would you please step out?" a nurse by the name of Lisa asked, wringing her hands as she stood in the doorway. "Miss Lawrence's family has arrived."

"I already told you assholes I wasn't leaving. Bring her family in," I said, my voice a low growl.

Her gaze ricocheted from Sirena's sleeping form to me before she visibly swallowed and darted away. A moment later, Dr. Conrad came in with who I assumed were her parents and a girl with a mass of dark hair just like my specter's. It had to be her sister.

"Uh, this is Dante Church," Dr. Conrad said, gesturing nervously to me. "It would seem him and Miss Lawrence are, uh, friends. He's been with her all night."

The woman stepped forward and held her hand out to me, tears in her eyes. I shook it, our gazes locked.

"Thank you," she whispered, breaking away quickly from me and going to Sirena's other side and running her fingers through her hair and doting over her.

The girl approached, taking me in, no sign of fear on her. She looked a lot like Sirena except her eyes were crystal blue, she was slightly taller, and she wore her hair in a shorter style that brushed the tops of her breasts.

Her gaze darted from me to my hand wrapped around specter's then back to me.

"Does my sister know you're touching her?" she demanded, an edge to her voice.

"She's sleeping, but it wouldn't be the first time I've touched her," I said back to her, my irritation rising. I was worse without sleep.

The girl narrowed her eyes at me as Dr. Conrad spoke to her parents. Or, if I wasn't mistaken, her mother and stepfather. I'd read her files, so I knew her real dad wasn't in the picture. The stepfather oozed cocksucker. I didn't even need to speak with him to know. It was in the way he stood. The way he ignored my specter lying in the bed. How he didn't even care to approach and check on her.

The girl moved to Sirena's side where her mother had been and leaned down to kiss her forehead.

"Hey, Rina. I'm here. So is Mom. We're going to take you home."

I bristled at her words. "You're not taking her anywhere."

The girl's blue eyes snapped to me. "Wanna bet?"

I ground my teeth, my fury already at the surface as we stared one another down.

"Mr. Church, perhaps we should let Sirena's family have some privacy," Dr. Conrad said, peering at me through his too small spectacles.

I hated the prick. He was the fuckwad who'd bundled Stitches up and shoved him into the hole. I'd nearly torn his head from his body when he'd denied us seeing him. It hadn't ended well. They'd had to subdue me by having some fucker sneak up and tranquilize me.

Then I'd proceeded to tear apart the medical ward when I'd broken free after waking hours later.

Doctor Conrad and I didn't like one another.

"I'm not leaving," I said firmly. I looked at her mother. "I'm staying. Sirena is my. . . "

Her sister scoffed. "Sirena doesn't let people touch her. She doesn't talk. She doesn't communicate. She's your *nothing*. So whatever delusion you have about my sister better end right now before I beat it *and* the rest of your bullshit out of you."

I rose to my feet, not releasing Sirena's hand. "Try me, little girl."

"H-he can stay," her mother cut in, giving me a quick, nervous smile. "He clearly cares for her. Sirena needs that right now."

"I think the boy should go. Take a shower. Rest," the stepfather said, his dark eyes skirting over me with disdain.

"Maybe you don't understand what I'm saying to you. I'm *not* leaving."

"It's fine. Really. I'm sure Sirena would appreciate having him with her." Her mother gave me another wobbly smile as the sister scowled. "My name is Melanie, by the way. My husband is Jerry."

I nodded curtly, not giving a shit what their names were. I settled back in my chair and continued to hold Sirena's hand. Doctor Conrad began his medical talk to her parents. I reached out and fixed her hair with my free hand.

"It's OK, specter," I murmured, running my fingers gently along her temple and jaw. "I'm not leaving you."

Her parents stepped out of the room with Conrad, leaving me alone with Sirena and her sister.

"What's your name again?" her sister grunted.

"Church," I muttered.

"Just Church?"

"Dante. Everyone calls me Church." I didn't look at her. I kept my focus on specter.

"I'm Cadence. Everyone calls me Cady."

I said nothing and kissed Sirena's hand in mine.

"Was she. . .did Rina talk or communicate at all?" she asked softly.

"She never spoke. Not in the traditional sense. The only time she used her voice was when she screamed for me to save her last night. But I was too late, and now she's gone."

"Rina screamed? She called for you?" Cady's question was sharp as she took specter's other hand in hers.

"Yeah. She was locked in a fucking coffin in the mausoleum with Asylum. I don't know the full story yet. I will though. Mark my words."

Cady was quiet for a moment. She didn't need to speak for me to know she was vibrating with rage. At least specter had family in her corner. It made me feel a bit better that she didn't grow up alone and sad.

"Who is Asylum?" Cady asked finally.

"Seth fucking Cain."

"S-Seth Cain?"

"Yeah. You probably know him. He claims he and specter were best friends growing up. He was the one locked in the fucking coffin with her."

"Why was he in the coffin with her? I don't understand."

"Join the club," I said, finally looking at her.

She sat staring at me. Sizing me up. It didn't take a genius to know Cadence Lawrence was a tough bitch.

"He moved away when we were kids. Right after Rina was. . . hurt. The cops tracked his family down since she was found on their property locked in a large toolbox. His mom had an alibi. Seth said he hadn't seen Rina after they'd ridden their bikes. Do you think. . . ?"

I sighed. "I don't know. He's fucked-up in the head. Everyone here is in one way or another. He's not called Asylum for nothing, so keep that in the back of your mind with anything concerning him."

"It doesn't matter. Mom is bringing Rina home. She never should've brought her here. This is all that asshole Jerry's fault. He's so embarrassed about having Rina as a daughter that he was eager to just shove her out wherever he could. Rina needs to be home where I can take care of her and keep her safe—"

"She's safe here." I snarled, glaring at her. "You're not taking her. She's not fucking leaving."

"And you're clearly a liar," she snapped back. "Because if she was safe, you and I wouldn't be having this conversation over her fucking body right now."

"Watch yourself." I glowered. "I'm not the sort of guy you want to talk to like that. The only reason I haven't torn your pretty head off is because of specter. I assume she gives a damn about you. She's your saving grace because if I had my way, you'd already be fucking buried beneath my feet."

She rolled her eyes at me. "Eat shit, *Dante*. You don't scare me."

"That's because you don't know me. Keep fucking testing me, and you'll soon find out."

She sneered at me. "What do you fancy yourself? Rina's boyfriend?"

"Yes."

The answer rushed out of me so vehemently I barely recognized the sound of my voice. I'd never had a girlfriend before, but specter was far from just a fun toy. She was mine. She was ours. It was that simple.

"One of," I added.

"One of?" Cady snorted. "You're really delusional, aren't you? That's why you're stuffed away here, huh?"

"One thing I'm not is a liar." My hand shook around specter's. "Sirena is my girl. She belongs to the watchers."

"You're insane. The sooner she gets away from all of you the better she'll be. I bet you and Seth are friends, huh? I always thought he was a damn weirdo too." She shook in disgust at me. "Rina wouldn't have one boyfriend, let alone however many your cracked brain is claiming."

"I don't have shit to prove to you. All I know is that she's not leaving here."

"Keep telling yourself that." She gave me a hard glare.

This bitch was testing my restraint.

But that was OK. If I had to, I'd wrap specter into my arms, and we'd leave this fucking place. I wasn't above taking what was mine.

And Sirena Lawrence belonged to me.

I'd do whatever I had to do to prove it.

STITCHES

My body screamed at me to stop, but I couldn't. I had to get the frustrated, pent-up energy out of me before it crushed me beneath it. My fists collided with the punching bag over and over as they had been doing since last night.

The burning in my chest intensified, but I pushed past it, my insides humming as I tried to focus on the pain in my body and not the pain in my heart.

Her soft, warm lips. Her silky skin. Her smell. Lavender. Coconuts. Something distinctly angel. Her eyes. Blue. Green. Bursts of gold. Beautiful eyes. Perfect, sweet girl. My angel. My fucking angel.

She was gone.

Gone.

Gone.

She wasn't coming back to us. Asylum had broken her. Shattered her. Shattered me.

My fists collided with the bag faster, my head spinning.

"You're going to hurt yourself," Ashes called out.

I hadn't heard him come into the gym in our basement. Not that I cared. But the last thing he needed was added stress from me. So maybe I did care. My brain hurt.

Rumors were flying at Chapel Crest. The watchers got her. Asylum got her. She was attacked by fucking Bigfoot. Danny Linley did it.

Fuck it all.

Her family was still staying in town. I hadn't met them yet. Her room was on lockdown. Church was the only one who had seen her. It had been three days.

It was killing me.

Breaking me apart.

Fuck, I missed my angel.

My muscles begged for mercy as I continued my onslaught. I hadn't been to classes.

"Stitches. Man. Stop. You're bleeding." Ashes's hand landed on my shoulder as I beat the punching bag.

I ignored him. I knew I was spiraling again. I wasn't stupid. It hadn't been that long ago that I'd done it, albeit I'd actually done something worthwhile and dug us a pool last time.

"Malachi. Stop. Fucking stop!" Ashes shoved me so hard I fell to my ass and slid across the floor.

I blinked at him.

He wasted no time kneeling in front of me and grasping my face.

"Focus," he murmured. "Don't fucking slip, man. Don't."

I blinked again. My body felt numb inside. Static. I was static.

"Do you remember when we were fourteen and we broke into that abandoned house? We found all those old newspapers from the forties?"

Another blink. I did remember that.

"You went out and bought a fedora because you saw an article about the mobster who was arrested and he wore one. You wore that damn thing until I set it on fire. You were so mad until you saw how happy setting that fire made me. Remember?" Ashes's gaze raked over me. He gave me a gentle shake.

I blinked at him again, the edges of my vision fuzzy.

"Slipping now won't be good for any of us. Stay focused, Malachi. Stay here, not inside your head. I want to escape too, but it's not fair that you're the only one who gets to. Come back, OK? Don't keep falling. Come back f-for angel."

"Angel," I murmured.

"Yeah." He cleared his throat, his hands still on my face. "Church just texted and said you can come see her. Her family agreed. But you can't go if you're fucked-up. Are you fucked-up?"

"No," I whispered in a hoarse voice.

"It's OK if you need to rest. I can tell Church. You've barely slept—"

"I'll go." I breathed out. "I can go. I can do it."

Ashes frowned at me. "OK. You don't look good. You need to sleep, Malachi. It's been three days. You've been down here for hours. . ."

"I'm OK," I repeated, blinking at him, my head spinning. I moved to get up and collapsed onto my ass.

OK. So maybe I wasn't OK.

"Come on." He held his arms out for me.

I grasped his hands and let him help pull me to my feet. I leaned against him, my muscles seizing and screaming at me.

"I'll help you to your room. Shower. Rest—"

"I just want to see her," I whispered. "I'll rest when I get home."

"Swear it?" He led me to the stairs and helped me climb them.

I winced and ground my teeth as we ascended.

Fuck, my body hurt.

"Promise," I mumbled when we reached the top of the stairs and came out into the living room.

That must have been good enough for Ashes because he continued to help me to my room. Once inside, he sat me on the edge of my bed and disappeared into the bathroom I shared with Sin. It was a Jack and Jill type setup.

I heard the shower turn on, and I was suddenly grateful we had a ledge inside it where I could sit. There was no way I'd be standing for this.

Ashes came back and took my hands in his, peering down at them. I followed his gaze to see the skin on my knuckles was raw and bleeding.

"I'll bandage and clean them after you shower. Come on." He helped me to my feet and led me to the bathroom where I leaned against the edge of the shower while he quickly pushed my basketball shorts and underwear down my legs.

"We're even," I muttered tiredly.

Ashes shot me a smirk. "We're even."

He helped me into the shower, and immediately I sank onto the ledge, letting the warm water pound down on me.

"I'll get you something to eat and drink then wait in your room. Call me if you need anything. Don't drown."

I was too exhausted to give him the finger, so I grunted instead. Moments later, I was alone, nothing but me and my feelings as they came to a head.

I buried my face in my hands and let out a soft sob I tried to choke down. I wasn't a crier. But fuck. Angel. I knew she was alive, but my baby was hurting. Sick. Lost. We had to figure out how to get her back.

What if she didn't come back?

I shoved those ugly thoughts away. Those were the same thoughts that had led me to the basement to torture myself with the punching bag. I had to keep my shit together. I couldn't slip. Fuck, I couldn't. I was teetering though. I could feel it.

I hadn't taken my meds the last few nights.

I just kept fucking up.

Focus, Malachi. Focus. Keep your head in the game. Angel. Stay for my angel. No spiraling allowed. Not yet.

I breathed out and reached for my shampoo, wincing at the pain in my body as I made quick work of washing my hair before I grabbed my body wash and scrubbed the sweat and dirt off me.

When I was done, I shut off the water and stepped out, regret at my weakness for nearly slipping coursing through me. I was a fucking mess. A real piece of shit. I hated myself in that moment for being so fucking weak when she needed me.

Slowly, I made my way back to my room. Ashes had set out a pair of sweatpants, boxers, and a gray t-shirt for me. After I had them on, I sat on the edge of my bed and grimaced at my shoes. Fuck, those were going to be a bitch.

"I've got it," Ashes said, coming into the room with a sandwich and a bottle of water. He thrust both into my hands. "Open," he instructed.

Obediently, I opened my mouth. He dropped my meds onto my tongue, and I swallowed down half the bottle of water before biting into my sandwich. Ashes went to his knees and pushed my shoes onto my feet and tied the laces for me before diligently doctoring my hands and wrapping them.

"Thanks," I mumbled, my eyelids heavy.

"You're welcome. Come on." He held his hands out to me.

I swallowed down the rest of my sandwich and finished my water before placing my palms in his. He helped me back up and out the door.

"Where's Sin?" I asked as we entered the living room.

"I don't know. Out," Ashes answered stiffly. "He didn't go to classes today either."

"Do you think he's hurting too?"

"I don't know. I want to think he is, but this is all out of character, even for him."

I nodded. He was right. Even when shit went down with Isabella, Sin still had his shit together. He didn't try to skip out on us. This was definitely weird. I was like Ashes. I wanted to believe Sin was just struggling like the rest of us were, and he just didn't want to show it.

"Did you call him? Text him?" I pressed as we made it outside.

"You know I did. But nothing back from him."

I grunted, wishing I'd have saved my energy to beat the shit out of Sin. I'd be sure to get a good night's sleep so I could. It was next on my list of things to do after I got to see my angel.

It took longer than it usually would to get to the medical ward. I was a slow fuck because of the torture I'd put my body through. When we got inside, Church was waiting for us.

His green eyes swept over me, a muscle popping along his jaw. "You good?"

I nodded wordlessly. It seemed good enough for him because he nodded for us to follow him.

"We only have a few minutes, but it's better than nothing. Her mom and stepfather went to get something to eat. Her sister is here. Her name is Cady. She's a pain in the ass, but nothing we can't handle."

"I take it you don't like her?" Ashes asked as we walked.

"Let's just say if she weren't specter's sister, I would've already buried her ass in the woods."

"That bad?" I muttered.

"Worse," Church said.

We stopped outside a closed door.

"Listen. Her mom wants to take specter back home. But I think her stepdad has been trying to change her mind. The guy is a grade-A cunt, but it works in our favor here. Cady mentioned he doesn't like specter at home. So we go in there and be with our girl, and then we show them she needs to be here. Show them she won't be alone. Don't fuck this up." Church's eyes locked on me.

"I'm a perfect gentleman," I said, not surprised he'd directed his words at me. I was barely holding my shit together.

Whenever I slipped, I tended to be volatile. I knew that. Fuck. Typically, I didn't give a shit. This was angel though. I'd struggle through it for my girl.

Church pushed open the door and stepped inside, with Ashes and me following. Seated next to Sirena, who lay in bed, was a girl with dark, wavy hair like angel's. Immediately, I could tell she was a handful by the way her brilliant blue eyes snapped to us, her mouth twisting into a deep frown. She rose, her small body tense.

If I had to compare her to something, I'd say a damn snake. Filled with venom. Cady Lawrence was both poison and a remedy. It didn't take a genius to figure out the girl didn't fuck around.

"Who the hell are you?" she demanded as she moved around Sirena's bed to block her from us.

"This is Stitches and Ashes," Church said, brushing past her to sit in the chair by angel's side.

"I'm Asher Valentine," Ashes said, stepping forward and extending his hand to her.

She peered down her nose at it but didn't make an effort to shake it.

"I'm, uh, Malachi Wolfe." I eased closer, desperate to get the niceties over with so I could go see angel. "They call me Stitches."

"I don't care what they call you. Why are you here?" She crossed her arms over her chest and stared us down.

"We're here for our girl," I said, a rough edge to my voice.

The vibration of energy was alive and well within me. My body ached like nothing else, but I wanted to see my girl.

"This is unbelievable. Does Rina even know you guys are obsessed with her? She'd never in a million years have given you guys the time of day. She doesn't communicate with anyone—"

"She talks to me," Ashes said softly. "On my palm. She writes words."

Cady's mouth opened and closed several times. "S-she does?"

Ashes nodded. "She started doing it a few weeks ago when we were together. I know her condition. I know she's withdrawn and has been for a long time, but I swear to you she isn't like that with us. We aren't here to harm her or frighten her. We just want to be with her. That's all."

Cady said nothing, her eyebrows crinkled.

I didn't have time for her to play gatekeeper. I moved past her on unsteady feet and staggered to the other side of the bed where I sat in a chair and took Sirena's hand in mine.

So cold. Angel was so cold.

I took in her face. Her eyes were open, but they were unfocused. Her lips were parted. I focused on Church, my heart in my throat.

"She's going to be OK," he murmured, bringing her hand to his lips and kissing it. "She will be. Right, baby?" He brushed her dark hair away from her face.

Ashes moved to stand beside me.

"Are they giving her anything for this?" he asked, his voice shaking. "What's the prognosis? It's been three days."

"Doctor Conrad and Headmaster Ass Nut have been speaking to my mother and my stepdad about some treatment options. I'm hoping my mom turns them down and just brings her home with us. So far, that's the plan." Cady stood at Church's side, her gaze darting around the three of us with uncertainty. "Is it true? Was she getting better?"

"She was," Church murmured.

Ashes nodded.

Cady looked at me. "What happened to your hands?"

"I almost fell," I said, clearing my throat.

Ashes gave me a gentle smile as I stared at angel. I hated seeing her like this.

"Angel, it's Stitches," I called out. "Ashes and Church are here. So is your sister. Come back, OK? Sin will hopefully be here soon—"

Her body twitched. Church looked at me, his eyes wide as Cady perched on the edge of the mattress.

"Rina? Hey," Cady said. "You there?"

"Sin should be here soon. He-he misses you too," Ashes said thickly.

Angel blinked rapidly and let out a deep breath before she parted her lips. The sweetest, softest sound left her mouth, albeit raspy and shaky. *"Sinful."*

Cady's eyes widened as she stared at her, her body frozen.

"Specter?" Church called out gently. "Hey, come on now. We can get Sin here really quickly if you want to see him. I already texted him."

I didn't want to release her hand to send that prick a message, but Ashes wasted no time in doing it, his thumbs flying over his phone screen.

"Sin is sorry he's not here," I added, not knowing if it was true or not.

"Sinful," she whispered. "Sinful."

Maybe she knew what a prick he was too. I knew he scared her. I'd been witness to her shaky body whenever he was near.

"Asylum," she whispered again, her voice cracking.

"You want Asylum?" Ashes asked tightly.

"Not fucking happening," Church said with a snarl.

"I haven't seen him yet," Cady said, shifting forward. "Rina? Hey. Can you look at me?"

Angel acted like she didn't hear her. Her plump lips continued to move like she was talking, only no words came out.

Then she started softly humming the same tune she'd been humming in the mausoleum when we'd rescued her.

Cady's face crumpled.

"What is it?" Church demanded, snapping his attention to her.

"That song. I-I haven't heard it in years. She and Seth... They made it up when they were kids. He'd hum it, and she'd sing it. I-I think she wants Seth."

I peeked at Church. A muscle thrummed along his jaw as his Adam's apple bobbed.

I knew what he was thinking.

It was the same thing I was.

Seth Cain really did win. She was his more than ours.

And that really fucking sucked.

SIN

I paced back and forth in the lobby of the medical wing. I'd gotten no less than ten messages from the guys telling me to get my ass there.

She's saying your name. Get here now.

If she was saying my name, it was only a matter of time until she spilled my ugly truth. I hadn't anticipated this.

Fuck, it was a flaw in the plan.

A plan I regretted in the deepest part of my soul. I'd really fucked things up. I'd spent the night it happened drunk and stoned off my ass, trying to force my worries for her out of my head. I knew Seth Cain had tried to kill her when they were kids. Sure, he'd claimed it was to protect her. *But seriously, who the fuck did that?*

A crazed, obsessed madman.

The same one you locked her in a fucking box with and made her go crazy.

I hated myself. Fuck, I did. I'd even contemplated ending my life just to escape the agony of what I'd done to her.

I knew she was bad. I'd seen it all over Stitches's and Ashes's faces the morning I'd stumbled in. I'd broken what I'd desperately been trying to save.

Drawing in a deep breath, I knew I had to face the music. I nodded to the nurse at the desk and marched down the hall. There were a few patients in rooms. Most faking ailments so they could skip classes. A few were restrained to their beds as I passed by. Danny Linley was wrapped in bandages and staring at his ceiling. Overall, there seemed to be a lot less students stuck in here today than what I'd seen before. I supposed that was a good thing. The place had been packed when Stitches had lost his shit.

"Hey, buddy," a familiar voice called out to me as I passed a room.

I paused and backtracked to find Asylum sitting on the edge of his bed, his face badly bruised and scratched.

I hesitated for a moment before I stepped through his doorway.

"I see you made it," I said.

A tiny smile quirked the corners of his lips up. "So close, yet so far away."

I swallowed hard. "Does that upset you?"

He shrugged. "No." He didn't elaborate.

"What are your plans?" I ventured, my throat tight. I had to know how deep my problems ran.

His blue-eyed gaze locked on me. "I won. I plan on taking my forever girl. Those were the terms, right?"

I nodded tightly.

"It may become a bit of a problem since I don't think the watchers are going to play fair. I guess that means we won't play fair."

I moved farther into the room and closed the door. "What is that supposed to mean?"

"Well..." He licked his lips. "You did a very bad thing, Sinclair. You betrayed your friends to help me win. I bet they won't be too happy with you once they find out. Especially since the whispers in this place say she's gone a little. . . *mad*."

Nausea twisted in my guts. "What do you want?"

"For you to secure my win. I don't want to hurt anyone. Not really. But I will. If I don't have my forever girl, I'll take her with me. Death doesn't frighten me. Third times a charm, right?"

"So you're blackmailing me and threatening to kill siren?"

He cocked his head at me, his dark hair falling across his forehead. "I suppose I am."

"You just fucking said you don't want to hurt anyone—"

"I don't. That's why I'm telling you to get her for me. Then no one has to be hurt. You can go back to fucking Melanie and whoever else it is you four fuck." He looked sharply to his left, his eyes traveling up and down quickly before he laughed like someone I couldn't see was telling him a joke.

I stared at the empty space, my guts aching.

Fuck, I'd delivered siren into the hands of a fucking lunatic.

I hadn't realized just how unhinged he really was. He was fan-fucking-tastic at hiding his crazy and blending in like the rest of the world. It only made him more dangerous.

"Yes." He nodded thoughtfully before turning back to me. "I can take my forever girl away with us, or I can spill your ugly secret and take the watchers from you. The choice is yours. Choose wisely. I don't have a lot of patience. Not now that I've made her scream for me. We really bonded in the darkness."

"You drove her to insanity," I said with a snarl.

"Did I?" He cocked his head at me again. "Or was it you? I would've never been in that box with her if you hadn't put her there." He tapped his temple, a sinister smile on his lips. "Think about that for a minute."

I ground my teeth so hard I thought I'd break them.

"What will you do with her if Church and the guys let her go?"

"Love her," he said softly, his demeanor completely changing from an insane asshole to one who looked like he really meant his words. "Forever. She's our Rinny. We'll take care of her."

I didn't exactly know what he meant when he said *take care of her,* but I did know he had my ass between a rock and a hard spot.

"Do you swear you won't hurt her?" I asked, the words tumbling out of my mouth with so much worry I couldn't stop them.

He blinked at me, a slow smile forming on his lips. "You love her too."

"I want to know that you won't hurt her." I swallowed thickly as we stared one another down.

"I won't hurt her. Swear it. I'm going to save her."

I studied him. He was a fucking enigma. All I wanted to do was punch his already busted up face in, but instead, I nodded. I needed him to keep my secret. I was on the brink of losing everything.

"I'll do it." I hated the words. I hated them so much.

I just kept digging a deeper fucking hole, but this was me. It was who I was. I sabotaged everything in my life and always would.

Because who could ever love a piece of shit like me?

Not Sirena Lawrence, the girl I'd broken, that was for sure.

†

I KNOCKED LIGHTLY on the door with siren's name on it. It cracked open a moment later, and a blue eye peered out at me before the door was pulled open.

"Who the hell are you?" the girl demanded.

Church was on his feet in an instant, shoving the girl aside like she was nothing, and hauling the door open so I could enter.

"Where the fuck have you been?" he demanded, glaring at me.

"I...just out," I muttered. I noted Ashes and Stitches sitting on either side of siren's bed.

"Fucking asshole. I texted you to get over here." Church stepped aside for me.

"And I'm fucking here." I looked at the girl who was glaring at me. She looked like siren, only mean.

"Who is this asshole?" she asked. "Another one of your fucked-up friends?"

"This is Sin." Church jerked his thumb in my direction as he stomped back to siren's bedside. "He really *is* an asshole. Sin, Cady."

She rolled her eyes and returned to sit on the edge of siren's bed.

"I can't believe Rina made so many friends," she said, her iciness sliding away for a moment as she looked at siren in bed. "All dick-heads, but still."

"Then you'll like Bryce if you think we're dicks," Stitches said.

"He's sweet as pie. He was angel's boyfriend before she realized she loved us."

"I doubt that," Cady huffed. "Isn't it time for your meds?"

"Already took them," Stitches shot back.

She sighed and looked at me. I was still standing in the center of the room, staring at siren in bed. Her eyes were glassy as she gazed someplace faraway.

My heart cracked as I took her in, the memory of that night rushing back to me.

The fear in her eyes. Me pushing the pill into her mouth to knock her out. How her soft lips had tasted as I pressed my mouth to hers. The remorse I'd felt as I stared down at her perfect form in that cold coffin. The worries and fear I'd struggled with the entire night as I thought about what was happening to her alone with Asylum.

How I'd prayed she wouldn't die, and that someone would find her before it was too late.

How I'd wished I were a better man and had run back to save her. She'd trusted me, and I'd betrayed her. I'd betrayed my family.

It was over now though. All of it. She'd never be mine. Never be ours. Asylum would make sure of it. That much I knew.

"So what's your deal? Delusional fuckwit who thinks my sister belongs to him?" Cady called out.

"She's not mine," I said softly. "She never was and never will be."

"Not fucking now, Sinclair," Church snapped, glaring over his shoulder at me.

Cady grunted and focused back on her sister, ignoring me.

"Come see her," Ashes said to me. "You can sit in my spot."

Knowing if I refused it would cause a scene I didn't want, I stepped forward and settled in Ashes's seat and stared at siren. Her face was slightly puffy.

"Talk to her," Stitches demanded.

I cleared my throat. "Hey, siren."

"Sinful," she whispered, her voice sending chills down my spine.

My heart clenched despite it. She had a beautiful voice. And it was my name. Sort of.

"Uh, yeah. It's me," I mumbled.

"Sinful. Sinful. Sinful," she repeated softly in a monotone. Her voice rose, "Sinful. Sinful!"

I looked quickly around at everyone, all wearing various looks of concern on their faces.

"Shh," I pleaded, reaching out and taking her small, cold hand in mine. "Shh, siren. Please. Stop."

"Sinful! Sinful!"

I couldn't take it. I released her hand and nearly fell getting out of my seat.

"Where the fuck are you going?" Church shouted at me as I rushed to the door, desperate to get her voice out of my head.

She was a siren, screaming my sins.

They just didn't know it yet.

I ran from the room and didn't stop until I'd made it outside. I slid down the brick wall and raked in air as I struggled to keep my composure.

Fuck. Fuck. FUCK!

Sinful. That was me.

A disgusting fucking sinner.

She'd named me well. The man who'd tricked her and locked her up with the devil.

I was truly sinful.

It just made me hate myself even more.

I deserved this hell. Sinners got punished, and I wouldn't be an exception.

ASHES

I trudged across campus, my heart heavy.

It had been one week since Sirena had been put into the medical ward. As much as Stitches and I tried to get in to see her, it was nearly impossible. Even Church had to leave because of classes. Her mother finally convinced him to go, citing Sirena wouldn't want him to fall behind. Church had made her mother promise not to take her.

Surprisingly, her mother had agreed.

Church needed to be away from her. He hadn't been sleeping. His behavior was becoming erratic and more unpredictable than usual. Last night, he was supposed to be in bed sleeping, but instead, he'd taken to the woods with his knife and had returned just before time to go to class with blood splatters on his shirt.

So now Sirena was alone in the medical ward while we attempted to get back to some semblance of our lives.

We all knew it was a sham though. We were just going through the motions.

"Ashes. Hey," Stitches called out to me.

I paused and waited for him to catch up.

"Hey," I greeted him tiredly.

He looked as bad as I felt. I had to give him credit though. At least he was trying to sleep. He'd even gone to an appointment to get his sleeping medication refilled and was taking it. The dark circles beneath his eyes suggested despite his efforts, they weren't offering him the deep, restful sleep he needed, which was dangerous for him since he seemed to require adequate sleep to keep his disorder in check.

"It's the weekend," he said.

"So?" I wasn't about to have a damn party. In fact, I was appalled he was even considering asking me.

"Bonfire?" he continued, raising his brows at me.

"Hell yes," I said, breathing out.

Fires had always helped relieve my stress. It felt like forever since I'd had one when it had really only been a week. I'd actually considered starting a fire in the bathtub just this morning as a means to gain some semblance of control in my life. I needed the distraction.

"I figured you'd like that idea," Stitches said. "I already told Church. He's agreed to come too."

"And Sin?"

"He's coming," his voice was tight.

Stitches and Church were still on edge and pissed because Sin had disappeared the night Sirena needed help. I didn't want to stay mad at him. I knew he was fighting his own demons, and the last thing we needed was to be angry with one another.

Church and Stitches would eventually get over it. They always did.

I slowed to a stop as Seth came into view.

Asylum.

"They let him go," I murmured, watching as he turned his head and spotted us.

His eyes were still mostly black and blue, only just beginning to fade to an ugly shade of yellow and purple. Stitches had beaten him good in that mausoleum.

"Fucker," Stitches growled, tensing beside me as Seth took a step toward us.

"Brave fucker," I added, waiting for him. I had a lot of questions for him. I'd hoped to question him in private, but this would do if I could keep Stitches from pummeling him again.

"What the fuck do you want?" Stitches demanded when Seth stopped in front of us.

"I'll be brief. I made Sirena scream. It's my victory. I'm coming to collect."

I bristled at his words and immediately grabbed Stitches's arm because I knew he was going to launch himself at him.

"You didn't fucking win. She screamed *for* Church," Stitches spat, lurching forward.

Seth didn't seem the least bit phased. "She screamed his name, but it was me who made it happen. It's my win."

"You're insane if you think we're going to just hand her over to you," I said, keeping a firm grip on Stitches.

"I won't deny who and what I am. What you say changes nothing though. It's my win, my mental illnesses aside. Right, Sin?"

Sin stepped up beside Seth, a frown on his face.

"It's his win," he agreed gruffly.

"What the fuck, man?" Stitches tugged out of my hold and glared at Sin. "Have you lost your fucking mind too? You know she screamed for Church. We told you. She made her choice—"

"She doesn't get a choice. It wasn't part of the original agreement," Seth interjected. "The deal was whoever could make her scream. We did. It was us. I won. I'm not going to argue the fact though. I'm simply giving you the courtesy of knowing that I'm claiming my prize."

"Don't you dare even think about going near her," Stitches said with a snarl, shoving Seth in the chest.

Sin immediately intervened and pushed Stitches back, getting between them.

"Are you on his side?" Stitches demanded. "Is that it?"

"Now isn't the time," Sin said. "We can talk about it later."

"How when that fuck is staking claims to our girl?"

"She's not ours," Sin said. "He won. He's right. That was the deal."

"Oh, you'd like that, huh? *Fucking asshole.* You've been trying to shove her away since she got here. What the fuck is the matter with you? Why do you hate being happy?" Stitches was shouting now.

We were drawing a small crowd.

"Man, chill. Sin's right. Not here," I said, taking hold of Stitches's arm again.

He shoved me off and stormed across the courtyard without another word. He didn't need to say anything. The anger oozed from him. We didn't need this shit right now.

I glanced back at Seth, who met my gaze with his curious one.

"I think we should discuss this before anyone makes public claims. OK?"

"I'll agree to that," he answered with a shrug. "When?"

"Tomorrow night. Our place. We can sit and talk. We have questions anyway."

"And I have answers."

"Fine. Tomorrow night—" I started, ready to give him further instructions.

"At seven. You'll text me if anything changes. Meet you on the back patio," he finished for me, making me crinkle my brows.

"Uh, yeah," I said, confused about how he knew exactly what I was going to say. Maybe it was a coincidence.

"I'll see you then." He clapped Sin on the back. "You too. *Friend.*" And then he was gone, pushing past us and continuing on like we hadn't just had an encounter in the middle of the commons.

"What was that about?" I asked, tearing my gaze from Seth's retreating back and focusing on Sin.

"What was what?" Sin grunted.

"Seth. He called you friend."

Sin shrugged, looking troubled. "I don't know. Guy's a nut job. Who knows with him."

He had that right.

I spotted Church ahead of us. Melanie called his name, and he paused, a scowl on his face as she tottered toward him in her high heels.

"What's she want?" I murmured, making to go to Church.

Accosting him when he was sleep deprived wasn't a good idea. Sin followed me over, and we stopped when we reached them.

"So I was thinking I could come over tonight," Melanie said with a giggle.

"Why do you think I want you to come over?" Church asked, rubbing his bloodshot eyes.

"Because you didn't claim the mute. She's not even on campus. Rumor has it she tried to kill herself with Asylum and failed after they were fucking each other—"

It happened in a flash. Church's forearm was at her throat, and he had her pressed against the wall of the English building.

"Where did you hear that?" he roared, his body shaking with barely controlled rage.

She parted her lips to speak, but no sound came out because he was putting too much pressure on her neck.

I reached forward and rested my hand on his shoulder. Immediately, he released her. She rubbed her throat, her eyes glassy.

"Answer me," Church demanded.

She let out a cough. "E-everyone is saying it. You didn't do a public claiming—"

"Just because I didn't fuck her in front of anyone, doesn't mean I didn't fuck her. She's mine. She belongs to the watchers. I told you that you were out, and she was in. Or did you fucking forget?"

Melanie visibly swallowed. "Church, she's not right for you. She and Asylum—"

"Nothing happened between them. Do you hear me? *Nothing.* And nothing ever will."

"I could give you anything you wanted. I-I can do the group stuff too. I'm sorry I wasn't willing before—"

"Melanie, stop. We didn't pick you," I said, stepping in front of Church before he choked her out. "We chose Sirena. Rumors are just that. They aren't true. Sirena and Seth had a bad experience we're looking into, but that's all. She's recovering in the medical ward. Nothing has changed for us. OK?"

Her gaze darted between us for a moment. "But Sin said—"

"What did Sin say?" Church asked, glaring over at Sin, who had the decency to look ashamed.

"He said she lost her mind and wasn't coming back. That she might be leaving Chapel Crest."

"Is that all Sin said?" Church turned his fury on Sin. "Or were you too busy fucking to finish lying?"

"It was nothing," Melanie quickly interjected. "He was upset. I sucked his cock to make him feel better."

The words weren't even out of her mouth before Church's fist collided with Sin's face. I shoved Melanie back as the two tore into one another.

"She's fucking lying," Sin shouted, dodging Church's fist, but still catching a glancing blow to his shoulder. "I didn't! I fucking didn't!"

Church was gone, his rage taking over. He landed a punch to Sin's ribs, causing Sin to double over, gasping for air. It didn't take him long to recover though because he shot forward and tackled Church, taking the fight to the ground.

I grabbed Church, who'd flipped Sin onto his back after a brief scuffle, and hauled him off, throwing him to the ground away from Sin.

"Get the hell up," I snapped at the two of them. I caught Melanie smirking before she rushed away.

Both men climbed to their feet, chests heaving.

"Specter is *our* girl. You don't go fucking or getting your cock sucked by anyone else. You know our rules—" Church seethed.

"I didn't, dickhead!" Sin snapped back. "Yeah, I saw Melanie, but nothing happened between us. She asked if I'd talk to you about her coming back. I told her I wasn't fucking interested. She got on her knees, but I pushed her away, and she got pissed. I didn't. . . I fucking wouldn't do what you're accusing me. You know how much I fucking hate cheaters."

Church slowly approached him. A cut from Sin's ring against his cheek dribbled blood. I cautiously stepped closer to the two in case someone threw another punch.

"What did you say?" Church asked softly as they stared one another down.

I glared at the few people stupid enough to stop and gawk. They scurried away, leaving us alone.

"I said I didn't do what she said I did."

"No. About cheating."

Sin licked his lips. "I said I hate cheaters."

"You insinuated that you're with specter without saying it," Church's voice was quiet.

"I-I'm not. I don't want her."

"Why are you like this? You know you're fucked in your feelings over this shit, and yet you continue to deny it. Let fucking go so you can feel something besides anger," Church said.

"So I can be broken like you three? I told you it was a bad idea. I wasn't wrong. I don't want to hurt the way you guys are. I-I refuse. Not after what Isabella did—"

Church fisted the front of Sin's white uniform shirt and got in his face, his voice barely above a dangerous whisper, "*That cunt is dead.* We fucking put an end to her. Get. Over. IT!"

Church shoved him away.

Sin visibly swallowed. "She didn't kill your kid. She didn't make you love her. She just got you to fuck her."

"You have a chance to try again with someone new. Someone better. And you're fucking it up like you always do. Get your shit together or get fucking lost." Church stormed past him without another word.

Sin stared after him, his eyes narrowed. He wiped at the remnants of blood trickling from his nose as he watched Church go.

"I know you care about Sirena," I said gently to him. "It's OK to be scared and confused."

He was quiet for so long I didn't think he'd say anything. When he finally spoke, it took me by surprise. "I only wanted to save you guys from this. That's all. It's killing me inside to see you all barely hanging on. I tried to. . . fix it. But I fucked everything up."

I frowned. "What are you talking about? Just relax, man."

He shook his head. "I can't. I don't know how to make this right. It's killing me inside. And siren. . .fuck." His Adam's apple bobbed in his throat. "I'm sorry, man. I truly am."

He didn't elaborate past that. Instead, he strode in the direction of our place, his head down.

†

I KNOCKED LIGHTLY on the door to Sirena's room in the medical ward later that evening. After forcing Church to just sleep and promising I'd be with her, he'd finally gone to his room and laid down. Stitches was asleep on the couch when I'd left, and Sin was holed up in his bedroom like he had been for the last week.

"How is she?" I asked, stepping into the room.

Cady looked up at me from the chair beside Sirena's bed where she was reading a book.

"Same," she answered, closing the book and stretching.

I moved to Sirena's other side and leaned down to press a kiss to her forehead. She didn't respond. She simply continued to stare at the ceiling.

I settled into the chair beside her bed and turned to Cady.

"How are your parents?"

"My mother is fine. Jerry is a douche. I don't claim him."

I chuckled. Cady was funny once you got past her rough exterior. While Church and Stitches didn't get along with her, I was finding her a welcome relief. Even if they took Sirena from Chapel Crest, I was confident Cady would make sure she was OK.

"That bad?" I asked.

"Worse. I'm just giving you the Cliffs Notes." She glanced at Sirena before leaning forward. "Can I tell you something?"

"Of course." I held Sirena's cool hand in mine as I focused on Cady.

"I think you're probably a nice guy. I mean, your friends are dicks, but I like you and trust you. Do you love my sister?"

The question caught me off guard. "I-I do," I said, my heart swelling as I recalled our short time together.

Sirena was what my soul needed. She came into my life at the right time.

Cady nodded. "I can tell, you know? All of you, actually. Except maybe Sinclair. He's more dickish than the rest of you. He acts like he's scared to even look at her. But then again, I only met him the one time."

"Sin has trouble forming relationships. He's desperate to, but he's also scared. His illness and his past experiences can create many issues for him. He's getting better though."

"So you think Rina is safe with him?"

I looked at Sirena and smiled. "I'd like to think so. With all of us."

"OK." She swallowed and nodded. "OK. Then I'm going to tell you something." She breathed out as I waited. "Listen, I want my sister to be safe. I want her home where I can take care of her, but the thing is, home might not be the best place for her."

"Why?" My chest tightened with worry.

"Jerry. I-I told my mom, but she's under the correct impression that I hate that asshole, so she thinks I may be acting out and trying to dislodge him from our lives." She bit her bottom lip, clearly mulling it over in her head. "I came home from school early one day last year. Sirena had an appointment with some doctors that day. Mom took her but had some garden club meeting she had to get to afterward, so she left Rina at home. Jerry was there. I went upstairs to see Rina and make sure she was OK. I-I saw Jerry coming out of her room, and he was putting his belt back on. He didn't see me though."

My guts clenched at the possible implications.

"I went in her room right away. She was in bed beneath her covers. She refused to even look at me. Obviously, she wouldn't tell me what happened. All she did was cry a little and stare at the wall. I never found out what happened in that room. I-I don't know if he t-touches her or worse." Her hands trembled as she continued, "I don't think she's safe at home if Jerry's there. As much as I wished she was, I think he'd continue doing whatever he was doing to her if she came home. I don't want that for my sister. I need to find out what sort of monster he really is then burn him for it." Her words were so fierce they sent shivers through my body.

"If he hurt her, I'll burn him myself," I whispered, tightening my hold on Sirena's hand.

I'd kill the son of a bitch if he touched my heaven. I wouldn't hesitate. Violence wasn't my thing. It was reserved more for the other watchers, but when it came to my heaven, I'd burn the fucking world down in her name.

Cady breathed out and stared me down. "They're talking about doing some medical experiment on her to bring her back. To study her condition. If she stays, can you protect her?"

"I'd die to save her," I said immediately. "We all would."

"I'm scared for her to stay and scared for her to go," she said softly. "She's been through so much."

I released Sirena's hand and got to my feet, going to Cady and kneeling in front of her. A tear slid down her cheek. I reached out and swiped it away.

"You're a good sister, Cady. You remind me of my sister, Abby. She fought for me too."

Cady sniffled again.

"We'll do everything we can to make sure Sirena is OK. We want her back too." I leaned in cautiously and gave Cady a hug, hoping she wouldn't knee me in the groin.

Her small body shook against mine as she hugged me back. She stayed in my arms for only a moment before she pulled away and wiped quickly at her eyes.

"Thank you. I'm glad she found someone like you, Asher."

"Ashes," I said, getting to my feet and going back to my seat. "Everyone calls me Ashes."

"Why?" She tilted her head and studied me.

"I have impulse control issues. Fire in particular. I'm a moth to the flame one might say."

"You set fires?"

I nodded wordlessly, the anxiety rearing its ugly head. I tried to keep my shit together when I could. The lighter pressed to my thigh in my pocket was calling my name. I was desperate to open and close it.

I shut my eyes, trying to focus on keeping it together.

"Ashes, hey," Cady called out.

I opened my eyes and looked at her.

"It's OK. Whatever you need to do. I won't judge you for it."

I breathed out and let go, pulling my lighter from my pocket and flicking it opened and closed five times. Pause. Again. Five more times. Pause. Again. Five times. Five times. Five times. Breathe. Fuck. I let my leg bounce, the pent-up energy vibrating through my body.

Cady offered me a smile before she turned her attention back to Sirena.

Church and Stitches may think Cady was a pain in the ass, but I liked her. If they could see her as the doting sister the way I did, maybe they would too.

At least I hoped so because if my thinking was right, Cady wouldn't stay home for long either. Not if Sirena were here.

We all did crazy things to protect those we loved.

Cadence Lawrence would be no exception when it came to Sirena.

I knew it right down to my bones.

ASYLUM

I ran as fast as I could, forcing my body to endure the burning pain in my chest. It was in my nature to push the limits. It had only gotten worse as I'd aged.

I often took a similar route through the woods like Church did when he ran. Sometimes I followed him, lurking in the dark forest. He was fascinating to watch. Dante Church was an admirable machine. Clever, too. Protective of our Rinny.

Normally, any man with eyes on what belonged to me would upset me. For some reason, while the jealous monster inside me reared its head on occasion, it wasn't nearly as dangerous when it came to the watchers.

It was still ugly and unpredictable though. I supposed that was a danger in itself.

The only reason I hadn't struck them down was because of our Rinny. I saw the way she looked at them. I knew her heart better than she did.

She loved those assholes.

And I swore the moment she came back to life for me at Chapel Crest that I'd never take from her again. I'd only give.

Mausoleum aside, I thought I was doing pretty well. I honestly thought we'd finally find peace in the darkness. She hadn't liked it though. I was far too eager to be alone with her and had let myself go a bit.

Her screams though... While they'd made my heart race, they'd also been music to my ears. She hadn't forgotten me. *She remembered us.*

I ran back to my private dorm and went inside. I grabbed a quick shower, my mind on her the entire time.

My forever girl.

I was chomping at the bit to see her. The watchers had made sure I couldn't get into her room though. I'd seen her mother and stepfather on campus, and I'd watched Cady, her younger sister. Beautiful. Intelligent. Strong. . . Cady.

Cady was no Sirena though.

No one came close to her beauty or magnetism. She was one of a kind.

A knock on my door pulled me from my thoughts on our Rinny. I went to it and cracked it open to find Riley, one of only two real friends I had on campus.

"Hey, I'm supposed to tell you Sully wants to see you in his office. He said—"

"That I have fifteen minutes," I finished for him, opening my door and allowing him into my room.

He stepped inside as I went to my closet and pulled out a black hoodie, tugging it over my torso. If he would've knocked thirty seconds sooner, I'd have answered the door naked.

"How do you do that?" he asked, crinkling his dark brows at me.

"Do what?" I slid my feet into my shoes.

"Know what I'm going to say?"

"You always ask me that," I pointed out. "And my answer is?" I strode to my door with him following.

We stepped into the hall, and the door clicked and locked behind us.

"That you just do what the voices tell you to." He rolled his eyes, making me smirk.

"Exactly."

It was way fucking deeper than that, but explaining the intricacies of what the fuck I was wasn't something I wanted to dip my toes into. I was different.

"You should play the lottery," he said as we reached the elevator.

"How dull. There's only one thing I want in this world, and it isn't money."

"Sirena Lawrence." He nodded. "I know."

My friends weren't new to my obsession with her. The moment I'd seen her again, I was done for.

"How is she, by the way?"

I tensed. "I don't know. Alive. I'm hoping to be able to see her soon."

No one knew the sort of history we had with Rinny except *us*, her, and now Sinclair Priest. In all fairness, I really wasn't concerned about him telling our secret because he had a secret of his own that he didn't want to get out. It seemed secrets and souls were currency here at Chapel Crest, and I was a motherfucking banker.

It was just as well. I was good at finding skeletons.

"Hopefully, you'll get in to see her. Ask Sully when you see him. You know, if he doesn't beat you with his ruler." He winced.

Sully had beaten Riley's hands so hard with a ruler last year, his bones had fractured. He hadn't told anyone but me and Cody. And all because he'd failed to recite some Bible quote correctly.

Honestly, I'd wanted to kill Sully then. While killing wasn't my thing, I'd do it if I had to. Everything ended in death. It didn't bother me to take a life. I found little joy in it though. There were much more satisfying things to do, like feed people their eyeballs after I carved them out of their skulls with a dinner fork.

Maybe I didn't enjoy killing as much as the next lunatic because aside from small animals, Sirena had been my first human attempt. Maybe I had PTSD from it.

I had nightmares of her crying for me to stop for the first few years after I'd done it. In turn, I'd cry. I'd slipped into an awful depression as my life had spiraled further.

Then I'd gotten the chance to fuck up the asshole who'd caused *us* so much pain.

I wish I could say life had gotten better, but it hadn't.

There'd been a gaping hole in my existence, and it took seeing our Rinny again to realize she was what had been missing.

Now, I felt like I was on fire, and she was both the water and the gasoline. It was driving me insane. Well, *more insane* one might say.

When I'd gotten my chance to be with her, I'd snatched it up without contemplating exactly what it would mean. All I knew was I wanted her, however I could have her.

And now my forever girl was locked in her own mind.

I couldn't save her. It was fucking eating my blackened soul to know she was even further from me now.

It made me ache inside when I realized I might have to finish the job I'd started all those years ago just to put her out of her misery. But first, I'd try to get her back before I had to resort to such drastic measures. I'd go with her this time though. Without hesitation, I'd go.

Riley and I parted ways without a word, and I strolled to Sully's office and knocked lightly on his door.

"Come in," he called out in a gruff voice.

I opened the door and stepped inside his office, moving to stand in front of his desk. He gestured for me to take a seat, so I did.

"I'd like to discuss Sirena Lawrence with you," he started.

"Go on," I said evenly, my mind racing.

I knew Sully. If Chapel Crest was hell, he was a devil lurking in the darkness.

"Now, I don't typically discuss student health issues with anyone but the staff treating them. However, we're close to losing one of our own with her. Her mother would like to unenroll her and take her home. Her stepfather has agreed to leave her under my. . . *treatment*."

I stiffened in my seat.

She can't leave. I can't let her leave me. No. No. NO!

I'll stop them.

Take her. Fuck him and his treatment. Take her. Take her. TAKE HER.

"You see, I've spoken to her family. They say you and Sirena were once very good friends. Yes?"

"Yes," I said evenly.

"Aside from your scripture writing as punishment for the mausoleum incident, I had another idea. You being there with her during her ordeal in the cemetery, well, it prompted me to read her file again. You know what I found?"

I stared back at him, unflinching. Unmoving.

"I found she had an accident right around the same time you moved away from her. Interesting, don't you think?"

"Useless facts can be interesting to a simple mind."

He gave me a sinister smile that made me narrow my eyes. *Definitely the fucking devil.* He just didn't realize he was fucking with a god.

"I think it would be helpful if you were to aid me in this treatment plan I have in mind for Sirena."

I sat forward. "What treatment plan?"

"Sometimes it takes fear to scare fear away. And since I know you had something to do with her disorders, I figured you're the best one for the job. Of course, you could say no. I have it on good authority that Danny Linley also frightens her. I'm sure he'd agree to assist me if you're unable to...especially if he's offered certain...protections." He raised his brows at me.

"Fuck Danny Linley," I snarled, my body shaking with rage. "And fuck you for suggesting that piece of human garbage."

Sully nodded and steepled his fingers as he surveyed me. "It's you or Mr. Linley. I figure if we're going to get to the root of her problems, you're the first I should seek out. I'm sure Dante Church and his watchers wouldn't want to be such willing participants to her treatment plan. But I know you're a sick, twisted creature who might *enjoy* helping me. So it's either you on your knees or it's Linley. The choice is yours, but we'll work those screams from her lungs until she's the docile, sweet girl I know she can be. The kind of girl who obeys her... master. Don't you want that master to be you?"

I rose to my feet, my body still trembling.

"Having a beautiful girl on her knees, obeying your every

command. Isn't that every twisted monster's dream, *Asylum*? Her warm, willing mouth. Her sweet whimpers? Her acceptance that *you* are her master, and she bows to no one else?"

Kill him.

Kill him.

FEED HIM HIS OWN COCK.

Then the soft voice whispered to me. *She could be ours again. Taught and trained to obey. Desperate to be yours again. You could protect her from the monsters. If you say no, she'll be in worse danger.*

"But I am the danger," I whispered so softly I knew Sully couldn't hear my words. I'd break her again, this time to keep her alive...

Sometimes danger is what keeps the heart beating and the mind alert. We want her. . . here she is. Ours. Take. HER. Own. HER. CLAIM HER! FUCKING CLAIM HER!

She could be ours. Not theirs.

"Ours," I whispered, a thrill running up my spine.

Forever.

"Promise?" I asked softly.

Sully cocked his head at me and raised a brow again.

Forever.

I breathed out.

I'd do it. I'd save her. I'd save *us*.

And I'd punish any motherfucker who looked at her wrong. We'd own her. The thought of her on her knees for us. . .

Fuck.

"When do I start?"

Sully's lips twisted up wickedly.

"How about now?"

CHURCH

I slammed back my shot of bourbon and wiped my mouth, my blond hair hanging forward and wet with sweat from working out in our gym. My body was drenched, and I grabbed a towel and ran it quickly over my bare torso in an effort to dry off.

My fucking nerves were shot. Sleeping escaped me. I could only lie in my bed and stare at the ceiling. And if I wasn't doing that, I was in the forest, taking out my frustrations with my knife in the only way I knew how.

And specter. My fucking girl was bedridden and unresponsive.

I closed my eyes and let out a slow breath. Knowing I'd have that piece of shit Asylum in my presence in just an hour's time had me on edge. I wasn't so sure I wouldn't just kill him and bury his body in a place no one would find him.

I opened my eyes, grabbed my tank top, and walked up the stairs to the main part of the house. Stitches sat staring at a wall in the living room while Ashes worked in the kitchen, the smell of food permeating the air.

"Where's Sin?" I demanded. I'd been asking where the fuck he was a lot more lately, and that was another thing beginning to piss me off.

"His room," Stitches said with a grunt from his seat, his jaw slack and his dark eyes fixed on a point above the dark TV.

"I'm making some food. We haven't been eating lately. We need to eat. We need our strength." Ashes's voice was tight as he stirred the pot on the stove.

I nodded, knowing he was too busy to see the action. He was right. We weren't eating. We were barely living.

"It'll be done in a few minutes." He moved to stir the pan on the stove next to the bubbling pot.

I didn't say it, but I was grateful for Ashes. He always tried to keep it together. I knew it was hard as hell for him though. It was admirable. But falling in love seemed to have affected us in different ways.

"You OK?" I asked, sitting in my chair next to Stitches.

"No," he answered, not looking away from the wall. "You?"

"No."

We were both quiet for a moment before he spoke again, his voice low and shaky.

"I want her back, Dante. I can't fucking exist like this. Knowing she's stuck in a bed and lost in her mind? Knowing she's probably fucking terrified? It's tearing my goddamn heart out, man. I-I can't—"

"*You can,* Malachi. I fucking know you can, so get your shit together and do it. We don't need you losing it right now. *We fucking don't.* If you slip, what will that do to us? We're already losing her. We can't lose you too," I said, balling my hands into fists as I stared at him. Anger coursed through me knowing he was suffering so much. I couldn't stand to see him in the hole again.

He exhaled and nodded as he ran his hands up and down his thighs, his chest heaving.

"Did you take your meds today?"

His body shook as he snapped his attention back to me, his breathing faster.

I knew the answer to that.

I was on my feet in moments and in his bathroom. Within seconds,

I had his meds in the palm of my hand and was pushing them into his mouth.

"Swallow," I commanded, pressing a glass of water to his lips. "You don't fucking fall, Malachi. Not now."

He swallowed, water dribbling down his chin. Quickly, I swiped it away with my thumb and kneeled in front of him as Ashes walked to the back of the couch and looked down at me, his brows crinkled with worry.

I reached out and cradled Stitches's face. "Look at me, Malachi. Fucking breathe with me."

He sucked in a shuddering breath as his eyes focused on me.

"Again," I commanded, my hold on his face tight.

He breathed again, his rhythm slowing to match mine.

"What do we do when we feel like we can't breathe, brother?"

"W-we fucking do it anyway," he answered in a shaky voice.

"And what do we do when we get lost in the darkness?"

"W-we become the darkness." He breathed out, the trembling slowing in his body.

"Right. And what do we do when we need help?"

"We t-trust each other to protect our sanity."

I nodded and loosened my grip on his face. "Good. We'll see Seth soon. Once we do, we can do what needs to be done."

"What if he takes her?" Stitches asked, his eyes becoming glassy as his meds kicked in.

I clenched my jaw for a moment, knowing a win was a win. "He'll never take her from us. Only she can decide that. You know that, right? Even if he gets the chance to have her, she'll make the decision herself."

They were ugly words, but they were true. In the end, the decision belonged to specter.

"Promise she'll choose us?" He stared at me with worry in his eyes.

"We love her. She knows that. She knows where home is."

He visibly swallowed and exhaled. I studied him for a moment, hoping beyond anything she'd come back to us. But even if she didn't, I knew we'd work hard to convince her otherwise.

"I can't lose her," he whispered. "I'll die if I lose her."

"We will get her back," I answered softly. "Somehow."

We were all silent for a moment.

"Food's done," Ashes finally murmured.

I nodded and held my hand out to Stitches. He took it and I tugged him to his feet. He followed me into the dining room as Ashes went down the hall to get Sin.

We settled at the table, Ashes and Sin returning moments later.

Ashes had made fettuccine alfredo. The delicious smell made my stomach grumble. I dug in quickly, needing the food. Ashes devoured the pile on his plate at a pace that rivaled mine. Stitches ate at a slower, steady pace. It was Sin who stared at his food, his lips turned into a deep frown.

"Eat," I said.

He didn't look at me. He speared some noodles on his fork and stuffed the bite into his mouth, chewing quickly.

Shaking my head, I ate more. I knew he was pissed at me, but I was pissed at him too. The fact he was denying shit and fighting his feelings was enough to drive my insanity to its limits. I wasn't even sure what the next step in insanity was. Maybe I'd finally fucking lose it and revel in the blood and tears of those who'd pushed me too far.

We ate in silence before clearing our plates. Ashes loaded the dishwasher, and Stitches went back to the couch where he stared at the wall, his head resting against the back of the couch.

Sin's stare lingered on him for a moment before he stepped onto the back patio and leaned against the railing to peer out at the lake.

I pulled out a blunt and sparked it up, inhaling the first hit deeply and holding the burn in my lungs before blowing it out. I sat beside Stitches and offered him the weed. He hesitated for a moment before taking a hit and blowing out the smoke. He did it twice more before handing it back to me. He scrubbed his hand down his face and closed his eyes.

I took a few more fortifying hits before clapping his stoned ass on the thigh and going to my room, but not before noticing Ashes flicking his lighter as he watched Sin on the patio.

We were a fucking mess.

Once upstairs, I pushed my sweatpants off and got into the shower, letting my high blanket me as I washed away the day's bullshit.

All I wanted to do was see my specter. Hold her. Kiss her. Fuck her. Tell her I love her.

I vowed to remedy that soon enough. I'd lost track of how many nights I'd watched her sleep. If I went to her while she slept, would she feel me bury myself inside her heat? Would she explode onto my cock and cling to me like she did the last time I was deep inside her? Would she scream? Could I bring her back to me?

I hated I was this fucked-up monster, but the heart wanted what it wanted. And that was specter back in my arms.

†

A BIT LATER, I smoked another blunt as I sat in my leather chair in the living room. Stitches was glued to his spot on the couch, not saying a word. His silence worried me. Ashes was our quiet one. Stitches was always going a mile a minute. To see him sitting and staring wordlessly at the wall had me on edge.

"He's here. Asylum," Ashes said, coming into the room. "I see him on the path."

I took another hit before getting to my feet and handing the joint off to Stitches. He took a final pull then put it out and followed me like a damn zombie.

"Showtime," I said.

He nodded tightly, his eyes still glassy.

"I'll get Sin," Ashes muttered, darting to Sin's room where the prick was still holed up.

Stitches and I stepped onto the patio and watched as Seth approached. *Asylum.* Stitches tensed beside me. As much as I wanted to pummel Seth and rip his spine through his throat, I shoved those feelings beneath the surface.

"Easy," I said softly to Stitches. "Sit down and don't get up for shit. Got it?"

He said nothing. Instead, he backed away from me and went to the patio chair and sat down, his eyes narrowed as he took in Seth who was now climbing the steps to me.

"Church," Seth said, inclining his head at me. "Glad to see you have your dog on its leash."

"I'd be careful if I were you," I said with a snarl, not caring for his jab at Stitches. "You'd be dead if I let him free."

"I don't fear death, Dante. It fears me."

I scowled at the asshole and gestured to a patio chair. "Sit."

He moved past me and grabbed the chair opposite Stitches, who glowered at him.

Ashes and Sin joined us a moment later. We formed a circle around the gas fire pit on the back deck. The sound of the waves lapping the shore in the distance filled the silence for a minute.

"Let's get to the point in all of this," I started. "Sirena."

"I want her," Asylum said immediately.

Stitches sat forward. Ashes threw his arm out to stop him from fully getting out of his chair.

"We're aware," I said, reeling in my anger. "But we had a deal. Whoever could make her scream would get her. She screamed *my* name."

Asylum licked his lips, his blue eyes focused on me. "We did make a deal. However, the deal was that whoever *made* her scream would get her. That would be me. It was with me that she screamed. Yes, she screamed your name, Dante, but had I not been there to provoke her shout, your name would've never slipped past her lips. Yours may have been the name on her lips, but I'm the one carved into her fucking soul. She belongs to me. To *us*."

"She belongs to the watchers," Ashes snapped back.

I glanced at him. I didn't want Ashes to lose it. He was the sanest of all of us. If he slipped and fell, it'd be a fucking feeding frenzy of crazy. Asylum really would end up buried beneath a new hot tub.

Asylum leaned back in his seat, his blue eyes darkening. "I know what you did." His focus was on me.

"What I did?" I raised my brows at him.

He nodded slowly, his gaze raking over me. "You claimed her. You *fucked* her."

I stared back at him. "I did."

He narrowed his eyes. "She loves you, which is the only reason I haven't killed you… or any of you, yet."

Stitches lunged to his feet this time. Instead of Ashes holding him back, it was Sin who moved to get in front of him. He spoke in a hurried, soft voice to him as Stitches glared at Asylum. Finally, Stitches sat back down, and Sin returned to his seat.

"She's mine," Asylum said softly. "I won. You know I did."

I fucking knew he did, but there had to be something else. Something I could cling to because giving her to him didn't sit well with me. She was my girl. Fucking MINE.

"Why do you want her so badly?" Ashes asked.

Asylum snapped his focus to him. "Because she's my forever girl. She's *ours*. *We've* known her since *we* were children. She needs me—us — right now. Believe that."

Sin rubbed his eyes and looked at his lap, not saying a damn word.

"I'll explain it to you this way. As much as I know you want to kill me and bury me beneath a new hot tub…" He shot a quick look at me, a smirk on his lips.

I crinkled my brows. I'd never said that shit out loud. *How the fuck… ?*

"You won't. You may try, but you'll fail. I'm not alone, you know. I'm never *fucking alone.* I know all. I. SEE. All." He rubbed his hands down his thighs and shot a look to his right and he muttered something I couldn't make out before he looked back at us.

"You think you're saving her, but you're not. You think you're protecting her from me. You're not. She'll never be free of me. Of *us.* I'm entwined deep into her soul. I am *her roots*. I'm the one who'll keep her from losing her mind, even though I brought her to the brink of madness. You'd be wise to release her to me." He gazed at us each in turn, settling on Sin last. "Right, Sinclair?"

I shot a look to Sin as Ashes frowned at him. Sin studied Asylum for a moment. Shit was going on he wasn't telling me. Something niggled deep within my mind, but it didn't make sense. I pushed the nagging thought away, deciding I'd unpack it later.

"What do you plan on doing with her?" Sin asked, his voice rough.

The corner of Asylum's lips twitched. "Hold onto her and never let go. If *we* let go, she'll suffer."

"Are you threatening her?" I snarled at him.

He shook his head. "I am not. I'm only being honest. You want her back. I want her free. We are not the same."

"Free from what?" Stitches finally broke his silence, glaring at him.

"Free from the madness. The restraint. *The fear.* Only I can set her free. I'm her warden. Her punisher. *Her redeemer,*" he explained, his words soft and dangerous.

The hairs on the back of my neck stood on end.

"And in her fear of me, I will set her free. Wouldn't you like that? Her running back to you because she's afraid of me?"

I did fucking like that idea.

To get her back, we'd have to let him break her.

But why would he do that if he wanted her so badly?

"If you honor our arrangement, I promise to return her to you when the time is right," he said.

"You're just going to give her back? Like a broken fucking toy?" Stitches asked, snorting and shaking his head. "You're a fucking lunatic. No deal."

I held my hand up to silence him. I ignored the incredulous look on his face and focused on Asylum.

"How do you know you can bring her back?"

"Because she's always listened to us. You may be a god to her, Dante, but I'm her devil. The demon from her nightmares. We're the voices who's been with her since we first laid eyes on her. And good girls always do what the voices in their heads tell them to do. *I* am her voice now." He surveyed me evenly, challenging me.

"Where I'm from, good girls worship their god, not their demons." I pressed my palms to my knees, shifting forward.

"Where I'm from, we let gods think that."

We stared one another down for a moment.

The truth of the matter was, I wanted her back in whatever way I could have her. I knew Asylum enough to know he'd make our lives miserable if we didn't play along. Who knew what he was planning if we failed to keep our agreement.

As much as I wanted to kill him right then, he probably had a safety net in place making it impossible. Once he walked out of here if we didn't honor the bet, he'd rain hell down on us. On specter.

If we kept to the agreement, we had a very real chance of getting her back.

It was an ugly gamble, but one I was willing to take. For now. Because I'd be watching and planning too, and the moment I could, I'd take my specter from him. Then I'd kill him.

It had been a long time since I'd planned a murder. This could actually bring me some enjoyment.

"We'll honor the terms. She's yours. *For now,*" I said, my words carrying softly into the night.

Stitches jumped to his feet and glared at me before stomping back into the house. I knew this would hurt him, but to save her, we had to let her go. I'd explain it to him as soon as Asylum left.

"He won't listen," Asylum murmured. His gaze was fixed on me.

Fucking weirdo.

"And if you try to take her from me, you won't win," he continued. "So consider your next move very carefully, Dante. If you break the terms of our deal, I will break *you*. I'll tear apart everything you thought you had protected. Your friends. What's left of your family. Hopes. Dreams. Desires. *Nothing* is safe from us. Do you understand?"

"You don't scare me," I said, my words laced with honesty. "You and your fucking voices."

"That's because we haven't tried." He cocked his head at me. "Let's pray we don't have to."

I studied him for a moment before I spoke, "So we have a deal? You get her and will bring her out of whatever mess she's in then return her to us?"

"We have a deal." He rose to his feet with me and shook my hand. He pulled me in closer, his lips at my ear so no one else could hear his words, "When we return her, I will be taking something with me. Trust me. It's for the best. Will you give me anything for her?"

I swallowed thickly. "Yes."

"Perfect." He chuckled softly in my ear, making goosebumps erupt along my skin.

"Don't hurt her." This time, my voice shook.

"I would never," he whispered before pulling away from me. He turned to Ashes. "Keep that anger in check with those flames. We're going to need both later."

Ashes glared at him wordlessly.

"It was a pleasure doing business with you. Tell Stitches hanging himself won't fix the mess. I'd tell him quickly though since he's tying the rope now." He stepped down the stairs and looked over at Sin. "I'll be seeing you soon, Sinclair."

"Fuck you," Sin grunted.

Asylum let out a soft laugh. "Go cut your boy out of his closet. You have about thirty seconds."

And with those words, he departed into the night.

I glanced at Ashes and then Sin before darting into the house, something telling me just maybe Asylum knew what he was talking about.

SIN

I raced into the house after Church, Ashes on my heels. Church didn't bother knocking on Stitches's door. He burst through it, me and Ashes nearly crashing into him as he stopped and stared at Stitches's closed closet door.

I could feel the fear radiating from him as he lunged forward and yanked the door open.

He let out a garbled sob as Stitches hung from the bar in his closet, his face red, his body twitching.

I nearly fell to my knees at the sight, my guts twisting in fear and sickness. Church dashed forward and pulled the knife from his pocket, cutting through the rope quickly as Ashes and I jumped into action, holding Stitches's body so he wouldn't hit the floor.

We laid him flat, the ligature marks on his neck ugly and swollen.

But his chest was moving. He was breathing.

"Malachi. Fucking wake up," Church shouted, slapping him in the face before shaking him. "You stupid motherfucker. You promised. You fucking promised, man!" Church's voice broke as he slapped him across the face again.

I was going to throw up. *Fucking Stitches. What the fuck?*

"Wake up. You can't go. You promised. We don't break promises." Church gave him another shake while Ashes checked his pulse.

"His pulse is strong. We need to get him to the medical unit. Call the wards," Ashes said.

Quickly, I pulled my phone out and dialed the emergency number for the campus.

"The wards," a bored sounding female answered.

"It's Sinclair Priest. We need someone here. Now!"

"OK. What's going on?"

"Malachi Wolfe. He-he tried to kill himself. Hanging."

"Is he breathing?"

I looked at him and saw the rise and fall of his chest.

"Yeah. He's breathing. He has a pulse too. He's just unconscious."

"Elevate his legs higher than his head. Continue to check for breathing and a pulse. Please have the door unlocked. Someone should be there any minute."

"Thank you." I hung up, not waiting to hear the rest of her instructions. I ran over to his bed and grabbed a couple pillows and put them beneath his legs.

Church clung to his hand, his own breathing shaky as Ashes wiped a tear from the corner of Stitches's closed eyes.

Fuck. How did it get to this? And how the hell did I stop it? I knew shit would get bad, but I never thought this would happen.

Guilt surged through me as I knelt next to Church.

It should be me on the floor, not Stitches. I was the one who deserved to die.

Stitches's eyelids fluttered, and his eyes cracked open.

"Stitches," Ashes murmured. "Hey, man. Welcome back."

Another tear slipped out of the corner of his eye. And another.

"Don't you dare fucking do this shit again. I can't. I just fucking can't," Church choked out. "Not you, man. You fucking promised."

"S-sorry," Stitches rasped, his voice barely audible.

His eyes were so bloodshot it made my stomach roil. He squeezed Church's hand before his eyelids fluttered again, and he went silent, his breathing deep and even.

Church wiped at his eyes as the front door banged open.

Four of the wards—emergency service people from the hospital on campus—barged in with a stretcher and a bag of supplies. We stepped away from Stitches as they set to work on him. They gave him oxygen and hooked him up to a heart monitor before putting him on the stretcher, positioning his head between two blocks to stabilize it in case he'd done damage.

"We'll be right behind," Church said thickly as the men moved Stitches out of the room.

We followed behind to the living room.

"Give us a few minutes with him," one of the guys said. "Doc will want to assess him and all that. Might be a bit of a wait."

"Fine." Church nodded, his eyes fixed on Stitches as they hauled him out the front door. The last ward followed, closing the door behind him and leaving us in silence.

"He'll be OK," Church whispered, swallowing.

"How did he know? Asylum?" Ashes asked the question that was rattling around in my head.

"I don't know," Church murmured, finally looking over at us. "It doesn't make sense."

"He's a weird guy," I muttered, running my fingers through my shaggy hair.

My head was killing me. My stomach was still upset.

"He always seems to just know things," Ashes continued, shaking his head.

"Which is why I think we need to trust him about specter." Church looked at both of us. "Even if it fucking guts us. I think he was only demonstrating what he's capable of."

"I agree," Ashes said, rubbing his eyes and grabbing his jacket.

"Sin?" Church looked at me.

I blew out a breath, the nausea twisting like a snake in my guts. "I don't give a shit about Asylum right now. Right now, I'm worried about Stitches. We need to go. One thing at a time."

"You're right." Ashes strode to the door and pulled it open.

Church was quick to join him. I grabbed my cell phone off the coffee table and followed them, my heart in my throat.

†

IT TOOK hours for the doctor to let us back to Stitches. When he did, we just saw him for a few minutes since he was knocked out on meds.

"He'll survive," Dr. Conrad said as he looked at his chart. "He'll be sore. We're going to keep him on a mandatory ninety-six-hour hold, though. Headmaster Sully will come in and do an assessment as well. If we deem him unfit to leave, he'll remain here until he is well enough to go."

A muscle thrummed along Church's jaw. "If you so much as fucking think about putting him in the hole, I'll fucking put you in one. Understand?"

Doctor Conrad visibly swallowed. "Perfectly, Dante."

Church eyed him for a moment longer before stomping out of the room, Ashes and me following him.

"I hate that prick," Ashes grumbled as we walked.

"Me too," I muttered.

Guy was a tool.

We walked in silence for a few more minutes down the quiet hall. We were about to pass siren's room. Church slowed.

Cady stepped out of the room and waited for us.

"I saw them bring him in. Is he OK?" she asked as we stopped next to her.

Cady was a beautiful girl. Not the same mesmerizing way her sister was, but I bet she still fucked with the hearts of men though. She looked like the type.

"He's OK. He's under a ninety-six-hour psych hold," Ashes said as Church peered past Cady into siren's room.

Cady nodded. "What did he do?"

"Tried to hang himself," I muttered.

Her eyes widened at the information.

Church wordlessly stepped past Cady and went into siren's room. I watched as he approached her bed and stared down at her.

"He's just hurting. He's worried about Sirena," Ashes said.

"Real shit way to worry about her," Cady answered, shaking her head. "Trying to unalive himself doesn't seem like something he should do to help her. If he loves her as much as he claims to, why would he want to hurt her by killing himself?"

"There's a lot of shit you don't understand about the things that go through our heads," I started.

She held up a hand to stop me. "I'm going to stop you right there and tell you to shut the fuck up."

I glared at her. She definitely wasn't like siren.

"I don't give a shit what he's feeling for himself. If he wants my sister, he better fucking put her before himself or I won't let him within a mile of her. So make sure that message gets delivered. I don't need her to have a broken heart on top of the shit she's already dealing with. Got it, shrimp dick?"

"The fuck? Shrimp dick?" I snarled at her. "I don't have a fucking shrimp dick. I can prove it if you'd like."

She raised her brows at me. "By all means, prove it."

I scowled at her as Ashes let out a soft chuckle.

"Fuck that. Fuck you too."

"Unlikely to happen with a shrimp dick."

This bitch...

"Easy, man. She's just looking out for our girl. I'll make sure Stitches gets the message," Ashes said.

"Thank you." She shot me a sour look.

"Come on, Sin. Let's see Sirena." Ashes slipped past Cady.

I didn't follow. I stayed in the hallway, but so did Cady. She watched Ashes sit on Sirena's opposite side since Church was now sitting in the chair by her bed. She turned to me, her gaze raking over me.

"Why don't you go say hi, *Sinful?*"

"Fuck off," I muttered, tearing my focus away from siren and my friends.

"I know you had something to do with Rina being this way. Once I figure it out, I'll bring you down."

"What makes you think I did something?" I asked thickly.

"Because no one named Sin is without it. And you looked guilty as hell running from her room when she started screaming *Sinful.*"

I breathed out and glanced away from her to the guys gathered around siren's bed. Ashes kissed the back of her hand while Church brushed her hair away from her face. I knew if Stitches was here, he'd be right next to her too.

"She's too good for us," I finally said. "I don't want her. She'll only wind up ruined if she's near us too long. Everyone does. And then we'll be destroyed. It's an ugly, vicious cycle I don't care to repeat. Stitches tried to end his life tonight because the thought of not being with her was tearing him apart. The worry that she'd slipped away forever was eating him alive. I don't want that for any of us, and I don't want that for her. So maybe I am *sinful,* but it's only because I give a damn."

Cady studied me for a moment as we locked eyes.

"I think you're right. I think she'd be better off without you. But I won't ever stop her from loving who she loves. If it's you, so be it, but if it is—even all of you—then you better fucking be worth it. She's been through hell and back. The last thing she needs is another monster holding her down."

"It won't be a problem for much longer. We're going to be stepping away from her soon so she can heal."

"Good."

I focused back on the guys as they doted on her.

"Will you tell her goodbye?" Cady asked.

I shook my head, my voice thick and laced with my pain, "I already did."

And with those words, I walked away.

ASHES

When I got out of classes, I rushed over to the medical ward so I could spend every possible minute with my heaven while I could. I knew our time with her would be over soon … until Seth gave her back.

I sat next to Sirena's wheelchair and laced my fingers with hers. They'd gotten her out of bed today. She wouldn't walk, so the nurse and orderlies had lifted her and sat her in a wheelchair facing the wall.

I chuckled, thinking about when I'd first seen her. "I thought I was in love. The more I watched you, the more I knew I was," I continued. "I'd never considered what my life would be like past Chapel Crest, but you made me see a future. A real one. Me and you with the guys. Happy. Free of the shit in our lives. I still feel that way. I still see that future for all of us together." I swallowed thickly. "You just need to come back, baby. I'll take you to our spot at Pictured Rocks. I'll make love to you beneath the stars. I'll whisper to you how much I love you because I do, heaven. I love you so fucking much." I breathed out and swiped at the dampness along my lashes.

"Stitches isn't well," I said softly. "He misses you. He tried to hurt himself last night to escape his pain. We need you. Please, Sirena. Come back to us." I reached out and cradled her face.

She didn't acknowledge me as she stared at the wall.

"Come back to me," I whispered, clinging desperately to her hand.

Nothing.

"Fuck, baby, come on," I pleaded softly.

I rose from my chair and dropped to my knees in front of her, both my hands cradling her face. She stared straight through me, her pretty eyes dull in comparison to the sparkle and brightness that they used to have.

I released her face and took her hand, flipping her palm up. I placed my finger on her palm and began to write, desperate to get her to acknowledge me.

I miss you.

I finished and gazed at her. She simply stared straight ahead. My throat tightened as I thought of Stitches locked away and medicated in his hospital room. Of the pain in Church's voice when we'd taken Stitches out of his closet. How Church had held her when we'd found her. How he'd fucking begged for her to be OK. The desperation I felt in my heart to get her back to us so our world could heal. So *she* could heal.

I shuffled forward and pressed my lips to hers, kissing her gently.

Please, heaven, come back. PLEASE!

Nothing. Not a damn thing.

I deepened the kiss, probing my tongue against her soft lips as I continued to cradle her face.

When she didn't respond, I broke the kiss off and rested my forehead against hers.

"I fucking love you, Sirena," I whispered. "I can't do this without you. Come back. Please. I don't even care how long it takes. I'll wait forever if I have to."

I finally shifted away from her. Surprise filled me as I caught sight of Asylum leaning against the door jamb, watching.

He pushed himself off and sauntered toward us in his school uniform.

"Forever is a long time, Asher," he said as he took a seat on the edge of her bed. "Do you intend on keeping that promise?"

"Do you intend on keeping your promise to us of giving her back?" I shot back. All I wanted to do was shroud her from him and keep her tucked away safely beside me.

"Absolutely," he said solemnly. "I figure the payoff is worth it."

I snorted. "And what's the payoff?"

He smirked at me, his blue eyes flashing. "No spoilers, Valentine. Only cliffhangers."

I rolled my eyes at him.

"How is Malachi? Still *hanging* in there?" His eyes sparkled with amusement.

"Fuck you, Seth. How the hell did you know he was going to do that?" I demanded.

He shrugged and picked a piece of lint off Sirena's comforter. "Some call it crazy. Others call it intuitive. And then there are those who would say I got lucky. What do you say?"

I studied him for a moment. He stared back at me with bright blue eyes, his black hair a mess on his head, his white uniform shirt not buttoned to the top and his red tie loose.

"I say you're not telling us how the hell you *really* knew."

He gave me a Cheshire smile. "You're smart, Valentine. I like that. Perhaps if you comply, I'll tell you my secret."

"Do you always know everything?" I asked, curious.

He shrugged again. "No. But sometimes, yes."

"Do you know if Sirena is going to make it out of this?"

He licked his lips and looked over at her. A look of complete adoration washed over his face as he took her in. My chest clenched.

"I'll do everything I can to bring her back. I have no limits on that."

"But do you know for sure?"

"Yes," he whispered, still staring at her, the adoration replaced by hunger. "Or we'll die trying."

I had no idea who the *we* was that he spoke of, but I prayed it didn't include my heaven. He and his fucking hallucinations or voices or whatever the fuck haunted him could go straight to hell.

His brows crinkled, and he cocked his head. His words came out in a soft rush. "Her family is coming. Sully is coming. We must be cautious."

I frowned at him as Cady stepped into the room, a sullen look on her face. Her gaze jumped between me and Seth, her face morphing into one of anger as she openly glared at Seth.

Before she could speak, Sully stepped into the room with her mom and stepfather.

"Asher. What a. . . pleasant surprise," Sully greeted me, offering me a fake smile.

"I'm sure," I muttered, glancing at Sirena, who hadn't moved an inch and continued to stare at the wall.

"Seth. My goodness," her mother said, approaching him as he stood. "I haven't seen you in ages. You've grown into a handsome young man!" She stopped in front of him and offered him a smile.

He returned it, his entire demeanor changing. "It's been too long," he said, a charming smirk on his lips. "How are you?"

"I'm well. Mostly. Worried about Sirena. Professor Sully said you were there when she was found. Can you tell us what happened?"

Seth nodded, the grin still on his face. "A game of *ghost in the graveyard* gone wrong, I'm afraid. But don't worry. She'll get better. I'll make sure of it."

"We were told you were found in th-the coffin with her," her mother continued.

Seth nodded solemnly. "I didn't want her to go crazy alone."

Her mother's lips shook. "Right. Well, uh, we're just going to say our goodbyes to Sirena. We're leaving a little later. Professor—I mean, Dr. Sully—has created a treatment plan for her that we've agreed to. Jerry, my husband, thinks it's very promising."

"It's completely insane," Cady piped up. "And bullshit."

"Cadence, enough," Jerry snapped, glaring at her.

She glared right back at him. She crossed her arms over her chest and sneered at him. I watched the exchange, my body tense. I knew what Cady had told me about the asshole. I'd beat the shit out of him if he even thought about hurting her too.

"Sirena is staying?" I asked.

"Yes. She'll be here through her treatment." Her mother offered me a shaky smile. "We're very hopeful."

I nodded tightly. *Fucking Sully.*

"Asher, it may be a good idea to step out of the room so Sirena's family may spend some quality time with her. Seth, you as well," Sully said.

I'd have told him to fuck off if Sirena's mother wasn't in the room. Instead, I leaned in and placed a gentle kiss on Sirena's cheek and whispered in her ear, "I love you, heaven. I'll see you soon."

Seth raised an eyebrow at me as I scowled back. He followed me out of the room. The moment we were in the hall, he spoke, "Tell the watchers they should come say goodbye to Sirena tonight. After tonight, I won't tolerate you guys involved in her life. Not until we're done."

"Done?" I scoffed at him. "Fuck you, Seth. Seriously. What do you think you can do for her?"

"I'm not Seth. I'm Asylum," he said. "You don't trust me. And you shouldn't. But you can't deny that I made her scream. If I can make her scream, I can make her talk. So have a little faith, Asher. Everything happens for a reason."

Anger raced through me, but I pushed it down. Instead, I reached into my pocket and squeezed my lighter, the cool metal calming me.

"Don't fucking touch her," I whispered. "Don't hurt her more. I swear on everything I am, I'll set you on fire while you sleep and watch *you* scream if you hurt her."

He cocked his head at me. "We do love the suffering, don't we? We're sick. Twisted. Monsters who don't deserve life, much less love. Yet, we seek it. Perhaps to continue tormenting ourselves. Fascinating, isn't it? Tell me, Asher, if I offered you the chance to help me bring her back, would you take it? Would you leave the watchers and join me?"

I glared at him. "I'm never leaving the watchers. Just like she's never leaving us either."

"Ah, but what will you call it when I'm buried inside her warm, wet confines and she's clinging to me? When she's *coming* for me?"

I couldn't take it anymore. My fist collided with his face, knocking him back, blood trickling from the cut on his lip. I glared at him, my body shaking as he righted himself and let out a laugh which shook me to my core.

"That's the fucking spirit, Valentine. *That's* what I wanted."

"You're a sick, twisted *fuck*. If you touch her, I'll kill you, Cain. That's a fucking promise."

His blue eyes sparkled, making my anger boil harder. Nothing bothered the asshole. In fact, he seemed to enjoy my outburst of violence. Rather than give him what he wanted, I backed away. I knew if I didn't leave, I'd burn the entire place down and take Stitches and Sirena out of here while I let the world scream.

"See you around, Valentine," Asylum called after me as I turned and stormed away. "I meant what I said. Tonight. Say your goodbyes."

I said nothing as I walked away.

Fuck Seth Cain. Or Asylum. Whoever the fuck he was.

CHURCH

I couldn't concentrate as I sat in class all day. Knowing my brother was on a psych hold and my girl was struggling really had me on edge. I knew Ashes had gone to see her and had checked on Stitches. I hadn't heard back from him, which I supposed was a good thing because no news was good news. At least I hoped so.

The fact our group was shrinking had me chomping at the bit to figure out what the hell was going on. I knew Stitches was always toeing a delicate line with his sanity, but I never thought he'd do what he'd done. It broke my fucking heart. He was my brother, even if only by adoption. We'd been through way too much for him to try to leave me like that.

And specter… Fucking damnit.

"Dante, can you come up and read your short story?" Sister May interrupted my morose thoughts.

I frowned at her. "I didn't write one."

She blinked at me like she was stupid and didn't understand what I'd said.

"It's due today," she finally said as the class sat in silence.

I assumed they were waiting for me to explode. "OK. And I didn't do it," I snapped back.

She frowned and studied me for a moment, the act really pissing me off. Finally, she forced a smile onto her pretty face and moved on to Melanie, who was far too eager to jump up and read a story about a girl who was beautiful but ignored.

Shit had to be about her, although I'd have omitted the beautiful part. Even her soul was ugly. Not that I was one to talk. Mine wasn't much better in the grand scheme of things. I'd murdered before. I'd done plenty of fucked-up shit in my life.

I found it odd that the only thing lately I regretted wasn't the murders, but rather the fact I hadn't been with my specter when she'd been stuffed into that fucking coffin. I'd have killed whoever had done that to her. I was really beginning to doubt Seth had acted alone. There was just no way he could've lifted that heavy stone lid to close it over them. Not from inside the coffin.

I planned on finding out which of his leach friends had assisted him. Then I'd punish them accordingly. It may end up with me gutting whoever it was in the forest like I did to all the animals who were unfortunate enough to cross my path. I was getting rather good at carving.

Classes were dismissed, and I got to my feet, sauntering to the hallway, students, patients whatever the fuck we were called, giving me a wide berth.

I spotted Bryce in the corridor and zeroed in on him.

He froze when he realized I was headed straight for him.

"H-hey, Church," he greeted me, his gaze darting around like any of those assholes around us could save him if I decided his time was up.

"Sirena isn't well," I said, ignoring the proper social constructs to get to the fucking point.

Sadness morphed across his face. "I-I know. They won't let me see her. I've been trying—"

"Were you there? The night it happened? Don't lie to me. I need the truth."

He blinked at me. "What? No!"

I surveyed him and saw the fear and honesty on his face. "So you don't know who helped Seth put her in that fucking coffin?"

"So it's t-true?" His voice trembled.

I nodded tightly. "Someone lured her to the cemetery and put her in the fucking tomb in the mausoleum with Asylum. He's not really talking about if he had help. But I'm inclined to believe he did. There's no way she'd go out there with him alone. It had to be someone she knew. Someone she trusted."

"I swear it wasn't me. I'd never do that to her. Never," Bryce said fiercely.

I studied him again. "Get me information. You're always in the office working. See if you can find out what happened. If anything comes to Sully's desk. If anyone talks…I want to know everything."

"I'll do everything I can," he said evenly. "And if I find out who did this to her, I hope you make them pay."

His words surprised me. Bryce had always struck me as the nonviolent sort, but finding out he wanted retribution and punishment as much as I did was something I didn't expect. I knew he and Sirena were close—too close for my liking—but if he felt this way, then I had no reason to suspect him. Bryce was a smart guy. Easy to read most of the time. He was angry on her behalf.

Good. Hopefully, it would get us somewhere.

"They're already dead," I said before backing away.

†

"HE SAID we needed to say our goodbyes tonight. That he's taking over." Ashes stared at me as I sat in my chair in the living room later that night.

Sin was on the couch, his elbows resting on his knees as he stared at the floor.

I steadied my breathing to keep from losing my mind at Ashes's words.

"So that's it? We're doing it?" Ashes asked, his voice soft as he gave me a hopeless look from his spot next to Sin.

I breathed out, hating he was hurting. That we all were. And Stitches...

Fuck, my brother.

"We don't have a choice right now," I said. "Not until we figure out what happened that night. Not until he decides to give her back to us. He's dangerous, and we don't need her being punished because we couldn't honor our end of the deal."

Ashes nodded morosely.

"Sin?" I called out.

He looked over at me slowly.

"You haven't said shit about any of this. Care to fucking weigh in?"

He was silent for a moment before he spoke, "I think we lost. I think we're doing the right thing."

"Of course you do," Ashes said sourly.

Sin sighed. "I told you guys it was a bad idea from the start. I was right. Now look? Everyone is heartbroken, and Stitches tried to kill himself. See where all of this shit has gotten us?" He shook his head. "Sirena Lawrence will be the death of us. If we want to live, then we let her go."

"Tell that to Stitches," Ashes snapped, glowering at Sin.

Sadness washed over his face, and he said nothing else, opting to go back to his fascination with the floor.

So this was it.

"So we tell her goodbye tonight. Maybe by some miracle she'll come back to us," I said softly. "And then she can tell us what really happened."

"What if she gets worse?" Ashes asked, his eyes bloodshot from trying not to cry.

"She won't," I said. "I trust she's in there yet and will be back."

Sin sighed and gazed out the window, a muscle thrumming along his jaw.

"And when she's back, Sin can tell her how he really feels," I finished, staring at him.

He glanced over at me, sadness on his face. There was something else there too which I couldn't quite place, but I honestly didn't have time for it. We needed to see Sirena and make these last moments count. We needed to see Stitches.

We'd deal with whatever the fuck Sin had going on later.

†

SHE LAY IN HER BED, staring at the ceiling, her pretty, mismatched eyes focused on something only she could see. She seemed smaller to me today.

Her parents were speaking to Sully and Dr. Conrad. Cady had just finished feeding her, which based on what I'd seen, was an ordeal because they struggled to get her to open her mouth, chew, or swallow.

"Did she eat enough?" I asked, eyeing the half-eaten pudding cup on the table.

"No," Cady said, sighing. "But it was more than at lunch, so that's progress. They're talking about a feeding tube for her."

Ashes flinched at Cady's words and sat beside Sirena. He kissed her hand, whispering to her things I couldn't hear.

Sin stood on the edge of the room, his eyes focused anywhere but on Sirena, his hands buried deep in the pockets of his uniform pants.

"Are they going to?" I demanded, hating the idea of more shit being tossed at her.

"Maybe. Dr. Conrad said we'd see if she starts eating more this week before they do it. They don't want to keep force feeding her."

I looked to Ashes, still clutching her hand like a lifeline.

Fuck... come on, specter. Come back...

"We're leaving tonight," Cady continued. "I don't want to go, but my mom signed the papers. Sirena will be alone. I'm...I'm scared, Dante."

I snapped my attention to her.

"Will you make sure she's OK? Seth was here with her. He just kept staring at her. He got upset when I wouldn't leave the room. I don't trust him."

"I'll watch over her," I murmured. "No one will harm her while I'm at her side."

She let out a breath. "OK. I-I'll try to come back soon. Leaving her makes me sick to my stomach. Mom already said goodbye. Jerry the fuck noodle didn't even look twice at her. I'm supposed to leave now. I-I just. . ." Her voice trailed off. "Just keep her safe. She's really my only family now that Mom is on Jerry's side."

I nodded and watched as she shuffled back to Sirena and kissed her forehead, murmuring words of love and promising that we'd keep her safe.

I glanced at Sin. He was focused on the sisters, a frown on his face.

He caught my eye and looked away.

She would be safe because I'd find out who helped fucking hurt her and they'd pay.

ASHES

Cady left with her mom and stepdad, but not before giving me her cell number so I could keep in touch with her about Sirena. Church and Sin stepped out of the room so I could be alone with Sirena.

Knowing I had to say goodbye was breaking my heart. It shattered further when I realized Stitches wouldn't get the chance since he was in lockdown with no visitors for now.

Bad fucking timing.

I hoped it didn't make him worse.

"Heaven," I murmured, holding her hand. "I have to go. I don't want to leave you, but Seth won. Since he was able to make you scream, he won you from us. We fucked up by making that bet with him. Our egos were bigger than our hearts, and for that I'm so fucking sorry. I'm sorry you're going through this. I'm sorry you're scared. I'm sorry I can't be here. I just. . . please come back. Tell us what really happened. Seeing you like this is killing all of us. Stitches sends his love. He needs you so much."

I licked my lips as I memorized her features.

Still as a doll. Perfect as one too. She continued to stare at the ceiling.

"Can I kiss you, heaven?" I whispered, standing so I could lean over her.

She didn't move. Didn't answer me. I sighed and cradled her face as I leaned in and pressed my lips to hers, kissing her slowly and gently.

She didn't kiss me back.

I rested my forehead against hers after I broke away.

"You're in there. I know you are. Please. Find your way out. Find your way back to me. To us. I thought we were strong, but without you, we're not. This is breaking us."

I pulled away from her and wiped my eyes.

How was it possible to fall in love with someone so fast?

Because you've waited a lifetime for her.

I took her hand in mine and flipped her palm up. I gently traced letters onto it.

I love you.

"I'll wait for you, Sirena," I said, tears trickling down my cheeks. I wiped at them and released her hand. "We all will."

I left the room, forcing myself to not look back at her.

"You good?" Church asked as I stepped into the hall and wiped at my eyes again.

I nodded, my throat tight. I didn't want to cry. Fucking help me, I didn't.

I cast a look at Sin. He was staring back at me, his brows crinkled. He quickly turned away.

"Sin, go tell her goodbye," Church said gruffly.

"I'm good," Sin muttered.

"Fucking get in there," Church snarled before I could tell him the same thing. "I swear to fuck, Sinclair, you're working on my last nerve."

Sin glanced at me before closing his eyes for a moment to compose himself and opening them again.

"You may never get another chance," I said softly. "So if there's anything you want to say to her, do it now."

He said nothing, but after a moment, he pushed past us and marched into her room, closing the door behind him.

I moved next to Church. "It'll be good for him."

"I hope so. Right now, it's just me and you."

He was right. Stitches was laid up. Sin was having an internal war. Everything really was just me and Church right now.

"We've been through worse," I said.

"We've always come out on top. I'm not big on faith, Asher, but I think that's all we have right now." His green eyes glimmered with his sadness.

"We'll find out who helped do this to her," I said, my voice low, as I stared back at him.

"And then we'll punish the motherfucker."

"Or kill him," I finished.

A glint of darkness flashed through Church's eyes. "Or kill him. I know a good hiding spot for the bodies."

"I know a better one," I whispered, looking at the closed door to Sirena's room. "You can't find a body when it's ash on the wind."

Church chuckled softly and clapped me on the shoulder. "Let's get to work then, brother."

Let's get to fucking work.

I approached her bed, my heart in my throat. The last thing I wanted to be was in the fucking room with her.

But it was the only place I wanted to be too.

I hated the feelings that kept crashing into one another in my chest. Hearing her voice calling me *Sinful* was stuck on repeat in my head. It was my own silent hell as I wrestled with the demons of what I'd done to her. Knowing I was the reason she was suffering more now, locked in a prison going through God only knew what.

And if Dante and the guys found out. . . well, it was safe to say I'd have a whole host of new problems to deal with.

I sank down onto the chair beside her bed. She stared up at the ceiling. She didn't move. Her chest rose and fell, but if I couldn't see it with my own eyes, I'd think she was dead. Her eyes, which had once been so vibrant, were dull and lifeless now.

"I broke you," I whispered. "Fuck, siren."

She flinched at the sound of my voice.

I deserved it. If she even made it out of this, I'd never have a chance with her.

You don't want one. You don't deserve one. Look what happens whenever you love someone.

Love.

I barely knew her.

But fuck, I felt something I couldn't deny.

Something which made me desperate and terrified.

Something which made me do stupid shit I knew I couldn't come back from. From the moment I'd first seen her, I knew I was in trouble.

I blinked back my tears.

What the fuck, Sinclair?

I reached for her hand, fumbling with it when I realized how cold it was.

"I'm fucked-up," I whispered. "Siren. I-I made a mistake. Now you're hurting. I just want this to be over. I don't want you to hurt. Fuck, I don't. I-I wish I could go back in time. I wish I could change the things I've done. I'm a sinner, and you're a saint. I'm scared, siren. I'm fucking terrified." I breathed out, tears slipping down my cheeks. "But I'll accept whatever punishment you deem fit for me because I know I deserve it. Is this how you're doing it? By leaving and making us hurt? Making me witness the pain I've caused?"

I stood up and leaned over her.

Her breathing picked up.

"What do I do?" I choked out. "Siren. Please."

"Sinful," she whispered in that tiny, sweet voice.

"Siren," I answered back thickly. "Punish me. Please, fucking punish me and put me out of my misery."

"Sinful," she said again.

"Yes," I whispered to her. "I'm Sinful. I'm a monster."

I brought her cold hand to my lips and kissed it. My tears dripped onto her knuckles. I sniffled as I stared down at her before I placed her hand on her stomach and leaned down.

Gently, I swept my lips over hers.

"Siren," I said softly against her lips. "Please. Put me out of my misery."

I didn't know what I meant by my plea. I just knew I wanted it to end. I wanted to be free of the guilt and regret. I wanted to see her big, luminous eyes peering back at me from Church's side. I wanted to hold her and taste her and tell her how fucking sorry I was for ruining everything.

Instead, my tears trickled onto her cool, porcelain-like skin as I pressed my lips harder to hers, desperation soaring through me in the hopes she'd snap out of it and slap me across the face.

Nothing.

She remained unmoving beneath me.

I pulled away from her and wiped my tears gently from her face.

And a single, solitary tear trailed from the corner of her eye. My heart caught in my chest.

She was in there.

She was fighting. She was trying.

I swallowed thickly and backed away from her.

"I'll await your return," I said softly. "I'll await my punishment."

I wiped my eyes again and left the room.

Life would only get harder now.

But I had no one to blame but myself.

CHURCH

Sin didn't stop.

He pushed past us as he left her room and strode to the lobby without looking back.

"He's struggling," Ashes murmured.

I nodded. "He is, but it's not an excuse to be a dickhead. We're all struggling."

Ashes said nothing, but he blew out a breath. "I'll go talk to him. I'll see you back at the house, OK?"

"Yeah," I said, watching him go.

I didn't know what the fuck to do with Sin. He always got caught up in his emotions, or lack thereof. It had never been this bad before. He didn't need to tell me he cared because I saw just how much he did with his reactions to all of this.

He never did well with emotional conflict.

Clearly, this was no exception.

I couldn't deal with his shit right now though. I had one last night to see my specter, and I wasn't going to waste it dwelling on shit I couldn't fix for Sin.

I stepped into her room and locked the door behind me before I dragged a chair over and barred the handle.

If I only got one last night with her, I wasn't going to be disturbed.

I moved to her bedside and stared down at her. Her gaze was focused on the ceiling.

"Hey, specter," I greeted her softly. I leaned down and brushed my lips against her cool cheek. "I missed you today."

I took up residence in the chair at her bedside and held her hand.

"I didn't write some paper for Sister May. She tried to call me out in class, and I barely reacted. That has to mean something, right?"

She didn't answer me. Not like I expected her to.

"I don't know if anyone told you yet. But Stitches won't be visiting anytime soon. He hurt himself. He tried to h-hang himself in his closet because I accepted that Seth w-won," my voice cracked. "I don't really think he won, baby, but I don't have any proof to fight him with. All I know is I heard you screaming my name. But it wasn't me who made you scream. It was him. So to the victor go the spoils."

I grew quiet as I sat beside her, watching through the window as the sun gave way to the horizon and night fell, my hand wrapped firmly around hers.

I fucking missed her. It was eating my soul. My heart. My fucking mind. And this was my last night with her.

Knowing I wouldn't be able to touch her. Kiss her. Fuck her again.

She had to be in there. She had to come back to me.

Ideas swirled rapidly through my brain as I tried to come up with a last-ditch idea to make this right. To keep her mine.

I finally settled on one.

I rose to my feet and stared down at her.

Gingerly, I reached out and eased her blankets down her body then ran my hand along her silky thigh. She didn't move.

I let my hand wander higher until I was at her panties. Gently, I brushed my fingers over her cotton-clad heat, my cock growing hard in my pants.

She didn't react to my touch.

Come on, Dante. She's in there. Fucking force her out. . . It's your last shot.

I pushed her hospital gown up, revealing her bare breasts. Bending down, I kissed along the soft mounds, sucking and nibbling as I went. When I reached one pink, pebbled bud, I sucked it gently into my mouth, swirling my tongue around it before I moved to the other one.

Still nothing from her.

Anger began to eat at me.

She loved me. I knew she did.

I dragged her panties down her thighs, spread her legs apart, and climbed onto the bed. Settling between her legs, I licked up her hot center. She flinched beneath my tongue, making me eager to get more of a reaction from her.

I did it over and over again, listening as her breathing grew quicker. I flicked my tongue over her clit before I sucked and nibbled, putting all my moves on repeat until warmth flowed from her pretty, pink pussy onto my waiting tongue.

Her lips parted, and she whimpered softly.

There it was.

A reaction.

I unzipped my pants and stroked my cock as I stared down at her. She continued to look at the ceiling.

Something came over me. The desire to fuck her like this. To make her remember me. To make her scream my name again. To force her to just fucking come back to me.

I ran my cock along her pussy, collecting her release on the head.

I exhaled, my eyes fixed on her pretty face.

I pushed deep into her heat.

Her breath hitched, her eyes wavering.

Yes. Fuck yes.

I forced my way in until I was buried completely inside her. I loomed over her body, kissing her lips and neck, my thrusts into her pussy perfectly timed.

Faster. Faster. Her body jostled beneath mine as I fucked her. Made love to her. Desperate to bring her back to me.

"Come on, specter," I choked out, staring down at her lifeless body. "Baby, please. Come back. Please, fucking don't leave me."

Oh God, she was so fucking tight.

I sighed, relishing in her heat. Fuck was I desperate.

"Specter. Baby. Come on. Come back to me," I rasped before kissing her again.

Fucking nothing.

No. No. NO!

I thrust harder into her, fucking her rough and fast, my anger at the world taking over. I knew if she was in her right mind, she'd cry for me because I wasn't being gentle. The slapping of our skin met my ears along with my harsh breathing and her soft gasps.

"You don't get to fucking leave me," I said, my eyes burning as tears slipped past my lashes and onto her pale cheeks. "I'm not letting you leave me, Sirena."

My release came to a head, making me groan softly. I pulled out of her and came on her pussy, biting her breast and marking her as I unloaded myself on her core, knowing I'd gotten her off too by the way she shuddered beneath me.

I balanced my body over hers for a moment before I sat up and stared down at the mess I'd made, my come glistening on her slit and thighs.

I reached out and rubbed it into her skin, sliding my fingers through the mess and pushing some of it back into her. I didn't clean her. I simply pulled her panties up so a bit of me could seep into her skin the way she'd seeped into my soul.

Within moments, I had her clothed and covered and my dick put away.

The orgasm had been one of the best in my entire life. I should've felt guilty, but all I felt was sorrow.

Sorrow that I couldn't bring her back. She was still staring at the ceiling.

"You're gone, aren't you?" I whispered, caressing her cheek. "You fucking left me, didn't you?" I bit back a sob. "Everyone leaves me. But you know what, specter?"

I leaned in and put my lips to her ear, my tears falling into her hair. "I'm never leaving you. You are my love. My *fucking obsession*. And the next time you leave me, we'll go in body bags together. I fucking promise you."

I pressed my lips to hers in a hard, deep kiss before breaking it off, my heart heavy and filled with agony before I forced myself away from her so I could leave.

When I got to the door, I unlocked it and pushed the chair aside before I paused and looked back at her.

"Just scream my name again, specter. Then I'll know. I'll know you're ready to come home to me."

And with that, I opened the door and stepped through it, leaving a piece of my heart behind for her to take care of.

SETH

I knew the plan. The treatment. The fucking cure.

And it wasn't anything Sully had in mind.

Not really.

He may have given us the ability to get close to her, but it was us with the fucking power here. He just didn't know it yet.

I watched as they brought her into the room in a wheelchair. Her black hair was limp and needed to be brushed. Dark circles rimmed her mesmerizing eyes. Her skin was paler than I remembered.

And my heart… It surged in my chest at the sight of her.

My Rinny.

"I want you to get into her head. You made her scream before. I know you can do it again. You'll be given a new task each day to complete with her. Get it right and you get to play another day. Get it wrong and I get to," Sully said, his voice was soft and dangerous. "I expect you to not succeed in all of them."

The way he said that made my skin crawl.

His time is coming…

Keep him alive until we bury ourselves in her mind so deeply she'll never be able to escape us.

Break her. Break her and make her mind your new home.

Save her. She needs you to save her, you fucking monster.

So much fucking noise!

I breathed in deeply and cracked my neck, allowing the voices to fade away.

Sully handed me a slip of paper.

The wards lifted Sirena from her wheelchair and sat her in the overstuffed, red velvet chair in the lavishly decorated room. Definitely no hospital vibes in here. No asylum look with padded walls and dim lights. I surveyed the space. It was . . . a red and black room. The colors were dark and warm. Bookcases filled with books lined an entire wall. There was a fireplace and a couch, an ensuite bathroom. A table and two chairs. A sitting area where they'd put Sirena. Plush, thick rugs.

And no windows.

Interesting.

I'd never seen this room before. While it seemed comfortable, I knew it was anything but. It was meant to relax a patient. But this wasn't a place to feel comfort. It was a place to scream without being heard.

A bigger tomb for me and Rinny.

I looked down at the paper Sully had handed me. The task was typed onto it.

Make her remember your childhood. Start from the beginning.

How would they know if I made her remember?

My second thought was that I didn't like the idea of anyone listening in on our special memories because I knew Sully would be listening. Probably watching too.

I said nothing, not wanting to give him any ideas about my feelings.

"You'll spend the day with her," Sully said softly. "You have until this evening with her. Do not fail me. If you do, you fail her. We don't want that, do we?"

I remained silent until he left the room with the wards, locking the door behind him.

Slowly, I approached her, wondering if she'd respond to me.

Her eyes continued to stay fixed on a point straight ahead as I kneeled in front of her.

"Rinny," I murmured, eye level with her.

She stared right through me.

"Do you know who I am?"

A tiny whimper left her lips.

She knew who I was.

Of course she does. She could never forget. She always loved you. Nothing had changed. Except her fear.

"Are you afraid?" I asked, reaching for her.

She rocked slowly in her seat, a soft hum slipping past her lips.

Our song.

She's humming our song.

I hummed along with her as she continued to rock.

"Oh, Rinny," I murmured as I gazed at her.

My pretty, little princess was broken.

Ask her about the first time you met.

Ask her if she remembers what she was wearing.

Ask her if she remembers the first time you made her scream playing hide-and-seek.

Ask her if she remembers the fireflies. . .

I shook my head, willing the noises to quiet before I spoke.

"Do you remember the first time we met?"

She didn't answer. I looked around and saw an ottoman, so I got up and grabbed it, placing it in front of her so I could sit. I took her cold hands in mine. I didn't want that fucker to hear our memories. I hated Sully.

He'll get what's coming to him after I get our forever girl back.

I licked my lips and leaned in so I could press my forehead to hers. I began to recount our memory.

Ours.

Not fucking Sully's. These memories belonged to us and only us.

This was our circus. *My* fucking show now.

And we were going to have a hell of a lot of fun before we got to the main event.

SIRENA

I knew his voice, and I knew his sins. In this darkness I was locked in, he was a treacherous prayer I screamed in silence. He was everything I knew to fear. An angel with the soul of a devil and the master of my terror.

I knew him.

Asylum.

"Seth," he said softly, his deep voice sending a current of fear through my body. "Rinny. I'm Seth. Your best friend. I see you hiding in there. Come out and play, pretty girl. I've been waiting forever."

Seth. My best friend?

Seth was gone.

No. This was a lie.

Seth hurt me.

"I'm your Seth. Remember me? Please, remember me. We met when we were four. Do you remember what you were wearing that day? Think back."

There was warmth on my thighs.

His hands.

He was touching me.

Up and down, he rubbed my legs. Slowly. Tenderly.

"A little, yellow dress that tied at your shoulders with ribbons. Your black hair was long. The longest I'd ever seen on anyone before. It was in twin braids down your back. And your eyes... Your eyes were the northern lights. So bright and colorful. I thought you were magic, Rinny. Pure magic made just for me."

I breathed out.

I remembered that.

He'd asked me if I was magic.

His dark hair and blue eyes had mesmerized me too. He was bigger than me. Louder. Stronger. He took my doll and made me chase him when I wouldn't answer him.

"You let me keep it," his voice called out through the fog. "The doll I took. I still have it. I'd like to show you once you're better. It's in my bedroom."

It was quiet for a moment as I stayed locked in my safe place.

"Rinny," Seth's soft voice called out. "Do you want to come out and play with me? It's been so long since we played together."

Seth. . .

"Remember us? Best friends. We were going to get married someday. You were my pirate princess. I rescued you. Don't you remember?"

My chest felt heavy.

He saved me.

But . . .

I couldn't breathe. I couldn't fucking breathe!

The world shook. My body trembled.

Please help me. It's so dark in here. I'm scared. Seth, I'm so scared!

"Come on, sweet girl," he cooed. "It's me. Your Seth. Let me take care of you. We're going to play pirates and princess again. This time, you're stuck in a castle because your wicked stepfather stole you from me. And there's a cruel wizard who wants to hurt you. We're coming to save you. You just have to help me find you. Let me find you, Rinny."

My heart beat faster.

I was trapped.

It was dark here.

Scary.

I wanted to go home.

Please, let me go home.

I couldn't find my way out.

Seth. Seth. SETH! HELP ME!

"Where are you, Rinny?" his voice grew urgent as my chest tightened. "Come on. You're right there. Come out."

I was cold here. So cold. *Why wasn't there any warmth here?*

Seth swore softly through the darkness.

All went quiet as I panted.

"Do you remember when we'd save our money, and my mom would take us out? She'd go shopping and let us sit at the ice cream shop. Do you remember that, Rinny? You loved strawberry ice cream. They'd put chocolate syrup on it. Loads of whipped cream. Sprinkles. Do you remember you'd always give me the cherry they put on top?"

He'd open his mouth, and I'd try to toss the cherry in. He always caught it even though I had terrible aim. He'd laugh and tell me I'd get better at throwing someday.

I missed him.

Was this real?

"I'm here," he called out softly. "Come find me. It's like that time we played hide and seek at your house. You always hid in the shower. When I asked why you never hid in the closet, you said because there were monsters inside."

He waited a moment before continuing, "You don't need to be afraid of the monsters, Rinny. I won't let any of them ever hurt you."

My eyes burned. My face was damp. I couldn't wipe the tears because my arms were too heavy. I was too weak. Too tired. Too. . . gone. Stuck. Broken. Terrified.

"Rinny, the monsters are here, and you're stuck in the closet. I can see you, but I can't reach you. I need you to help me this time. I can't save you if you can't help me."

He continued to recant tales of our happier times. Memories popped up and disappeared, each story making me desperate to find him in the darkness and cling to him. To beg him to save me. To tell me I'd just been living in a horrible nightmare.

"Rinny," he called out in a sing-song voice after a long time of silence.

Seth!

"Rinny, where are you?"

I'm here. I'm right here!

Why can't I call out to him?

Why am I in this darkness?

"Take my hand," he called out. "I'm right here. Reach out for me."

I focused everything I had on my arms. I wanted to leave this place. I wanted to find my best friend. I wanted to find Seth and be safe and have him tell me everything was OK. That none of the things that happened were real.

"Rinny. Right here. Just. . . try. We're running out of time."

I wept softly, unable to do anything. I was chained down. The evil wizard had me.

Then there was. . . a light.

Seth's blue eyes danced back into my vision. His messy, black hair.

I see you. . .

"Hey," he said, worry laced into his voice. "Rinny. Now. Please. Reach for my hands."

I crinkled my brows.

Seth.

"Fuck," he snarled, looking over his shoulder as the door creaked open. "Rinny. Rinny!"

It was too late. The evil had arrived.

I slid back into darkness as rough hands gripped me painfully. I was moved. Trapped inside this dark prison.

Was I in my head?

My body was jostled as Seth called out for me.

Then the pain came. Blinding white light. Searing agony ricocheting through my body.

Seth screamed.

"Sirena!" A hiss. A cry. "Sirena!"

He was hurting too.

He was hurting so much.

A crack of pain hit me over my back. Again. Again. Again. An angry voice rang out in the darkness. *"Beat the demons out of you. Kill the demons residing in your soul. The ones who have your mind."*

Seth, help me.

He screamed again before there was a thud and no more noise.

Except the heavy breathing of the evil wizard as he leaned down and spoke into my ear, "Submit yourselves therefore to God. Resist the devil, and he will flee from you. Or we will beat him out of you. . ."

I didn't hear the rest. The pain took over, and the darkness grew heavier until it was all I was.

All I'd ever be.

STITCHES

I lay in the cold, hard bed and stared at the ceiling. Food and drink were passed through the slot in the door. I'd woken up several hours ago, still alive and in even more misery.

And I'd completely freaked the fuck out.

I'd been restrained, medicated, and brought to this fucking hole like a prisoner.

There was nothing in this place but a mattress without a sheet, a camera out of reach in the corner, and four walls. Four white walls that reminded me of the nothing in my life.

It wasn't the hole, but it was really damn close.

Maybe I shouldn't have punched that ward. . .

Fuck it.

It didn't matter. Nothing did. Angel was gone. Church gave her away. Asylum had her now.

My poor, sweet angel.

I had nothing without her.

It was extreme, but ever since I'd met her, I couldn't get her out of my damn head. I'd wanted her so much it had hurt, and when I'd had her. . .I was so fucking close to getting everything I'd ever wanted then she'd been torn from me.

I inhaled.

If I concentrated on it enough, I could almost smell her. Almost taste her sweet lips. Feel her warm mouth on my cock as she sucked me to completion.

I groaned and rubbed my eyes. They fucking hurt. So did my neck and the rest of my body. It was reasonable to assume it was from my suicide attempt.

In retrospect, I'd overreacted. I should've waited until everyone was sleeping then done it. Of course, the other side of that was the pain I knew I'd leave behind whenever they would've found my cold body.

I winced at that. Hearing Church calling for me broke my heart. Seeing the look on Ashes's and Sin's faces had made the reality of my poor decision set in.

I'd fucked up. Plain and simple.

A midnight death would've been better planned. Then I wouldn't have these shitty thoughts in my head.

If I had a way right now, I'd finish the fucking job. I didn't want to be in a world where I couldn't have Sirena. I'd lived a life without her before meeting her. There was no way I was going back to that cold, harsh existence. Sure, I had Dante and the watchers, but I didn't have her.

And I fucking wanted her more than I'd ever wanted anything in my life, including my mother to give a damn about me.

Sighing, I stared at the ugly ass walls, hating that I was on a ninety-six-hour mandatory psych hold. It felt like an eternity.

I wandered back and forth, pacing. For hours. Then I lay down. Stood up. All on repeat. Being stuck like this was driving me insane.

Grinding my teeth together, I stomped over to the door and peered through the slit of a window. My breath caught in my chest as I saw Sirena on a stretcher being wheeled down the hall. Sully strode along behind her in his fucking brown suit.

Furiously, I pounded on the door, shouting her name as they passed by. She was so fucking pale. Her eyes were closed. Her black hair was tangled around her. She looked sick.

My baby looked awful.

"Sirena! Angel!"

Fuck.

"Sirena!" My voice cracked, giving way to a rasp.

That was it. My voice was toast. I mouthed her name instead, my chest aching in desperation as they continued to wheel her down the corridor, the fluorescent lights flickering and buzzing overhead.

My room was soundproof. They couldn't hear me.

I slammed my fist repeatedly against the door, her name a silent plea on my lips.

And then there he was. Tied in a straitjacket and in a wheelchair.

The son of a bitch who was taking everything I'd ever wanted from me.

Seth fucking Cain.

I glared at him as one of the wards pushed him down the hall. Seth's eyes were black and blue again, and his lip was cut. He looked like hell.

His icy blue gaze locked on mine. There was so much pain in them it made me sick to my stomach.

What the fuck was going on? Had he touched her? Did he get caught? Did he finally fucking snap? Did Church lose it on him?

My mind raced as Seth continued to stare at me as he passed by, three more wards behind him.

I couldn't take this shit. I couldn't stand knowing she was out there and something bad could be happening to her while I was stuck in this fucking prison.

I tugged furiously at my hair and let out a silent scream, letting my nails dig deep into my flesh as I slid down the wall and onto the floor where I started rocking.

Sirena. Angel. Fuck. I should be sane. I should be helping. What do I do? What do I do?

Nothing. There was nothing I *could* do.

The thought had me vomiting on the floor, my throat screaming for mercy. I collapsed onto the ugly white tiles, my head and heart a tangled mess. I lay there forever it seemed.

When the door to my room opened, I didn't even bother to crack my eyelids open. It didn't fucking matter. I just knew I was being lifted and carted off to be cleaned up. That meant I'd be sprayed down in a cold shower, naked, before they shot me up with one of their miracle drugs.

The pinch of the needle in my vein made me realize that they feared me. It was just as well. I scared me too.

They'd drugged me first.

When the first wave of the medicine washed over me, everything dulled, even the pain in my heart for Sirena. I was wheeled down the hall and placed inside a cold room. My eyes were too heavy to open, so I didn't bother to fight, but the burn of tears was there.

"Why do you cry, Malachi?" Sully's soft voice called out as a tear slid past my lashes. "Do you miss your mother?"

"S-Sirena," I rasped, the words barely audible.

Warm hands cradled my face.

"Leave us," Sully murmured, his warm breath on my face.

The thud of doors closing sounded out.

I exhaled. My heart felt slow and sluggish. My head was heavy with fog.

They'd put my ass down for sure. There was no way I'd be able to stand let alone think straight.

"Did you think I didn't see you in the window when I passed by tonight?"

My body trembled. I was so cold.

"You're quite a beautiful creature. Fascinating, really," Sully continued, his hands moving to my chest. "So many tattoos you've etched into your flesh. So many sins."

My body was bare. I had no idea when that had happened. I must have slipped from consciousness at some point during the journey and been undressed.

Had I passed out? Why couldn't I remember?

The hands moved south, stopping on my pubic bone.

"So beautiful," Sully continued in a soft voice. "The devil picks the best. Always has. It's such a shame."

His fingers moved to my cock, where he stroked me.

I let out a soft cry of protest before the feeling on my dick left. Another prick in my arm caught my attention. I struggled weakly against my restraints.

I was restrained. Flat on my back on an ice cold slab.

Fuck.

God.

Help.

"Shh. Don't struggle. You'll only make this worse. We have many demons to fight together. Save your strength."

"N-no," I rasped, my throat burning.

Warm lips brushed against my ear. "It's either you or her. Take this nightmare and cradle it close or she will."

The medicine he'd given me washed through my body, choking my protests down.

Another tear slid past my lashes as he touched me. As someone else came into the room. A voice I recognized. My brain couldn't put the pieces together though.

Darkness descended.

And then silence.

ASHES

I flicked my lighter opened and closed. The clock was moving painfully slow. I'd barely slept. My brain felt like mush.

I hated this class. Sister Elizabeth was a bitch, who assigned way too much work. It took all my willpower not to set her and her economics book on fire then toast some marshmallows over it.

"Let us pray," she called out.

Students bowed their heads at her words.

I didn't.

All I knew was that God must have stepped away from his desk when it came to getting my messages. I was on my own here.

I flicked my lighter opened and closed again.

"Asher, join us," she urged in that false sugary sweet voice of hers. "And please put the lighter away."

I clenched my jaw.

If I put my lighter away, I'd lose it. It was the only thing keeping me in my seat right then. All I wanted to do was rush to the medical wing and check on Sirena. Talk to Stitches. Neither were allowed visitors now though. And I was going mad with worry.

No news was good news. That was what Sin had muttered this morning as he smoked a joint on the back patio, a scowl on his face.

"Asher? Mr. Valentine—"

I couldn't handle it any longer. I got to my feet and stormed out of the room, knowing I was a breath away from complete destruction.

Dealing with that place wasn't going to work for me today, so I went home. When I got there, I closed the door behind me and sighed. It was only then that I realized I'd been holding my lighter so tightly that I'd bruised my palm with it.

I was ready to explode. Too much stress was building within me. It was like each bit of bad shit was a piece of kindling.

And I was the raging pyro who couldn't help himself. Life had gotten hectic, so we hadn't been able to go out for me to burn things. I couldn't fight the urge anymore.

I dashed across the living room and went into my bedroom where I grabbed a few notebooks, magazines, and anything else made of paper I could burn, my economics book included. With those items in my hands, I rushed into my bathroom where I threw them into the tub before darting back out to my closet to get lighter fluid.

I squirted the fluid over the papers, eager for a fix and the high flames.

I lit a twisted piece of paper and chucked it into the tub, watching as everything burst into beautiful orange flames which soon licked the ceiling.

"Fuck," I groaned, inhaling the smoke, my body relaxing as the crackle of the fire sounded out around me.

"What the fuck are you doing?" Sin demanded, pushing past me and turning on the faucet in the tub. "Ouch. Fuck."

He shook his hand out as the shower sprayed out, the flames having licked him.

"Are you trying to burn the fucking house down?" He reached out and shook me. "What the fuck, man?"

Somewhere in the distance, the smoke alarm rang.

"I was trying to get some relief," I murmured, dazed as the flames were drowned by the shower, my high deflating. "I don't ruin your high."

"I don't try to burn the damn house down either," he shot back, his gray eyes flashing at me. "What the fuck? You're supposed to be the strong one. You're the one we count on to hold your shit together. Don't fucking slip, man. Not right now." His Adam's apple bobbed as he stared at me. "Come on. Please."

I tore my gaze away from the now dead, waterlogged fire and sighed.

"I'm sorry. I-I shouldn't have let go like that. I'm just worried."

"I know," he said, frowning. "I'm sorry too."

"Why are you sorry? You're not the one who set the tub on fire. Church is going to punch me in the throat when he gets back. I promised no more fires in the house."

Sin sighed. "I'm sure he'll overlook it. Everett is here."

I blinked at him. "His dad came?"

Sin nodded. "Yeah. Made an appearance because of Stitches I suspect. He's his guardian and all that."

"Fuck," I muttered. "I didn't know he was here."

"I only found out because I saw him in the hall with Church earlier." Sin walked out of the bathroom, and I followed him to my room. He sank down onto my computer chair and rubbed his eyes.

I sat on the edge of my bed and stared at him for a moment.

"Are you OK? You've been gone a lot lately," I said softly.

I needed to open the windows. The stench of the fire still hung thick in the air, but at least the smoke alarm had stopped blaring.

He shrugged and studied the floor.

"You can talk to me. You know you can."

"I don't have anything to say, man. I'm just worried about Stitches."

"And Sirena?"

He was quiet for a moment. "I-I can't worry about her."

"You can, Sin. You can let out your emotions—"

"No, I fucking can't, Asher!" he snapped at me. "It's not that fucking easy for me. I can't just set a fire and feel better. If I let myself feel, I'd burn up like the fucking shit you set on fire in there. It would kill me." He pounded his fist on his chest. "I can't let this shit consume me because it would end me. You need to understand that. I'm already struggling." His voice cracked, and he quickly looked away from me. "I just. . . I just want to forget. Float away. Be someone else for a fucking change. I-I wish I'd died when my father shot me."

"Why?"

He shrugged. "So I didn't have to hurt. Be afraid. *Feel.*"

"What are you afraid of?" I watched as he continued to scowl at the floor.

"I don't know," he mumbled. "Losing what's important to me. Fucking up."

"Stitches is OK," I said. "He'll be out soon—"

"And then what?" He fixed his gray eyes on me. "What happens if he tries again? Because it's fucking Malachi, man. You know how he is when he falls. He tumbles in an endless, black abyss. What if he can't come back this time? What if he feels how I feel and just doesn't fucking want to keep going?"

My heart constricted.

"I don't want to lose either of you."

Sin shook his head, his blond hair loose around his shoulders and falling forward. "I don't want to lose you either, but I'm scared I already have."

"How? I'm right here—"

"You love her," he said softly. "And she's hurt."

I frowned. "What does that have to do with me and the guys leaving? We're in this together. You know that. We're not going anywhere. We love you, Sinclair. I know you think you're not worthy of love, but you are. If we, by some miracle, get her back, that doesn't change our group. We're *still* in this together." I studied him as he continued to look at the floor. "Let a little love in."

"Look where love got me last time."

"Right here," I said gently. "Right on the cusp of falling in love with someone wonderful and perfect for us. It wasn't a mistake to love Isabella, Sin. She was a light guiding you to these moments."

"We're monsters, Ashes." He peered at me, his eyes filled with sorrow. "It doesn't matter if we're capable of feeling love. At the end of the day, a monster loves his meal. He loves to feast, and Sirena is a fucking delicious meal we'd devour and tear apart. You know we would."

I swallowed hard at his words.

"At least, I know I would." He got up and ran his fingers through his hair. "I'm going for a walk. Don't burn the damn house down. Church will be pissed."

I didn't try to stop him. I let him stomp out of my room. Moments later, I heard the front door open and close with his departure.

Sighing, I flopped back onto my bed, his words on repeat in my head.

Yeah, we were monsters.

But even monsters deserved to be loved.

Maybe Sirena was a different kind of monster, one who could save us.

A good monster.

"The best kind of monster," I murmured.

I'd cling to that thought.

SIN

I hated being home. I hated being away. I just fucking hated everything.

I raked my fingers through my long blond hair and tied it up into a bun atop my head then pulled my hood up around my ears as I marched across campus.

Coming home and smelling smoke let me know we were all fucking spiraling. It wasn't just Stitches. Ashes was losing it too.

I wasn't watching where I was going as I walked, my mind on my friends. I crashed against a hard body.

"S-sorry, Sin," Bryce Andrews said, trying to right himself as he stumbled back.

Instinctively, I reached out and snatched him upright. "My fault," I muttered, noting his eyes widening as I released him.

Bryce was Sirena's best friend here. Her ex-boyfriend or some shit as well. They seemed to have had a clean break, although I did notice him moping around after it had ended. Of course, they'd also hung out afterward as well, which had pissed off Church.

Hell, it had pissed me off too.

He said nothing as I stared him down.

"H-how's Sirena?" he finally asked.

"Not good."

"Will…I mean…is she going to be OK? I can't get in to see her. I've tried. I asked Church about her, but he didn't really tell me much."

"I don't know," I said. "But it's best if you don't go around her. She's with Asylum now."

"What?" He crinkled his brows. "She is?"

I nodded, nausea churning in my guts. "She is."

"I thought. . . I thought she was with the watchers."

"Was," I said, my voice rough. "Past tense. Asylum got her."

"I don't understand—"

"And you don't need to," I snapped. I hated talking about this shit.

Church had named her well. She was a fucking specter. A ghost who wouldn't stop haunting me because everywhere I went, she was there. In my head. My heart. In fucking conversations. Every-fucking-where.

Bryce visibly swallowed. "Right. It just doesn't make sense. Sirena was scared of him, or at least that was the impression I got from her."

"Things change."

I had no idea why I was still standing there, but I was. Maybe it was nice to be close to her like this. It was nice to not feel the accusations in unsaid words when I knew damn well I deserved the punishments.

Why the fuck did I want to be close to her? Fuck. What was happening to me? I was letting her go. Wouldn't I have had to have had her first though?

Not knowing was pissing me off.

Or maybe I did know, and that was what was pissing me off. Whatever the hell was happening, I didn't like it. I hated all of it.

I'd meant what I'd said when I'd told Ashes that I wished I'd died with my old man. Life would be a fuck of a lot easier if I wasn't around to dick everything up.

"I'd really like to see her. I'm going to try tomorrow." Bryce cut through my morbid thoughts of throwing myself off Pictured Rocks and drowning in the lake.

"What-the-fuck-ever," I muttered. "Do what you gotta do. But if it was me, I'd stay away."

My social meter was on E, so I turned and walked away from him.

"Hey, Sin?" Bryce's voice followed me.

I paused and looked at him over my shoulder.

"She cared about you, you know? I could tell. It was in her eyes when she'd watch you. So, um, if you're feeling upset or something, just know that she cared. Figured I should tell you."

I said nothing and turned away from him then kept walking.

Fuck.

Fuck.

Fuck.

I didn't want her to care.

I made it around the edge of the science building before I couldn't take it anymore and slammed my fist into a tree. Pain shot through my knuckles and up my arm.

It hurt but not as much as the pain in my chest did.

My jaw quivered as I pulled my fist back, letting the blood drip onto the grass.

I wanted to get out of this fucking nightmare. Church wasn't going to let this go. He was going to dig until he unearthed my skeletons. Ashes would help. I'd seen the looks on their faces.

And Stitches.

He'd nearly killed himself because of me. Because of some fucking shit I'd done.

My demons were feasting on my black soul.

The guilt was becoming too much to take.

Quickly, I wiped my cheek with my uninjured hand. I was crying. *Fucking crying.*

I sniffled and ducked my head before I pushed forward, not wanting anyone to see me like this.

I shuffled along the edge of the tree line until the sound of Church calling my name forced me to stop and wipe at my eyes again. Once I figured I had my shit in order, I turned to see him storming toward me, his face twisted like he was pissed off.

I swallowed thickly, waiting for him to punch me in the face since that seemed to be pretty much all he wanted to do to me lately. Honestly, he had every fucking reason to.

"Ashes set his bathtub on fire." He stopped in front of me, his green eyes filled with his anger.

"I know," I muttered, averting my gaze from his.

"What's next? Huh? Are you going to tell me you're losing it too?"

I shook my head. "I'm not losing it. I'll go back and help him clean up the mess." I moved to step around him, but he wrapped his fingers around my bicep and stopped me.

"If you have anything you need to say to me, Sinclair, now would be a really good fucking time for it."

I stared back at him, my heart dangerously close to beating out of my chest as fear pummeled me. If Church knew, I was done for. He'd bring the punishment. I'd really lose him and the guys. My family.

Fuck. I couldn't. I couldn't lose them. They were all I had in this world. They'd never forgive me...

I exhaled. "I'll go help Ashes."

"Something is bothering you," he pressed in the only way Church knew how.

Fucker was too smart for his own good.

"Well, Stitches was hanging in his closet not too long ago, and Ashes set his bathtub on fire. So yeah, I guess something is bothering me." I jerked out of his hold and set my face into the emotionless mask I wore so well. "I'll go help Ashes clean shit up."

Church didn't say anything, but then again, he didn't have to.

It was really only a matter of time.

That was how Dante Church worked. He'd watch. Wait. Then he'd fucking attack.

I'd take it. I'd take it all.

I knew it was coming for me. For now though, I needed to try to fix things.

But fucking how?

ASHES

I dropped my cold slice of pizza back onto my plate. My appetite wasn't there. Apparently, neither was Sin's and Church's because they hadn't touched their food.

"Stitches is out tomorrow," I finally said. "It's already been seventy-two hours. Did your father say anything, Dante?"

"He didn't seem to care one way or another." Church grunted.

He scrubbed his hand down his face. He was exhausted. Black haloed his green eyes as he stared down at his cold dinner.

"So. . . everything is cool?" I ventured.

Sin shot a quick look at Church as he pushed his pizza around on his plate.

"He actually seemed. . . happy. It was odd. But it's probably only because he got something good to play with later," Church muttered.

I cast a quick glance to Sin, who frowned. We all knew Everett Church was into some fucked-up shit. He was only ever in a good mood when he had an upcoming snack to play with.

"Well, tomorrow," I said, hoping my excitement at seeing Stitches was contagious.

Sin rose to his feet and dumped his pizza into the garbage then made to leave.

"Where are you going?" Church demanded.

"Out," he answered. He didn't bother to explain. He simply pulled his hood up and left the house, the door clicking closed behind him.

I sighed. "He's struggling."

"Aren't we all?" Church muttered.

I said nothing and decided to just force the food down. I took several bites and swallowed before Church spoke again.

"Do you think she still loves us?"

I dropped my pizza onto my plate. "I'd like to think so."

"She doesn't even acknowledge us. Do you think she's scared?" The pain cracked his voice.

"Yes," I whispered, wanting to be honest with him. "I think she's terrified. But she's also brave too. You know she is. She's coming back, Dante. Believe that."

"Do *you* believe that?" he asked, his green gaze locked on mine.

"I do. I believe it with everything I am."

His Adam's apple bobbed. "I tried to bring her back. I fucked her."

I froze at his words. "*What?* When?"

"When I said goodbye. I begged her to come back. I thought maybe she'd remember me," his voice wavered. "She didn't. She laid there as I fucked her."

"What *the fuck*?" I snarled, pushing away from the table. "What if she didn't want that?"

"Does it fucking matter?" He scoffed, getting to his feet. "If she didn't, she could've told me no. She didn't fucking tell me no, Asher! Didn't even goddamn flinch as I pushed into her or when I came on her pussy or marked her with my bite. *Nothing.* I want to believe she's in there, but I'm more inclined to believe she's just a fucking shell," he shouted, his voice cracking as his eyes glistened with his tears.

I breathed out, pissed at him for what he'd done but understanding why he'd done it.

"What if Asylum is doing that shit to her? Huh? What if she can't tell him no either?" He wiped furiously at the tears on his cheek. "Or anyone else for that matter? God, I'll kill anyone who touches her. You fucking know I will. We're killers, Asher. We're murderers. We *are* the bad guys. The fucking monsters under the bed. But we aren't the only ones. You know it. You fucking know it. This world is filled with guys like us."

"She'll be safe," I whispered, hating that he might be right.

"She's not fucking safe! No one is safe here! Fuck!" He kicked his chair over. "I'm running on a fucking prayer here, and it ain't to the guy upstairs. You know God has forsaken all of us. I prayed to the devil to keep her safe. How many people have we killed? Huh? Have we hurt?"

"If you're feeling guilty about that shit, remember why we did it—"

He let out a criminal laugh. "Guilt? *Me?* Fuck no. I don't regret killing anyone. I only regret not keeping the ones I love safe. You know I'll even kill those I love if it means death is a better alternative." His voice faded out as he swallowed.

I winced. I knew what he was referring to but didn't want to open up that memory with him. He hadn't spoken about it in years. I'd assumed he'd buried the pain like we all had.

"She's going to come back to us. I know she will. In the meantime, we need to sort out who the hell did this to her and deal with that. It'll be retribution in a way. We need to focus on that and on Stitches right now. You had faith in Asylum, and honestly, I do too. We saw what he did with Stitches. He knows shit, man. I think he knows about Sirena too. Let's just roll with it. It sucks so bad, but sometimes we have to eat shit to get what we want."

He nodded and let out a whoosh of air. "You're right. I need to focus on finding out who helped Asylum. I think we need to start with his friends."

"Then let's do it."

"I'll get my tools."

And just like that, his entire demeanor changed as he rushed from the room to get his *tools* from his room.

His hammer. His favorite skinning knife. His razor blades.

They'd get the job done or we would.

I wasn't a good guy either, so I went to my room and grabbed my own tools.

The night was about to get lit.

CHURCH

I didn't knock on the door to room three-one-five.

I simply kicked it in and strode through the entrance like I owned the place.

Riley Danvers stared at me with wide eyes before he stumbled out of his chair and backed up. His fear ramped up as his jaw quivered.

Maybe it was the look in my eyes that got him. Maybe it was the knife in my hand. Or maybe it was the fact he knew I'd kill him first and then Ashes would burn his fucking corpse before he got to kiss his mama goodbye.

"Hey there, Riley," I said softly. "Looks like you're about to have a really bad fucking day."

"Church, man, whatever it is you think I did, I swear I didn't." He held his hands up, his back against the wall. "I've been here all day. I-I swear."

I cocked my head at him as I stepped deeper into the room.

"Oh, I'm not interested in what you did today," I said.

"I-I haven't done anything, man. I fucking promise I haven't."

"We're just here to get some information on Asylum," Ashes said, flipping his Zippo. "No one has to get hurt as long as you're honest."

I smirked at Riley. "Probably. I may need to prove a fucking point."

Sweat dotted Riley's forehead as his gaze darted to the closed door.

"Door or window, Riley," I said. "Either is going to fucking hurt."

He made his decision. Then he snapped forward, rushing at us like a scared rabbit, attempting to dart around.

It was nothing to me.

Ashes swept his leg out and knocked Riley to the ground.

I kicked him onto his back then kneeled beside him as he quivered, my knife in my hand. I twirled it and smiled at him.

"So. Here's the thing. My girl was hurt a few days ago. Asylum was found with her. I want to know who helped him get her into the fucking coffin they were in."

Riley's eyes widened. "I-I don't know. It wasn't me."

"Wrong fucking answer." I swung my knife down and caught his hand as he tried to block my blow to his face.

Blood oozed out as he let out a cry. He tried to scoot away from me, but I swung my knife again and put it through his pant leg, pinning him to his floor.

"Just tell us what you know," Ashes said gently. "Then we'll go. We won't tell anyone how we found out."

"I-I don't-don't know anything!" Riley said, clutching his hand, fear making his body quake. "Asylum never said anything to me about it. He doesn't tell me shit about what he does, and I don't want to fucking know."

I licked my lips. "He doesn't tell you anything? *Ever?*"

He shook. "No."

"Did he tell you he has a thing for Sirena?" I raised my brows at him.

He was quiet for a moment. "He-he just said they knew each other before. That they were friends."

"That's it?"

He breathed out. Blood still oozed from the wound on his hand.

"He-he loves her. That's all I know. He's never gone further than telling us that she's his. We never asked."

"Loves her?"

The anger surged in my guts.

He nodded. "She's his forever girl," he murmured. "That's all I know."

"So you just lied to me when you said he never tells you anything," I said, desperate to find an excuse to let this anger and rage out of my system. I needed something to fucking break.

And Riley Danvers looked like it might be him.

"No!" he shouted as I reached for him. "No!"

He kicked at me, but it only fueled my fire. Ashes reached out and grabbed hold of his arms, holding him down as I sat on Riley's legs and pushed his shirt up.

Riley squirmed and wept beneath me as I took in his pale flesh.

A perfect canvas to paint on.

My specter would love it.

I pushed my knife into his abdomen, breaking the skin as he squealed.

"Don't move. It'll be over soon," Ashes said.

"Please. Please." Riley wept, his body trembling.

I carved each letter deep enough, so he'd remember his place in this fucked-up world.

His sobs finally quieted as he passed out. Blood trickled from his stomach. I finished carving the last letter into his flesh and got to my feet as he came to and Ashes released him.

A sheen of sweat covered his skin as we got to our feet and stared down at him.

The ragged letters spelled out what he was.

LIAR.

"Little much, Dante," Ashes murmured.

"Not even close," I answered softly. I locked my eyes on Riley's glistening ones. "If you find out anything, you'll come tell me. Right?"

"Y-Y-yes," he rasped weakly.

He was bleeding everywhere. It was smeared on everything, me included. My fingers were sticky with it.

"Go get cleaned up," Ashes instructed gently. "And always tell the truth. Next time won't be better."

"Come on," I said, wiping my bloody blade on my pants. "Let Riley sort himself out. Tell Asylum I send my fucking love." I spat on him, turned on my heel, and left the room with Ashes right behind me.

"Find Sin," I said as I pushed my knife back up my sleeve into the sheath I kept beneath the material. "He needs to fucking help us."

Ashes said nothing. He simply walked away from me to do my bidding.

I stared out at the cemetery in the distance, the memory of my specter beneath me flashing through my mind's eyes.

"We'll find out who the fuck did this to you, specter," I murmured. "And I'll teach them what happens when you fuck with what belongs to us. Promise, baby."

STITCHES

My head felt like it was going to explode. I had no fucking idea what had happened to me after I'd seen Sirena and Asylum. All I knew was that I'd fallen asleep on the floor and had woken up in my bed, wearing a thin hospital gown, my body aching.

I rubbed my head and let out a hiss.

"Shit," I rasped, my voice still fucked.

I gasped. It felt like razor blades slicing through my throat.

Slowly, I got out of bed and shuffled to the door and peered out the tiny window to see an empty hall. Turning, I looked at the small camera in the upper corner of the room.

"W-water," I rasped. "Please. W-water."

I shivered and hugged myself. Something wasn't right. In fact, something was very wrong. My head didn't feel right. My body felt hollow.

Flashes of light and soft voices filled my head. Memories I wasn't sure why I had.

I clutched at my head and sank onto the bed, rocking.

I wanted to crawl out of my fucking skin. It didn't feel like mine anymore. It felt tainted and used. Wasted. Broken.

Not my fucking body.

I wasn't Stitches.

I was something else I didn't quite understand.

The door swung open, and Sully came in with a doctor named Jenkins. I hadn't had much experience with him.

"Malachi, how are you this morning?" Sully asked, strolling closer to me with Jenkins at his side.

Two wards stood at the door, watching me.

"I need water," I choked out.

Sully looked at Jenkins, who nodded. One of the wards came in and handed me a Styrofoam cup. I downed it quickly and winced at the ache in my throat.

"I want to leave," I said, my voice barely audible.

"Unfortunately, that's not going to be able to happen," Sully said.

"What? W-why?"

"You were uncontrollable last night. We had to sedate you for your own safety. Because of your erratic behavior, it's under both Dr. Jenkins's and my recommendation that you remain here for a few more days."

I crinkled my brows. "I just want to go home."

"I know you do," Sully said. "But it's not going to happen. We have several more tests to run on you. Your teachers have been made aware of the situation."

"T-there isn't a fucking situation," I argued, almost too exhausted to do so. "I've done my time. Let me out." I stumbled to my feet, my heart in my throat. "You can't fucking k-keep me here."

The orderlies rushed in and took me by the arms as Sully nodded to Jenkins. My heart jumped hard as Jenkins produced a syringe and approached me.

"No! No!" I struggled weakly against my captors, knowing I wasn't strong enough to fight all of them.

If this were a few days ago, I would've killed them all. The best I could do now was slam my head into one of the orderly's head, knocking him back.

His nose gushed blood as I went in for the next one.

I didn't make it halfway into my next attack before the needle was plunged into my body. The hold of the drug was immediate. I sagged, and Sully caught me.

The heaviness grew, making it feel like I was being weighed down by lead.

Sully maneuvered me back to my bed.

I couldn't fucking move.

Panic rose in my chest as a numbness washed over me.

All I could do was breathe and move my eyes.

Terror. Pure fucking terror.

"Get the gurney. We'll take him back now," Sully said.

Please, no. Don't take me. Don't fucking take me. I don't want to go. Mama, please. Help me.

"Relax, Malachi," Sully cooed softly. "You're perfect for what we need. This is a place of healing. You can't heal while demons infest your soul. You may be a lost cause in that respect, but your body is still useful."

Fear clawed at my chest as a gurney was wheeled in. The orderlies moved me easily onto it as I lay there, my gaze darting around.

Fuck this. Fuck THIS.

I strained so hard to sit up that my guts ached.

But I had nothing left.

I couldn't move.

I could only blink my fucking eyes. My brain was beginning to feel foggy.

"We'll get to round two of the medication soon," Sully continued. "Soon you'll be able to listen without issue. You'll do what you're told. We just need a few more tweaks to the dosages. You did so well last time. So well. I was quite happy with your performance." He reached out and raked his fingers through my hair. "Beautiful."

They pushed me into the hall. I kept trying to look around.

Church. Fuck. Where are you? Ashes? Sin?

God, what if they're doing this to Sirena?

My angel.

I was taken to a dimly lit room. The gurney was locked into place.

"Leave us," Sully said as Jenkins pulled out a vial and another syringe before handing it to Sully.

"Do you know what the best part of all of this is, Malachi?" Sully drew up a dosage of the amber liquid as Jenkins tied a band around my arm.

My insides quivered as I waited for the inevitable.

Sully pushed the needle into my vein and depressed the plunger.

"It's that you already wanted to die, so if you don't make it through our little experiment, we're covered. The suicidal, manic ones are really the best."

Fuck. FUCKER.

I was going to kill him. I was going to fucking kill . . .

The fog in my head grew as Jenkins removed my hospital gown, leaving me naked.

Sully drank me in, a wicked, twisted smile on his face before he reached out and stroked me.

"Let go, Malachi. Let the drugs do what they're best at. Controlling you."

My heart thundered in my ears as the ability to clearly think began to leave me.

Where was I?

"Breathe," a voice called out softly. "In and out. Good boy."

Who was I?

Hands on my groin. Heat. Wetness.

Fuck, help me.

Whoever *me* is.

"Spread his legs," the voice said.

My body was jostled, my legs spread.

Dizziness swept over me.

I was dying.

I was fucking dying.

I hoped they remembered me.

Whoever they were.

Who was I?

Help me.

God? Was there a god?

There was a devil.

Demons.

I was a demon.

No. I was the devil.

I was scared.

Mama. . . please. . .

Pain. So much pain.

I couldn't scream. I couldn't fucking scream!

Please, Mama. Help me. Help me!

I was being torn in two.

The ring of fire burned my center as the silent scream lodged in my throat.

Mania.

Tears.

Was I crying?

I hurt so much. Mama, please help me.

Sirena. . .

Do I know you, angel?

I love you.

I fucking love you.

Darkness.

Cold.

Thank fuck.

SIN

"What's going on?" Ashes demanded as we walked next to Church.

"I called the wards to see what time we needed to be there to pick Stitches up. They said he's not being released." Church's face was a hard mask as we stormed across the campus.

Ashes had made it perfectly clear the night before we were on a mission to find out who had helped Asylum get Sirena into the coffin.

My fucking days were numbered if she spoke or if Asylum ratted me out.

Fear didn't adequately explain the feelings I had. Dante and the guys were my best friends. My family. They were everything to me. Losing them was unacceptable. I just couldn't.

Vomit threatened my throat as we continued forward. My heart pounded hard.

Stitches was a prisoner to the fucking wards. To the facility. To Sully.

It made everything a million times worse.

My guilt soared.

If I hadn't fucked up, none of this would be happening right now.

"What do you mean they aren't releasing him?" Ashes demanded.

"Exactly what I said. They said he's being held."

"How long?" I asked as we climbed the steps to the hospital.

"Didn't say, but I'm going to find out."

When we got inside, Dante moved swiftly to the front desk. The nurse immediately picked her phone up and made a call.

Back up. Reinforcements.

She was scared.

Church surged forward and grabbed the phone from her hand. She cowered beneath his rage.

"Where is Stitches?" he asked with a growl, looming over her.

She shook, her brown eyes wide, her bottom lip wobbling.

He reached out and cradled her face. I watched, mesmerized as he shifted into the monster he was.

"If you don't tell me, I'm going to strangle you with this phone cord," he cooed softly, moving his fingers to grip her chin tightly. "Then, I'll peel the skin from your body and make my Halloween costume with it. I thought I could be a fucking clown this year."

She let out a choked cry, tears streaming down her flushed cheeks.

When she tried to look away, he jerked her attention back to him. I glanced at Ashes to see him watching intently.

It was clear he was with Church on this.

Good.

It meant we were all on the same page because I wanted Stitches out of this place more than I wanted my next breath. I needed him free. I needed to tell him how sorry I was for all this shit.

When the nurse didn't answer, Church slowly began wrapping the cord around her neck. She blubbered softly, her small form quaking as she stared up at him.

He tugged the cord suddenly, jerking her toward him. She collided with his chest, gasping, her face tear soaked.

"I'm going to ask you again. Where *the fuck* is Malachi?"

"H-he h-he's w-with—"

"Dante, what a pleasant surprise!" Sully boomed out as he strode to us, wearing his stupid fucking suit, with his hair slicked back.

Church released the cord and gave the nurse a shove. She

toppled to her ass before she fumbled with getting the cord undone. Then she ran off, practically tripping as she knocked shit off her desk.

"Fuck you. Where's Stitches?" Church demanded, rounding on Sully, who had the decency to look nervous as he took a step back and adjusted his ugly, purple tie.

Six wards rounded the corner.

Ashes pulled out his lighter and flicked it opened and closed on repeat.

I sighed deeply. This wasn't going to end well if they decided to attack us. Someone would end up dying, and I could guarantee it wouldn't be us.

"Dante, please. Let's discuss this in my office—"

"We'll discuss it right fucking here," Church snarled back. "Don't tempt me, motherfucker. You know what I'm capable of."

"OK. OK. Here." Sully offered us a smile, which didn't reach his beady eyes. "Stitches isn't well. He's in one of his manic episodes. It's unsafe for us to let him go. Your father, Everett, has already agreed this is the best decision. He's paying for his. . . treatments."

"Stitches is old enough that nothing my father says should have any impact on what the fuck he does," Church argued.

Sully inclined his head. "I know you think that, but Malachi isn't coherent right now and can't make those decisions on his own. Your father, he cares deeply for your brother. We all do—"

"You're pissing me off. Stop lying!" Church's deep voice reverberated around us.

Sully winced and held his hands out. "Dante, please. Malachi needs help. He's not even in his own mind right now. We think his attempt may have caused more damage than we originally thought. He needs to recover—"

"I want to see him. Show him to me," Church snapped. "Now."

Sully hesitated for a moment before he nodded. "Of course. Come on. I'll prove to you he's not right."

Sully gestured for us to follow, and we did. The wards remained at our back as we took the elevator to the third floor. No one said a word as we ascended. When we reached the floor, we took a left and followed Sully to a room down the dimly lit hall.

My heart thrashed hard in my chest as my concern for Stitches took over everything.

God, please be OK, Malachi.

I'm so fucking sorry, brother.

"See for yourself." Sully nodded to the small window set in the heavy, locked door we'd stopped in front of.

Church shot him a glare before he stepped forward and peered through the glass.

He stared for so long I wasn't sure what he was going to do. Finally, he backed away. I was quick to take his place and look through the window.

My breath caught as I gazed at Stitches strapped to his bed. He was uncovered, and his hospital gown was twisted around his legs like he'd been fighting for a while. His forehead glistened with sweat as his chest heaved. White foamy spittle surrounded his lips. Even the tattoos on his face seemed pale in contrast to his natural color.

"What did you do to him?" Church snarled. "Stitches was fine when we brought him here. This isn't him! He's never done this shit before!"

"I understand your concern, but please…you know Malachi's history. You know how he struggles sometimes. This is just a more severe occurrence. We're working through some new medications that are going to help him," Sully explained. "He just needs time to adjust. I promise you he'll be better in no time and will return home soon."

I glared at Sully. "If he isn't better soon, you better fucking hope your god answers prayers."

Sully gave me a tight smile. "We'll get him right as rain in no time, or we'll die trying. You have my word."

Something about the way he said that sent chills rushing over my skin.

Church backed away, a muscle thrumming along his jaw. "Where's Sirena?"

"Resting comfortably. There's nothing new to report on her condition."

Church nodded and turned to us. I stared back at him, letting him silently know that I'd go to war with him if it was what he wanted. Judging by the slight nod Ashes gave him, it was safe to assume we all would.

"I'll be checking in," Church said softly, dangerously. "If I'm unhappy, believe me, it'll pale in comparison to what you'll feel."

Sully said nothing as we spun around and strode away. It wasn't until we'd nearly reached the elevator that he finally spoke.

"Your father approved his treatment, Dante. He knows how sick Malachi is. He knows how important your brother is to you. Getting him back is all he wants."

Church didn't say a damn word. He simply stepped into the elevator, and Ashes pushed the button for the first floor.

"Church?" Ashes called out quietly.

"It isn't about what my father wants. It's about what he's capable of," Church whispered. "Stitches is strong though. He'll get through this."

"And if he doesn't?" Ashes whispered. "Then what?"

"Then we kill all of them." Church stepped out of the elevator without a backward glance.

I looked at Ashes and sighed.

"Looks like we should start digging holes," I muttered.

"Not necessarily. We could burn them all instead." Ashes followed Church, leaving me to stare at their backs.

I swallowed hard as I watched my two friends walk out the hospital doors, their heads together.

Everything was fucked.

SETH

Who the fuck am I?

I stared at myself in the mirror, taking in the bruising on my face. I could hold my own in a fight if forced to, but lately I'd been letting my ass get beaten.

Of course, it was hard to fight off people when they were jabbing needles into my flesh and forcing me to my knees.

Forcing me to watch as they hurt Rinny.

Forcing me to comply.

Forcing me to fucking obey.

I breathed in and out deeply as I continued to study my reflection. My blue eyes seemed dull. My bottom lip was swollen slightly. Bruises peppered not only my face but also my body. I worked out. A lot. My body could take an intense beating, but this? This was something else.

We must hold on.

Don't let go.

For Rinny.

We suffer in silence for our forever girl.

Retribution will come once she's ours again…

I licked my lips.

"And then what?" I whispered. "What will we do once she's ours?"

Teach them a painful lesson before we kill them all.

"I don't like killing people. Much. I do like to torture them though. . . like you do."

We do what we must to protect what's ours. They'll be punished. We owe it to her. Say it. Say what we must do.

"We'll kill them all," I murmured.

Again. Say it again.

"We will kill them all," I repeated fiercely, Rinny's face flashing in my mind's eye.

No survivors.

"None," I said softly.

I closed my eyes for a moment, desperate for some peace. I shook my head, willing silence to fall over me and shut out the noise in my head.

When all was quiet, I opened my eyes and pushed away from my sink then dressed quickly.

I had a lot of work to do today and not much time to do it.

There wouldn't be a repeat of my last time with Rinny. Neither of us would be hurt today. At least not by Sully.

†

I STARED down at the slip of paper in front of me and frowned.

Kiss her.

"What is this?" I glared at Sully.

"I thought perhaps you needed a reward today after the misfortune of last time." He offered me one of his shitty smiles, which made me want to shove nails through his fucking eyeballs.

"That's not how a reward system works unless you want me to continue my bad behavior. My failures."

"You're a smart one, aren't you, Seth? That's what has me so fascinated by you." He scrubbed his hand down his chin. "Then don't consider it a reward. Consider it. . . an incentive, an enticement. I'm enticing you to break into her mind and own her."

"And what does that do for you?" I frowned at him. "How would me violating her mind benefit the great and mighty Dr. Sully?"

He's using her to break into your mind.

He wants to use her to get to you.

Kill him.

Kill him.

KILL HIM.

We can't kill him. We must wait until the time is right.

WAIT.

I ground my teeth and glared at Sully.

I wouldn't kill him. Yet. The prospect of torturing him for a long time brought me great pleasure. He'd be wise to tread carefully.

"I'm a scientist," he said with a chuckle. "I'm here to observe. To learn. You're a remarkable creature. You're. . . different. It fascinates me."

"How am I different? I'm crazy like everyone else here. Yourself included."

He flashed me a toothy smile and nodded. "You know things. We both know you do. Your diagnosis of schizophrenia isn't accurate. We both know that."

"Do we?" I raised my brows at him. "We both know I hear voices. Maybe I'm just really good at paying fucking attention and don't actually *know* things. Maybe I just get *lucky* sometimes."

He shook his head at me from behind his desk and sat forward. "I'm inclined to give you a diagnosis of dissociative identity disorder. Tell me, Seth. How many voices are in your head? Who am I speaking to right now?"

I smirked at him. I'd heard this diagnosis before. I'd heard them all. Bi-polar. Narcissistic. Dissociative identity disorder. Schizophrenia. Disruptive behavior and dissocial disorders, particularly oppositional defiant disorder. And my favorite. . . neuropsychiatric disorder. Basically, they called me a psychopath.

It was a nice umbrella term as far as I was concerned.

I humbly accepted it because why the fuck not? It made them tiptoe just a bit lighter around us.

And *that* I liked.

"Who do you *think* you're speaking to?" I asked, studying him.

It was in the subtle way his hands shook that told me he was losing control with talking to me. He was desperate to act, but he knew I'd react. Knew I was a ticking time bomb, and he needed me for whatever his nefarious plans were.

I'd play.

I loved to play.

He's sick.

Sicker than you.

He wants you. He wants to touch you.

Taste you.

Experience you...

Us.

I licked my lips and raked my gaze up his torso.

"Or who would you like me to be?" I asked softly. "Because we both know I'm capable of playing games. Any game. Pick one. We'll play."

His Adam's apple bobbed, and his hands shook again.

"Complete your task. Your reward is her. We'll discuss what else I can provide you once she's broken. You'll need a pet once you've realized how fun they can be. I can give you many. I can give you anything... *Asylum.*"

I quirked my lips up at him, burying my rage and disgust deep down like I tended to do. It was kindling for the fire I'd build later. The fire *we'd* build.

His screams will be worth all the pain. All the tears.

I got to my feet and followed him to the red room and stepped inside. I turned to face him before he could close the door.

"You're trying to break me too," I said softly.

He stared back at me with no emotion on his face.

I leaned in, his powerful cologne burning my nose as I breathed him in, my lips brushing against his ear. "Trouble is, I'm already fucking broken. If you play with me, it's only because I let you."

He jerked away from me quickly as I let out a wicked laugh and backed away. The door closed in his wake, but not before I noticed his face flaming red with anger.

I smirked, enjoying the game we played.

But now it was time to start a new game. One that was infinitely more enjoyable…

One with my Rinny.

SIRENA

It hurt in the darkness. Everything hurt. Breathing hurt.

"Your ribs are probably bruised," a soft, familiar voice called out to me. "Mine are too."

Seth?

"It's me," came his voice again before the warm touch of his hand landed on my bare thigh.

I couldn't see him.

It was all darkness here.

I was a prisoner in this cold world. I wasn't even sure if I existed anymore.

"Seth," he continued. "Your Seth. And you're Rinny, our. . . forever girl."

Church. I was Church's girl.

Ashes's

Stitches's.

Sinful's. . .?

I was their girl, or had been, not Asylum's. He'd tried to kill me. He'd trapped me.

"I'm Seth, Rinny. Not Asylum."

The soft hum vibrated my lips, the familiar song my response.

"Our song," Seth murmured.

"Just scream my name again, specter. Then I'll know. I'll know you're ready to come home to me."

Church.

Dante.

He'd promised to come. To save me if I called for him. He hadn't. I screamed alone and for nothing.

"He let you go," Seth continued. "They all did. You're mine now. It was a bet. I won. The watchers are honorable. Mostly."

Gone.

I remembered that. They'd used me in a game. Sinful. . . he'd used his occurrence to punish me.

My face felt damp.

A soft touch removed the wetness from my cheeks.

"I'll always protect you, Rinny. I always did. Nothing has changed. I'm here now, protecting you from the evil wizard."

Seth.

Not Asylum.

Seth had protected me.

Warm hands touched mine. "Come back to me so we can slay the evil wizard and leave this place. I won't hurt you."

"Asylum," I rasped.

"No. Just Seth. I'm here. Come out of the darkness and join me in the fire, Rinny. Don't be afraid. I won't hurt you."

"Seth. . ."

"My princess locked in hell," he whispered, his gentle fingers cradling my face. "Come out, come out, wherever you are."

So heavy.

This world was so heavy.

I liked the darkness despite the cold.

No one could hurt me here.

I couldn't see the evil in the world.

I was safe. No one could see me. They could beat my body, but they couldn't get my mind here. They couldn't hurt my heart.

"If you don't come to me, I'll go to you." Warmth brushed my cheek. Trailed to my jaw. To my ear. "And then we'll stay wrapped together forever in the darkness."

I shivered against him.

"No one can get you in the darkness but me, Rinny. It's because I was made from the darkness. It's my kingdom. My empire. I want it to be ours. Didn't I always promise forever to you? You promised it back. We remember."

I felt like I was falling slowly.

My back hit the cushions, and he loomed over me.

"Come back to me. Please, come back *to us*. I'm sorry you were hurt. I only wanted to save you. Now you're trapped in this hell with me." Warmth brushed against my cheek again. "I'll give you a crown of daggers and slay anyone you want me to. Then I'll make love to you over their remains. Whatever world my pirate princess wants, she will have. Just come out of hiding. I need you, Rinny. Fuck, I need you." His voice cracked.

He needed me.

Seth needed me.

It was Seth.

He seemed like two people.

One I loved. One I feared.

But I knew that wasn't possible for him to be two people. Asylum and Seth were more different than they were alike. I just ... didn't understand what it meant. All I knew was something was off.

He hummed our song softly. I couldn't see past the darkness, but I knew he was there. That he was looming over me. Watching me. Wanting me.

I was so scared.

I missed Seth. My best friend.

He leaned in, his lips brushing the shell of my ear.

"If we don't play the game, they'll hurt us. They will destroy you, Rinny. It's how they'll destroy me. Please, come back to me. I don't want to break you, but I will. I swear I'll shatter you into a million pieces before I repair what I've broken. *Let me in. . .*"

He shifted and dragged my limp body into his arms, where he held me with our song on his lips.

I breathed in and out evenly, falling deeper into the darkness.

And then a gentle heat brushed against my lips before it disappeared. So soft. So fast.

Through the darkness I saw him peering back at me, his blue eyes bright.

"The next time I kiss you, you'll kiss me back," he whispered. "I'll be buried so deeply in your body and mind, you'll never escape me. You'll become another part of me, and I'll be a part of you. I embedded my hooks long ago into your soul. Nothing will tear me from you, Rinny. *Nothing.*"

He stared back at me as I blinked slowly at him.

Seth Cain.

Not Asylum.

Holding me.

Making promises.

I belonged to him now.

"You see me," he murmured. "Stay with me. Don't go."

Fear coursed through me as I retreated back into the darkness before I let the numbness take over to shield me.

"*Fucking stay*! Rinny! NO! Come back! Don't fucking leave me. Please. Don't leave me again." He wept softly, shaking me roughly. "Please... I need you. We fucking need you..."

All went silent.

And I was safe once more.

STITCHES

My groan was a rasp as I rolled over on the cold, hard mattress. The hospital gown was much too thin to keep me warm.

I shivered and curled into a ball, a soft hiss leaving my lips because the pain I was in. Rocking softly, I tried to keep myself warm, but it wasn't much use. The agony I felt was far too great, and after a few minutes, I had to stop.

The door to my room opened. I didn't bother to look at my visitor. It didn't fucking matter. My head felt like it had been beaten with a sledgehammer for as much as it throbbed. When I tried to rack my brain to remember anything, I was hit with a brick wall. I had no fucking memory of what had happened to me, but judging by the way my body felt, it hadn't been good.

I wanted out.

I needed out.

I was going to die here.

Fucking die in this hell.

Fuck.

"Malachi," Sully's voice greeted me. "It's good to see you awake. You gave us quite a scare yesterday."

I said nothing. I didn't move. Fuck him.

"Sit him up," Sully called out.

A moment later, rough hands pulled and tugged on my body, lifting me into a sitting position. My head felt too heavy to hold up. One of the wards tangled his fingers in my hair and jerked my head up so I was looking at the cocksucker in front of me.

"You're upset," Sully said. "It's understandable. You're going through a big change right now."

"Fuck you," I mumbled.

"Yes, well, later." He chuckled, the sound sending chills down my spine.

A flash of a memory cracked through the wall, making me blink rapidly.

Crying.

Begging.

A hot mouth against mine.

Pain. So much fucking pain.

My chest ached as the memory faded away, the wall firmly back in place.

My pulse thundered in my ears.

"You were hallucinating yesterday." Sully's voice brought me back to the moment. "Babbling incoherently. Saying things that hadn't happened. Then you passed out on us, and we couldn't wake you."

I blinked at him.

I'd never hallucinated a day in my fucking life.

"Your brain was without oxygen when you tried to kill yourself. That kind of event can cause damage. We're trying to fix that."

I licked my lips.

"I-I want to go home," I rasped.

Sully nodded. "I'm aware, but you need to understand that this is for the best. Your father approved your current treatment plan. He was here yesterday when you slipped and fell. That was when your hallucinations began. You had a seizure, Malachi."

I breathed out.

I'd never had a seizure before in my life either.

"It could've been from the new medications or. . . something else. In the end, you're still here with us, which is a good thing. So we can resume treatment."

"I want to g-go home," I repeated, my throat aching. "I want Church. Ashes. Sin. And angel. Please. Let me see her. Sirena."

Sully kneeled in front of me as the ward released my hair. I struggled to hold my head up as I stared back at him. He reached out and brushed my dark hair off my forehead.

"If you do well today, I'll let you see her tomorrow. How does that sound? If you obey, you can see her."

I hated this prick, but I was desperate to be with my angel, so I nodded weakly.

"Good boy," Sully cooed, smiling at me. "Very good boy. Let's take your medicine, OK? Then tomorrow you can see your angel."

I jerked away from him as he reached for my arm.

"Malachi," he warned softly. "You're not being very good right now. What happened to my good boy?"

His words sent nausea churning deep in my guts.

He reached for my arm again, and this time, I didn't yank away. Quickly, he tied a band around my bicep and slid a needle into my veins. When he pushed the plunger, the amber liquid heated my arm as it raced upward.

"Oh f-fuck," I choked out, an incredible euphoria hitting me.

It had to be the best high I'd ever had.

"Keep doing good things for me," Sully said softly. "And I'll reward you. You like this reward?"

"Y-yes," I choked out.

"Good. Very good. Come on. Let's get you to the treatment room. Then, tomorrow, you'll get to see Sirena." He held his hand out to me, and I placed mine in it, my head a jumbled fucking mess of pleasure and happiness.

I'd never felt so fucking happy before.

At least I thought it was happiness.

I wasn't quite sure. It wasn't *my* happiness though. It was artificial, but fuck, it felt good.

"We'll give you the rest of your medicine if you need it," Sully said after I sat in the wheelchair.

I licked my lips. "I like this medicine. What's it called?"

"Of course you do. The name isn't important. It is by far one of the best drugs available. You can only get it from me here though, so you'd best make sure you're doing what you're told. Each time you do, I'll reward you with some."

I hated this prick, but I definitely loved the way I felt. The pain in my body was gone as the static blanketed me.

For once in my life I felt like maybe I could make it.

Like I could do this.

Whatever *this* was.

Was it life? Could I do life?

I'd give it a hell of a shot if it felt like this.

This high was definitely where it was at.

†

I GRUNTED, my arms straining against the leather bands which held me in place on the bed. The drugs had worn off long ago, and I'd been given something else that intensified the agony in my body.

"P-please. No," I cried out, my mind completely blitzed, confusion running rampant. I couldn't tell what was real and what wasn't.

The people in robes. In masks. I couldn't see their faces.

It was dark. So dark.

I couldn't tell if they were real or not.

They didn't move like they were real.

They jerked and twitched before moving fast, almost like they were lagging, glitching.

And they kept praying in a circle around me.

It wasn't a prayer I'd ever heard before though or a language I knew. I spoke both English and Spanish. This was neither.

Then there was the touching.

My naked body.

Hands on my groin.

"Mama," I choked out. "Please. Please, Mama!"

Silence.

"Malachi, look at me." Sully's face appeared.

There were no masked people. No chanting. The room was bright white, not dark now. I wasn't strapped down anymore.

I let out a whimper.

What the fuck was happening to me?

"I hurt," I sobbed. "Please. It hurts."

"I know," Sully said gently. "That's what it feels like when the demons fight back. If you want the pain to go away, you have to listen. Can you listen for me?"

"Y-yes," I stammered, desperate to do anything to make this end.

He brushed my hair from my forehead. I shivered beneath my thin hospital gown.

"Pray with me," Sully murmured.

He recited the Lord's Prayer, and I said it with him, my voice trembling and nausea rolling deep inside me.

"Amen," Sully finished.

"A-amen." I shook violently.

"Get him up," Sully demanded.

Wards came into the room and sat me up. One shoved a basin beneath my face just before I heaved violently, emptying my guts into it.

I quaked, shivering at the cool air. But I was burning inside like I was on fire. My throat ached like hot pokers were digging through it.

Tears streamed down my face as water was pressed to my lips. I drank hungrily until my belly was full. Someone wiped my mouth.

"You're unwell, Malachi," Sully said softly. "You know that right?"

"W-who are the men in masks?" I whispered. "Why are they hurting me?"

"They're your demons." He cradled my face. "They're fighting back. They don't want to leave your body. There's a war within you. You just need to submit."

"To who?" I asked, my body continuing to quiver.

"To God. To me," he said, his voice barely above a whisper. "If you submit to me, I can save your soul. I can make sure God loves you. That he forgives you. Wouldn't you like that, Malachi? To be in His grace? To not feel pain anymore? To be happy?"

"How?" I was done. I was ready for these feelings to leave me. For this pain to go away. I just wanted to go home. I wanted my friends. My girl. I wanted to sleep. Fuck. I wanted to sleep forever.

"By doing what you're told. By accepting me. Let me in. You keep fighting me. Stop fighting me. You've done terrible things. God wants to save you. He's using me to do it. You just need to accept me into your heart. Your mind. Let me guide you."

I wept softly. Pain ebbed through me like an electric current. I ground my teeth so hard I feared they'd snap off and I'd choke on them.

Please, Mama. Make the pain stop. I hurt. I hurt so much. Please...

"The pain will go away if you let me in. You're such a strong boy. Defiant. Beautiful. Your skin is a beautiful canvas that you've destroyed with your markings. It's the first way to make this end."

"What do I do?" I peered at him through bleary eyes. I wanted this ache to go away. I wanted the drug he'd given me. I wanted my freedom. I just wanted to be normal.

"You cut away what burdens you," he said in a soft voice that sent chills over me. "Make the first cut. To be free. Carve the sins from your body."

Something cold was pushed into the palm of my hand.

"I'll stay with you to make sure you're safe from the demons."

I cried, my chest throbbing.

"Freedom is only a slice away, Malachi. Cut the demons out of your life. Be free. Be happy. Submit to me. Prove you want your sanity, and I'll give you a life you never dreamed possible. Where you don't have to think anymore. Where you aren't haunted. Where you aren't sad."

Tears leaked out of my eyes and fell onto my lap as I stared down at the blade he'd given me. He was asking me to cut parts of my skin off. To remove my tattoos as punishment for letting the demons in.

My entire body was tatted. Even spots on my face. And he wanted me to cut them away?

His warm fingers met my temple. "Start here."

"Do you promise the pain will stop?" I gasped as it intensified like it had a mind of its own and knew I was trying to expel it from my body.

I fell back onto the bed, my body stiffening as my misery grew.

A scream tore from my lips as my chest heaved.

I thrashed violently on the hard mattress, the pain turning into fire, incinerating my insides. Cold hands pressed me down as I ground my teeth painfully hard. My jaw ached.

Mama. Please. Help me. HELP ME!

"No one is coming to save you, Malachi," Sully's voice broke through the agony. "You're a wicked boy who needs to prove himself. Who needs to show me and God what your freedom means to you. The pain will go away once you submit. Your reward will be your angel. Don't you want to see her again? I promise. Rid your body of your demons first."

I screamed again, vomit and spit spewing from my mouth as I lurched to the side. Everything felt like it was moving in slow motion. Like it was a fuzzy, agonizing nightmare.

I twitched on my side in a puddle of vomit and piss. I saw the knife on the mattress. With shaky hands, I reached for it.

"Set yourself free," Sully whispered.

Free.

My angel.

I grasped the handle of the knife and pressed the blade to my temple.

It was hard to see through my tears as Sully bent and put his face in front of mine.

"Cut the demons out, Malachi. Prove yourself."

The pain began to build again.

But it was because I was carving at my skin with the knife in my hand, ridding myself of the demons.

ASHES

I couldn't sleep.

I'd been tossing and turning for hours. I hadn't been able to burn anything since the bathtub. I was supposed to be able to go out and get my fix at my barrels off campus, but that had gone to shit.

I was going nuts.

Sitting up, I rubbed my palms against my pajama bottoms, my heart thudding hard. I was going to fucking lose it. Something had to give, and I really fucking hoped it wasn't my willpower to not burn the house down.

I needed help.

I was smart enough to recognize that part. If I didn't get it now, we'd have a real situation on our hands.

Abby flashed through my mind. Holding her small body as the flames danced in my eyes.

No. I wouldn't fucking slip again. . .

Quickly, I went to Sin's room and pounded on the door.

"S-Sin. Sin. Man, open up. Please. I need help." My hands trembled as I shifted my weight from one foot to the other. I was breathing too fast. I felt like I was going to pass out.

Great. Anxiety too.

Unable to wait any longer, I flung his door open to find his bed empty and his sheets rumpled.

Fuck.

I raced to Church's room and barged inside. He looked peaceful as he slept. I knew how stressed he was. How close he was to losing it too. He and Stitches were brothers, after all. Knowing Stitches was suffering was hurting us all.

I crawled into bed beside him, my body shaking. I didn't want to wake him. God, I didn't. He needed to sleep. He needed the escape, but shit, I was spiraling.

I couldn't fucking breathe!

"Asher?" Church called out in a sleepy voice. "What's going on? What's wrong?" He rose up on his elbow and rubbed his eyes before frowning down at me.

I was breathing too hard now. Everything I'd tried pushing away felt like it was tumbling down. It was crushing me.

The loss of Sirena. Stitches's suicide attempt and him being locked up. Sin withdrawing and never being here. Church's pain. My fears. The worry that something terrible was happening to my heaven and my best friend under the thumb of Sully. Concern that Sin was drifting from us and fighting his thoughts alone. Fear that Church might lose it and hurt someone without having a plan.

"Help me, Dante. Please," I managed to say.

He lay beside me and cradled my face as I panted.

"It's OK. I'm here. Everything is OK. You're safe."

"I-I can't—"

"Fuck you, you can," he said in a fierce growl. "You're not going to fucking leave me too, Valentine. Get your shit together."

I sucked in breath after breath, desperate to not disappoint him. He was all I had right now.

"Remember what we do when we can't breathe?"

"We d-do it anyway," I said.

"That's right. We fucking do it anyway." He wrapped his arms around me and held me against his body as I tried to get my shit together.

"Do you need fire? It's been too long," he murmured.

"Y-yes."

"OK. Try to calm down. I'm going to get dressed. I'll take you to the barrels."

I said nothing as I continued to focus on keeping myself in check. Church kissed my forehead fiercely before he released me and slid out of bed.

I was too focused on holding myself together to hear what he was doing. A moment later, his hands were in mine as he helped me out of bed and led me to my room.

Quickly, he pulled a hoodie over my head as I tried to sit on my mattress. My body wasn't having it though. I needed to go. I needed air. I felt like I was suffocating in this madness. My hands wouldn't stop trembling.

Church slid my shoes on my feet before tugging me upright and leading me out of the room and to the front door.

"What's going on?" Sin asked, coming through the front door, wearing his jacket.

"We need some therapy," Church muttered, grabbing my coat and helping me into it.

Sin's gray eyes swept over me, a pained look on his face. He reached for my hand.

"Come on, Asher," he said softly. "Let's go."

I took his hand and followed him out of the house while Church locked the door behind us. Within minutes, we were cruising down the road in Church's new Bronco, the top peeled back and the cool air hitting my face.

No one spoke as we drove.

My chest ached with the cool night air filling my lungs. My body was shaking, my mind racing.

Hurry. Please hurry.

When we got to the spot where my barrels were, Sin helped me out while Church grabbed my stuff from the back. He placed it at my feet and pushed my lighter into my hand.

"Burn it all," he murmured.

I swallowed hard and pushed past him.

I squeezed lighter fluid into the barrel then lit it while tears streaked down my cheeks and flames licked toward the sky. I watched them for several long minutes, my breathing ragged, until I was finally able to focus.

Within minutes, I'd gathered more kindling to feed the flames, urging them higher into the night sky. This was the middle of nowhere, so we were safe. The heat from the fire warmed me, calming my heart and soul.

I stared into the flames, my heaven flashing through my mind. *Her soft lips. Her smile. The way it felt when she touched me.*

Stitches. His laughter. The way he smirked when he was teasing and happy.

My family.

The ones I fought for now.

I stayed lost in the positive thoughts for a long time, desperate to make them a reality again.

When I'd gotten a decent fix, I turned to my friends.

Sin and Church were leaning against the front of the Bronco, watching me like they always did.

But there was no Stitches.

He needed to be here.

I turned back to my fire and closed my eyes.

I need both Stitches and Sirena.

†

"We need to talk," I said the following morning when I came into the living room.

Surprisingly, Sin was sitting with Church. They'd grown quiet when I'd come into the room, so I knew they'd been discussing my near-breakdown last night.

"I'm feeling a lot better now," I said, dropping onto the leather wraparound. "So you guys don't need to be out here discussing my mental health. It's shit, but yours all are too, so let's move past that, OK?"

Church nodded solemnly at me while Sin remained wordless.

"I want Stitches home." I looked from Church to Sin.

He crinkled his brows at me but nodded.

I focused back on Church. "Let's go get him."

Church sighed and rubbed his eyes. "I want him home too. But I don't necessarily know if he's ready to come home. I don't want to get him here and him try to hang himself again. I-I don't want to lose him."

"Then we need to see him. Get an idea of how his mental health is. See where he's really at. If he seems good, we break him out if they won't release him. I know a way to smoke them out if I have to."

Church's lips quirked up at that. "Let's do it."

I glanced at Sin, who sat forward, his gray eyes locked on me. I didn't think he'd agree. He'd been all over the place lately with his actions, but he nodded.

"Yeah. I'm in."

I grinned. Maybe if we were lucky, we'd get to see Sirena too. Two birds with one stone wasn't a bad plan.

We needed this.

For the love of our sanity, we needed it.

CHURCH

I marched into the hospital and straight to the nurses station. The same nurse from last time was on duty. Immediately, her eyes widened.

"I'm looking for Stitches," I said evenly. "You're going to step aside and not call anyone to come interfere, right?" I tipped my head toward the phone. "We both know that phone cord makes a really beautiful necklace on you."

Her lips parted, and she nodded.

"If you do call someone, you'll have to become a patient here. I'm sure you don't want that."

She visibly swallowed. "Right."

"Good girl." I grinned at her. She blushed and ducked her head.

Fucking beautiful sluts. I loved them all. So easy to manipulate and maneuver when I was thinking clearly and not losing my mind in rage.

We moved past the station and took the elevator up to Stitches's floor and got out. I didn't really have a plan. I just knew I wanted to see my brother.

The hallway was empty the entire way, which made it easier for us.

"Those doors are locked," Sin said as we marched down the hall. "We need a key if we want to get inside."

"We'll get inside," I murmured as we approached his room and slowed to a stop. I peered through the tiny pane of glass and saw his bed empty and rumpled.

My heart lurched.

"What? What's wrong?" Ashes demanded.

"He's not here." I stepped away from the door, frustration rolling through me.

"What?" Ashes peeked through the window. "Where the fuck is he?"

"Visiting hours aren't for another two hours," Sully's voice called out.

I snapped my head up and narrowed my eyes at the prick.

"We make our own hours. You know that," I said, glaring at him as he approached with a smug smile on his stupid fucking face.

"Of course." He stopped near us and widened his shitty smile into one he must have thought looked sincere, but it looked like bullshit to me. "Malachi took a turn for the worse last night, I'm afraid. Your father is back."

"What?" My blood ran cold. "What happened? Why wasn't I notified?"

"Your father needed to be notified first. We follow protocol, regardless of who the students are. While I know your family is important to Chapel Crest—"

I shoved him hard in the chest, sending him stumbling back to the wall. I didn't hesitate to get in his face.

My father was a fucking monster. If he was here, shit was going down. He'd warned me that he'd step in if he had to return.

"Where *the fuck* is my brother?"

Sully visibly swallowed and smoothed down his tie. "Right. Come with me."

I let him move past me and looked back at Sin and Ashes, who were both pale. They followed wordlessly as we were led down the hall and around the corner.

We didn't stop until we were at a new room. I stepped inside. Stitches was in bed with an IV in his arm and his face bandaged. Bright red blood peeked through the white gauze on the side of his head. His eyes were closed. His lips were dry and cracked. Ugly purple bruises haloed his eyes, and the ligature marks on his neck were still apparent from where he'd tried to hang himself.

I ground my teeth tightly as Ashes sucked in a soft breath.

Sin stared at Stitches, his hands trembling.

I turned on Sully.

"What the fuck happened to him?"

"Malachi is very sick—"

"*Malachi* is very fucking injured. Explain why and how," I snarled, ready to beat the truth from his body.

"Malachi, as you know, tried to kill himself in your home. We hoped he'd be on the mend by now, but because of his mental issues, it's not worked out that way. His brain was without oxygen for a little too long, and it's caused him to start having seizures and hallucinating. Last night, he hallucinated that we wanted him to hurt himself. So he broke free and managed to get hold of a scalpel then he tried to cut his tattoos off his face because he was convinced he'd be released from here if he did."

Horror spread through me at Sully's words. Bile threatened my throat.

"Stitches wouldn't do that. He's fallen into darkness before. It was never like this. What *the fuck* did you do to him?" I shoved Sully again as Ashes ignored us and went to Stitches and held his hand. I recognized that he was speaking to Stitches, but I didn't register his words.

Sin moved behind me but didn't try to stop me.

"Dante. Please. We will detain you—"

My fist met his face in a satisfying crack. "Detain this, bitch."

I was just about to kick the fuck out of him when a strong hand landed on my shoulder and gripped me tightly. I knew that fucking touch.

"Enough," my father's deep voice boomed out.

It took everything I had within me to back away from Sully and his bloody fucking nose, but I did.

I whirled on my father, the hatred boiling hotter within me.

"You're letting this happen to him, you sick, twisted fuck."

"I do not control Malachi's illnesses," he said softly to me, his dark eyes emotionless. Like always.

The man was just a voice except when it came to harming people. That was where his sickness was. I fucking loathed him and wanted nothing more than to skin him alive while listening to him scream the entire time. It was a sweeter, kinder end than his fucked-up soul deserved.

"No, you just control the cunts making it worse," I said fiercely.

He inclined his head at me. "I understand your frustration, Dante, but we're trying to help your brother. I'm here to approve treatment for him so he can return home and to his studies. Do not think for a moment that I want him stuck here, imagining things. Malachi needs to get better. He can't do that if you're in here with your friends attacking the staff."

I swallowed hard. "I want him released immediately into my care—"

"Unfortunately, Son, that's not your call. It's mine, and I say he stays."

I glared at him, doing everything in my power to resist flattening his ass. I knew my father. If I hit him or lashed out at him, Stitches would be punished as a means to punish me. Or worse. That was just how the prick operated. He controlled people through the power he wielded. Through his abilities to harm those closest to us.

"What have I done to offend you, Father?" I whispered. "For you to hurt my brother like this?"

He reached out and cradled my face. "Your brother is sick. He's sicker than you, Dante. He needs this treatment if he is to return home. If I wanted him dead, don't you think I'd have done it already? You remember who I am, don't you, Son?"

"The fucking devil," I whispered.

He smirked at me, making me want to spit in his face. "Ah, and you're the prince of my darkness. Now return home and let the professionals deal with Malachi. If I catch you here again, you will be punished." The way he said it let me know he meant Stitches. He knew how to hurt me.

He leaned to speak into my ear as I stiffened. "That pretty, little thing down the hall really is magical, isn't she? It would be a shame if she became my new toy. Now *fucking* leave and think about what you *know* I want from you."

My breath caught in my chest as he pulled away and gave me a look to let me know he wasn't playing. But I knew that already. My father never played. If he made a threat, he followed through. We were cut from the same cloth, he and I. We were both disgusting monsters.

I glanced at Stitches in bed, my eyes burning.

"D-don't fucking hurt him," I choked out. "He's my only family."

My father let out a soft, dark laugh. "I'll make sure he's in good hands. Don't worry, Dante. Malachi will return home soon enough. Then we'll talk about you finally joining the family business."

The family business.

The flesh trade.

Sex. Body parts. Lives. Fucking souls.

My legacy.

He backed away from me as Ashes got to his feet and Sin moved to my side.

I knew I couldn't fight this battle like this, so I turned and left, taking my friends with me.

"What the fuck is going on?" Ashes snarled. "Stitches wouldn't do that shit. You know he wouldn't!"

"I know," I said tightly. "We're all fucked. FUCKED!"

"We need to get him out of here," Sin murmured. "I-I'm sorry. Fuck. How? How do we do it?"

"He can't leave until he succumbs and accepts," Asylum's soft voice called out.

I stopped and pivoted to find him leaning against a doorway, clad in pajama bottoms and a white t-shirt.

I stormed toward him. He didn't back away or look scared. Instead, he simply peered back at me.

"You know something," I said to him. I hadn't forgotten how he knew Stitches was hanging himself in his closet or the other shit he'd said to us in the past.

"I know many things," he answered, no emotion on his face.

"What the fuck is happening here? Why are you still here? Shouldn't you be out lurking in dark corners by now? Or luring girls into fucking coffins?" I demanded.

"You act like I'm always making girls get into coffins with me." He waved his hand dismissively at me. "That was a one-time thing. Let it go, Dante."

"Fuck you, you piece of fucking human garbage."

"You want information? You have to play nice. You're not being very nice."

I tried to calm my breathing and rage. "I will fucking kill you."

"Foreplay. My favorite," he said, smirking at me. "Meet me at midnight at the mausoleum. We'll talk then. Maybe I can seduce *you* into a coffin with me."

I balled my hands into fists.

"Don't take to violence so soon, Dante. I promise if you hold onto it, it'll be much better placed later on. We can even discuss your sweet, little specter. Midnight. Take the woods, not the path. They'll be walking through there at 11:53. Don't need you getting caught." He winked and backed away before closing his door in my face.

"Are we meeting him?" Ashes asked softly.

I ground my teeth. *What choice did we have?*

"Yes," I said softly, noting the look of fear which flashed across Sin's face.

I ignored it.

I had bigger things to worry about, like what the actual fuck was going on here.

ASHES

Beneath the cover of darkness, we slipped through the pitch-black forest to the cemetery, all three of us dressed in black to keep us invisible to anyone patrolling.

None of us spoke. Our entire evening had been spent in silence as we'd tried to come to terms with what Church had told us his father had said. Sirena was in danger. Stitches certainly was.

Something had to give.

Regret at having let Sirena go so easily weighed heavily on me. If she was in the same condition as Stitches. . . well, I might be inclined to burn this fucking place and its inhabitants to the ground. If Church didn't murder someone first.

When we reached the mausoleum, we stopped.

"What if it's a trick?" I asked, apprehension rolling through me.

It was becoming more apparent that Asylum wasn't the normal sort of insane.

"Then he dies," Church answered as he stared at the mausoleum. "We'll bury him out here."

I turned to Sin and found him staring at the mausoleum too, his lips turned into a deep frown.

"Why are you still standing here?" Asylum's voice from behind us made me jump.

He winked at me before he passed clad in all black too. Turning, he walked backward and gestured for us to follow him. I glanced at Church again. A muscle thrummed along his jaw beneath the dim light of the moon.

He stepped forward, and we followed, letting the door to the mausoleum swing closed behind us. Old man Morse's coffin was still in its place, minus the bones. Who the hell knew where those even were. I was sure if Asylum had anything to do with their disappearance then they were probably hiding in his closet or some shit.

We went from pitch-black to a soft, warm glow of light as a battery-operated lantern was lit. Asylum's face shone eerily in the pale light as he held it.

"Don't want any ghouls to play grab ass with us in the dark," he said softly.

Had this not been a serious situation, I would've laughed. Instead, I simply kept my focus on him as he placed the lantern in the center of the circle we'd formed.

"Speak," Church growled.

"Always straight to business," Asylum said with a sigh. "I can't give you all the answers you seek because I simply don't have them. Yet."

"So why the hell did we have to meet you here?" I demanded. "Stitches is clearly getting fucked with. We need to know what's going on and how to get him out."

Asylum cocked his head at me. "I remember the way she sounded when she screamed."

"What?" I frowned and glanced to Church and Sin.

Church took a dangerous step forward while Sin appeared confused.

"Isabella," Asylum continued.

My guts twisted at her name. I hadn't thought about her in forever. Sin's ex-girlfriend. The one who'd killed their unborn child.

The one we'd killed and scattered as ashes on the lake.

"Don't fucking say her name," Sin said with a snarl, stepping forward to stand next to Church. "She left here."

"Yes. Gone. Dust to dust. Ashes to ashes. Bells's death was a must after Sin's seven deadly lashes." He let out a soft laugh at his fucked-up nursery rhyme.

It was the fact he knew what had happened which made chills rush across my skin.

There was no possible way. . .

"How do you know. . . ?" Sin asked, his voice wavering.

Asylum cocked his head to the other side. "How does a creature like me know anything? Must be the voices." He let out another burst of laughter that echoed around us as he tapped his temple, his blue eyes sparkling with madness in the light from the lantern.

We stared at him, transfixed at what a lunatic he really was.

"He's fucking with us. He doesn't *know*," Church said. "Why is that bitch even important to this? She has nothing to do with Stitches or specter."

"Doesn't she?" Asylum stared right at Church. "She's a little key to a vast kingdom, I'd say. You still don't believe me, though." Asylum let out a sigh and shook his head. "Fine. Test me. Ask me anything. If at the end of your questioning you aren't convinced I know things, then I'll go back to the shadows with my prize, and we'll never speak again."

"Your prize is *my* girl," Church said, his voice laced with barely controlled rage. "When you return to your dark corner, it'll be alone."

I was glad he was doing the talking because it was taking all my willpower once more to not just say fuck it all and burn down the hospital, and grab my heaven and best friend from there, then leave this place for fucking good.

I dipped my hand into my pocket and brushed my fingers against the cool metal of my lighter as I tried to calm myself.

"Fair enough," Asylum said without missing a beat. "I won't argue that for a period of time in the near future I'll be without her."

I didn't feel like playing any longer. I just needed answers. We all did. "Get to your point."

"Then simply ask your questions. Some are harder to answer than others. Know that going in."

I snorted. Of course they were. I couldn't shake the fact he'd known about Stitches trying to hang himself though. It was still weighing heavily on me.

I pulled my lighter out then opened and closed it five times before starting over. Everything was stressing me out lately. Being in this damn place not only gave me the creeps, but it sent ugly memories of finding my heaven in that damn coffin with Asylum, filling my head with heartbreaking images.

"Fine. What's happening to Stitches?" Church asked.

"Wrong question. Ask me something you've never told anyone before. Or something I shouldn't know."

Church let out an exasperated sigh. The fact he was still playing along surprised me. I was ready to just storm the hospital and take back what belonged to us.

"What's my favorite color?" he asked.

"You like. . . white."

I blinked in surprise and looked to Church quickly. White *was* his favorite color.

"Mine is yellow," Asylum continued. "It's quite cheerful."

Sin let out a soft snort.

"What's wrong, Sinclair? You don't think I'm deserving of cheer?"

"I think psychos like yellow. I mean, I think that's what I heard during one of my group sessions." Sin stared back at him.

If it bothered Asylum, he didn't show it. Instead, he simply winked at him.

"Where is Bells buried?" I asked softly, wanting to get to the heart of the matter.

"Trick question, Valentine." Asylum's focus snapped to me. "For she is *not* buried. She swims in the water. The flames grew hotter. She floats on the wind. She became the ultimate sin." He smiled widely at me. "Church lured her in like a spider waiting, and then he and Sin killed her. She screamed for them to listen to her as you flicked your lighter. *Open. Close. Open. Close.* Five times. A pause. Five more times."

He closed his eyes and breathed in deeply as my guts churned. "Mm. Yes. The watchers removed her body when life left it, and you set it ablaze to become nothing but ash and bone. Her bones are. . ." He snapped his eyelids open and cocked his head as I held my breath.

How the fuck did he know?

Church's body was tense, his eyes narrowed, his chest heaving.

And Sin... Sin looked like he was going to throw up.

"She liked Poe," Asylum said softly after a moment. "'The Tell-Tale Heart' was her favorite." He focused on Sin and cocked his head in the other direction as if he was listening to someone nearby we couldn't see. "Why do you keep her there, Sinclair?"

Nausea twisted my insides as Sin licked his lips. "Keep her where?"

"Don't play dumb with me. I know your level of depravity," Asylum murmured. "Beneath the floorboards, of course."

I widened my eyes as I looked to Sin. I had no idea what he'd done with the bones. He'd said he'd take care of them. We'd figured it'd be best if only he knew. Besides, he'd wanted it that way even though I'd offered to be with him when he'd gotten rid of them.

"Tell me there aren't bones in my fucking house," Church hissed, his hands balled into tight fists.

"There aren't," Sin answered, his voice strained.

"No, not in the house. They're in Sully's office. Clever, clever," Asylum said in a sing-song voice. "*Very* clever."

Church and I both gaped at Sin. I felt like the air had been knocked out of my lungs. Killing Isabella hadn't been a crowning moment for me. I never let it enter my mind if I could help it. I didn't like the memories or the way it made me feel. In all actuality, it wasn't a bad feeling. When I thought about it, I felt accomplished. Satisfied. The woman who'd hurt my friend so deeply had been punished for her crimes.

The guilt at having those satisfying feelings sickened me. Hence, why I kept them tightly locked away in my mind.

"Is that where she is?" Church demanded.

Sin stared at Asylum like he didn't recognize him. Finally, Sin focused back on us. "Yes."

"How did you know?" Church turned and glared at Asylum. "How did you know Stitches was going to hang himself? How do you know any of this shit?"

"*I* don't know. *We* know," Asylum answered, gesturing widely around him. "Special little parlor trick. How am I doing so far?"

"Are you even crazy or are the voices real?" I rasped, my mouth dry like I'd been sucking on a cotton ball.

"Good question. Maybe a little of both, Valentine." He nodded. His eyes unfocused in the lantern light as it became silent in the cold room.

When he spoke, agony clenched my chest.

"She doesn't blame you, you know. Abigail. She loved you." His voice adopted a girlish tone as he continued, "*Asher, you're so silly, but the flames are going to burn someone if you're not careful. . .*"

My heart froze in my chest as his gaze bore into me, examining my tainted soul. He'd repeated words Abby had said to me the day before she died. I'd never told anyone her words before.

"Your parents, even they miss you sometimes."

I let out a snarl and launched myself at him. Sin and Church grabbed me before my fist could connect with his face.

"Don't talk about her. *Never* fucking talk about her," I shouted, fighting against my friends. "You fucking piece of shit! Let me go! Fucking let me torch him!" I didn't even realize I was sobbing until I fell to my knees, my cheeks damp with tears.

I hated being reminded of my sins against my twin. My best friend. She was everything to me. She was a good person, and because I couldn't control myself, she was dead.

It was something which ate my soul every fucking day of my life.

My chest heaved as I tried to get a handle on myself. I flicked my lighter opened and closed quickly, working to get myself together.

"I don't say things to hurt you," Asylum called out softly. "Only to inform you. To offer you proof of my. . . knowledge. Rinny wouldn't like it if I hurt you, even if she is upset with you."

How. How. HOW?

I wiped my eyes as Sin's warm hand rested on my shoulder and gave it a squeeze.

"How do you know she's upset with us?" Church asked. "She doesn't fucking move, let alone talk."

"Because I know," Asylum answered. "You played a game and lost. She knows she belongs to me now. I've been tasked with a very special assignment."

"By Sully?" Sin helped me to stand.

"Well, he'd like to think so, but it's by. . . fate. Yes. Fate." He looked to his right.

His lips moved, but I couldn't hear what he was saying.

"Stitches is being harmed, but I think I can help him," Asylum said, turning his attention back to us.

"Sully?" I wiped my eyes and peered at Church to see he was focused intently on Asylum.

"Eh, yes and no. Stitches is slipping, but not because of his mind. It's because of. . ." his voice trailed off, and he let out an angry grunt before he tugged at his hair and rocked back and forth on his heels. "Fucking. . . no. Come on. Fuck. Focus, Seth."

He was certifiably insane. I hated him, and I didn't make it a point to hate people. Very few people made that list for me.

"His mind isn't in a good spot. It's. . . foggy. I can't fucking see..." Asylum let out a groan and tugged his hair more, words I couldn't decipher spilling from his mouth. "Touch. Touch. Touch. He cries for his mama and cuts his sins from his face. He will. . . join us. Join us. Yes. He'll join us soon. Rinny. . . Angel. . . Firefly. It'll work. It will work. Fall in line. Fall in line."

He snapped his head up, his blue eyes wild. "We won't kill the wicked just yet. When Stitches walks free, he'll be broken. It's up to you to care for him. His angel will help." He frowned. "Sirena. Only when he's accepted himself and the situation will it be time to end it. He'll make love to her on a Thursday, and on Friday, the world will burn. *Ashes.*"

I swallowed thickly as he stared at me. "You'll burn the world with Mirage at your side."

"Who the fuck is Mirage?" Church demanded.

I didn't know anyone named Mirage. None of us did.

"You know Mirage. Mirage is one thing outwardly but something else completely inwardly. Mirage wants revenge."

"But you don't know who Mirage is?" Sin asked. "Some fucking prophet."

Asylum tilted his head, his attention focused on Sin. "I know what you're capable of, Sinclair. And I know the date and time of your fall. A Tuesday at one-oh-eight in the morning. Your name will be called, and you'll fall. The ropes will hurt, my friend. And I'll be there to set you free."

Sin said nothing as he took a step back.

"All will come to fruition ," Asylum whispered, his voice shaking.

I had no idea what that madman was talking about, but I was all funned out with his weirdness.

"Is Sirena OK?" Church asked. "Is she safe?"

"She will be," Asylum answered simply. "I am with her. Always."

"If you fuck this up and she gets hurt—" Church started.

"I know, Dante. This matters to me too despite who I am. *What I am*. Rinny, my firefly, is my entire world. She always has been. Since the day she waved to me while I stood in my attic window. Whatever is set to meet her will meet me too because I won't leave her side while she's in the hospital. Tonight, she rests peacefully. Alone. Her room is next to mine. I can hear her heartbeat. *Thump-thump. Thump-thump. Thump-thump*." He pounded his chest in time. "It calls to me. She always calls to me. Fucking trust our process."

"Why does it seem like you're trying to steal her away from us and deliver her back all in the same breath?" I asked softly.

He offered me the smallest of smiles and a wink. "Keep your distance and let me work. When the time is right, everything will fall into place."

"That's not good enough," Church said. "Not with Sirena and Stitches both suffering—"

"Sirena suffers in silence because she wants to. Anything she faces will be faced with me at her side. Get that through your head, Dante. I am with her. I'll make sure we come out of this. As for Stitches, he'll soon join us." He crinkled his brows. "Yes. Soon."

"What's happening there with you? Why are you staying at the hospital? What does Sully have you doing?" Sin asked.

A look of sadness swept over Asylum's face.

"Just. . . politics. Science. Sickness. But it must happen to get us to where we're going. We'll grow from the pain. I promise."

"If Sirena is being harmed..." I choked out, unable to finish. "Just. . . let us get her and Stitches out. I know you know how."

"I do know how. And I will. I have to get into her head first. I have to bring her back. Then she'll be released. As for Stitches, it's a tragedy. I'll do my best, but she will always come before him. Know that."

Church nodded stiffly. "He'd want that."

"I know," Asylum murmured, his brows crinkling again. "Trust the process. All of you. I said I'd bring her back. I will. Someday. Just. . . wait for the right time. I know what I'm doing."

He got a faraway look in his eyes. "They think I'm crazy. I am...I am crazy. They wonder why I don't just leave with her. Why I don't drag him out of the loony bin...They don't know...No, they don't know what's at stake...I only take the lives of the unworthy, but this time. . . They need to understand."

He was talking to himself again. Or his voices. I had no clue. Whatever he was doing, his mind was there and away from us. I cast a quick look to Church and Sin, noting the confusion and worry on their faces.

"Trust the process," Asylum repeated. "No one ever trusts the goddamn process! Always with the questions. Just. . . listen to me. The crumbs are right here. The answers are here. Pay attention!"

"Do you want us to trust the process. . . or you?" Sin called out.

Asylum's blue gaze snapped to Sin, and a frightening grin carved his lips upward. "*Trust the process.* Don't trust me. I'm crazy."

"Fucking lunatic," Church snarled. "You have one fucking chance to make sure everything goes OK. If something happens to Sirena, if she's hurt, I'll kill you. I fucking swear I will. And my brother... If Stitches gets fucked-up because we put some faith in you—"

"The gallows I go so that I can swing below," Asylum said in a sing-song voice. "I get it. I caught on the first time you thought about burying me beneath a new hot tub. We haven't forgotten."

Church let out a sigh. "Just. . . fucking go back to your room, you nut job. And keep my family safe."

"Surely not all your family? Your father. . . we should bury him with the bones beneath Sully's office too. Yes?"

"Yes," Church said fiercely.

Asylum's eyes lit up. "We won't kill him right away."

"No," Church murmured. "Not right away. He has sins to pay for."

Asylum's lips quirked up at one corner. "Perfect. Foreplay."

Fucking nut. I couldn't take any more of his riddles. I felt like I'd fallen into Wonderland whenever I had to speak to him. He'd already pissed me off enough for one night. Getting out of there before I lost my mind to him was important. He was good at getting into people's heads. I'd give him that one. I felt like I needed a psych evaluation after spending the last thirty minutes with him.

"Asher needs air. I'm making him a little. . . *mad*," Asylum said with a laugh, offering me a wink. "I'll go. Don't take the path back. They're watching it. Not smart enough or brave enough to go through the trees."

He ambled past us and paused when he reached the door.

"Halloween. The party. Send me an invite. You never invite me to that."

And with that, he left us.

Sin stared at the doorway, and Church turned to me.

"Are we crazy for giving him the benefit of the doubt?" I asked.

"We're crazy for a lot of reasons, but I don't think that's one of them. I think we're just out of options," he said.

"We should've asked the Cheshire fuck who helped him get Sirena into the coffin with him. Once we know that, we can tie up that loose end and punish the asshole who did this to all of us. Stitches wouldn't be slicing his fucking face off, and Sirena wouldn't be catatonic and with that weird prick," I said fiercely.

"One step at a time," Church murmured, his mind seeming far away.

Sin reached down and picked up the lantern before speaking, "Let's stop thinking about who helped him and start thinking about what we're going to do to the fucks who are hurting Stitches and siren. Those are our enemies." He turned out the lantern, his voice wavering.

He was right. We needed to get a game plan because if we were trusting Asylum's process, the time would come when we'd need to act.

I gripped my lighter tightly.

I'd incinerate anyone who hurt my heaven and Stitches. Without a doubt, I would.

STICHES

I didn't feel like myself.

My head felt full and fuzzy. Even the world looked hazy as the wards held my arms and led me down the hall. My body didn't want to move, so I shuffled, stumbling every now and then.

I didn't know where we were going or why, but I prayed it wasn't to the place that had hurt me. I didn't want to hurt anymore.

"Might just want to kill yourself," one of the wards said softly as we stopped outside a massive wooden door.

"I tried," I mumbled. "I'm immortal."

"Too bad for you," he said as the other ward pushed the door open and hauled me inside.

Red. Everywhere.

The walls. The ceiling. Everything was fucking red. Except the black leather sofa and accompanying furniture. Bookcases lined one wall. There was a fireplace with low flames crackling.

I breathed out as I pushed onto the sofa.

"What is this?" I asked, blinking as I tried to keep my head together.

"Your reward," the ward who'd spoken before said softly as he leaned down and wrapped a band around my bicep to give me a dose of something. "Or your punishment. Depends on how you look at it."

I swallowed thickly. "Since when do wards get to administer drugs?"

"Since you scare the fuck out of the nurses," he answered, pushing a needle into my vein.

I didn't even bother to fight him. If it killed me, so fucking be it. I clearly wasn't one able to make it through pressure and trauma, so it was what it was. Hallucinating shit wasn't helping me, so I may as well fucking die. *What good was I like this?*

Fuck it.

The high of the meds hit me hard and fast. I let out a soft groan at the pleasure, every fiber in my body coming to life.

"What's this drug?" I asked, licking my lips.

"It's some tainted form of a new drug they're experimenting with. You're the lab rat. Good luck. You'll need it once the dose kicks in." The ward moved away and left the room without a backward glance.

I lay with my head on the back of the couch, watching as the red swirled above me. I felt like I could fly if I wanted to.

Stumbling to my feet, I ambled over to an ornate mirror hanging on the wall and stared at myself. I looked like I was made of colors. The aura ebbed around me in varying shades, pulsing and pounding as if it had a life of its own.

I continued to stare at myself, taking in my dark eyes, the fading bruises on my neck. Gingerly, I touched the bandage on the side of my face.

I did this. I'd cut off a tattoo. Or maimed it enough to render it unrecognizable.

Nausea churned in my guts before the pounding of the high pushed it down. I winced beneath the pleasure. This had to be a different drug. I hadn't seen colors before. I hadn't felt so. . . invincible before.

The door opened, and two more wards came in pushing my angel in a wheelchair. I stood staring as they wheeled her in. Quickly, they lifted her out of the chair and placed her on the couch then left us without a word.

I blinked rapidly, trying to get my mind right as her head rested on the back of the couch, her focus someplace I knew I'd probably never be able to reach.

Staggering forward, I fell to my knees in front of her.

"Angel," I whispered, my voice shaking.

My reward for being so good.

I reached out for her and brushed my fingers along her soft skin. She didn't even flinch. She simply continued to stare at the nothing only she could see.

"Angel," I choked out again. "Baby. Hey. I-it's me. It's Sti-Stitches."

I grasped her cool hand in mine and gave her a gentle tug to sit her up. She couldn't sit upright on her own. She simply flopped back against the cushions, her body limp.

"No," I called out, my voice trembling. I got to my feet and sat beside her, her hand still in mine. "Angel. Sirena. Hey. Baby, it's me. It's Stitches."

She didn't react.

I ground my teeth, anger racing through me.

"Malachi," Sully's voice called out.

I snapped my head to see he'd entered the room. I'd been so focused on her, I hadn't heard him come in.

"Sh-she's not responding to me," I said thickly. "Is she really gone?"

"No." Sully took a seat on the ottoman he'd dragged in front of the couch. "She's in there. We get reactions from her sometimes. She reacts quite a lot with Seth Cain."

I clenched my jaw at that.

"You let him in to see her?"

"Seth sees her every day. In fact, he's gotten rather *close* to her." He offered me a smirk which made me sick to my guts.

I trembled inside even as the high blanketed me. I winced, confused about why it seemed to be controlling me. While I could feel the anger and sickness within me, there was something else there. Something I couldn't quite figure out.

"Don't you want to be close to her too, Malachi?" Sully asked softly. "I know you care about her. Tell me, have you had intercourse with her?"

I snapped my attention to him and away from my pretty, little doll lying motionless in front of me.

"What?"

"I know she visited the watchers' home often. I know she had a relationship with all of you. She was chosen, wasn't she?"

As much as I tried to be pissed, my anger was tamped down, allowing only euphoria to soar through me. I groaned softly beneath it, enjoying the high so much more than anything in a long ass time. I didn't want it to end. Silently, I begged it to do another sweep over me.

"That means you four had to have done things with her," he said. "And if you haven't, that's a shame because she's a beautiful girl who could never tell you no."

I looked from him to her and crinkled my brows.

How dare he talk about her like that...

The high rushed over me once more, pushing away my anger. My focus returned to her.

She looked so beautiful as she rested. *My perfect slice of heaven.*

"She still can't tell you no," he continued softly. "And you don't have to share her here. You can have her any way you want her."

I licked my lips, the waves of the high crashing over me again. I trembled beneath the heaviness and pleasure of it.

"The drugs I gave you will heighten every experience you have. Don't you want to feel even better? This is your reward. I promised you'd have her. And now you do. No one is here to tell you no."

"I can't," I whispered, my hand trembling as I held hers.

"Why can't you?"

"Because. . ." I groaned again, my cock aching as pleasure rolled through me once more. "Fuck." I panted hard as Sully's words rolled through my mind.

I could have her.

Any way I wanted her.

No one would tell me no.

All mine.

"I give Seth the same drug as you as part of his treatment here. After he was found in that coffin with her, it was an immediate decision. He needed to be treated as well. To change his behavior and expel the demons from his soul." Sully paused as I stared at my angel.

I had no idea if he was telling the truth. Picturing Seth being rewarded with the same things as me didn't sit well.

Sirena breathed evenly, her breasts rising with every breath, her nipples barely visible beneath the thin material of her hospital gown. I yearned to be near her. With her. My focus returned to her.

Inside of her.

"He is a dreadful creature. He takes what he wants and never thinks of the consequences. Like Sirena here. I left him with her because she's his reward too."

I snapped my attention on Sully. I wanted to be furious, but the drug wouldn't allow it. Instead, I breathed harshly, another wave rolling through me.

"You need more," Sully said softly, eyeing me. "Do you want more, Malachi? Of the drug? It'll last throughout the day. You won't feel a bad thing while on it. Just pleasure. Wouldn't you like that? I must warn you though, the crash is a hard one. The side effects are. . . unsavory. We're working on that."

I swallowed hard and nodded. I hated being inside my head. I wanted more. Fuck the side effects.

"Tell you what I'll do." He pulled out a vile and doled a portion into the syringe he'd brought out. "I'll give you what you crave, and then I'll simply leave you to do what you want. How does that sound?"

"Do you leave Seth with her? Like that?"

He smiled as he finished drawing up the dosage. "I do. It's what he asks for, and he's very good when he wants something. So you can imagine how much fun he has in here with her when he's alone."

My heart lurched at that information.

"I may even go as far as saying that when Sirena snaps out of it, it'll be him she wants. Not you. Especially if you don't show her how much she means to you."

I crinkled my brows.

It wasn't right.

It wasn't right.

I couldn't. . .

I didn't want to hurt her.

To take from her.

But if Seth already was.

Or would be.

The nausea and anger threatened me again but was quickly doused. I knew I should be pissed, but I couldn't be.

I just wanted her.

Even like this, I wanted her.

I wanted to be inside her.

Deep inside her, showing her how much I loved her.

Love?

I love her.

Fuck.

"She can't tell you no," Sully murmured as he wrapped the band around my bicep. "She'll take what you give her."

"Do you. . . give her. . .?"

Sully let out a soft laugh. "I do not. She's a reward for you and Seth. That's all. He takes it. Will you?"

I trembled at his words as he plunged the drugs into my veins. They hit me like a ton of bricks, sending me rocketing through pure euphoria. I didn't want Seth to touch her. Only me. I wanted her.

"Fuck," I moaned softly. "Fuck."

Sully chuckled softly. "You have the day with her. Do whatever makes you feel good. What makes *her* feel good. You might be able to bring her back if you know what you're doing." He winked at me and rose to his feet. "She's your toy for now. Make her remember why she belongs to you and not to Seth Cain."

He paused at the door and looked at me. "Good boys get rewarded. Bad boys get punished. I'm sure you remember what that's like."

And with that, he left the room, the door locking softly behind him.

A wave of fear raced through me, the thought of being tied down and hurt again making me sick. A breath left me. Another. And another. The pleasure hit me again.

I stared down at my angel, feeling so goddamn good I couldn't think straight.

The only thing I could focus on was wanting her. Making her want me too. Making her realize she could come back to me. To the watchers. Showing her we were better than Seth fucking Cain.

I'd kill him.

Asylum.

Dead.

I fucking wanted him dead.

That feeling, that emotion, rocketed through me without pause.

I could make her feel better than he ever could.

He *thought* he won.

He didn't win shit.

I won.

Me.

The watchers.

Us.

Fuck. Fuck. Fuck.

I smashed my lips against my angel's, kissing her deeply. She remained motionless beneath me, but I didn't care. I'd bring her back. I'd show them all.

Quickly, I tugged her hospital gown down her small body, revealing her pale skin to me. Her bare breasts. Her pink, pebbled nipples which begged for me to suck. Taste. Bite.

"Fuck." I exhaled, taking in how beautiful she was. "Angel."

Mine. Mine. Mine.

All fucking mine.

I cradled one of her full breasts, my cock aching beneath my hospital gown. I wanted her. Fuck, I wanted her so much.

Church had her already. He'd be happy I took what belonged to us. That I'd tried.

I kissed her again, eager to feel her pussy wrapped around my thick cock. To feel her come on it, hugging it deep inside her small, perfect body.

My heart pounded hard with desire. With desperation. I pushed her gown completely off and let it fall to the floor, revealing her naked body to me. Goosebumps popped up along the pale flesh as I tried to control my breathing and my touch along her skin.

Gently, I eased her to her back, my gaze locked on her.

She didn't acknowledge me, but it was OK. I'd still try.

I spread her legs apart, revealing her pretty, pink pussy. Without hesitation, I dropped down, licking up her hot center and tasting her.

I let my eyes roll back as I let her flavor sink into my tastebuds. Then I ate. Starved. Ravenous for her to come in my mouth.

Diving deeper, I buried my face into her core, earning the smallest of whimpers from her. Flicking my tongue over her clit, I did it on repeat, drinking in what she gave me with each stuttered breath that left her. Each drip of moisture from her heat.

Gently, I slid one finger knuckle deep into her, envisioning what it would feel like to be buried in her hot, tight confines with my cock.

I finger fucked her harder, continuing my onslaught on her clit until her body tensed and her pussy hugged my finger. Then she came hard in my mouth, her breathing fast and ragged.

I swallowed all of it, taking her deep inside me.

Then it hit me.

Everything.

What I'd done.

I jerked away like I'd been burned and stared down in horror at her.

"Angel?" I rasped, moving to loom over her as she breathed harshly.

A tear trickled out of the corner of her eye.

"Fuck. Fuck!" I shouted, shoving away from her and fisting my dark hair and tugging it violently. "Fuck! Fuck!"

I'd hurt her. I'd treaded where I didn't have permission. I'd never done anything like that to anyone before. I may have been a prick, but I wasn't a fucking rapist.

I fell to my knees and wept, my body quaking with my sins.

Get it together.

Fucking get it together!

Fix it. Fucking fix this.

Crawling back over to her, I reached out and draped her hospital gown over her before wiping my eyes. When I could see clearly, I hastily redressed her, making sure to tie her gown as I rolled her onto her side.

Then I slid in behind her on the couch and held her against me. These drugs were fucking me up worse. I was trying to see through the haze, but it was so fucking hard. It was like I was being controlled. The thought terrified me.

"I'm sorry, angel. I'm so sorry." I kissed her forehead fiercely, squeezing my eyelids closed as she hummed that fucking song softly, her voice faltering, her breathing harsh.

Sully had promised a high all day. He'd lied because I was crashing hard and fast. The dark, hopeless feelings I'd had before twisted around me like an ugly snake.

"I want to go home," I whispered, clinging to her. "I want us both to go home, baby. Together. I'm sorry. I didn't mean to. . ."

But I did. I fucking knew I did.

I'd wanted her, and under the influence, I'd taken a small bit of her. I'd let the drugs control me.

I'd stolen it.

Like a thief.

Like a disgusting piece of shit.

I breathed out, trembling as I held her.

"I-I promise, angel. I promise I'll make this better." I kissed her forehead again and closed my eyes, listening to her soft, sad song as I cradled her against me.

I wanted to die.

I wanted to hang in a closet. Throw myself out of my window and break on impact. Slit my wrists until I'd drained the monster from my body.

I twined my fingers through hers, sobbing softly.

And maybe it was my desperation, but I could've sworn she gave my hand a tiny squeeze, her quaking body relaxing against mine.

"You're still here," I whispered, my voice wobbling and hoarse.

A tiny blossom of hope bloomed in my chest. I breathed out.

It hurt.

This life hurt so fucking much.

And the pain was growing.

But. . . I had her. We still had her.

For that, I'd fight until my body broke.

"I'll stay too, baby. I'll stay too."

SIN

I couldn't shake the shit Asylum had said from my head. Lying in bed, I stared up at my ceiling, watching as the shadow of a branch danced on a moonbeam.

I had no idea how he knew what I'd done with Isabella's remains, but he did. One of my gifts was being able to break into places without being detected. I'd done that to dispose of her remains, thinking maybe one day I'd use it to get Sully tossed out on his ass if he ever pissed me off enough.

That day seemed to be here.

I couldn't do it though. Not without making sure everything was set for it. I didn't want that shit to come back on any of us. I'd let Bells go a long fucking time ago. Or maybe I hadn't, which left me in the lurch I was currently in.

Closing my eyes, I breathed deeply. Then again. And again. Until I drifted off, my mind on my crimes and Sirena.

The dream came quickly.

I stared around the cemetery, inhaling deeply as the smell of summer hit me. The sun heated my skin, making me uncomfortable.

I took off my leather jacket and placed it beside me on the stone bench near the mausoleum.

Movement behind the tombstones caught my eye.

I was on my feet and moving toward the statue of the weeping angel. My heart sped up at the prospect of what I'd find lurking behind it. Peeking around the edge, I saw Sirena sitting on the grass in a gauzy, white dress, her black hair spilling around her.

"Siren?" I called out, my heart lurching in my throat.

She snapped her attention to me, her colorful eyes wide. Quickly, she stumbled to her bare feet and backed away from me, fear flickering across her face.

No... please don't be afraid.

She turned on her heel and dashed away from me, her long hair whipping behind her.

No! Don't run!

I raced after her, jumping over crumbling tombstones to reach her. Finally, when I was close enough, I shot out my hand and snatched her by the bicep. She spun to face me, silent as always.

I backed her against a massive headstone as her chest heaved. Her dress showcased her full breasts as she panted heavily, her pink lips parted.

Saying nothing, I moved my hand to her cheek and cradled her face. My heart hammered loudly in my ears. I crinkled my brows as I took her in.

She was so beautiful.

I said as much.

She desperately tried to back away from me, but there was nowhere for her to go. She twisted her head from side to side, looking for a way out. I closed the space between us and pinned her to the tombstone, trailing my hand down to her neck where I wrapped my hand gently around her delicate throat.

"Don't be afraid, siren," I whispered. "It's me. It's Sin."

Her body trembled as she stared into my eyes.

Something came over me that I couldn't stop.

So many emotions rushed through me, finally stopping on one I knew would be the end of me.

Leaning in, I pressed my lips to hers. She didn't kiss me back. Her mouth remained stiff beneath mine. I kissed her harder. Deeper. Silently begging her to kiss me back. Needing her to feel something for me besides hatred. Besides disappointment.

"Come on," I mumbled against her lips. "Kiss me back. Please, siren."

I brushed my lips against hers again, and she still didn't react.

"I fucked up. I fucked up bad."

She didn't seem to care. Anger surged through me. Snarling, I tightened my hand around her throat, giving it a squeeze. She gasped against my lips, her fingers digging painfully into my chest through my t-shirt. Flashes of Isabella went through my head as she'd cried out for me to stop. To not hurt her. I was a repeat fucking offender it would seem.

I tore our clothes off like they were on fire and forced my knee between Sirena's legs and pried them apart. My dick was already weeping with excitement at the thought of having her. I didn't give her a chance to fight me. To show me she didn't want more. I shoved into her heat, forcing my way deep inside her tight body. Tears gathered in her eyes as I fucked her against the tombstone.

"Love me," I choked out, fucking deep into her. "Please, fucking love me."

She whimpered, tears streaming down her face. She squeezed her eyelids tightly together as her body clenched around my dick, her release blanketing me as she shook beneath the pleasure.

"I hate you. I fucking hate you, siren. You're ruining my fucking life." I rasped as she sobbed silently.

My cock swelled with my release until I couldn't hold it any longer. I jetted my come deep inside her, breathing hard as she continued to cling to me.

I rested my forehead against hers, gasping for air.

"But I also think I love you," I choked out, crying with her. "And I'm scared. I'm so fucking scared of these feelings. T-They're different this time. So much different."

"Sinful," she whispered. "Sinful."

That soft, melodic voice.

My name.

"Sinful," I repeated, pulling away to peer into her eyes.

My heart ached when I realized she was no longer with me. The dead look

I'd been witnessing from her was all that was left, her body cold and stiff against mine.

"Don't go. Please. . ."

But she was already gone.

I jerked up with a shout, my eyelids snapping open as I took in my dark bedroom in confusion.

"Fuck," I muttered, calming down and rubbing my eyes.

It took me a moment to realize my groin was damp as siren's pretty face faded from my mind.

I'd fucked her in the dream, but apparently, my cock hadn't gotten the memo that it wasn't real. Groaning, I went into the bathroom and started a shower. Quickly, I jumped in and cleaned myself.

Once I was clean, I stood beneath the warm spray, my heart pounding as I cried silently, tears running down my cheeks. The emotions from the dream hit me all at once, but this time, my brothers were on my mind along with siren.

My mind raced from Stitches, hanging in his closet to siren silent as a tomb in her bed. The devastation on Church's face. The pain flickering in Ashes's eyes whenever they met mine. Everything was fucked-up because of me. I always ruined things. Always.

I couldn't handle what Bells had done to me, so I took it out on my poor, sweet, innocent siren.

Fuck, I was a monster. A villain. A demon.

And she was a perfect angel I knew I didn't deserve, but fuck me, because I wanted her. I wanted her so badly I was willing to come clean with the guys if it meant it brought her back to us.

Us.

Like she'd ever want me.

But it struck me hard in that moment. It didn't matter if she never wanted me. I'd leave for her. I'd let the guys take her and find their happiness. Mine didn't matter. I deserved punishment. And a fitting one would be for me to forever be without her and my brothers by my side. It was a fate that was all too kind after the shit I'd done.

"I'll make it right," I whispered into the spray. "I swear I will. And then I'll take my punishment. I'll kill myself if it'll stop the pain I created for my family. For siren."

And I would.

I couldn't live with this secret. I couldn't live knowing I'd hurt my family. Knowing that Stitches was suffering. That Sirena was. That we all fucking were because I was a piece of shit who couldn't let go of my anger and hatred. Who couldn't see the good there was. Or could be.

Everyone I loved left me.

Now, I knew why.

It was because I wasn't worth staying for.

But this time. . . I'd fix everything.

Then I'd say my goodbyes.

Forever.

CHURCH

Trust the process.

That was what Asylum wanted us to do.

Fuck the process.

I ran faster through the woods, my knife in hand. It was best I was out there in the woods rather than on the main campus grounds because I needed to blow off some steam. All I could think about was gutting Sully like a fucking fish and doing worse to my father.

For as long as I could remember, all my father had wanted me to do was join the family business. I'd been forced to carve and hack on people. Sometimes they'd still been alive. Sometimes they'd been dead. And then my mother. . .

I ground my teeth harder as I picked up my pace. A small rabbit darted ahead of me beneath a bundle of brush. Within moments, I was doing what I did best when I caught an animal.

It was better I played out here rather than where I really wanted to play.

My father had taught me—had demanded— that I learn how to tear a body apart perfectly. He'd created the monster I was. He was sick. Fucked-up. He needed to be in a cage somewhere. Or at the bottom of the lake. The man wasn't fit to walk this earth.

But I was his son, and the apple didn't fall far from the asylum. Or what-the-fuck-ever. I'd always been fucked-up in my head. Killing came easily to me. Plotting. Watching. Taking. Most of the time it didn't faze me to do it, but lately, something was wrong in my head. I didn't feel like myself. I felt. . .something different.

If I had to sit and think about it anymore, I'd go nuts.

Love did fucked-up shit to men.

At least that was what I was diagnosing myself with. A case of love.

I loved my specter, and not having her with me was tearing me apart. I was close to losing my damn mind.

After taking the life of the rabbit, I built a small fire near a couple of tree stumps. It was a quiet day. Unseasonably warm. Or maybe I was just hot from all the running I'd done.

I carved away at my victim, not even noticing the tears dampening my cheeks until they fell into the small puddle of blood at my feet.

I wiped furiously at them, probably smearing my face with the blood on my hands. Once I put the meat on a stick, I arranged it over the fire and watched as it sizzled in the flames.

"I know you're there," I called out softly, not looking away from my dinner. "No sense in continuing to creep around."

Footsteps crunched on the leaves behind me, and a moment later, Asylum sank down onto the stump across from me.

"Why are you here and not with specter?" I demanded.

"She's with Stitches...again," he answered in a monotone.

I raised my brows at that information and sat up straighter. "She is? Are they OK?"

He shrugged. "I assume so. Sully said Stitches gets her today for his treatment. I know they're together because I saw the wards take them to the red room."

"Red room?" *What fucking red room?*

"There's a red room," Asylum said, like he'd been reading my mind. "It's where our treatments are. Usually, it's me and Rinny. Today, Stitches gets her."

"You're angry about that," I said, surveying him.

He seemed closed off, his blue eyes darker than normal. There wasn't as much pep in his fucking step today.

"I'm not," he answered softly. "I'm not upset because Stitches is with her. I'm simply angry because I'm not. I don't like to be left out."

"Well, I'm glad Stitches is with her." I grunted, rotating the rabbit. "He needed to be with her. He was hurting."

The news offered me some relief. It meant Stitches was at least able to think. I'd been fucking terrified since seeing him in his bed when my father was there.

"He was dying," Asylum murmured.

I swallowed hard. "He was."

We were quiet for a moment as we both stared into the flames. I still had nightmares about finding my brother dangling in his closet. As much as I tried, I couldn't get the image out of my head.

"He's still dying," Asylum continued in a soft voice. "We all are. If we're not careful, some will leave sooner than others. Very tricky situation we're in. The. . .it's not so clear anymore."

I rotated the rabbit again.

"What's not clear?" I asked, glancing up at him.

His blue eyes locked on mine. "Everything."

I was quiet for a moment, contemplating my next words. "Do you. . . see the future or some shit?"

He looked to his right, his gaze darting around. I wasn't even sure he was going to answer until he snapped his attention back on me.

"No."

"No?" I raised my brows at him. "Then what is it? You really just get lucky?"

His forehead crinkled. "No."

I sighed. He was difficult to talk to.

"I'm really not," he said, studying me.

"Not what?"

"Difficult to talk to."

I gaped at him for a moment. "You're in my head right now, aren't you?" I wanted to get to the bottom of whatever the fuck he was.

"No. You're in mine," he whispered.

His words sent chills up my spine. I wasn't easily unnerved, but Seth Cain had a way about him. Maybe it was the same way I had about me that set people on edge whenever I was too close. I let my thoughts flow, testing him, wondering if he'd pick up on anything. I could kill him out here and bury his body. No one would know. No one would miss him.

I watched as his Adam's apple bobbed, and his bottom lip wobbled.

"That's the hardest part," he finally said.

"What's that?" I took the rabbit off the spit and tore a chunk of meat off, popping it into my mouth.

"Not the killing. Not me being dead. It's that no one would miss me. That's sad, isn't it, Dante? That no one has ever cared enough about me to miss me?"

I swallowed the meat, trying to hide my surprise and discomfort.

What the fuck else could he see inside my head?

I said nothing as I continued to eat.

"Rinny was the only one, and I fucked that up," he continued. "Don't hate me for trying to find someone to give a damn about me. I know it's easy to hate someone like me after all my crimes, but I'm human too. Or at least I think I am."

"You think she'll forgive you for what you did to her?"

"Do you think she'll forgive you?" His gaze narrowed on me. "You fucked her when she couldn't fight back. In her hospital room. When you were alone with her. You're the one who made a bet that created all of this. Do you deserve to be forgiven?"

"No." I shook my head. "I don't, but I want to be. So I see where you're coming from."

We were quiet again for several minutes before he spoke.

"May I have some?"

I hesitated for a moment before I handed over the rabbit and watched as he ripped a piece of meat off and placed it into his mouth. He took several more pieces before giving it back to me to finish off.

"May I ask you a question?" he asked.

"Sure you don't already know the answer?" I muttered.

"I. . . don't." He cleared his throat.

This Asylum seemed uncertain and cautious. It put me on edge.

"Ask," I said, chewing.

"When you cut up the body parts for your father. . . did you also dine with him?"

I stared at him, my body tense. "Why would you ask me that?"

He appeared genuinely confused as his forehead wrinkled like he was thinking hard. "My mind is really fuzzy lately," he finally said. "I-I don't like it. Everything's coming and going."

"What the fuck does that have to do with me?"

"I. . . know the trade. I know your sins. Most of them. These are just not speaking to me."

I let out a soft chuckle. "And I bet the suspense of not knowing is just fucking killing you, isn't it?"

He licked his lips. I took note of his trembling hands. Something was wrong with him. He rubbed his temples, his face scrunched up before he rocked on the stump.

"No. No. Don't... Fuck." He staggered to his feet, his chest heaving as he continued to rub his temples.

He muttered and babbled shit so low and fast I couldn't understand him. I simply watched his meltdown, almost hoping his ass would fall into the fire and end his shit.

"Rinny... Sirena."

I got to my feet at the mention of her name.

"Asylum? What the fuck is going on—"

He stumbled past me, his face flushed. "I'm Seth. Not Asylum."

Quickly, I turned and kicked out the fire so I could follow him, but when I finally swiveled back around, he was gone, having disappeared into the dense foliage of Northern Michigan.

I stood in the silence, my heart pumping hard, my breathing heavy.

Something was wrong.

I just didn't know what.

Or maybe Asylum had just finally lost his shit.

I'd seen the look on his face though. This was bigger than just an episode. Deciding I needed to get back to campus, I broke into a run.

When I reached the house, I rushed through the door to find Ashes and Sin in the living room talking.

"What's wrong?" Ashes demanded, his lighter snapping closed as he rose, worry on his face.

Sin sat forward, frowning at me.

"I-I met Asylum in the woods. I think something's wrong."

"What do you mean?" Sin demanded.

I shook my head. "I honestly don't know, but he called out specter's name and took off."

"Do you want to check on Stitches and Sirena?" Ashes asked.

I nodded tightly. "Yeah."

Ashes barged past me and right out the door with Sin following.

I wasted no time in joining them.

Maybe I'd let Asylum get into my head. Maybe he'd just had an episode and was off his meds or some shit. He'd said Stitches and Sirena were together. That offered me some comfort because I knew Stitches would die to protect her in the event Sully decided to try anything.

"Everything will be OK," Ashes said softly as we jogged to the medical building.

I said nothing. I didn't have to because Sin said it for me.

"And if it's not, we'll break them out and kill the fuckers."

I couldn't have said it better myself.

ASYLUM

I felt her. She was scared.

I rushed down the hall to get to her, my soul knowing the way. When I reached the door I knew she was behind, I pounded on it hard, my breathing heavy.

"Let me in!" I shouted. "Fucking let me in!"

The door creaked open, and Sully peered back at me.

"Seth. Good. You're here." He opened the door wider so I could come in.

I didn't hesitate to shove past him into the dim room. I'd run the entire way here, the urge to be at her side overwhelming me.

And there she was.

In bed. Strapped down with leather bands, her black hair a wild mess around her. Her pretty eyes were wild and wide as she struggled against the restraints, her entire body quaking.

"What the fuck?" I snarled, darting to her side.

Two wards stepped forward to bar me from her, but Sully gave a slight shake of his head, allowing me to get close.

"What did you do to her?" I demanded. "Why is she strapped down? Why is she shaking like that?"

"We tried a new medicine on her to see if it would help. It's causing some mild side effects. It'll pass soon though. She just needs time," Sully said.

"Fucking unstrap her! Get this shit off her!" I reached out and undid her wrists as fast as I could, surprised I wasn't being stopped.

Not that it mattered. I wouldn't fucking stop. I'd kill someone if they tried to make me. Fuck the plan. Fuck fate.

I managed to get her legs undone then reached for her, tugging her into my arms. She struggled against me, bucking and kicking, but I held tight.

Her mouth came down hard on my shoulder, her teeth sinking deeply into my skin. I let out a snarl of pain, but it was fine. I deserved it. She could pay me back in small increments if that was what it took. Bite by bite. I'd offer my flesh at will to my Rinny. She could devour me whole if it meant she was fighting.

I ground my teeth as her bite tightened. When she released me, her nails dragged down my arms. Across my face. Down my neck. I knew she wasn't in her right mind, and I knew she was drawing blood.

Good.

I wanted to bleed with her.

I bit her back, sinking my teeth into her shoulder. A gasp fell from her lips as she quivered against me, the fight finally leaving her.

I withdrew my teeth, tasting her sweet blood on my tongue and whispered in her ear, "Relax, Rinny. Me and you. We'll suffer together."

Sully let out a soft laugh behind me, making me want to tear into *his* flesh with my teeth. Only I wouldn't be kind to him. I'd rip him apart without batting a lash. Opting to hold it together, I breathed out, willing myself to relax.

I raked my fingers through Sirena's hair as she sagged against me. Her body still trembled, but I'd hold her through it. It was the biggest reaction I'd seen from her.

"Lie down with me," I murmured in her ear before I lifted her small body easily into my arms and placed her back in bed. I crawled in behind her, spooning her, as she shivered.

She curled into a tight fetal position, and I matched it, drawing her into my arms.

I tried to steady my breathing as Sully moved to stand behind me.

"You have only days left to work your magic," he said. "And then we will move on to the next part. Bring her back. There's a lot of money riding on her cure. Her stepfather is paying to see results. So far, we have none. I have no problem shifting to other means."

I said nothing as he left the room with the wards.

When he was finally gone, I gave her a squeeze, noting the smear of blood on her bare shoulder I'd left behind. A beautiful rose-colored bruise was forming around my teeth marks on her pale skin.

"Rinny," I whispered. "We're in a lot of trouble here. I need you to come back, OK?"

She didn't acknowledge me.

I exhaled.

"The evil wizard is back, and he's angry. If we don't defeat him, he'll continue to hurt us. He'll hurt others. We don't want that, do we?"

I licked at the bit of blood still beading out from the wound I'd given her. She flinched beneath my tongue.

Fuck, she tasted like my kind of hell.

I lapped at her wound again, loving the way she tasted on my tongue. Sweet. Bitter. Rinny. Rinny. RINNY.

Our forever girl.

I pressed my lips to the bite and sucked against it, desperate to taste more of her. Her blood slowly pooled into my mouth, and I swallowed it down like some sort of psychotic vampire.

"Did you know Church's dad eats pretty, little girls like you, Rinny?" I whispered into her ear.

She shook against me.

"He does. He's the kind of monster with teeth and claws. He traps those poor girls in his house of horrors and then makes them scream. It's different from the screams we made you do." I paused and licked her flesh again. "Actually, it's probably the same. Those girls really do stay dead though. But Dante needs to tell you the rest. It's his story, after all. I'm just here to bring you home."

I sucked at the wound again, getting a little more blood from her.

"They're going to hurt you, Rinny. He's going to hurt me. He's hurting Stitches. We can't keep doing this. You have to come back to me. Let's go home. Please. Let's go home."

Her trembling slowed, and her breathing grew deep.

I sighed and ran my fingers up her bare thigh, relishing in her smooth, warm skin.

My mind wasn't working the way it usually did. Everything seemed cloudy.

You're going crazy.

Gone crazy.

Cuckoo.

Why not just fuck her? Why wait? You want it. I bet her pussy is tight. Hot. Wet. Made for us.

She'll never know.

Just do it. End this.

Then kill him.

Give Stitches back to the watchers. Take Rinny.

No.

No.

Retribution is best had once the suffering permits it.

Why is everything so foggy?

I hate it.

She will have a baby someday.

Fuck.

"I want it to be mine," I whispered.

Not mine.

Yes?

Mine.

Can it be mine?

Fuck her. Come deep in her pussy.

She's on a shot.

She can't have your baby.

Yet.

Will it be mine?

I'm so lost. Stop.

Never.

Stop!

I clenched my teeth and shook the voices away, my chest aching. Nothing was fucking working like it should.

Who the fuck am I? What am I?

Who are we?

I closed my eyes and hugged my forever girl closer to me.

"Tomorrow, Rinny," I said softly. "We'll make progress. If we don't, we die. And Malachi will die with us. It's that simple."

And it really was.

ASHES

"We're here to see Sirena," Church said as he stared down the nurse.

"Uh, sh-she's in room four-ten."

Church moved past the desk, us following closely behind. I should've been more surprised at the nurse's usefulness, but honestly, I wasn't. We'd been holding back during this fiasco because we knew what Everett could do if pushed. With Stitches and Sirena stuck in here, we had to tread lightly. All Everett had to do was give the word, and we'd never see either of them again. It was just a fact.

That was why we weren't storming the keep and taking what was ours. We could control a bunch of in-patient assholes and nursing staff here on campus, but Everett Church was the big leagues. We had to be more cautious. We had to play the long game.

Silently, we went to Sirena's room. Church peered through the small window.

I stood behind him, waiting for him to say something. I cast a glance at Sin, who wore a frown.

I cleared my throat. "Church?"

He backed away and stared at the door.

"What is it?" I demanded.

I pushed past him and looked through the glass rectangle to see Asylum and Sirena in bed together. It looked like they were sleeping. His large body was curled around her small one, and he held her tightly against his chest. I swallowed hard as I took in his fingers twined through hers.

"What the fuck is going on?" Sin demanded as I backed away from the window, my heart in my throat.

That didn't look like a girl who was frightened of the man she was with.

I cast a quick glance at Church, who wore a grim expression on his face before I glanced to Sin.

"She's sleeping," I said softly.

Sin rolled his eyes and moved to the door, peering inside for a moment before backing away.

"She's sleeping with Asylum," he said.

A muscle feathered along Church's jaw. "It would appear so."

Worry crept up on me and put me in a stranglehold. I flicked my lighter open and closed.

Again. Pause. Again. Pause. Five times. Breathe, Asher. Think.

"Did we lose her?" I finally whispered.

Church strode by us. "I don't fucking know, but something isn't right. The Asylum I saw today was different."

We followed him down the hall. I wanted to run back to my heaven and tear her away from the demon who held her. I knew we had to just get over this bad patch, and I wanted to just trust whatever process Asylum spoke of, but shit. This was too much.

What if he was just playing us?

It would be an Asylum thing to do too. Get into our damn heads and then trick us.

"Where the hell are we going?" Sin demanded. "Are we done with siren?"

Church whirled around on Sin so fast I nearly tripped over my feet trying to stop myself from running into him.

"We're *never* done with Sirena," Church snarled. "*Ever.*"

I looked to Sin to find him holding Church's glare. This entire thing was still a touchy subject. We didn't need to be fighting in the middle of a psych ward though.

"Enough," I said softly. "We love Sirena. We'll do what we can for her, but Asylum has her right now. We need to just. . . back off. We'll focus on Stitches."

Church stepped away from Sin and nodded. "Ashes is right. Stitches needs us."

"I agree," Sin murmured. "Let's go see him. Maybe. . ." his voice trailed off.

"Maybe everything will be OK, and we can just trust the fucking process," Church said, his hands twisting into tight fists at his side.

He was angry and frustrated. I couldn't blame him. I was drowning in it too. All I wanted to do was rush back to Sirena's room and hold her in my arms. To tell her I was so sorry and promise I'd fix it all.

But I'd basically already done that and hadn't been successful in carrying out my promise. The best thing now would be to find out who'd helped Asylum in the first damn place. So far, nothing had turned up. Naturally, no one wanted to talk if they knew. Face the wrath of the watchers or face the wrath of Asylum. There was no lesser of two evils when it came to that choice. We were all wicked and screwed up.

"Let's just get out of here before we have to deal with Sully again," I said, interrupting the growing tension. "She seems fine. Asylum is with her."

And I hated it. I really, truly did, but there wasn't anything we could do about it. At least, not yet anyway. We'd fight for her once we were on even ground. We'd go to war if it came down to it.

I stepped away from my friends and went to the elevator and hit the button to go to the third floor, where I knew Stitches's room was.

Church and Sin got into the elevator with me, neither saying a word for a few moments as we stopped on the third floor.

We stepped out and were walking to Stitches's room before Church finally spoke.

"Do you guys know how Asylum hurt his wrists?"

I shook my head. "I didn't know he had."

"He has scars. I saw them today in the woods. On his wrists."

"Maybe he's a cutter," I said, grimacing. I cast a quick look to Sin to see him frowning.

"I've never seen scars on his wrists," Sin said. "Not that I've spent a lot of time looking though."

Church grunted but didn't say anything else.

We stopped in front of Stitches's door. Again, we let Church go first.

He peered through the window for a moment before Stitches's dark hair came into view. Church pressed his hand to the window. Stitches's tatted hand met his, trembling on the glass.

I swallowed hard, my heart in my damn throat.

He was responsive.

"You'll come home soon, brother," Church called out.

The room was soundproof though. I knew Stitches couldn't hear him.

"Soon, Malachi. I'll get you out of here. I love you. Stay strong. Fuck, stay strong." Church stayed at the window for a long time before I moved forward to see Stitches's dark eyes peering back at me.

A look of pure, heart-wrenching sadness was on his face, a bandage covering the side of his head yet.

He appeared thinner. Gaunt. Sick. His eyes were bloodshot, and his dark hair hung limply.

He mouthed my name, a tear snaking down his cheek.

And a sentence I could make out plain as day.

I'm sorry.

"Stitches," Sin murmured, looking into the window with us. "Fuck, man."

"We'll get him out. He's coming home," Church choked out. "We just. . . I don't know. We have to get them out. I just don't know how. What the fuck do we do?"

Church looked at me, turmoil on his face. I knew how he felt. There'd never been a situation we couldn't figure out. Even with Isabella, we'd overcome. But this? Fuck.

"I don't know. Your father could take them," I said thickly. "And then. . ."

"No. No." Church turned back to Stitches. "No. We won't let him take him. We just. . . fuck. FUCK!"

Stitches wept on the other side of the glass as Church continued to hold his hand against Stitches's through the clear pane.

"Keep holding on. We'll be back. We'll get this sorted."

It was almost like Stitches could hear Church. He nodded, his face damp with tears.

"Soon," I said, resting my hand over Church's. "Soon, man. We'll figure it out."

Stitches nodded again before his hand fell away, and he took a step back from the door. It was tearing my heart apart to witness him like this. He'd always been so strong and so full of life. This was a shell of him.

I hated it. God, I hated it.

"We need to go before Sully finds us," Sin urged softly. "It could end badly for Stitches if we're caught. If he tells your father. . ."

"Let's go." Church grunted, stepping away from the door and turning.

I cast a final look back at Stitches's room before following Dante to the elevator where we rode it in silence. He didn't say a word until we were outside.

"We have to save them," he said.

"We will." I breathed out.

There was no damn way we wouldn't. I didn't care what I had to do to make it happen, it would happen.

We walked back to our place in silence. No one commented on the tears on Church's face or the way I sniffled or how quiet Sin was.

When we reached the house, we opened the door and stepped inside.

"I was wondering when you assholes would get here," Cadence called out as she stood from where she'd been lounging on our couch.

"Cady?" I asked. *She was here?*

Church wiped quickly at his eyes. "Why the fuck are you in my house?"

"Why the fuck isn't my sister here?" she countered.

"It's complicated," I muttered, confused about her sudden, unannounced arrival.

"Why are you here?" Sin demanded, eyeing her wearily.

"Because you guys would rather cry than save the ones you claim to love. I'm here to save the damn day," she sassed back, crossing her arms over her chest.

"What does that mean?" I narrowed my eyes at her nervously, praying she wasn't here to take Sirena away from us.

"It means, Asher Valentine, that you have a new roommate."

"What?" I crinkled my nose at her.

"You're not staying with us," Sin said immediately.

I followed Church's gaze to Cady's suitcases near the couch. She shot us a mega-watt smile.

"I'd like to see you make me leave." She pulled out a knife and did some fancy little twirl with it. "Really, I would. Fucking try me, dickheads."

I blinked at her. She was the complete opposite of our sweet Sirena. Cady was fire.

I liked fire.

I grinned at her. "What did you do to get thrown in here?"

"Set Jerry's car on fire." She smirked widely at me. "You gave me the idea with all your talk of flames."

Church scoffed. "That's hardly enough to get someone thrown in here."

Her grin widened. "I guess I forgot to mention he was in it at the time."

And with that she spun with her knife in one hand and a suitcase in the other before heading to the stairs.

"Whichever room I get to first becomes mine," she called out over her shoulder.

I looked back and forth between Sin and Church for a moment, all of us dumbstruck, before Church snapped into gear.

"I'll kick your fucking ass if you go into my room." He raced after her as she ascended the stairs.

"What the fuck is even happening?" Sin muttered.

"Good things," I said, smiling. "Finally. Good things."

SIRENA

I felt so weird inside my head. Inside my own body. It was like a prison I couldn't escape. In the darkness, I could hear Seth calling to me. Reminding me. Begging me.

And Stitches.

He'd been lost in the dark too.

He'd made me feel good once he'd found me. He'd made me want to wake up. He'd hurt me though. All of the watchers had. If I woke up, I'd just be hurt again.

"Rinny, come on," Seth begged through the blackness I surrounded myself in.

I had no idea if it was day or night. I just knew I didn't want another shot. I didn't want to feel the way the evil wizard had made me feel.

"You have to come back. We're running out of time. We're a fucking experiment. I may be destined to be a lab rat, but you're not. Come on, Rinny! It'll be scary, but I promise we'll be OK. Just. . . trust me, OK?"

Trust him. Seth.

"You can trust me," he called out.

The pressure on my hand moved to my face. He was cradling my face.

I wanted to pull away as much as I wanted to lean into him.

I missed him.

My best friend.

"Let me save you. I owe this to you." His warmth radiated through me as his body touched mine.

I retreated deeper into the darkness to a memory long forgotten. A light. Hope. Seth's soft voice begging me fading as I embraced the old memory.

"I don't want to play dolls." Seth looked at me, his bottom lip jutted out, my doll in his hand. "Can't we just play pirates?"

"Pirates aren't pretty, silly." I giggled, brushing my dolly's hair with the brush Mommy had given me for her. Daisy. That was this one's name.

Seth sighed and flopped down across from me on my bedroom floor. "Can I at least be a boy doll?"

"I don't have a boy doll," I said, blinking at him. I'd never thought to ask for one from Mommy and Daddy. Girl dollies were far prettier than boy dollies. Maybe I'd ask for one for my seventh birthday.

"Rinny, I don't like playing pretend with dolls." He pushed the doll away from him and frowned. "Can't we please play pirates?"

I squinted my eyes at him, contemplating his request. Seth always did lots of nice things for me. This would make him happy.

"OK. But promise I can be a nice pirate?"

His face lit up as he got to his feet and held his hand out to me. "You can be a princess. I'll be a pirate."

"I can be a princess?"

I took his hand, and he pulled me to my feet. I wasted no time as I danced happily around him, making him laugh as our hands fell away from one another.

"I'll kidnap you, Rinny. You'll have an evil stepfather. He'll hurt you."

I stopped dancing and stared at Seth. "I will? What about Daddy?"

Seth reached for my hand and held it as he stared down at me. "Your daddy is going to leave. Then you'll have a mean stepdad. But don't worry because you're a princess, Rinny. I'll save you. I promise."

I nodded. I always believed Seth. He was my best friend.

"How do we play pirate and princess?"

He leaned in. "You have to run and hide, OK? I'll find you. When I do, I'll rescue you. Ready?"

I steeled myself, ready to make a run from my evil stepfather so the very best pirate in the world could come rescue me.

"Count of three, Rinny. One. . . Two. . . Three!"

I bolted from him and ran as fast as my feet could carry me down the hallway. I had to get away from my evil stepfather. When I reached the downstairs, I skidded to a stop in front of the basement door. I didn't like the basement. It was scary, but I knew if we were playing this game, I had to play it right. I didn't want to disappoint Seth.

With as much bravery as I had, I opened the basement door, the creaking of it on its hinges sending a shiver down my spine. Holding my breath, I took the first step down the stairs into the darkness.

Another. And another, until I reached the bottom. I fumbled with the light switch on the wall. The dim, yellow glow lit a portion of the basement. Quickly, I rushed to a corner where Daddy was building a strange big box. I slid behind the boards as carefully as I could, but I wasn't careful enough. Another pile of boards crashed down, trapping me inside the small space.

Panic rose in my chest as I banged my small fists against the heavy wood. I couldn't move it. I was stuck.

One had fallen on my hand, making it hurt.

"Seth?" I called out. "S-Seth!"

Nothing.

Silence.

Scared, I curled up into a small ball on the cold floor, hoping he'd find me soon. He promised he'd save me.

Time crept by in the dark. My legs began to tingle from being stuck in the small space for so long. Finally, I heard footsteps on the stairs as I cried softly.

"Seth?"

The footsteps moved faster until they hit the concrete floor.

"Rinny?"

"Seth!" I called out frantically, my voice cracking from my crying. "Seth! Help!"

"Rinny?"

The boards clattered and shifted until the dim glow filled the space and Seth's hand reached for me.

I took it and let him help me out.

"Are you OK? Your hand is bleeding," he said, staring down at the small cut on my hand from the board.

"It hurts." I sniffled and wiped at the fallen tears on my cheek.

"Do you know what makes things that hurt feel better?"

"Mommy?"

He laughed softly. "No, Rinny. Kisses." He pressed his lips to my cut for a moment.

I watched as he pulled away and gave me a sweet smile, some of my blood on his lips. He quickly licked it away.

"See? You stopped crying. My mommy taught me that kisses make everything better."

I swallowed and smiled at him. "It does feel better."

"And I rescued you just like I promised," he proclaimed, his smile turning into a full-on grin. "Do you know what that means?"

"No."

He gave my hand a gentle squeeze. "It means now we have to get married. You can be my pirate princess, and we can fight off all the bad guys."

"Aren't pirates bad though?" I wrinkled my nose at him. "I don't want to be a bad guy."

"You won't be, Rinny. We'll only hurt the ones who hurt us. I'll be the bad guy, so you won't have to, OK?"

"Promise?"

"I swear it." He began walking backward, my hand still in his as he led me. "Do you believe in magic?"

I nodded. I loved magic and fairies and unicorns.

"Do you believe I'm magic?"

"Yes."

A serene look covered his face.

"Then as long as you believe in my magic, nothing will ever harm you. Pirate's honor."

"You're a magic pirate?" I giggled at the notion.

It only made him grin wider.

"I am. You'll see someday, Rinny. You'll see."

I twined my fingers with Seth's, the light infiltrating my dark prison. He'd saved me then. He promised to save me now.

I blinked rapidly, the light from the flames in the fireplace hurting my eyes.

Seth's blue eyes greeted me.

"Rinny," he breathed out. "Hey."

I crinkled my brows, ready to retreat as fear gripped my heart.

"No. No! Don't go. Stay. Fuck. You have to stay. Just. . . listen. Sully has Stitches. He's here. He's experimenting on him. We need to get out of here, but we can't because you're not well enough to leave. If you stay here in the moment, you save us all. You save Stitches, Rinny. Remember Stitches? Malachi? You-you love Malachi."

I licked my lips.

Malachi.

Stitches.

I was his angel.

I stared at Seth. He seemed different. Darker. Tired. Worried.

Asylum. He was crazy. He hurt me. . .

I retreated from his stare, but he was quick to squeeze my hand.

"I'm not as crazy as you think I am," he whispered. "I'm not him. I'm not Asylum. You *should* fear us, but you should fear Sully more. Right now, I'm not your enemy. Stay. Save Stitches if not yourself."

I parted my lips.

I was scared.

"Don't be," he murmured, cradling my cheek with his other hand.

Butterflies flapped wildly in my chest.

How did he hear me?

"My head hurts, Rinny," he said, his voice choked. "So much. I think they're drugging me through my food or something. I really need you to stay. Can you do that for me?"

For him. Seth.

He wanted me to stay.

The light felt nice. But I was scared. I was so scared. I didn't want to get put into another box.

"The next time you're in a box with me, I'll be buried deep inside you," he said fiercely. "And you won't be screaming out of fear, I can promise you that, Rinny." He shifted closer so his nose was nearly touching mine. "Stay. I need you."

You need me? Where were you when I needed you?

I wanted to scream it at him, but my voice. . . not for him. He didn't get my voice.

"We get your screams," he finished softly. "They belong to us. They always have. They always will. If you don't stay, Sully gets them. Stay, Sirena. *My pirate princess*."

My eyes prickled with tears.

He remembered.

"How could I ever forget our pirate princess?" he asked, bringing my hand to his lips and placing a soft, warm kiss on my knuckles. "We're supposed to get married."

I remembered that promise.

But then he'd broken it when he'd tried to kill me.

"I love seeing you here with me," he continued. "Your eyes. I've always loved your eyes."

I swallowed thickly at his words.

"Things are going to get really scary, Rinny. OK? When you're with me, stay. When Sully comes and it scares you, hide. I'll protect you from him. You can shimmer in and out and be whoever you need to be to stay safe. My sweet pirate princess or. . ." He cocked his head at me.

Your vicious little monster.

"My monster," he murmured. "Yes, you're the monster we created, aren't you?"

He winced and shook his head before he looked back at me.

"Sometimes it's loud in my head," he said, grimacing. "Sometimes it's hard to. . . *hear* you."

We stared at one another for a minute. I willed myself to hold his gaze rather than retreat back into my mind like I was tempted to do.

"Just play the game, Rinny. It's all we can do until we're free. Can you do that? For me? For Stitches?"

I contemplated his words. I wanted to go home too. Being here was hurting me. My body was so sore now that I was in the light. As much as I wanted to dart back to my safe spot, I knew I couldn't. Not if Stitches needed me. Not if... Not if Seth did.

My killer.

Or attempted murderer.

Was that what he was to me now?

"I'm your Seth," he said thickly. "That isn't going to change. And you're my Rinny. Our forever girl. You belong to us."

And you belong to me...

"Always," he said, resting his forehead against mine. "Now let's get the fuck out of here, so I can give you a proper rescuing. You ready, Rinny?"

No.

But definitely yes.

I needed to get out of here. I needed to be away from it all so I could breathe. So I could think. So I could...

"*Live*," he finished. "Good. Because I don't plan on doing it alone."

Funny he should say that considering he'd tried to kill me before.

He pulled away and gave me a smile I hadn't seen in years. My heart raced as I stared at the boy I'd once loved with every ounce of my being.

"Love," he whispered. "Still love. There is no past tense with us, Rinny."

No past tense.

So the fates seemed to have decided.

I squeezed his hand.

He'd rescued me. He was inside my head somehow. *Just...how?*

"Magic." He thumbed my bottom lip. "Now get ready. The evil wizard is coming. Hide if you have to. I'll find you."

I let out a shuddering breath.

Hide.

I was good at that.

I receded into the darkness again where I was safe but not alone.

Not now.

"Not ever," Seth's soft voice called out to me again.

Not ever.

That offered little comfort.

SIN

"You can't go into the fucking bathroom and take a damn hour!" I shouted through the door at Cadence, who'd taken up residence in my bathroom. "How the fuck did you even get in here?"

"Why are you so mad, Sinclair?" Cadence yelled back. "I mean, you should be excited there's a girl this close to your bedroom. I'm sure that's a new experience for you."

Oh, this fucking chick. . .

I hammered on the door again. "Hurry the fuck up! I have to take a piss!"

"Then go jump in the shower with Dante. I'm sure he'll let you piss down his drain!"

I snarled and banged on the door again before storming back into the kitchen. I paced for a moment, irritated. Then I went to Ashes's room. There was no way in hell siren and Cadence had come from the same fucking womb. Cadence was a complete nightmare and siren was. . . fucking perfect.

Goddamnit to fucking hell.

"What?" Ashes mumbled from beneath his covers as I strode into his bedroom.

"Fucking Cadence is in my bathroom and won't get out. Can I use yours?"

"Yeah," he mumbled.

Sighing, I went into his bathroom and drained the piss which was strangling my cock, then I washed my hands and walked out to find Ashes still buried beneath his blankets.

"Hey," I called out.

He grunted again.

"Ashes. Come on. I need to talk to you."

"What is it?" he mumbled, not bothering to pop his head up from beneath his blanket.

"Cadence is in Stitches's room. She can't stay in there. She needs to sleep in the basement or something."

Ashes was quiet for a moment before he let out a heavy sigh and sat up. He rubbed the sleep from his eyes.

"Have you spoken to Church?"

"No."

"Then talk to Church. She annoys him too. I think you guys need to relax. She's Sirena's sister. We should be nice to her."

"Fuck that. She's being annoying on purpose."

"She's Sirena's sister," he repeated evenly. "We aren't going to be mean to her. She's here because she cares about Sirena."

"She's here because she's fucking nuts."

"Aren't we all?" Ashes raised an eyebrow at me.

I exhaled and raked my fingers through my hair.

"Fuck, man. I can't deal with the fucking estrogen." I tugged my hair again. "I can't. She's been here less than twenty-four hours and already I'm ready to pull my fucking hair out."

Ashes sighed. "She's actually a cool chick. Give her a chance."

I paced his room for a minute. "Whatever. I just want this shit over with."

I strode to his door.

"I'll be down in a minute. Try to not strangle this one," Ashes muttered.

I gave him the finger and stomped back to the living room, a little irritated he'd made that jab at me. It didn't matter. He was probably irritated that I'd woken him. A jab was far less than what I knew my treacherous ass deserved.

Sighing, I shuffled into the kitchen and poured a bowl of cereal before chowing it down, vowing to make a point to stay the fuck out of the house if Cadence was going to be here. Then again, she'd probably lay claims to my room.

I rinsed my bowl then went out to the patio to smoke a joint, needing the escape.

"Bit early to be getting high, isn't it?" Cadence called out.

I closed my eyes and took another hit. *Fuck this day.*

She snagged the joint from my fingers and took a deep hit as I scowled at her.

"Hello, kettle," I muttered.

She blew the smoke out, her blue eyes locked on me. "Hello, douche."

I took back my joint and finished it off, not bothering to look at her.

Fuck, she was an asshole.

"Why are you here?" I asked, not taking my focus from the lake.

"I told you why—"

"No. Why are you *here* in our house and not in the dorms with the other nut jobs?" I finally looked over at her.

"They gave me a dorm. I gave them the finger, and now I'm here and I'm not going to leave either. Because I'm keeping an eye on you."

"Me?" I rolled my eyes and turned to fully face her, my arm on the deck railing as I leaned against it.

"Not *just* you," she said, rolling her eyes right back at me. "All of you watchers or whatever you call yourselves." She mirrored my stance and raised her brows at me.

"So you set a fucking car on fire with your stepdad in it? All to annoy the shit out of us?"

"I set his car on fire with him inside it in the hopes it would kill the prick," she said. "Not to annoy you. I needed to be here for my sister. She needs me. I'm her ride or die."

"Then you better tell the rest of the guys that you're her partner in crime because I think you'll have competition."

"And you're *not* competition?"

"Nope." I pushed off the railing. "I'm a prick who doesn't deserve happiness."

"How melodramatic," she said, smirking at me. "Is that part of your mental disorder? Feeling sorry for yourself classifies a person enough to be here?"

"Fuck you," I snarled at her. "You don't know shit about me."

"I know you hate yourself. That you run. That you're a grouchy prick. That maybe you know what really happened to my sister."

I got in her face, my pulse roaring in my ears. She didn't back away from me as I stared her down, my chest heaving. In fact, she pushed back, clearly ready to fight me if it came down to it.

"Don't fucking come at me with that shit. You'll find yourself dead."

"Don't threaten me with a good time," she grumbled back, poking her finger hard into my chest. "Fuck with me, and I'll fuck with you right back. And fuck with my sister? You'll be the one who fucking wakes up dead. I'm going to find out who did this to her. So if it was you, I'd start running. This is me giving you a head start."

"Yeah?" I breathed out, my hands trembling.

"I'm fast as fuck, Sinclair," she said softly. Dangerously. "I promise that you don't want to find out just how fast. If I catch you, you're a dead man."

I swallowed thickly. I'd never met a girl, or person for that matter, who'd ever stood up to me. I wasn't even sure how the fuck to navigate it. Backing down seemed like a pussy thing to do, but deep down inside, I wanted to run. And she was right. I wanted to die.

"Everything OK?" Ashes called out, strolling out onto the patio as Cadence and I stared one another down.

"Yeah," she said, stepping away from me. "We were just getting to know one another better."

I glared at her. "Yeah. We were. It's cool."

"Good. Cady, what's your first class?" Ashes shot me a quick look. I knew he felt the tension in the air.

"I don't know. English? Or maybe some shit on plants."

Ashes chuckled. "Either way, both are near my first class. I'll walk you."

She smiled at him. "Cool. I'll go grab my bag."

She sauntered into the house, leaving me alone with Ashes.

"I know she's a lot to handle, but just. . . be cool, OK? For Sirena?"

I let out a sigh. "Fine. Whatever."

He gave me a nod and clapped me on the back as we went inside.

I caught Cadence's gaze when I came back in. She winked at me, making me want to launch myself across the room and pummel her tiny ass.

Instead, I opted to give her the finger.

She acted like she caught it in mid-air and then gave me one right back.

Fuck, what a nightmare.

STITCHES

I didn't know how much time had passed. It had to have been a few days at least since I'd seen Church and the guys outside my door. In those hazy days, I'd been shot up with drugs again, had hallucinated that I'd gotten on my knees and begged for freedom, and I was really fucking certain I'd been sucked off.

But each time I questioned things, I was reassured I was just hallucinating. Again. More delusions. More drugs. More. . .crazy.

It didn't matter though. The memories or whatever the fuck was happening were so fucking cloudy in my mind that there was no way in hell to tell what was real and what wasn't. I wasn't even sure if I'd really spent a day with my angel or not. If I'd really eaten her sweet pussy like a slice of juicy watermelon while she'd came on my tongue.

Nothing was real, and yet it all was.

It was fucked-up. I was fucked-up. This life was fucked-up.

I wanted out. Still. I wanted out.

I'd definitely hacked away at my face though. I knew I had. I didn't know why though. I only remembered the pain. It was still healing. I didn't like to touch it. It was tender, and I had no idea the extent of the damage. Sully assured me it wasn't terrible.

I didn't believe him because fuck him. Truly. He was the root of evil as far as I was concerned.

I paced the short length of my room, counting the steps.

One. Two. Three. Four. Five. Six. Seven. Eight. Turn. One. Two. Three. Four...

Breathe.

Angel.

Help me, Mama.

Fuck. I feel nuts.

Church, man. Come on. Ashes. Burn this motherfucker down. Sin. . . prick. I'm still pissed, but I miss you.

When the doorknob jiggled, I snapped my head up. My door swung open. I stopped pacing and stared at Sully as he came into the room with two wards. And my father. Well, Church's father. My adoptive father.

Everett. Wicked fucker.

I licked my lips, telling myself to keep my shit in check. Any slip-up and Everett would have my ass down in his butcher shop, hacking away at vital organs some poor bastard out in Ohio was missing.

I hated the family business, but I was sure Dante hated it even more than I did. I knew Everett was hellbent on forcing Dante to join and help with all the fucked-up shit he had his hands in.

There'd been a time when we'd been forced to watch some of the shit that happened. I was a wicked guy with a soul made of pitch, but Everett Church? That man was the face of pure evil. *Hands down. Tag, I'm out.*

Fuck him and his shit.

But I knew the game. I knew I had to keep myself in line. I needed to appear like I had my shit together in front of him if I wanted out of here.

"Malachi," Everett called out, opening his arms for me.

I pushed a fucking grin onto my face and rushed to him like I gave a shit. I fell into his arms as he held me tightly, his hand smoothing down my mess of dark hair.

"Father," I murmured, breathing in the smell of his rich cologne and cigars.

"How are you feeling?" Everett asked, pulling away and holding me at arms' length.

"Like I'm getting better. I feel. . . happier now." I was lying out my ass, but I knew the happiness would come once I was released.

"Excellent." Everett beamed at me. "Has Dante come to visit?"

I hesitated for a moment, not knowing how I was supposed to answer since I wasn't sure if shit had gone down between Dante and his father.

"Uh, no. Not really. He looked at me through the window twice. That's it," I said, feeling like that was vague enough. And truthful considering I hadn't actually been close to my brother and best friends.

"I'm surprised he hasn't made more noise than that. God knows he's been wanting to see you," Everett commented, his gaze swooping quickly over me, a brittle smile on his face. "Tragic, really. He knows you need the help, and yet continues to demand your release. Shame on him, right, Malachi?"

"I miss him," I said immediately. "I want to go home. I'm ready." I stared Everett right in the eye. "Father, please. I promise I'm well enough."

Everett surveyed me for a moment while Sully and his dogs lurked along the edge of the room. I wanted to gut the fuckers so badly, but I held it together with the hope I'd soon be free from this place.

"I'm not so sure about that, Malachi. We both know you need much more help," Everett murmured.

"Father—"

"How about we make a deal since you're so desperate to leave?" He raised his brows at me.

"What is it?" I was cautious.

Everett Church was a monster, and making a deal with a monster always ended in casualties. I'd sworn I'd make sure it wasn't my dick on the line if it came down to it. Church and I had promised one another we'd never fall prey to Everett's evil ways. So far we'd done a great job, but as I stared back at the monster in front of me, I realized all good things must come to an end.

"Our headmaster here has informed me he is working with two more patients. Well, students." Everett smiled at me. "He hasn't been able to make as much of a breakthrough with them as he has with you."

He had something up his sleeve. I knew the prick did...

"Oh?" I swallowed thickly, waiting for the hammer to fall.

"I was discussing the situation with him. He seems to believe you may be the key to cracking open these. . .nuts."

Fuck. Fuck. Fuck.

"And if I crack open the nuts, what's in it for me?" I asked, my heart pounding in my ears.

"Your freedom. And theirs. Well, one is already free in a way, but both could proceed to the next level of treatment, which is being released from here to continue their education. Education is important, don't you think?"

I nodded. I was smart enough to know the right answers this time. Hopefully.

"Yes, Father. Education is important."

Everett's grin widened. "Excellent. Sully has done well with you. You're so. . . compliant. I love it."

Was I compliant? Or desperate? Was there a difference?

"Anyway, if you participate, I think it'll do you some good. It'll train you. Enlighten you. Teach you things I still believe you're missing."

"What am I missing?" I frowned at his statement.

"That little bit of pizzazz that drives us wild. Not crazy, Malachi." He gave me a stern look. "*Wild.* Something that brings out our emotions. Something that'll test you and make you understand how very bad things could get if you step out of line. You tried to kill yourself. Hanging. Of all the disgusting ways to leave this world, you chose that one." He shook his head at me, disappointment evident on his face. "No son of mine will leave the world like that. Do you understand?"

"Yes," I said softly, feeling remorse over my actions. Not that I wouldn't try it again if it came down to it, but really, it did suck. If I'd had a gun, I'd have made it more permanent. I'd simply worked with what I had.

"If you help the headmaster in his next step of treatment, we'll see to it that you're free. Can you be wild for me, Malachi?"

I glanced at Sully to find him eyeing me closely. Almost like a hungry, rabid dog. Chills raced over my skin. Whatever Sully had planned wouldn't be good. I already knew it involved my angel and most likely Asylum. But when it came down to it, I knew this wasn't all Sully's plan. Everett had his dirty hands in it too.

He always fucking did, the prick.

"And the students?" I questioned. "They'll get to leave once it's over?"

"Of course. As long as we see what we're looking for. You have to do everything the headmaster says, or the treatment fails. Do you understand? Saying no or declining to participate could end not only in your punishment, but in theirs. I'm sure you don't want to hurt the others because of your feelings, right?"

"I don't want to hurt anyone, Father. I told you. I feel better now —" I was a lying motherfucker. All I wanted to do was gut these pricks and walk out with their entrails around my neck like a bloody necklace.

"Malachi, sometimes hurting people makes them stronger. You want her stronger, don't you? The pretty girl with the colorful eyes and long, black hair? She's truly a beauty. Her stepfather has said he's willing to sell her to me should she become too damaged here. I'm sure you know what sort of use for her I'd find. Right. . . Son?" He cocked his head at me, his eyes glittering with his wickedness.

I hate you. I fucking hate you. Evil, worthless prick.

I exhaled.

"Yes. I want her stronger. I just don't want her to hurt. I lo—" I stopped myself from speaking, but I knew the damage was done.

Hell, he probably knew weeks ago how I felt about her.

"If she's the one, Malachi, then you could turn her inside out and rearrange her soul and she'd still come back to you." He approached and drew me in against his body as he whispered in my ear, "Do you think she's the one?"

"Yes," I answered in a trembling voice, knowing better than to lie to him.

He'd simply find a way to prove I was a liar. Then my angel would suffer for my lie.

"She's the one."

"Then make her stronger. Show Dante. Show him what happens when you listen to your father and do as you're told. He needs a lesson in that. Can you teach it to him?"

I nodded wordlessly, my chest aching.

"Good boy. Such a good boy." Everett dragged his lips along my jaw as I stiffened beneath him. "Help the headmaster and earn your freedom. *No* won't be a part of your vocabulary, right?"

"She'll get to leave here too? And so will I? Together?"

"Yes." His lips lingered on my jaw.

"Promise, Father? Swear it to me."

He chuckled softly and trailed his lips to mine where he placed a soft kiss on the edge of my mouth. "I promise. You have my word. But if you fail, I'll take her from you and Dante. There's a debt that needs to be paid. For now, if you abide by the rules, she'll remain yours. If you fail. . . well, then I'll take her flesh. That's my vow to you."

I shivered at his words.

"Do we have a deal?" Everett asked, his hand resting on my waist and his body entirely too close to mine.

I hated it. Fuck, I hated it, but I had to promise. I had to save her. I owed her this. I owed Dante and the watchers. Screwing up had led me to this moment. So to hell with it.

"Yes. We have a deal," I confirmed, my throat tight.

"Excellent." Everett stepped away from me without hesitation and turned to Sully, the weasel who kept slinking on the edge of the room. "We're set. Continue on. Call me if he steps out of line. Punish him the way we discussed if he does. Reward him if he doesn't. Although, I think it'll all be a reward to him."

"Of course." Sully inclined his head at Everett.

"Malachi, be a good boy for Daddy, OK? I'll need your services if you manage to pull this off. It's part of our deal."

Nausea twisted in my guts, but I nodded.

He smirked at me. "I'll see you soon."

And with that, he left the room, taking Sully and his dogs with him.

I blew out a shaky breath as the door slammed and locked behind them.

Something told me I'd just made a deal with the devil.

ASYLUM

You can't keep running out like that.

I do what I fucking want.

Not when it comes to her.

I ground my teeth. It was the truth. I'd been slacking. In my defense, I'd been busy doing other things to help pave the way. Deep in my mind was a terrifying place. It was where all my demons hid. Where plans were made. Where plots were sorted. Where I decided who lived and who died.

Usually, I let them live just because I had a hard-on for making people scream. *Was that a kink?* Fuck it. It was mine.

I needed to focus. Always a fucking issue with me. The only time I could keep my shit sorted was when I was asshole deep in blood.

I'll try harder.

Fucking BE better.

I shook my head and cleared the noise. I blew out a breath as I stared up at my ceiling in the shitty hospital room I was in.

Ah, poor boy. So sad.

Many tears this one cries.

No, many tears she'll cry.

Here comes the deep wound and the remedy.

Stitches. Stitches is coming.

"Shut the fuck up," I snarled, panting as I glared to my left before I shook my head again. *Malachi Wolfe.* The predator himself was coming.

It was fine. I'd deal with that shit like I had every other time.

I know.

Of course you fucking do.

Just do what you promised.

Oh, I will and so much more.

Silence washed over me again, allowing me a moment to gather myself.

It was hard for me. This life. All I really wanted to do was tear Sully and his posse to shreds. Getting myself talked down daily was becoming a chore I was tired of participating in. But I'd promised. I guessed. Or maybe it was an unspoken promise because maybe I felt a little... I didn't know.

Unhinged?

No, that wasn't it. I mean, it was, but not in this instance. Responsible? Yes. That was a better word for it. I was responsible for her. For my forever girl. My firefly. If she only knew...

I raked my fingers through my mess of hair, glad it was me doing today's schedule of events. I'd been away far too long it seemed. But even crazy men needed a day off. In my case, it just meant I was taking my frustrations out elsewhere.

I grinned at the memory.

Blood.

Fuck, so much blood. The money was good though, so I shouldn't complain. And I wasn't. I was reveling in it. If the skies could rain blood for me, it would be perfect. Mostly. I did like sunshine on occasion. I had to prove to the watchers yellow really was my color.

Just go.

Shut up. I'm going.

Fuck. Cut me some slack.

I let out a breath and shook out the tension from my body, preparing for the mess I knew I was going to get into.

This was by my own doing. Me and my sweet side, trying to save someone by killing them.

My poor forever girl.

Fuck, I missed her.

I'd be near her soon, and then we'd play.

We'd play until she screamed my name for me.

I wanted to hear her say it.

Asylum.

Not Church. Not Seth.

I wanted it more than my next breath. Something had washed over me in the night it seemed. I was prepared to go to war for this girl. I had been before, but there was more here. Her eyes. Her lips. The way the light cast around her beauty as I saw her in my mind's eye.

Awake.

She was awake and back.

And fucking mine.

Ours.

Fine. Ours.

I smiled as I reached for the door handle.

But today she's mine.

SIRENA

I felt him before he came into the room. Making sure to keep my eyes focused ahead of me, I exhaled.

As far as Sully knew, I was still locked away in my mind with no hopes of a return.

That was what Seth had told me to do.

I trusted him for the most part.

I'd been brought into the vibrant red room minutes ago and left alone on the couch after a ward had lifted me like I weighed nothing at all and placed me there. I was hungry and thirsty. Tired. Homesick for a home I didn't have. And I missed my paints and canvases.

Seth approached and kneeled in front of me as the door clicked behind him.

I remained looking straight ahead, waiting for further instruction.

"Look at you being such a good girl," he murmured in his thick voice.

Something wasn't right though. He didn't sound like Seth. Or maybe I'd been gone so long I'd lost touch with what his voice sounded like. This voice was more commanding. Darker and more threatening. The Seth I'd come to know had a gentle tone whenever he spoke to me. Even when he was begging me, he was gentle.

I shivered.

"Sirena. Look at me, pretty girl."

I quivered, fear washing over me.

What was happening to me?

"Nothing. Yet." Seth reached for my hands and took them in his. "You don't pretend when you're with me, Sirena."

Sirena.

Not Rinny?

"Do you want me to call you Rinny? I was under the impression. . ." his voice trailed off.

I frowned at that. Nothing had changed, yet it felt like everything had.

"Rinny. I can do that if it's what you want."

I cocked my head at him, finally focusing on his handsome face.

My heart jumped hard in my chest as his crystal blue eyes locked on mine.

"Hey there, firefly," he murmured, leaning forward. He reached out and brushed a lock of hair away from my face.

I shivered at his cool touch.

Firefly.

"I remember one night when the fireflies were all over the lawn. They lit it up like a tiny city," he continued softly. "Your hair was loose and whipped around you as you ran through them, disturbing their peace. My little bit of chaos." He smiled sadly.

I remembered that night. It was right before I was hurt. Before he'd left me. Before. . . we'd changed.

"You laughed so much. I heard it. It made me realize how very special you were to us, and how I wanted you to always be that perfect girl." He licked his lips. "Then I hurt you in order to keep you that way. I have a lot of groveling to do, don't I?"

I said nothing as I studied him. He was so different. . . yet the same. So Seth. . . but Asylum.

"I don't deserve your forgiveness, my little firefly, and I won't ask it of you. Not today. Today is for new beginnings. Today is for. . . us. I wish to dance."

I blinked at him as he gave my hand a gentle tug.

"Come," he instructed softly. "Let's waltz through the darkness. You light the way for me like you always have."

Could I? Was it safe? What if Sully. . . ?

"You can do anything you want. As long as it's by my side, I'll make sure it's safe. It's my promise to you. I owe you that much and more. As for Sully. . . we can gut him together if you'd like then fuck in his blood."

My breath hitched at his words.

He leaned in suddenly, a smirk on his lips, darkness dancing in his eyes.

"Trust me when I say it'll be the time of your life. Now dance with me."

I swallowed and let him help me to my feet. I was like a newborn fawn on my feet, all wobbly and weak from not standing in what seemed like forever. If it bothered him, he made no mention of it as he placed his hand on my waist and took my other hand in his.

Our song spilled from his lips in a sweet hum as he guided us around the room, his pace increasing as I got my bearings about me.

A smile teased my lips as his eyes sparkled, the room whipping wildly around us.

We made several rotations around the space before I became breathless with a grin on my face.

I wasn't sure what had come over me, but I finally felt free. Like having Seth back was changing me. The dark clouds which had been blanketing me for nearly a decade were giving way to sunshine again.

To us.

"To us," he whispered as he slowed us to a stop. Without hesitation, he leaned in and brushed his lips against mine. "Forever my girl."

I stared up at him with parted lips, my heart racing.

"Mine," he murmured, running his nose along my jaw. "Ours." He inhaled deeply and dragged me tightly against his hard body. "And I *will* fuck you in the blood of our enemies, my little firefly. That's a promise."

And then we were dancing again as if nothing in the world was wrong.

And maybe nothing was.

Maybe it was right.

Maybe this was how it was supposed to be.

Seth.

"Asylum," he whispered in my ear before dipping me low and staring down at me in my thin hospital gown, his dark hair a wild mess and a gleam in his eyes that made me realize who he really was. "I'm Asylum, and I'm yours."

Asylum.

My Asylum.

He hauled me back upright against him, and we moved through the room again, slower this time.

I clung to him when we slowed to a stop.

He had a lot of make-up work to do. Forgiving him wasn't easy, but. . . I was losing my mind. I felt like I was slipping. Like I needed this. Like it was fate. Like it could work. . .

"Fate has a funny way about her, doesn't she?" he asked, swaying with me gently. "If this is how it's supposed to be, then I regret nothing."

Funnily enough, I was beginning to regret a lot less too.

He smirked. "That's why we dance. To prove we're still alive. That we're still fucking screaming inside. That we're fighters. That we'll *never* let them take that from us. So keep fighting. For all of us. Promise me?"

Promise.

"Good girl," he murmured. "And I promise the same. Now, we need to see Stitches. He's coming."

Stitches.

Malachi.

A watcher.

"Brave face. No tears. No screams. You never give them your screams. Those belong to us. Right?"

I said nothing as I stared at him.

He reached out and gripped my face tightly. “Say it. Tell me your screams belong to us.”

My screams belong to you.

A triumphant smile spilled onto his lips.

“Then get ready because these men wish to steal them. More evil wizards and cunts, firefly. Watch the magic, OK? Pay attention. This is the part where it gets good.” His blue eyes shifted from mine, and he looked to the door.

I followed his gaze and swallowed hard as the handle twisted.

I really hoped things got good.

I was tired of the bad.

ASHES

"Your house is cool," Cady said as I walked beside her along the path to school.

Church said he wasn't attending today, opting to probably carve up some defenseless creatures in the woods, and Sin seemed too pissed off to do much more than stomp around, so our walk was just the two of us.

"It's really Church's place. It's basically the home for his family on campus."

"His dad own this place or something?" She cast me a quick look.

I shrugged. "Or something. Church's family founded it years and years ago. Guess they liked crazy or some shit. Whole family is a little, uh, dark."

She nodded and blew a bubble from her gum. The fruity smell of the berries met my nose.

"I figured he was a bit of a headcase, but then again, look where I am and who's talking. I set my stepdad's car on fire in a bid to get here."

"But not to kill him?" I glanced at her and raised a brow.

A grin spilled onto her face as she winked at me. "Maybe a little. Guess that makes me a little crazy too, huh?"

I chuckled. "Welcome to Chapel Crest."

She bumped shoulders with me. "So really what's your deal, Asher?"

"My deal?"

"Yeah. Like you're nice. Way nicer than the ass nuts you live with. What gives?"

"I'm really not," I said softly. "I have my moments. Believe me on that."

"Ah, a sinner. My kind of people." She flashed a smile at me again, and I offered her a return one.

Cady was a lot cooler than Church and Sin gave her credit for. I actually liked her. I wondered if maybe Sirena was a lot like her. Or if she would be if she spoke.

Deep down I knew better though. I knew my heaven was soft and sweet and absolutely perfect. I smirked at that thought, a pang shooting through my heart from missing her.

Cady cleared her throat. "So… Sirena…"

"Yeah?"

"Was she really getting better? You said she communicated with you."

"She was," I answered, nodding. "She wrote on my hand. I took her on my motorcycle to look over Pictured Rocks. She loved it."

Cady's lips pursed in a reflective expression. "I never thought I'd hear someone tell me Rina was on a motorcycle. Then again, I guess I don't really know my sister past when she used to talk or who she was before she left."

"What was she like? Before. . .?"

Cady was quiet for a moment before she spoke. "Bit like she is now. She's always been quiet and sweet, you know? But she used to sing. She was amazing. Our father got her lessons, and she was even doing auditions for commercials and stuff. Then she was hurt, and everything changed."

My chest constricted with that information. Knowing Sirena had been a singer made me even more desperate to hear her voice.

"I bet she was amazing."

"You know what? I have a video on my laptop. I'll show you when we get back if you want."

"Hell yeah," I said, my eagerness shining through.

Getting to see Sirena perform would be a godsend.

Cady laughed for a moment before going quiet again. "I keep the video to remind me of before. It was the last time our dad was around. It was her last performance. She won some cash with it too. She was on the local news. Seth was there to see her."

"Seth cares about her," I said softly.

Cady grunted. "Fuck him. I know he had something to do with her getting hurt. Plus, he was in that fucking coffin with her. He'll get his moment with me, that's for damn sure."

"You don't want to go poking around Asylum," I said gently. "I know you want to help Sirena, but Asylum is dangerous. Even we tend to stay away from him. We can handle that aspect—"

"We don't fight alone when it comes to my sister," she said, stopping to look at me.

I stared down at her, taking in the fierceness she had about her. I didn't believe for a minute she'd let this go. Not wanting her to get harmed if Asylum slipped, I nodded.

"OK. We don't fight alone. You want in?"

She nodded eagerly.

"I'll talk to the guys and see what we can do. You're already staying with us. If Church wanted you out, he would've never let you go to sleep, so there has to be something there."

"He knows I can help. Or at least I hope he knows. I mean it, Asher. I want to find out who did this to my sister. I want her out of that hospital and back. . . with you guys, I guess. I mean, as long as I get to be there too. I'm not leaving her side this time, so we're a packaged deal."

"Call me Ashes, and no offense, Cady. You're beautiful, but we only want Sirena," I said awkwardly.

She snorted and rolled her eyes at me. "Fuck off. I don't *want* you assholes. Four dicks with attitudes? That's like dick squared. I'm good on that. A girl can only deal with so many pricks at a time."

I chuckled and shook my head. She was something else. I really liked her and could see us becoming good friends.

"I'll just be there to make sure the dickish boys don't toe out of line."

"Dickish boys?"

"Yeah. It fits. That's how I refer to you guys in my head."

"Nice." I laughed.

We started walking again.

"Just. . . don't hurt her, OK? I think you genuinely care for her, but the other three. . .it makes me nervous."

"They love her. Sin is harder to understand, but I know he cares. He just has a shitty past, and his issues sort of cause self-sabotage. He's worth it though."

She grunted but didn't say anything else on the subject of Sin. I knew she didn't like him. It was in her eyes. Her voice. The way she said his name. Sin would have to get on his knees and beg for Cady to take him seriously, and even then I was sure she'd laugh at him. He had his work cut out for him.

"Ashes! Hey!" Bryce called out.

I frowned and turned to where Bryce was. He approached cautiously, eyeing Cady with a clear set of nerves.

It was rare for Bryce to approach. He'd been getting brave lately it seemed.

"What?" I asked as he stopped in front of us.

"I, uh, was just wondering if you had any news on Sirena." He visibly swallowed. "I tried to see her again, and they wouldn't let me. Nothing has come through the office on her either."

"Oh. It's the boy from the office." Cady cocked her head at him. "I heard you were involved with my sister."

Bryce glanced at her and drew himself up. "Yes. We're friends."

"He's her ex-boyfriend," I said sourly.

Bryce was a nice guy and all, but I had a little bitter jealousy inside me from their relationship.

"I heard." Cady smirked at him. "You're weak. That's why she left you."

Bryce narrowed his eyes at her. "I'm not weak. We were just better off as friends. I'm worried about her. I didn't come over here to be made fun of. I genuinely give a shit about her. I don't like that she's stuck in that place with them doing God knows what to her."

"Why? What have you heard?" Church's voice sounded out over my shoulder. He must have decided against his morning hunt.

I watched him approaching, his blond hair windswept and his Chapel Crest uniform a mess. He never tried with these uniforms. Always unbuttoned and untucked. He simply didn't give a fuck.

"I, uh, haven't heard anything. That's why I'm here."

"I told you to get me fucking information before coming back to us. Do you have any, or are you just being a nosy little cunt?" Church demanded as he stopped next to us.

"You know what? Fuck you guys. I've been trying to help. I can only do so much, which is basically nothing but care about her. I haven't seen shit come through the office or paperwork. Nothing. If shit is happening in there, then I don't know about it. I'm only speculating, like you lot are. So answer me if she's OK or not, and I'll go back to my damn corner." Bryce's chest heaved as he balled his hands into tight fists.

"Easy there, killer," Cady said before I could reprimand him. "She's important to us. We're just trying to figure out how to get her out and if she needs saving or is really getting help."

"I know," Bryce snarled. "But treating me like shit isn't the way to make things happen."

"Why? Because if you don't like what we say you'll what? Withhold information about the girl you claim to care about?" Church snorted. "Fuck off. Get me information or don't darken my fucking door, Andrews. Fucking piss-willy twerp."

Bryce's face reddened before he turned and stormed away.

"Unnecessary," I said with a sigh. "He cares. You know he does. I know he's annoying, and it's hard for me too—"

"Fuck him. He has no right to her," Church snapped.

"He's her friend—"

"He's nothing to her." Church glared at me. "*We* care about her."

"It's good that others care about her," Cady said thoughtfully, like she hadn't just insulted Bryce moments before.

"I swear to fuck, Cadence, I'm ready to drown your ass in the lake. Shut the fuck up, and stay out of this." Church rounded on her, his green eyes flashing.

"You shut the fuck up, you overbearing ass muncher. That guy may be a little. . . odd. . . but at least he's trying. More than I can say for you. If you cared half as much about her as you claim, she wouldn't still be under that perverted headmaster's thumb!"

Cadence breathed heavily as she and Church had a stare down. They were nearly chest to chest with neither of them looking like they planned on backing down.

"Cady, come on," I said, wanting to cool things off before they got further out of hand. I managed to get between them. "It's fine. We'll get this worked out—"

"I like you, Ashes, but you're wrong. *I'll* get this worked out, not you guys, because unlike you, I don't have shit to lose *but* my sister. She's why I'm here."

"Thought it was because you decided to play tough girl and set your douchebag stepdad's car on fire," Church said, fixing her again with his piercing stare.

Cady opened her mouth to fire back, and Church took a step forward again. I placed my hand on his chest, feeling his heart hammering hard beneath my palm. I gave him a slight shove back, hoping to snap him out of his rage.

"Cady, please. Let's just try to get things worked out without creating more problems. You don't know what you're getting into. Church's father—"

"She doesn't care. She's selfish," Church growled. "No point in explaining it to her. Let her find out the hard way."

"The hard way is losing Sirena!" My voice came out far louder than I'd intended. I sucked in a deep breath. Then another.

Shit.

I was going to lose it. Quickly, I stuffed my hand into my pocket and pulled my lighter out, flicking it opened and closed five times.

Breathe, Asher.

Open. Close. Open. Close. Open. Close. Open. Close. Open. Close.

Flame.

I fucking needed fire.

I let the flame out this time, letting out a shaky breath as I stared at the dancing light pouring from my lighter.

We couldn't lose her. I wouldn't lose her. There had to be another way...

"I'm open to negotiations," Cady said softly, breaking through my near meltdown. "But if we don't have a solid plan soon, I'll go in. Alone. And hell have mercy on the monsters' souls because I won't have any."

And with that, she pivoted and strode away from us, leaving us to stare at her retreating back.

"She's a fucking nightmare," Church complained with a grunt, scrubbing his hand down his face and sighing.

"So are we," I murmured.

But two nightmares could only make a night terror. At least that was the hope I had as the heat from my flame burned my thumb.

SIN

My head felt like a drumline was bashing its way through it. I was high as fuck in an effort to stop the pain. It was helping, but not as much as I'd hoped.

It didn't help that I was sitting on our patio with the sister from hell openly glaring at me.

I took another hit of my joint, praying it would just put me to sleep if it didn't make the shit in my head chill. Ashes had called us all together tonight after classes. I knew it was because of some bullshit Cadence had going on.

She was quickly becoming a thorn in my ass. The sooner we could get her out of our lives, the better. She was pissing me off to the point where I was seriously considering helping Church plot her death.

But I'd already fucked up enough.

I blew out the smoke and stared right back at her.

She continued her glare.

She was a tough bitch, I'd give her that.

"So we need a plan," Ashes said, his voice cutting through my thoughts.

"No shit. That's why I'm here," Cadence said, tearing her scowl from me to focus on Ashes. At least she didn't look at him with pure loathing.

But why would she? Out of all of us, it was Ashes who was closest to saint status. He might be able to smile his way to the pearly gates. The rest of us were doomed.

Especially me.

I took another hit off my joint, desperate to not seem like I gave a shit. But fuck, I gave a shit. I wanted to say that Cadence wasn't an issue, but deep down I knew she was. If I didn't make it to hell, the devil brought it directly to my doorstep in the form of Cadence Lawrence.

She was a fucking weasel, here to announce my sins.

I knew determination when I saw it. Sirena's sister was the picture next to determination in the dictionary.

I had to give up something or lose it all. I knew that. But fuck, I didn't want to add more shit to my laundry list of bad deeds.

At the same time, I knew I was a piece of shit and deserved all the heartache headed my way.

Fucking damnit.

"Right," Ashes said, offering her a quick smile. "I was thinking maybe one of us should go into the med ward and try to see Stitches. When I say one of us, I mean maybe just me. Or Sin. Not Church."

Church frowned and leaned forward in his chair. "Why can't I go? Stitches is my brother."

"Your father," I muttered. "That's why."

"I don't give a shit about Stitches," Cadence broke in. "I'm here for Rina—"

"Stitches gets to see her. He may be able to give us information on her. I don't think us all barging in there is a good idea. We have to play the long game." Ashes peered at me for help.

I sighed and glanced at Church to see him frowning.

"We can't go near Sirena," I finally said.

"What? Why?" Cadence rounded on me, her eyes flashing.

Great. Here we go...

"Because we lost a bet with Asylum. He won. He gets Sirena, not us. We agreed to let her go," I said, the words searing my chest.

Fuck. How many times was I going to tamp down these fucking emotions?

"Wait. What?" Cadence snapped her focus to Ashes. "Is he serious? You guys played a fucking game with my sister and lost? And now she's *property* of a psychopath?"

"It's not like that. Asylum said he's going to bring her back to us," Ashes answered softly.

"Oh, fuck that." Cadence stood from her chair and tightened her dark ponytail. "I'm done. I'm going to get my sister."

She stormed off the patio and into the darkness. It only took moments for Church to snap into action. He nearly knocked Ashes over rushing off the patio to chase Cadence through the darkness.

"Should we go after them?" Ashes asked, flipping his lighter opened and closed so fast it was a blur. He was getting upset.

"No." I took a hit from my joint. "Fuck her. She won't get two feet into the facility. You know she won't. She'll raise hell and end up getting tossed in the hole. Might be the best place for her."

Ashes winced. "She loves Sirena."

I nodded. "People do crazy things when they love someone."

A small, sad smile graced Ashes's face. "Yeah. They do, don't they?"

I swallowed thickly as I thought about Bells and all the shit I'd done.

Deciding it wasn't the time to wallow in all my bullshit, I cleared my throat. "Let Church and Cadence sort it out. Church will win. He always does."

"I don't know." Ashes peered into the darkness where the pair had disappeared. "Cady might give him a run for his money."

"Church is good at running. I'm not worried." I waved Ashes off. "Besides, I don't hear any screaming or fighting."

"You wouldn't," Ashes murmured. "Not with Church. He's a stalker in the dark. He could be drowning her in a mud puddle right now, and we wouldn't know it."

"Good riddance."

Ashes sighed but settled back in his seat. "Do you want to talk?"

"About what?" I grunted, staring at the night sky.

The stars twinkled overhead, reminding me how insignificant I was in this world.

"Anything. Sirena?"

I caught the expression in his eyes. Ashes was struggling. It wasn't a surprise. I knew he was.

"Not really, but if you need to talk about her, I guess I'll listen."

Ashes breathed out, relaxing a bit more in his seat. "She kissed me. Before. . . everything."

I nodded. "Yeah?"

"Yeah. Her lips were so soft. I could tell she was nervous, but man, I loved it. I loved that she was a bit hesitant. I had all these feelings pouring into me." He stared at me with wide eyes. "Like, here was this absolutely perfect girl for all of us, and she needed us. She needed me to take things slowly. To show her. To let her explore. I don't know. I-I've never felt this way about anyone in my life, man." He grew quiet for a moment. "Is this love, Sin?"

I sighed and finished my joint. "Can't be hate, right?" I repeated the words he'd said to me back when I was struggling with Bells.

A tiny smile shadowed his lips.

"I feel so small compared to my feelings. I just want to give her everything in the world. I want to make her breakfast in bed, rub her feet, kiss her, and tell her how I really feel. I even want to have kids. I've never wanted any of that before, but with Sirena?" He nodded. "I want it. I want it all with her."

I didn't know what to say. My heart ached. I'd made a vow. A promise to the watchers. A girl for all of us, and here I was, taking it all away. Hell, I'd already taken it away.

I should've been honest then. I should've told them I was out. That they could have a girl for the three of them. That I was too broken to love. That I wasn't worth the fucking effort.

But then. . . I'd kissed Sirena. Touched her. Guilt and shame had warred it out in my heart. I wasn't capable of giving her anything good. And she'd only break me further. I knew that. I fucking knew it all the way to my core.

If I could go back in time, I would've walked away. I wouldn't have hurt her. I know I wouldn't have. I would've let the guys have her and would've left to give them what they deserved. That perfect girl Ashes spoke of.

Instead, I'd ruined everything like I always did.

Story of my fucking life.

And once they found out about it, I was a dead man.

My days were numbered.

"Sin?"

"Yeah?" I rubbed my eyes.

"You love Sirena too, right?" The way Ashes said those words let me know one thing. He was worried.

"I'm incapable of loving. You know that," I said softly. "I don't even know what loving a girl even fucking is."

"You're not. You just have to let go—"

"I'm really not interested," I said firmly. "I can't be. I-I keep thinking about leaving. About just letting you guys take her and getting your happy ending. I'd be good with it. You know that, right? I want you guys to be happy. I-I just don't think I'll ever be. Not now. I don't deserve any of it."

"We're a family. You're not leaving," Ashes said. "We won't let you. You deserve every ounce of happiness in the world, Sin. You know you do. Or you will once you let it into your heart again. So you're staying. Got it?"

"No matter what?" I whispered, my heart in my throat as I stared at him.

He leaned closer, a frown marring his lips. "I get the feeling you're not being honest with us. Sin, man, if you need to talk, you know I'm always here, right? I'm worried about you. You don't tell us where you're going. You stay out late and sometimes don't even come home at all. Where do you go? Who are you with? Is-is there someone else?" His voice trembled with the last sentence.

"There's no one else," I answered. "I-I just walk. I sit at the lake and stare at the stars. Sometimes I go to the mausoleum."

"Why?" Ashes crinkled his brows.

I rubbed my eyes, hating we were having this conversation. At the same time, it felt good because I couldn't live beneath all this guilt.

"I sleep in the coffin where Sirena was."

Ashes blinked at me. "You. . . what? Why?"

I opened my mouth, ready to spill it all out for him because I was tired of living the lie. "I-I hurt h—"

"Put me down, you fucking barbarian psychopath!" Cadence's voice interrupted my confession.

Ashes jumped up and stared into the darkness, me joining him.

A moment later, Church appeared with Cadence thrown over his shoulder, her pounding her fists into his back as she struggled against him. He held her tight though, despite her hits and kicks.

He marched right past us as he took her into the house.

We wasted no time and followed him inside. He took her straight to Stitches's room and tossed her onto the bed. She bounced and shot right back to her feet, but he simply pushed her back down.

She glared up at him, dark strands from her ponytail unleashed and tangled around her. Clearly, they'd been fighting. Judging by the cut on Church's lip and the glint in Cadence's eye, it had been a good one.

"Sit your fucking ass down. Go to sleep before I put you to sleep, Claws."

She crossed her arms over her chest and sneered at him. "You're not my boss."

"When it comes to the girl I love, the girl I'd fucking die for, I'm everyone's boss. Learn to deal with it or get fucking lost. If you ruin this, none of us will forgive you."

She opened her mouth to speak but quickly snapped it closed as Church continued.

"Sirena won't forgive you."

She visibly swallowed. "She'd understand."

"She'd hate you for taking away any potential happiness she could have. Trust me when I say that if you intervene the way you want to, it'll be the nail in Sirena's coffin."

"Then we need a plan," she whispered, her voice wavering.

For the first time since I'd met her, she showed vulnerability. It did something to my chest.

I'd fucked up everyone's life because of my actions.

If only I had a time machine. . .

"Sin will go in and see Stitches. He'll get all the information we need. OK? Trust in Sin."

"Fuck Sin," she snarled, glaring at me.

"Fuck you right back, bitch," I snapped.

She stuck her tongue out at me, and I stuck mine right back out at her like a damn child.

"For fuck's sake," Ashes mumbled, rubbing his neck.

"Claws, do you understand what I'm saying to you?" Church demanded, pulling her attention from me.

"Yes," she muttered. "I get it. I'll hold off. For now."

"Thank you," Church said, actually sounding grateful. "But if you fuck this up, I'll kill you and pretend like you never existed. No one will find your body."

She rolled her eyes. "I said OK, dick weed. I won't. I'll wait. For now."

Church nodded.

I studied her for a moment. Beautiful and fierce.

Just like Sirena.

We had our work cut out for us it seemed.

I didn't think Cadence Lawrence would back off for long.

Which meant my end was really fucking near.

STITCHES

The room was so bright and white that I winced as they led me into it. It took my eyes a moment to adjust, but when they did, I noticed her.

Angel.

Sitting in a chair, her skin pale and her hair hanging limply around her. Dark circles haloed her dull eyes, making her look exhausted and unwell. There were belts around her, keeping her fastened in her seat.

She stared straight ahead and didn't acknowledge me.

"What is this?" I rasped. "What's going on?"

"We're going to do that fun experiment we discussed the other day with your father. Good money was paid. You know how it goes. Sirena's stepfather wants her healthy and at least not a statue. Her mother too. And others. . . well, like I said, good money was paid for this." Sully winked at me.

I blinked in confusion at him in his ugly brown suit and slicked back hair. If I could launch myself across the room and beat his skull in without Sirena coming into the crossfire with the repercussions, I'd have been on the useless prick in a hot minute.

"Seth. Come," Sully instructed as two wards led Asylum into the room.

They sat him in the chair next to mine.

"What the hell are we doing?" Asylum demanded, his black hair a wild mess and his blue eyes filled with fury as he glared at Sully.

Whatever we were doing was nothing good.

"Everett needs you tested," Sully said, smiling that smug as shit smile. "I obliged because it's for science. . . and for him."

"What do you do? Suck him off when he comes to visit?" Asylum snarled. "He controlling you with his cock?" He cocked his head at Sully. "Who am I kidding? You'd do anything for some cock."

I glanced quickly at Sully, whose cheeks reddened. He struck Asylum across his face, snapping his head to the side.

It didn't take a genius to know Asylum was ready to do what I'd been thinking about. A muscle thrummed along his jaw as he straightened himself.

"You touch me again and you'll be sorry," he whispered in a voice that sent chills down my spine.

I didn't spook easily, but seeing Asylum glowering at Sully the way he was, I had zero doubts he'd make good on his promise. I was fucking here for it too.

Sully said nothing at that and focused on Sirena instead. Instantly, my fear ramped up.

"Hello, Sirena," Sully said softly as she stared straight ahead, her focus on Asylum.

Something flickered in her colorful gaze which made me crinkle my brows. *Movement. Behind her eyes.* It was so brief I wasn't even sure if I'd actually seen it or was just hoping for it.

"Don't fucking touch her," I shouted at the same time Asylum did.

Sully smirked back at us as he cradled her cheek. He dropped his hand away from her.

"Oh, no worries, boys. It's not me who's going to touch her."

The fear which had been a tightly wound ball in my guts burst into strands of complete freakout as my breath caught in my chest over what his words could mean.

I'd kill someone. I knew I would.

I had to hold it together. He'd come after Sirena worse. He'd go for Church. He'd punish me. I knew it.

Everett fucking Church.

Breathe, Malachi. Fucking keep breathing. For her. For angel.

I held my breath as Sully went to a machine and grabbed some electrodes from it. He began fixing them to Sirena's forehead and temple.

"What are you doing?" Asylum demanded as Sully returned to the machine and turned it on.

A nurse came into the room and began messing with the equipment as Sully turned back to us.

"It's very simple. Miss Lawrence is sick. She's catatonic. This is a last-ditch effort to bring her back before her stepfather gives her up. He's been in talks with Everett Church. Everett has a lot of interest in obtaining her for various reasons, but most of it has to do with who her real father is and just how much money a girl with her eyes and looks could fetch at the market. So we bring her back and have a little fun in the name of science, or we let her go. It's that simple."

"Fuck you," Asylum snarled. "I'll kill you. I swear to the fucking devil, I will murder you."

Sully offered him a smile. "The dogs of Everett Church never bite unless he lets them off their leash. I feel pretty safe, Mr. Cain."

Asylum got to his feet, but two wards shot into the room and shoved him back into his chair and held him there as the nurse left the room.

I had no fucking clue what was going to happen, but I wished more than anything that it wouldn't.

"Now, watch and learn how we get hands-on here at Chapel Crest." Sully moved to the monitor and stared down at it.

"Firefly," Asylum said in a fierce whisper. "It's going to be OK. It'll be OK. Breathe. Just keep breathing for us."

I glanced from Asylum to Sirena and saw a sweep of fear shoot through her eyes.

She was . .back. She was already back!

"No! No!" I shouted, launching myself up as everything moved in slow motion.

Two more wards dashed in right as Sully hit the button on the machine. I wasn't fast enough. They caught me before I made it to her.

Her eyes squeezed closed as she shook in her seat.

They were shocking her. The monster was shocking her.

Electroshock.

Her lashes fluttered for a moment before she trembled violently.

Asylum and I were both fighting with our captors while she continued to quiver.

"No! Angel! Fuck! NO!" I punched one of the wards in the face and was going to tear the head off the other one when a needle was jammed into my neck, dropping me to my knees as my chest heaved with every ragged breath I tried to drag in.

It looked like the same thing had been done to Asylum because he was sagging forward, breathing hard.

"Don't do this to her." I sobbed as she slumped over, finally going still. "Please. Don't."

My pleas fell on deaf ears because Sully hit the button again, and she shook once more. Helplessly, I watched as her fingers twisted and her body quaked violently. As her mouth foamed a little and her eyes rolled back.

Fuck. No. They were going to kill her.

Not my angel. Please, not my angel.

"What do you want? What do you want me to do?" I wept. "Please! I'll do anything. Just stop. Don't hurt her!"

Sully turned off the machine, and Sirena quaked in her seat, clearly having a seizure. If Sully cared, he made no show of it as he approached me. Asylum was quiet, but he was focused on Sirena. His lips were moving but his words were so soft I couldn't hear him.

Sully squatted in front of me. "Give me what I want, and I'll stop. You'll all be free."

I let out a shuddering breath. "What do you want?"

Sully offered me a sinister smile as he got to his feet. My body felt like lead as I tried to keep my head up. This wasn't the typical drug they'd been giving me. This was something to slow me down. Weaken my body. I felt like I could sleep forever if given the chance.

Sully stood and backed away from me.

Sirena finally stilled in her seat. Two nurses came in and cleaned her, blocking my view of her. Several minutes passed in silence before the nurses left and Sully spoke again.

"Malachi, would you be so kind as to undress Miss Lawrence?" Sully stepped back so I could see her in her chair, her head hanging forward and her face covered by a curtain of dark hair.

I wasn't even sure if she were conscious.

"What? No!" I practically spat. "Fuck you."

"You do recall your promise, don't you?" Sully grinned. "I can make a call and ensure Miss Lawrence loses her clothes. Wouldn't you rather it be you who does it?"

I ground my teeth so hard I thought they were going to snap off.

"Please, don't do this," I whispered, trying to figure out what the hell I should do in that moment. "Whatever you're planning, you can be better than this."

"Remove her clothes, Mr. Wolfe," Sully said evenly. "We're paid by the job here, not the hour, so we have all the time in the world."

"I-I won't do it. She wouldn't want that," I said. "Please. Tell Everett I'll do anything else—"

Sully stalked forward again and stood in front of me. Asylum hadn't moved an inch and was staring intently at Sirena as his chest heaved. He was pissed. Or he was doing some of his freaky mind shit to her. I had no idea, but if he let go of his rage, I'd follow and help the crazy fucker gut these pricks.

We'd all die though. I knew we would if we moved. Maybe not today, but Everett would send men to find us, and we'd hang for it. And so would Church. Maybe even Ashes and Sin. I couldn't do that to my family.

Fuck. FUCK.

"If I have to drug you again, Malachi, I will. Everett will know you weren't willing and broke your promise to him. Regardless of what you think you want, *this* is happening. Either remove her clothes or I will."

I peered around the stark white room and saw a mirror I was sure was actually a window where we were being watched. Everett and whoever the fuck else who'd paid to watch this violation was probably standing behind it, jerking their tiny cocks.

"It's an observation room," Sully said, noticing me staring at the mirror. "We observe science and the depths of depravity to get answers. We watch the human mind and all the reactions that go with it. Remove Miss Lawrence's clothes. Now."

I didn't want anyone in that fucking room or beyond to see my precious angel bared for twisted, sick men to see. But if I didn't do it, they would. I'd be drugged and useless.

"Motherfucker," Asylum snarled as I got to my feet.

I didn't know if he was talking to me or Sully, but either way, we were both pieces of shit in this moment.

I staggered over to Sirena and fell to my knees in front of her.

"I-I don't want to do this," I choked out softly. "Please, angel, know that I don't want to do this. I-I just don't know what else to do. We'll all be hurt if I don't. I'm sorry. I'm so fucking sorry, baby."

She didn't move.

I reached out with fumbling fingers and untied the back of her hospital gown. Then I let it fall to her waist, revealing more of her pale skin and her full breasts.

I swallowed thickly, wanting to cover her back up. My hands shook as I reached out and cradled her face, tears sliding down my cheeks.

"Undo her belts." Sully grunted.

With shaking hands, I undid her bindings, freeing her. She fell forward against me limply, her body still trembling slightly.

"Angel." I wept softly. "I'm sorry. Please. Be brave."

"Take her to the bed," Sully instructed. "She needs to be in bed."

I lifted her naked body into my arms as her gown slipped away. I forced myself to focus and ignore the heaviness of my body. Carefully, I took her to the hospital bed in the room and laid her in it.

Right in front of the fucking mirror.

Of course it was.

Fear choked me as I brushed her hair from her face. Her eyes wavered as she stared at the ceiling, her lips parted.

I blew out a shaky breath, dreading what would happen next.

"Asylum," Sully called out. "Your turn."

"Go fuck yourself," Asylum said, glaring at Sully.

Sully let out a soft chuckle. "I'm sure I'll get the opportunity soon. For now, comply or I'll have Mr. Wolfe put her back in the chair and see if she can handle another round of *therapy*. Not like it matters if we lose a catatonic patient. They're a bit useless anyway."

Asylum jerked free of the wards holding him and strode toward me and Sirena, his blue eyes darkened with rage.

I'd never seen anyone look quite so frightening before, and I lived with the watchers.

This Asylum was the guy who'd force you to eat your own eyeballs. That much I knew.

"Mr. Wolfe, if you'd be so kind to hold Miss Lawrence down for this next part." Sully offered another grin. "This is what our audience paid for. We want to give them a good show."

Dread overwhelmed my fear as I stared at Sirena.

"I sometimes allow audience participation," Sully murmured. "So consider that before you tell me no."

Bile burned my throat as I realized I had no choice. I knew what was going to happen. They were going to watch us defile her. Defile my angel for their sick pleasure.

If we were going to do this, I was going to make it as painless as I could.

I crawled into bed with Sirena and hauled her limp body into my arms, situating her on my lap. Her small body fit easily between my legs as I cradled her against me. I'd be sure to hold her through this nightmare.

"Mr. Cain, show us the wicked you're capable of," Sully said softly. "If you fail, I'll take over."

I watched, nausea and pain choking me, as Asylum got onto the bed and pushed Sirena's legs apart.

"Don't," the words slipped from my lips as he unzipped his pants and pulled his cock out. He stroked it to get it hard.

He said nothing, but his body trembled as I held my angel in my arms.

"Don't hurt her," I choked out as he positioned himself between her legs. "Please. Seth. . . don't."

"My name is Asylum," he whispered, his eyes wavering as they locked on mine. "Not Seth."

And with those words, he pushed into her body, jolting her in my arms.

A tear slid from the corner of her eye as I held her. As Asylum fucked her for all the sick fuckers to witness. He wasn't rough with her. In fact, I'd never seen him be so gentle before as he pushed in and out of her trembling body.

"Just keep breathing," I whispered softly against her ear as Asylum jostled her body gently against mine, my own tears flowing. "Just keep breathing, angel."

Her tears continued to fall as Asylum fucked her.

She was a prisoner inside herself. I hated it. I hated it so much.

"I'm sorry," I whispered over and over to her as I wept. "I'm so fucking sorry."

Her body arched as she came, her breathing ragged.

Asylum's eyes remained fixed on her face. I chanced a look at him to see a tear trail out of his eye too, his bottom lip wobbling.

He didn't want this either.

His Adam's apple bobbed as he reached out and cradled her face. He leaned down to hide her body from the sick perverts watching behind the glass. He whispered in her ear as he continued to move in and out of her.

He. . . loved her. Just like I did. Everything in the way he did this showcased how much he gave a damn. I never thought I'd see the day.

I swallowed my pain and focused on the angel in my arms and

continued to whisper to her about how beautiful she was. How brave she was. How it would be over soon.

"And when we're strong enough, angel, we'll kill them all. I fucking swear it," I croaked into her ear. "For you, baby. For us."

"They'll all suffer for what they've done to us in this moment," Asylum whispered, his forehead brushing against my head. "We'll revel in their blood. Stay fucking strong, *Malachi.* Many secrets are set to be revealed. We must have patience. Trust me."

I remained silent, absorbing his words as he pulled away.

Asylum came with a soft groan a moment later. His chest heaved as I stared up at him. Sirena was still limp in my arms, her tears still flowing.

Asylum reached out and stroked her cheek again before tilting her head so she was staring at him.

"They're dead, firefly. All of them. They just don't know it yet," he murmured. "Sully. Everett. The monsters behind the glass. I'll kill them all for you." He leaned in and licked her tears before he pulled free of her body and tucked his dick back into his pants.

He looked at me this time. "Want to help me?" he asked softly.

I nodded without a word.

A tiny, wicked smile curled his lips upward.

"Let's get out of here. We have business to tend to."

We sure the hell did.

CHURCH

When I'd hauled Cady back to the house after she'd run off like a little bitch, she'd locked herself in Stitches's room and had refused to talk to us, which was fine with me. Several hours of not having to deal with her had been a welcome reprieve. Cadence Lawrence was a swamp bitch and a complete pain in my ass.

And she'd emerged from her lair ready to make my life hell once again.

She winked at me as she ate the sandwich she'd swooped in and taken out of my hands before I could even bite into it.

Ashes laughed, which made her grin wider.

"Don't reward her shitty manners," I said, shooting her a look of disdain. "She'll keep doing it."

"I'm not a pretty, little princess," she said around a mouthful of ham and cheese as she sat on the couch in our living room. "I'm the fire who'll burn your house down."

I rolled my eyes at her, but I knew she wasn't lying. Sirena's sister was a crazy bitch and probably would torch us if given the chance and the mood struck her. She kept her cool now simply because Sirena was on the line.

In all honesty, I worried about what would happen if we couldn't free specter and Stitches.

Specter was Asylum's though.

For now.

I'd told myself a hundred times that Asylum would bring her back to us. I felt it deep within me that maybe he wasn't playing us the way I originally thought he was.

I had no proof either way and could only fucking hope.

If he failed to bring her back, I'd chop his ass up and sell him to my old man. Seth was pretty. He might fetch good money at the market. Father wanted me in the family business and all. If pushed too far, I'd start killing indiscriminately, starting with Seth Cain.

Many forest animals had lost their lives in my pursuit for some semblance of peace lately.

Stringing up and gutting Seth might help soothe my wounded soul if I found he was just fucking with me for the fun of it.

"So. Plan?" Cadence swallowed and raised her brows at me.

Sin hadn't said a word from his seat on the end of the sectional. He was quiet. Too quiet. He was worrying me lately, but he was also pissing me off. I hadn't seen him this bad off since Bells.

"You need to understand my father to understand how this needs to go down," I said with a sigh. The last thing I wanted to do was kick those skeletons out of my closet, especially to her, but Sirena and Stitches's safety were on the line. "My father is a monster. He runs the underground and plays all sides of the field. I suppose you could say he's neutral in the sense that he doesn't get involved in warring syndicates and such. He's just the guy you go to if you need to procure delicate things."

"What things? People? Jewelry? Uranium?" Cadence bit into the sandwich again and chewed.

I nodded. "Yeah. All of that and more. Say you're a sick fuck who's looking for a pretty, little, red-haired girl with pigtails and sparkling eyes. You give him your shopping list, and he sends out his shoppers to get what you want. You pay for it. Blood. Money. Tears. Whatever. My father is good with a lot of currency. He doesn't care what you do with your product once you've gotten it and paid. Fuck it. Kill it. Eat it. Nothing is off the table."

"Wait. Cannibalism?" Cadence dropped her sandwich on the coffee table, looking queasy.

"Of course. Anything goes. He trades in flesh as well. You have someone you want to trade him for, and he'll do that as well as long as he comes out ahead with the trade. It's an ugly business and an ugly world. Sirena is in danger of becoming part of it." I paused, watching as Cadence balled her hands into tight fists, her nostrils flaring. "He owns a lot of places you wouldn't even consider as his property. The Family Fun Center in the Sault? He owns it. It's the perfect place to shop for delicacies."

"Fucking disgusting," she whispered.

"It is," I said softly. "It's the world I was raised in. He wants me back. He knows he can use Sirena to get me. He knows he can use Stitches. He's the man behind the curtain in many places, Chapel Crest included. He funds a lot of what happens at this place. When I say to you that you need to fucking relax and play the long game, I mean it. Going off the rails, as much as I fucking wish we could, can't happen. When I tell you to back down, you back the fuck down. Understand?"

She visibly swallowed. "I want to save my sister."

"And we will. Safely. There is a way. We just need to figure it out."

"What about this Asylum thing? *She belongs to him.* How is that going to factor in?"

I looked to my hands as I leaned forward in my chair. "We're putting a little faith in his brand of insanity and hoping we don't have to kill him for it."

"So blind trust?" she asked sourly.

"For now."

We were all quiet for a moment. I took the opportunity to survey Sin, who simply stared at his feet. He hadn't spoken much lately. In fact, I was surprised he was here at all. He liked to be alone even more these days.

Ashes got up, a frown on his face.

"What?" I asked, watching as he went to the front door.

"I-I could have sworn I just saw Malachi—"

The front door swung open just as Ashes reached for the handle. I rose as Stitches filled the doorway, his dark hair hanging limply around him, his eyes darkened, and a scar forming along the side of his head from where he'd cut himself.

"Stitches?" I stalked forward, my throat tight, and wrapped my arms around him. "You're home."

He hugged me back, his body shaking. "I'm home," he whispered as Ashes joined in.

We stayed that way for a long time before breaking apart. When I turned to see what Sin was doing, I found him standing, his gray eyes wavering.

"You going to stand there like an idiot or fucking hug me?" Stitches rasped, his cheeks damp with tears.

Sin surged forward and wrapped his arms around Stitches, the two holding one another. I chanced a peek at Cadence to find she'd gone back to eating her sandwich, her eyes glued to us.

"Enough hugging," she called out around more food. "Where the fuck is my sister?"

Sin let go of Stitches.

"She's free too. She's with Asylum." A pained look swept over Stitches's face as his voice cracked.

Ashes peered at me, fear on his face as Sin cleared his throat.

"He's going to bring her back," I said softly, hoping it wouldn't set Stitches off again. I couldn't fucking deal with him swinging in his closet.

"He will," Stitches murmured. "When the time is right."

The fact he accepted it so easily immediately set off alarm bells in my head.

"Well, guess what? The time is right fucking now." Cadence stuffed the remainder of her sandwich into her mouth and stalked past us to the door.

"You fuckers coming or should I send you a written invitation for this ass kicking I'm about to deliver?"

I smirked at her. "I can't stand you."

"Good. Then you'll hurry your ass up and get this over with. The sooner this shit is over, the sooner I'll leave you twerps alone. I want answers."

I silently checked with Ashes then Sin and finally Stitches. They all wore varying looks of determination.

"Fuck it. I'll try anything once," I said. "Let's see what the plan is."

"Follow me, boys."

"Lead us not into temptation," Ashes muttered.

"But deliver us from evil," I added.

"Amen," came Stitches's soft voice.

Something was wrong with him, but we'd deal with it later. Right now, we had an ass kicking to deliver.

SIRENA

"Here," Asylum said, brushing the hair away from my face. "Let me help you."

As much as I wanted to return to my own room, it didn't look like that was happening. Asylum had brought me to his place, and that was where we'd been since walking through the door. We hadn't spoken. We'd simply sat in silence as I tried to hold back the tears.

What had happened in the medical ward. . .

Asylum took the chocolate chip cookie from my hand. I wasn't feeling great. I'd had a seizure. *Twice*. I'd been shocked. My entire body had seized beneath the electricity Sully had delivered to me. I'd played along. Asylum had told me to.

I wasn't sure what would've happened if I'd have just come to before that moment, but it probably would've ended the same. Cruelty and monsters wouldn't change directions just because I decided to blink.

I was quickly learning that here at Chapel Crest.

The fact Sully had just let us leave after everything put me on edge. I hadn't been able to walk out on my own. They'd given Asylum a wheelchair to use for me. He hadn't hesitated. He'd lifted me easily and placed me in it before bringing me back here.

I needed a shower and a decent meal.

My body was refusing to cooperate though. I felt like I was made of lead, and my head felt fuzzy and weird.

Static.

That was what my insides felt like.

"Like an old TV," Asylum murmured.

I locked gazes with him, feeling my cheeks flush. He'd been forced to fuck me for the sick pleasures of whoever the hell was behind that mirror. Nausea twisted like a snake in my guts at the memory.

I hadn't wanted that.

I hadn't wanted him to do that to me, but I knew. . . I knew worse would happen if I hadn't just taken it.

On the other hand, he *was* gentle and didn't hurt me. In fact, through my fuzzy, scattered recollection, I recalled some pleasure.

But I was so out of it, who knew.

A lot of those ugly moments were blank spaces in my mind.

Stitches's arms around me. Him begging me to breathe.

I couldn't recall much past that. In fact, I felt like sleeping a million years. Everything within my body just felt so. . .heavy.

Seth.

"Asylum," he said softly, offering me the cookie once more after breaking off a small piece. "I'm not Seth. Seth isn't here, firefly. We don't like it when you mix us up. Him for more obvious reasons than me."

I frowned. I had no idea what he was talking about.

He sighed and raised his brows at me. "Seth isn't the one who beat you with a shovel and tried to kill you. That was me. Asylum. Seth would never harm a hair on your head."

I trembled slightly beneath his confession.

"Open," he whispered.

I parted my lips and let him drop the cookie into my mouth.

"Chew."

I chewed, my gaze on him.

"Seth is the one you've always loved, but I think you can love me too if you give me a chance." He cocked his head at me. "I won't ever hurt you again. I've learned my lesson. It really fucking hurt to not have you in our lives. We all suffered so very much."

I swallowed and parted my lips as he offered me more of the cookie.

"This isn't an adequate meal for you," he murmured, watching me chew. "What do you want to eat? I'll make it happen."

I was far too tired to eat. I wasn't even able to feed myself.

"Then I'll feed you," he said, like he was inside my head.

I crinkled my brows at him.

Seth... can you hear me?

"I'm not Seth, firefly. I'm Asylum," was his answer. "Please stop making me repeat myself."

I shifted away from him, realizing he probably was inside my head. *How the hell?*

He let out a soft chuckle. "Fun, right?" He offered me another bite. "I have so much to tell you, my sweet forever girl. I just don't think the time is right. So we'll wait until it is. Now, what would you like to eat?"

I just want to sleep. Please. I want to wake up from whatever nightmare this is.

Wordlessly, Asylum stood in front of me. He pulled the sheets and blanket back on his bed. He came back to me where I sat in his computer chair and lifted me into his arms like I was just a rag doll. Tenderly, he placed me on his bed and tucked me in, dropping a soft kiss on my forehead, his lips lingering.

"I'm sorry for what happened at the facility," he whispered. "I never wanted to do that to you. Ever. Not like that. I promise you the next time I'm inside your body, you'll beg me to stay. And I will. We'll talk more after you've rested. Sleep, firefly. We have some revenge to plan."

He moved away from me and cradled my cheek as I stared up at him.

Asylum terrified me.

God, he terrified me.

But he also drew me in.

I'd missed him. Seth.

I'd missed him so much, but the man before me wasn't Seth. He wasn't my best friend. Weakly, I reached up and rested my hand over his. I let my thumb trail lightly over his smooth wrist as he stared down at me.

"You missed me too," he said in a soft voice. "You just didn't know me well then. I promise you'll know me now though. That promise comes with many strings I plan on tying you up in, my sweet forever girl. I'll never let you go again."

I swallowed, my lips parting as we stared at one another.

He rested his other hand over my chest. "Calm, Sirena. I'm not the worst monster on these grounds."

Please don't hurt me. . .

"Never again. I promise." He thumbed along my bottom lip. "Now sleep for us. Things will be different tomorrow. Seth will be here. I know you miss him."

I closed my eyes, really hoping he wouldn't bludgeon me to death in my sleep.

He let out a soft laugh as his finger brushed against my jaw.

"We've moved on from such things. Sleep, my love."

I kept my eyelids closed as he hummed our song softly.

It sent shivers down my spine.

Just not in the way I expected.

These shivers excited me.

Maybe I'd lost my damn mind too.

ASHES

We walked in silence across campus. I knew we were going to see Asylum. But what we were going to do confused me. Church had just said we were going to take things slow and wait it out. He'd said that Cady needed to chill.

But now we were making our way to his place with Stitches moving slower than the rest of us.

I fell back to walk beside him as he shuffled along in a pair of dark sweatpants and a white t-shirt.

"How are you?" I asked.

Cady shoved Church. He pushed her back before they launched into calling one another colorful names. Sin shook his head and moved ahead of them.

"Alive," Stitches muttered, his stare on his feet.

This Stitches seemed so reserved. It was unlike him to be so quiet. Even after his break before his suicide attempt, he was still all teasing and laughter.

"I'm glad you are."

He let out a soft huff of air.

I cleared my throat after a moment of silence. "Do you want to talk about it?"

He shrugged as he kicked a pebble on the path. Cady was now walking backward in front of Church, taunting him. She kept darting away every time he tried to grab her. I knew he'd throw her in a bush if he managed to get her.

"Ashes, man, shit was fucked in there. I-I don't even want to see angel right now. The shit that happened. . ." He blew out a breath. "She'll never forgive me."

"What happened?"

Fear roiled deep in my chest.

He shook his head. "I-I can't talk about it. I don't want to talk about it. All I know is I have a lot of work cut out for me if I'm ever going to get her to love me. She'll never forgive me."

"Stitches, what happened? You're scaring me."

"I-I can't say. Just know any hatred she has for me would be well-placed. The fact she's with Asylum right now. . . Fuck."

"Should we be more worried than we are? We'll take her from him. You know Dante will. He won't hesitate if you say the word—"

"She's not safe anywhere, man. This world is fucked. But if I had to pick a place for her, it would be with Asylum. He took care of her in there."

His words hurt, but the look on his face let me know he meant it. Considering what Stiches had done over the thought of losing her to him, this new approach made me uneasy. Something big had happened. I didn't want to dwell on it because my mind only went to the darkest of places. If I found out she was harmed in some screwed up experiment, I'd burn this place to the ground.

We reached Asylum's building and went inside.

"Hurry up," Church called out, looking back to us as he shoved Cady into a Ficus tree in the lobby.

"Prick," she muttered, catching herself on the wall.

"I'm not going in. I'll wait here." Stitches visibly swallowed.

"I'll wait with him," Sin said immediately.

"What the fuck is the matter with you two jerks?" Cady demanded. "I thought you guys loved my sister? I'm confused. So it's just Deputy Dipshit and Ashes who want her?" She jerked her thumb at Church.

"Fuck off, Claws." Church sneered, giving her the finger.

She rolled her eyes at him.

"I'm just not ready," Stitches said softly. "That's all."

Cady shrugged. "I get it. You tried to kill yourself because of her. I'll let you off this time. But you..." She rounded on Sin, her finger pointed at him. "What the fuck, shit for brains?"

"Don't point your tiny finger at me, you fucking nightmare. I'm not interested in your sister," Sin snapped, glowering at her. "I thought you got that memo."

"Whatever. Fuck you, pretty boy. I don't have time for this shit. I'm going to see my sister." She spun on her heel and pushed the button for the elevator.

I glanced at Sin. A muscle thrummed along his jaw. I wished he could get over the shit he went through with Isabella. She really messed with his head. Sighing, I flipped my lighter opened and closed five times. Pause. Five more times.

I stepped into the elevator as Sin joined Stitches.

Stitches's dark eyes wavered as he stared back at me. Something big had happened in that facility with him and Sirena. I needed to find out what. He wasn't the same guy who'd left us.

And Sin...

Damn him.

He was so stubborn.

We'd get there though.

We had to. We'd vowed one girl for us all, and I knew Sin loved her or he would if he'd just let go.

Sin inclined his head at me as I shifted my focus to him.

The doors closed, leaving me with Church and Cady.

"I hate that shirt," Cady muttered to Church as he adjusted the collar on his black button down.

"I hate your face," he said without missing a beat.

I sighed and looked to the ceiling.

The moment the elevator dinged on Asylum's floor, I stepped out with Church and Cady on my heels. We took the turn around the corner to Asylum's room and stopped. He was leaning against the wall beside his door.

He pushed off it and offered us a dark smile.

"Took you long enough," he said, staring us down as we approached.

"Where's specter?" Church demanded as we reached him.

"Asleep in my bed. She'll remain there all night. She's had a bad few days. She needs the rest."

"Not good enough. I want to see her," Cady demanded, pushing past me and Church.

I reached out to grab her hand, but she tugged out of my hold and went nearly nose to nose with Asylum. Or she would have if she was as tall as he was.

"Cady cat." Asylum smirked at her.

"Fuck off, you kook. I want my sister, and I want her now."

"You're aware she's mine," he said, his voice shifting to something darker and more violent.

"Cadence knows we had an agreement," Church said. "Sirena's still ours."

"She's in my bed. I'd say she's mine." Asylum grinned.

"Don't do this, man," I said softly. "Come on. You said—"

"Did I say something?" Asylum shook his head and sighed. "Are you sure it was me? There's a lot in here." He tapped his head before he gestured around to the otherwise empty hallway. "And in the shadows. Can never be certain who's really talking and making promises."

"Motherfucker," Church snarled.

I grabbed his arm as he stepped forward. The last thing we needed was a fight in the hallway.

Asylum's blue eyes sparkled. "OK. Fine. I won't fuck with you. She's asleep. She's mine. For now. As agreed upon. She'll remain with me until it's time to return her. Then she's yours, and I get what I want from you. That was the deal, right?"

Church nodded, his green eyes narrowed.

"I didn't make any shit deals. I need to see my sister," Cady cut in.

"You're right. Technicalities." Asylum waved her off. "I'll let you see her. Don't wake her." His voice grew soft, his entire demeanor changing. "She had several seizures earlier. She needs the rest."

"What?" My heart jumped into my throat.

Church's breathing picked up as worry filled Cady's eyes.

Asylum sighed. "Like I said, she needs her rest. Don't wake her." He stepped back and opened his door.

Cady stepped through it, Church following.

Asylum put his hand on Church's chest, stopping him. Cady closed the door behind her, her eyes catching mine, the fear in them evident.

"Cady cat can go in. You know our arrangement."

"I want to see her," Church said through gritted teeth.

"She belongs to us," Asylum murmured. "That was the deal. I'm honoring it. You'd be wise to do so as well."

"Seth, come on," I said, feeling desperate. "Please—"

"My name is Asylum." He snapped his attention to me. "I'm not Seth."

"Right," I muttered, assuming this was some multiple personality thing he had. "Asylum, please. We just want to make sure she's OK. We miss her."

"Cady will let you know," he said. "You'll keep your distance from her. It's for the best for now."

Church snarled and shoved Asylum in the chest. Asylum stepped back with the move, his blue eyes flashing as he righted himself and got into Church's face.

They glowered at each other. It was going to get bad.

I jumped into action and got between them, pushing Church back.

"We're sticking to the arrangement. He won," I whispered. "We already agreed. Don't fucking ruin this, Dante. Please. I'm begging you."

Church huffed and locked eyes with me. "We won. You know she screamed for me."

"We've been over this," Asylum cut in. "Without me, she wouldn't have screamed. The victory is mine. For now. So just fucking let me have it."

"Once I find out who helped you, I'll fuck your world up, *Asylum*," Church spat. "And whoever helped. Don't think I've forgotten."

"I'd hope not," Asylum said. "It's the key to unlocking everything. We just have to go through the motions. Believe us, we don't like it either."

"Fucking nut," Church snarled. "I swear—"

"You'll butcher me and sell me by the pound to your father. I'm aware. Not exactly how I want to go, but it is what it is, right, Dante? Just following in your father's footsteps. My, how wicked."

"Fucking prick." Church lunged forward again, but I shoved him back.

"Please. Just. . . please, Dante. Focus. Not right now. We need her. We need her back. This won't help."

He stopped trying to get past me and breathed out.

"We'll find out who helped him. That'll be our focus until she's back in our arms," he said, breathing hard.

I nodded. "OK. I want that too."

He swallowed. "Fine."

"Good. I'm glad you're listening." Asylum smiled. "I promise only good things will happen now. At least for us. The rest of the world will burn. . . right, Ashes?" He cocked his head at me, his brows crinkled. "You'll be summoned soon. A creature. A Fox. Ah, what a web when you help to *kill* him. Interesting. . ."

"What? Dante kills foxes and rabbits. Not me."

Asylum let out a soft laugh. "Perhaps you're right. How would I know?" He pointed to his head and let out a cackle. "I'm just crazy." He made a circular motion with his finger next to his head. "Bat shit crazy this one. All this noise. Fuck. Can you imagine? Sometimes my wires get crossed. It's fine. It's all fine." He clapped his hands. "Now, let's get that fucking tiger out of my room."

And with that, he opened his door and stepped inside.

"What the fuck. . ." Church muttered.

I managed to peek into the room to find Sirena sleeping peacefully in his bed, the blankets pulled up around her. Asylum ushered Cady out and closed the door as he stepped back into the hall.

"I want my Halloween party invite, Dante," he said. "If you'd be so kind."

"Fine. It's next weekend. Dress up." Church stared him down.

"Can I bring a guest?" Asylum asked, grinning brightly.

"It had better fucking be Sirena," Church snapped back.

"I promise to bring her if you promise to stay away from us. She's getting better now. I've helped her. I've helped us. Soon, we'll be united, and all the secrets will come out. Then. . ." He turned to me and cocked his head. "We'll burn it to the ground."

I nodded without even thinking things through. He knew something. I knew he did. If I had to guess, it was the same thing Stitches knew.

Fuck yes, I'd burn it down for my girl and my brother.

No questions asked.

SETH

I'd slept on the floor as Sirena took up the bed. Walking into the room and finding her curled up into a tight ball had made my guts clench a bit.

We'd come so far. . .

But we still had many miles to go if we were going to rise above.

Bile burned my throat at the knowledge of what she'd gone through in the facility beneath Sully and Everett's sickness.

Had I been there. . .

Damnit.

Mother. Fucking. God. DAMNIT.

It had to happen.

Fuck you.

She came at least.

Fuck you twice.

We will.

I shook the voice out of my head. Fucking Asylum. It was me now. Seth. While I loved Asylum dearly, he needed to be leashed sometimes. I understood why shit had to happen. I just didn't fucking like how.

Rinny didn't deserve this shit.

She hadn't deserved any of it, but I was a fuck up and hadn't locked the fucking door on Asylum ages ago, and he'd barreled through it like the damn Kool-Aid man.

And now here we were.

Fucked.

We aren't. You know we aren't. When have we ever been fucked?

Shut up.

I didn't want to do that to her either. Not like that. I'm a monster, but I'm not that fucked-up. I joke to take the pressure off. You know that.

I rubbed my eyes. I hadn't been around nearly as much as I should have. The stress from the entire thing was driving me over the edge. I was barely hanging on at this point.

Answer me. You know I didn't want it, right? You believe me?

Of course, I believe you. That doesn't make me any less pissed off that it happened though. And what about Rinny? She was hurt. You fucked her...

She understood. She didn't fight it. Her understanding of how to break free was there. When she opens those eyes we love so much, you'll see. You'll see. You already know. You see what I see. What is to come. What has passed. You know this is how it must be.

I didn't know you'd be fucking her!

I was as gentle as I could be. I tried.

I don't want to talk about this anymore. We'll chat later.

Of course, we will. Brother.

I rubbed my temples to clear my head, breaking the voice off from my mind. Quickly, I got up and took a shower in the small, attached bathroom. When I came out. Sirena was still asleep, her arm curled around her old doll that I'd tucked in bed with her. I dressed quickly and sat on the edge of the bed, not really knowing what else I could do.

A soft knock had me rising to answer the door.

I cracked it open to see Cody peering back at me.

"I got the food you asked for."

"Thanks," I muttered, opening the door wider for him.

He handed me a bag I assumed was filled with our breakfast.

He peered past me to the bed. "How is she?"

I glanced back to see she hadn't moved. "Alive."

He nodded grimly. "Aren't you scared the watchers are going to come for you like they did to Riley? Church and Ashes fucked him up."

"The watchers are the least of my concerns. Thank you for the food."

Cody backed away, a grim expression on his face.

I closed the door, not wanting that grim feeling to cling to me. Quietly, I went back to the edge of the bed and sat down. I placed the bag on my other side as I stared down at Sirena.

My Rinny.

Our forever girl.

At least that was what Asylum said about her.

He liked to argue that he saw her first. The only difference just happened to be I was the sane one who got to make first contact while he simply watched from the prison we kept him locked in.

I wasn't sure if the story would've been different if he would've met her first. I knew he tried to say he claimed her first. Ignoring that bit helped keep me calm because in my mind, she was always mine and always would be.

And then shit went down with that shovel...

She'd blamed me for years. It wasn't me. . .it fucking wasn't. Not really, but I did accept the blame in my heart for what happened.

Of course, I wasn't stupid. When it all came down to it, I knew about the depth of her love of the watchers so if I wanted her, I'd have to join her with them.

If they'd let us.

They will. We've seen it.

We haven't really seen it. It's another assumption. And didn't I tell you to go away?

I got bored.

She's awake.

I silenced the noise in my head and watched as Rinny's eyelashes fluttered, her pretty eyes opening.

"Hey," I said softly, reaching for her hand.

She stiffened for a moment before she relaxed.

"I-I had Cody get us something to eat. Are you hungry?"

She didn't move, but she was here. Her eyes trailed over me, her brows crinkling and lips parting.

"Rinny?" I licked my lips. "You can talk to me. It's me. It's Seth."

She sat up and winced, her hand slipping away from mine. I hated the distance. I'd hated the distance for years, but now that she was back, I hated that distance even more. I wanted her on my lap. At my side. In my arms. I didn't fucking care. Just. . . *with* me.

I knew she wasn't going to speak. Nothing had changed in that respect.

At least for the average person.

I tapped my head gently. "Here. Speak to me. I can hear you."

She blinked at me for a moment before I heard her soft voice around me.

"Seth?"

I smiled at her. "Hey, Rinny. I'm sorry I was away."

"I don't understand. . ."

"It's hard to explain," I said, sliding closer to her. She jerked away and cuddled into herself.

I breathed out.

I knew she was afraid of me still. I couldn't blame her after everything that had happened over the years.

And that fucking shovel.

I kept it. The shovel.

Fuck off. Seriously. Not now.

I loved him, but he pissed me off too.

"I want to explain it to you. I just. . . can't. Not right now. It has to happen a certain way. That's what I've learned over the years. It's dangerous to tempt fate." I offered her a shaky smile.

All was silent.

I cleared my throat.

"It's easier to communicate with me when you open your mind. You're a pretty tough nut to crack." I let out a soft chuckle at my attempt at a joke.

She bit her bottom lip and reached for my hand. Without an ounce of hesitation, she took it and swept her thumb up my wrist.

"You were always so smart, Rinny," I whispered.

"Why did you hurt yourself?" her soft voice called out in my mind.

"I blamed myself for what happened to you. For us. For. . . everything. I wanted to join you in heaven but was always too scared. Asylum always stopped me before it could get out of hand. He doesn't like the scars on my wrists."

Or the ones littering your body.

I shoved his voice out of my head again and fixed a smile on my face.

"I'm better now that you're here. Things will be different now."

"You won't try to kill me again?" She blinked once more at me.

"You know that wasn't me. That was Asylum. He escaped. . . it's so fucked-up, Rinny. I should've told you about him years ago. I-I just couldn't. My mom said I had to keep it a secret. She said people would look at us differently because of the sickness in our family. I'm sorry," my voice cracked. "I didn't want any of this. Especially you getting hurt. He-he was trying to save you. He thought killing you would save you from the wicked in the world so you wouldn't have to endure anything bad. I-I didn't know he was going to do it. I swear to you. I never would've left. . ." I wiped quickly at my eyes as she stared at me, her thumb still running gently over the scars on my wrist I usually kept covered.

The fact she was still here had to mean something.

I took that small bit of hope and ran with it, laying it all out for her as much as I could.

"I don't want you to be afraid of me, Rinny. Please. I've always loved you. You know I have. I was your pirate, remember? You were my princess."

"And his. . ." she called out softly, her thoughts audible to me.

I closed my eyes as I heard her voice in my head. I wasn't crazy. I was gifted. Or cursed. I supposed it depended on how one viewed it.

But it looked a lot like crazy from the outside.

This was real.

It was all fucking real.

"And his," I finished. "We're magic, Rinny. You believe that, right?"

She remained quiet as she studied me.

"I'll show you magic," I whispered. "I'll show you how beautiful it is. We-we won you from the watchers. The bet? You screamed for us."

"You scare me. . ."

"I don't mean to," I said, reaching for her hand as she pulled away. "Please. Stay with me. Let me explain." I captured her fingers with mine and held tightly.

"I came here for you. *The calling.* It jolted me out of a deep sleep. I'd been gone for so long, and then Asylum. . . He was here. It was time. I was so angry at him for what he did to you, but he said you were back. So I came. We vowed to keep you safe and with us, so we made a bet to keep you. To save you."

"You hurt me."

"I know, Rinny. I know. I'm so sorry. But it won't happen again. I swear to you. Please. Believe me. It wasn't me. It was him. Asylum. He told you already, remember?"

She was silent as a tomb as she stared back at me. My heartbeat thundered in my ears as I waited for that tiny, sweet voice to fill my head.

"Why didn't you come back for me?"

Fuck. I hadn't wanted that question to come up.

I licked my lips.

"I-I couldn't. Mom said you were dead. She cried for weeks over it. She knew. She knew Asylum had done it. She never told, just like you never told. I-I shut down after it happened. I didn't want to live anymore." I held up my other wrist to show her the jagged scars. "But I kept on breathing. If I would've looked and found you alive, I know I would've done something terrible. So I let it go to keep you safe from him," I whispered. "From Asylum."

She frowned and tugged her hand from me.

"He's not bad. He's not. He's just. . . misunderstood, but he loves you. I know he does because I can feel him. Everything. I feel it all." I pounded my chest. "You're safe with us. I swear to you that you are. It's me, Rinny. It's your Seth. You'll always be safe with me." Tears prickled my eyes as I gazed at her. "Please. I need you to believe me."

"Where is Asylum?" she finally asked softly, her words swirling in my mind.

"Nearby. Always nearby."

"I-we. . . in the facility."

"I know," I said thickly. "I'm sorry. Fuck, I'm so sorry."

A tear trickled down her pale cheek. I scrambled to my knees before her and swiped it away with my thumb.

"Look at me," I whispered, tilting her chin up.

Her glistening eyes locked on mine.

"They're all going to pay. I swear it to you. We're getting the names of the men behind the mirror. We'll kill them all."

"Promise?"

"Fuck yes." I pressed my forehead against hers, taking in the way her chest moved as she breathed quickly. "You like when I touch you."

She remained silent.

"I won't make you do anything you don't want to do. Neither will Asylum now that you're free. The ball is in your court, Rinny. For us. All of us. I want us together if that's what makes you happy. I just want. . . you. My little ghost."

"Dante says I'm his specter."

I let out a soft chuckle. "I know. He loves you just as much as I do. Do you. . . love him?"

"I-yes. But I'm also mad."

"It'll fade eventually when you realize just how much he adores you. He's been going crazy trying to get to you. But we made a deal—"

"I belong to you. You won me."

"You've always belonged to me, Sirena. Not death nor distance nor time will ever change that. Do you understand me?" I pulled away and stared at her. "Tell me."

"You've always belonged to me too, Seth."

I couldn't help myself. I went for it. Fuck the ball and the court.

I pressed my lips to hers in a soft kiss which quickly turned dangerous when she parted her lips for me, allowing me to claim her mouth.

With both my hands cradling her face, I kissed her so deeply she let out a soft whimper against my lips before her tongue slid along mine.

Tender. Ravenous. Delicious.

I hauled her against my body as I explored her mouth with my tongue, my heart in my damn throat.

So this was my Rinny.

"Ours," I whispered as we broke apart, both of us breathless. "You're ours."

"Y-yours," she whispered back to me, the word falling from her lips.

I smiled at her, my heart soaring at the sound of her voice. "I'm in your head, aren't I?"

"You never left it."

"And we never fucking will." I kissed her again, knowing we'd really won.

But this was just the first game.

We had a fuck ton more to play.

We'd start with Sinclair Priest.

SIN

"Hey, you sneaky fuck," Cadence called out to me two days after Stitches had returned home.

I scrubbed my hand down my face as I stopped my walk through the outdoor commons and turned to her. The leaves were nearly off the trees, and it had cooled down substantially.

She walked quickly toward me, her face a mask of annoyance.

Me too, Claws. Me too.

"I just saw Seth." She stopped next to me.

"And?"

"And Sirena wasn't with him. I asked him and he laughed at me. Can you believe that? He was always a jerk. Where do you think she is? Church and Ashes aren't answering my texts either."

"Church is in therapy right now and Ashes is probably setting a Bible on fire," I said, looking to the overcast skies. "Why do you need them?"

"Weren't you listening to me? Seth was here without my sister. I want someone to go with me to his dorm to make sure she's there. I haven't seen her since that day he let me in."

I studied her and saw the worry in her eyes. For as annoying as she was, she sure cared for Sirena.

"You're asking me to go with you?"

"Yes." She tapped her foot impatiently.

"Not going," I said. "Can't."

"Why?" She glared at me. "I thought you gave a damn—"

"Listen, I care about her, OK? And that's why I can't go. She. . . she would never forgive me," I finished softly.

Cadence's frown deepened. "What does she need to forgive you for?"

"I just. . . I fucked up with her. She hates me because of it. I don't want to hurt her any more than I already have. She needs peace, not my ass skulking around frightening her." I looked at the ground and swallowed hard.

I wanted to see her though.

I wanted to apologize. Fuck, I was scared though. What would happen once I did? I'd been so close to telling Ashes that night and hadn't. The guys would banish me. Kick my ass. Probably kill me.

It was less than I deserved for my crimes.

"You don't know my sister," Cadence whispered. "She's a good person. She doesn't hold hate in her heart. I mean, she's with Seth. In his room. Not fighting him on it, and I'm sure that asshole is the one who tried to kill her when we were kids."

I let out a huff of air. She was right on that. He'd confessed all that shit to me when I'd stuffed her away in that coffin with him.

I remained quiet.

"Sin, what if he's hurting her and she can't get help? Please. I'm begging you to help me." Her eyes wavered as she stared up at me. "If you ever gave a damn about her, come with me. Take your hatred of me out of the equation."

I chewed the inside of my cheek for a moment before nodding.

"I'll go."

"Thank you." She let out a whoosh of air and grabbed my hand. She gave me a tug to move me, and I fell in step with her. Her hand moved up to my wrist, where she wrapped her fingers tightly as she continued to hold on.

"I said I'll go. You don't need to lead me like I'm on a leash," I muttered.

"You're a flight risk," she answered back. "Speaking of your disappearing acts, where do you go? Do you have friends outside the watchers?"

I sighed as we walked through the courtyard, several students looking at us curiously. And why shouldn't they? I was Sin. A watcher. And she was the new girl with her hand on me. No one touched a watcher.

I bet rumors would fly soon enough.

"I go to the lake. Or cemetery."

"Why?" She gave Melanie the finger as we passed by. I didn't know if they'd been introduced or not, but I was guessing they'd had an interaction or two given Cadence's waving middle finger as Melanie scowled back, her eyes dark and filled with quietly controlled rage.

Great. Like we needed more problems.

"To be alone. To think. To... pray."

"Pray?" She glanced at me. "You don't strike me as the praying type."

"We all pray, Claws. We're all begging for help in one way or another. Some of us do it on our knees. Others whisper it when they sleep, but trust me. Everyone prays."

She grunted but didn't push the subject.

"Do you like the cemetery?"

"Yes."

"Why?"

"It's quiet there. Everyone is already dead," I answered as we pushed through the doors in Asylum's building.

She released my arm in the lobby.

"Do you want to die too?" She turned and stared up at me.

I swallowed thickly and looked past her, feeling my eyes burn with impending tears. The last thing I wanted to do was cry in front of Cadence Lawrence. She'd never let me hear the end of it.

"I-I want to be normal," I finally whispered. "Only death makes everyone equal. So yeah. I guess in a way I do. I don't deserve to live."

"Why do you think that?" She crinkled her brows at me.

I shrugged. "I'm not a good person, Cadence."

"You're a prick," she said quickly.

I let out a soft laugh. "Yeah, guess I am."

She narrowed her eyes at me. "You're hiding something. It's really tearing you up. I've been hiding stuff too, so I know how it can eat you alive."

"What are you hiding?"

The corner of her lip twitched, her eyes sad. "I'll show you my skeletons if you show me yours."

We stared one another down for a moment.

Tell her. Just fucking tell her what you did to Sirena. She'll hate you for it and will tell the guys for you. If she doesn't kill you first.

"You'll hate me," I finally said.

"News flash. I already do," she countered.

I let out a sad laugh. "Go check on siren. Then maybe. . ."

"Fine." She turned and walked to the elevator. I didn't move an inch as I watched her push the button. The doors opened and she stepped inside.

"Get your ass over here. You're going with me."

"I'm not going up there," I said.

She slapped the door back open as it made to close.

"I'm sorry. I don't remember that being part of the agreement when you said you'd come with me. That meant all the way, Priest. Now get your ass in this elevator with me." Her voice lowered. "I-I don't know what I'll find up there. So please. Come with me. I need your help."

I hesitated for a moment.

I didn't want to know what awaited us in Asylum's room. If he'd hurt her. . . fuck.

I stepped forward and joined her in the elevator. "Fine."

"I knew you'd bend, Sinclair. You love her too."

I didn't argue anything back because she was right. I did.

So fucking much.

SIRENA

A knock on the door sounded out as I sat in my wheelchair. I still felt weak and promised Seth I wouldn't try to get up until someone was here with me.

The way he'd said *someone* made me think it might not be him.

That maybe Asylum would be back instead.

Or worse.

Sully and the men from the mirror.

I shook in my seat as I gripped the armrest, my breathing heavy.

The doorknob jiggled for a moment. I knew I'd seen Seth lock the door before he'd left this morning for classes.

He hadn't wanted to go, but I'd insisted. He'd done enough for me.

Plus, I'd seen him smacking himself in the head and muttering while he was brushing his teeth in the bathroom. The door had been cracked open, and I couldn't help peering inside from my perch on the bed.

Seth scared me.

Asylum terrified me.

But I was beginning to. . .

Hell, I didn't know.

I was leery for sure, but something had come alive inside me the past few weeks. I wanted him. Them? I didn't even know how to navigate that. I knew I cared for Seth. I'd missed him. Asylum was new to me, and he'd done such bad things to me. He had a lot to prove if he wanted me to open my arms for him. I didn't even know if I'd ever be able to. Trying to kill me was a big freaking deal.

I also wanted the watchers, as upset with them as I was.

I felt betrayed by them. And Sin. . . He'd put all of this into motion. He was the reason why I was locked in my mind. It was his fault Asylum had fucked me in front of those men and Stitches had wept.

I blamed him.

I blamed them all.

I didn't want to though. I just hurt. At least Seth and Asylum never made me wonder about the level of their depravity. I knew what they were. It was all beginning to fall into place. The drawn curtains all the time in his home when we were kids. All the times he said I couldn't come into his home and play, so we'd played at my house or outside instead or when his house was empty of his mom.

An old memory filled my mind.

Seth was late. He was supposed to meet me at the park to swing.

I looked to the blue sky and came to a decision. I was going to go to his house and see where he was. Quickly, I walked back to our street and to his house.

I went onto his front porch and knocked on his door. When no one answered, I knocked again, worry seeping through me.

Where are you?

Seth was never late to see me.

I reached out and tried the door. It swung open easily. I knew the rules. I wasn't allowed inside his home without him, but I was scared something was wrong, so I stepped inside and climbed the stairs to his room.

The house was silent.

No one was in his room, and it was tidy just like it always was.

When I stepped back out, the stairway at the end of the hall caught my eye. Seth said we weren't allowed there. To play in the attic. That it was dangerous. That the door at the top of the stairs was to remain locked at all times.

Something pulled me in that direction.

I went to it and took the first step upward.

"What are you doing?" A warm hand wrapped around my wrist and pulled me back down.

I stared up into the pretty face of Seth's mom, Jackie.

"I-I'm looking for Seth," I said. "I thought he might be up there."

"No, honey. He's not," she answered tightly, giving the attic door a fearful look. "Seth is. . .busy right now. He'll come see you tomorrow, OK? Why don't you go home and tell your mom we really loved that pie she sent over yesterday and that I'd like the recipe if she's willing to share it."

She led me back downstairs and straight to the front door.

"OK," I said, frowning. "Can you tell Seth to call me?"

"I will. Please don't come in here without someone, OK? It's important. Promise?"

I nodded. "Promise."

She offered me a smile before she closed and locked the door, leaving me to stare at it. After a moment, I stepped off the step and walked across the lawn to my house next door. Something made me look behind me though. To the small attic window. It was always boarded up, but today, two slats were missing.

And there he was.

Seth.

Staring back at me from it.

I paused, confused, before I waved at him.

He cocked his head for a long time and stared back at me before he raised his hand and waved.

Another knock on the door.

"Seth? Someone's here," I called out feebly in my mind, not knowing if his apparent superpower reached this far. *"I'm scared. Please. Come back."*

The door clicked and creaked open.

I sucked in a sharp breath and squeezed my eyelids closed.

Please God, don't let it be Sully and his monsters. Please don't send me back. Please. Asylum. Seth. Help me. HELP.

If ever was a time for Asylum to prove himself, now was it.

I trembled in my seat as warm fingers brushed against my cheek.

"Rina?" Cady's soft voice called out. "Hey. It's me."

How. . .How is she here? Am I being taken home?

I don't want to go.

I'm scared.

"Open your eyes," she pleaded softly. "Come on, Rina."

I peeked through my lashes to see her worried face peering back at me.

She was really here.

And so was he.

Sinful.

The one who had stuffed me into that damn box in the mausoleum and left me to scream. To be hurt by Sully and those monsters behind the mirror. They saw me. They saw us. Doing things. Things that made me cry. As fuzzy as those memories still were, I knew it was sick and twisted.

I shook as I locked my eyes on him.

He crinkled his brows and took a small step toward me. His hair was tied up neatly into that blond bun atop his head. Nose ring. Lip ring. Ears pierced. Hands that forced me into a fucking box and lips that whispered his sins. His truths and his lies.

Sinful.

Pitiful.

I rocked, my breathing so fast I thought I was going to pass out.

My head spun.

"Rina. Hey. Come on. Let's go. I want to get you out of here. I have some money. We can run. I won't let them find us. I brought Sin to help." She reached forward and unlocked the brake on my wheelchair.

I couldn't leave. Not with him.

I rocked forward and tumbled out of my chair as Cady made to wheel me out.

"Damnit! Sin! Help me. I-I have to get her out of here. Please. Please help me save her." Cady's voice cracked as I curled into a tight ball, my face wet with tears.

Seth. Asylum. Where are you? Please. WHERE ARE YOU?

If someone had asked me anytime before this year if I'd call to Seth for help, I'd have told them they were nuts, but Sin had done something to me that had shattered my very being.

He was the reason for my current trauma. For Stitches's. For all this madness.

Seth and Asylum had been there to guide me through that darkness while Sin. . . I didn't even know what he'd done while I'd suffered. While I'd hid. While my body had been exposed to those disgusting monsters behind the mirror.

"Fuck," Sin snarled, his warm hands lifting me.

I couldn't take it. I couldn't take his touch.

A scream tore from my lips as he held me against his body.

"Siren. Stop. Come on," he whispered frantically as I continued to scream. Cady covered her ears, tears trickling from her eyes.

"Sinful! Sinful!"

"Fuck. Baby—come on," Sin continued as he rocked me in his arms. "Don't. Don't scream. Damnit! Fuck! Siren—"

The door to the room slammed open and I was torn from Sin's arms.

"What the fuck are you doing in my room?" Seth snarled. I gripped around his wrist tightly with one hand.

No. *Asylum.*

I clung to him and buried my face in his neck, his arms moving to wind tightly around me.

"Shh, firefly. All is well. No more tears. No more screams." He was on his knees as he whispered to me. "It's Asylum. I'm here. Your screams belong to me, remember? They're mine. You're giving them away for free and that's unacceptable. Shh. Quiet. There you go. There you go, my love. We're OK."

I stopped screaming as I breathed heavily.

I didn't know what the hell was wrong with me. I'd been trapped in a coffin overnight with Asylum. He'd tried to kill me years ago... and yet, he was who I wanted. Seth. Asylum. I'd snapped. I'd completely lost my damn mind in that box.

That was the only reasoning I could come up with that made any sense to me.

"Get the fuck out of my room," Asylum said in a dangerous voice after a moment.

"No. I'm taking her with me—" Cady choked out, her voice trembling.

"And where would you go, my dear Cady cat? Huh? That old cottage your father used to take you to when you were children?" Asylum tsked as I twisted my fingers tighter into his uniform. The white button down strained against his neck, giving way to a red welt from my grip, but he didn't seem to care.

I loved my sister so much... but I couldn't leave. We had too much to do here. If Sin was going to be there, I definitely couldn't go.

"H-how did you know?" Cady asked thickly.

"Because we fucking do," Asylum snapped back. "The road trip into Canada? The detour if you need it? The friend you have in Chicago? What's his name again? Trent?" Asylum scoffed. "His time isn't now. He's much too busy weaving his own web. You would be caught within hours of taking her from here."

"You don't know that," Cady said. "We could make it—"

"Everett would get you, Claws," Sin said softly. "He would. He has eyes everywhere. You'd both suffer then. His underground stretches across the country. No place is safe from him if he wants you."

"Fuck Everett Church. I'd get you first and believe me, you don't want to be caught stealing from us. Unlike Everett Church, we don't take prisoners to keep. We take them to kill." Asylum tensed beneath me.

I pressed against him harder, wanting him to stop talking to my sister that way.

"I'm sorry," he whispered to me.

Don't talk to her like that.

"We just don't want anyone taking you," he murmured quickly. "We just got you back, and we have no plans of ever letting you go again."

Please make Sin leave. I want my sister. I'm afraid of him. Please. Make him go.

"Sinclair, get the fuck out of my room," Asylum snapped as soon as the words were floating around in my head. "Now."

"Whatever," he muttered after a moment of silence. "Come on, Claws."

"She stays. You leave." Asylum adjusted his hold on me.

"I'm not leaving both of them with you," Sin said, his voice wavering.

He was worried.

"I don't believe you were given an option. If you don't leave, I might spill your little secret. Pretty sure you're not ready for that to come out." Asylum's voice was low and threatening as he enunciated each word.

I shuddered against him, remembering the betrayal. Remembering Sin shoving that pill into my mouth that made my body weak and tired. Remembering that mirror on the wall as I was violated in front of it.

Sinful.

So fucking Sinful!

"Go. They'll find out soon enough. Let's not be so hasty in our reveal, Sinclair."

Sin's heavy boots thudded across the floor before the door closed softly.

What secret?

"The one with the box, firefly," Asylum murmured. "You remember."

Did the watchers know he was doing it?

"No, my love. They did not."

I swallowed thickly at his words. The watchers hadn't known. Sin did it on his own. Dante... he hadn't wanted me hurt. Ashes. Stitches.

"You'll see them soon," Asylum assured me softly. "For now, let's see Cady cat, OK?" He lifted me and placed me back into my wheelchair and leaned in and licked away my tears before his lips brushed against mine.

"There's our princess." His blue eyes sparkled as he pulled away and we stared at one another. "I'll be right back, OK? Have a visit with your sister."

He got to his feet without another word to me. "I'll be right outside. Don't try anything. I'll know if you do."

Cady said nothing as Asylum backed away. He disappeared through the doorway a moment later, leaving me alone with her.

Immediately, she kneeled in front of me.

"Hey, Rina. I-I'm sorry if I scared you. I didn't mean to. I know Asylum is really scary, but if you want to leave, we can. I know we can make it."

I gave a slight shake of my head.

She sucked in a sharp breath and took my hand in hers.

"You want to stay?"

I squeezed her hand. A tear trickled down her cheek.

"Rina, there are so many monsters here. It's not safe for any of us. Church told me about his father. He's... terrifying. If he hurts you..."

I gave her hand another squeeze.

"Please," Cady whispered, wiping at her eyes with her other hand. "Stitches. That guy? He's so messed up over you being with Seth. He-He tried to hang himself. He almost died from it."

My heart lurched at that information. I hadn't known that was why he was at the facility with me. He'd tried to kill himself because of me. *Because of Sinclair Priest.*

Nausea rolled heavily through my guts.

He'd held me. Tried to protect me.

Not Sinful though. He'd thrown me to the wolves as a meal. Stitches almost died because of what Sin had done. His list of offenses kept rising.

"It's just not safe here, Rina. I want us to be safe."

I leaned in and rested my forehead against hers. She sucked in a breath as her hand trembled in mine.

"Stay," I rasped in a trembling voice.

She let out a soft sob and nodded her forehead against mine. "OK. OK. We'll stay."

We held onto one another for a long time.

"Rina?" she finally whispered, her forehead still against mine.

I said nothing, waiting for her to talk again.

"D-Did Sin h-hurt you? Is that why you're scared of him?"

I shook at the mention of his name.

She sniffled. "Did he put you in that coffin?" She pulled away and stared at me. "Did he help Asylum?"

I remained quiet, at an impasse. I loved the watchers. I knew I did. If they found out Sin had done that to me and had lied, they'd throw him out. Or worse.

It would hurt them. They were family.

I couldn't do that to them.

I was always a secret keeper.

And this would just be another I'd keep. For now.

"OK," Cady whispered, offering me a shaky smile. "OK. I'll find out another way then. You don't have to tell me your secrets. Not even about Seth."

I blinked at her. She knew about the shovel with him. Or rather, Asylum. Maybe it was just her suspicions.

I wasn't going to confirm or deny that either.

For now, all the secrets in the world were safe with me.

ASYLUM

I smiled at Sin in the lobby.

"I'm surprised you're waiting," I said, stopping next to him to look out the window.

"Just in case." He grunted.

"Of what?" I let out a snort as I *listened*. "Oh, I see. You think you'd be able to stop me if I went on a killing spree. Cute, Priest. Inaccurate, but cute nonetheless."

"Why don't you just let her come home?" he asked softly. "You promised Church and the guys."

"I did, didn't I?" I laughed softly. "I always keep my word too. My little firefly will be back in no time to light up the dark paths of the watchers. It just hasn't played out the way it should yet. Have a little patience."

He breathed out, a muscle thrumming along his jaw.

"You don't touch her when you're alone with her, do you?" Sin's voice was soft as he continued to stare out the window.

"No," I answered simply.

"You won't right?" He turned to me, so much turmoil rolling off him I had to take a step back.

Lines are fucking twisted. Pull it back. I exhaled, trying to push away the emotions swirling around me.

It's hard. You know that.

I hate feeling, and you *know* that.

Liar.

Fuck you. You know what I mean.

The noise stopped and the emotions rolling around me ended.

I offered Sin a smile. "Do you want me to do it?"

"No," he said, looking back out the window.

"Why do you lie, Sinclair? You were begging for your tongue to slip to Cady cat. Because you know. . . she'll tell on you. She'll lay it all out so you don't have to. Get on your knees for me and ask me to tell."

"Fuck you," he growled. "I'm not getting on my knees for you."

"You will." I cocked my head, listening again. "Cady cat is asking my firefly if you hurt her. If you're the one who put her into the coffin with me."

He visibly swallowed and balled his hands into tight fists.

"It's going to hurt when you fall. Don't worry though. We'll be there to catch you."

"Why are you like this?" Sin whispered.

"Why am I like what? Myself? Who else could I possibly be?" I let out a cackle. "Do you want me to role-play with you, Sinclair?"

He shot me a sour look. "You know what I mean. Where's Seth?"

I widened my eyes at him. "Seth? Why? Do you like him more than me? I'd understand if you said yes just because most people do tend to like him more. However, they don't know him like we do. They don't know what he's capable of. How much he loves to hurt people who deserve it. He's the right hand of Death."

"Then who are you?" Sin raised his brows at me.

"Me? I'm the left hand."

Sin's gray eyes stayed trained on me. "You asked me why I don't tell the truth. Why don't you?"

"I don't need to tell truths. I show them," I said with a shrug. "Expect the unexpected with us. We like to be fun like that."

"Are you really fucking touched in the head? The voices? How many are there?" He narrowed his eyes at me. His anger was showing.

"We are many," I said in a soft voice. "But I am me, and he is he. We are we."

He let out a huff of air and went back to staring out the window.

"So you're Asylum?"

"I'm always Asylum."

"And Seth is. . .?"

"*A mirage*," I said, smiling at him as he glanced over at me. "He is he. He is we. He isn't here."

"You have him chained up inside your head?"

I laughed at that. "I do so enjoy these games. So many people have it wrong. It's always been a good time for us."

He sighed. "So you're Asylum and Seth. Who else?"

"I'm only Asylum," I said, cocking my head at him. "And you're Sin. And the walls are puke green. I really much rather them be yellow."

"I hate talking to you," he muttered. "Why do you speak in riddles? Isn't it exhausting?"

"Life is exhausting. This is simply me passing the time." I grew quiet as I stared out the window with him. "You terrify her. It used to be me who scared her. Now it's you. Do you like that it's you, Sinclair?"

"No," he whispered. "I don't."

I nodded. "Isabella. She never feared you."

"She should have."

I clicked my tongue. "Indeed. I did warn her."

He turned to me. "What?"

"Her and I. . . we were friends. We went way back. I told her you were going to kill her. She didn't believe me. Narcissism and all that had a way of blocking reality for her. Pity, but really, she had it coming, didn't she? After killing the baby. After that little girl. After. . . Church."

Sin's bottom lip wobbled as he stared me down.

"It hurt, and for that, I'm sorry. But trust me when I tell you it had to happen that way so that you could stand here with me now.

So that later, you could find what your heart was so desperately craving. A pretty raven-haired girl with big, colorful eyes. A siren. A ghost."

His eyes glistened, and he quickly turned away from me and wiped at them.

"She says your name in her sleep," I said. "Calls for you. Begs you."

"Stop."

"Her voice. It's so soft and sweet. So innocent. *Sinful. Please. Please, Sinful. Help me.* That's what she screamed in her head when she realized you'd trapped her with me. She begged to God for you to come back and save her from her fate."

"STOP." He punched the wall, cracking his knuckles open. His blood dripped out from the broken skin as his body quaked.

I smiled at that. "My point is, it's easy to get lost in a nightmare. You'll wake up, Sinclair, and all will be well. I promise. . . just as soon as I cut you free from the ropes."

"If you're trying to comfort me, you're fucking shit at it," he snarled, wiping the blood onto his pants.

I looked to my left and smiled at the quick flash of light.

Stop playing. Get back to Rinny.

You're no fun.

Rinny. Now. Or I'll go to her.

I sighed.

Fucking voices.

"You could always fuck Cady cat," I said abruptly.

He glared at me. "Not fucking happening."

"Well, it was just a thought. I knew you'd say no. She's a little too wild for my tastes too." I frowned and cocked my head.

Secrets. Lots of secrets. A man. Dark hair. A blonde girl. A queen. Hiding. He's hiding.

The image faded. I tugged at my hair, irritated. Having these little flashes always irritated me.

"Message from another world?" Sin asked.

"Yes." I backed away from him. "I'm leaving."

"I figured."

"Halloween. You'll hang. You'll burn. You'll scream. Best prepare yourself. Retribution is coming, Sinclair. It's going to get you."

He stared at me as I walked backward from him. I offered him a smile and cocked my head.

"You'll get on your knees for me that night. You'll beg. I suggest making your peace with the consequences. *She knows.*" I reached the elevator and hit the button. The doors opened, and I stepped inside, taking in the fear on his face.

"And she's going to tell on you, Sinclair. Don't kill this one though. She means well. If you hurt her again, I'll kill you. Slowly." The doors closed before he could say anything to me.

Not that he was going to.

The fear of what was to come was already strangling him.

†

"Open," I instructed as I sat on the bed facing my firefly the following night.

She parted her lips for me, and I dropped a piece of orange into her mouth.

"Chew."

She did as I told her and swallowed and parted her lips for me to feed her again. I loved feeding my little firefly princess. I liked taking care of her. This felt a million times more enjoyable than smashing a shovel over her head.

"Come," I said softly, placing the piece of orange between my lips. I wanted to know what she'd do. If she'd be brave to come take it from me.

She stared at the orange in my mouth before she shifted forward, her eyes locked on mine.

My cock ached in my sweatpants.

She was such a sweet, scared kitten. It turned me on in ways no one else ever had.

I waited patiently for her as she leaned in.

She was so terrified. Trembling. But so brave too.

She wanted it.

Her lips brushed against mine as she took the orange from my mouth, sending a zing of electricity straight to my dick.

I watched as she moved back and chewed the orange, her eyes never leaving me.

"I want you," I said.

She blinked at me.

"You said I was yours," I continued. "That we were. That you were ours."

Everything about her was as silent as that tomb we'd been in.

"Sirena," I whispered her name. "You're too quiet. I don't like when you're quiet."

No noise. No sound. Nothing in my fucking head.

I tugged at my hair, growing more frustrated the longer I sat there.

"Talk to me. I hate your silence," I said, releasing my hair. "I fucking loathe it. We hate it. Do you want to scream for me? For us?"

She gave a tiny shake of her head.

I didn't like to be told no.

That was all the communication I needed.

I launched myself at her and put her on her back and stared down at her as her chest heaved.

"I want to fuck you the right way," I growled against her lips. "I want you to remember what it feels like to have a bit of crazy inside you."

Her breasts brushed against my chest as she breathed deeply with parted lips.

"If you don't want me to touch you, tell me to stop," I said, whispering in her ear. "And if I don't, scream it." I trailed my fingers along the curve of her full breast over her nightgown. Her breath hitched as she stared up at me.

I cocked my head at her, drinking in the way she reacted to me as I trailed my hand beneath her nightie and to her panties.

So terrified yet intrigued.

And wet. She was so fucking wet.

My fingers slid through her folds with ease.

Asylum. . . stop.

No.

Don't do this. She's not ready.

Her pussy tells another story.

I shoved the voice out of my head and pressed against her clit. A tiny, sexy whimper left her lips.

"Do you know why we're doing this, firefly?"

She said nothing as I rubbed her clit slowly.

"It's because I have to give you back soon. I don't want to do it with you never having known what it's like to be loved by me."

"You? Not Seth?"

I breathed out. There was our princess.

"Me." I licked along her lips, tasting the orange she'd had as I fingered her hot cunt. "Do you want to find out what my love is like, firefly?"

"I feel like I'm losing my mind. Please. I'm scared."

I chuckled softly at that as she quivered beneath me. I slid my finger into her tight heat, making her arch a little against my chest.

"Don't worry, baby. I love crazy." I crushed my lips against hers, my finger buried to the knuckle inside her as I tangled my tongue against hers.

I positioned myself better between her legs, pushing them apart as I withdrew my finger from her weeping pussy and pressed my hard length against her. She let out a gasp, her body shaking as I rubbed shamelessly against her wetness.

"We've fucked before," I breathed out against her lips. "This is nothing."

"Seth said we wouldn't—"

"I'm not fucking Seth. He doesn't speak for me." I bit her lip hard, earning a silent cry from her as her blood tainted my tongue. In a flash, I had her on her stomach and her ass in the air, her nightgown pushed up over her hips.

"Fuck, your panties are soaked," I murmured, taking in the wet spot that screamed at me to taste it on her white silk.

Fuck it. I was a wild animal when I wanted to come.

I buried my face into her silk clad heat and inhaled deeply before sucking the material into my mouth, my tongue brushing against her warm pussy.

My eyes practically rolled into the back of my head as I devoured the way she tasted.

Just like fucking candy.

A sweet princess.

I was losing it. It was hard to control myself. She struggled against me, falling to her stomach as I continued to ravish her.

I wasn't going to let her go. I loved it when she struggled against it. It made me want her even more.

I want her to come in my mouth.

I need to drink her down and make her a part of me. Forever.

Forever girl.

Don't. Control it. Don't do this. Not yet.

I can't. . . I can't fucking stop. She's letting me.

She's scared. Stop.

She wants it.

Together. Remember?

Please. . . I need this. She needs this. She needs to know. . .

I shoved her panties down her thighs and licked up her ass, enjoying the way she squirmed for me. The way she tried to get away.

Spreading her pert ass cheeks apart, I dipped my tongue into every hole she had, feasting like I was a saint at my last meal. Her breathing was ragged as she tensed her body, letting me do what I came to do. She knew she couldn't escape me.

I pushed my tongue beyond the tight ring of muscle of her backside, enjoying everything about her ass. Fucking it with my tongue. Eating it. Plunging two fingers in and out of her tight pussy.

That was a gourmet meal.

She shook violently beneath me as she came all over my hand. Having a girl shoot her load on me was worth the effort.

I removed my tongue from her ass and hefted her up so she was on her knees again and went straight to her pussy, drinking down her release as she shook beneath my tongue.

And this was dessert.

Sucking. Licking. Her clit was so swollen. Each nibble and suck made her jump.

I'd finally made it to heaven.

When I knew she'd had enough, I slowed to a stop, having cleaned her thoroughly with my tongue. I pulled her down beside me and held her against my body, her back to my stomach.

I wasn't going to fuck her.

I enjoyed the pain my aching cock brought me. It meant that when I finally got her again, it would be so fucking worth it.

She hadn't forgiven me for the shovel incident. That was fine. I didn't deserve her forgiveness for it, but I would make her see she was meant to be mine. I remembered the first time she acknowledged my existence. The way she'd stopped to wave up at me as I watched her from the attic window.

"Sleep," I commanded softly to her. "My forever girl. Tomorrow will be busy."

Her body relaxed against mine as I held her.

I hadn't been lying. Tomorrow would be busy.

Tomorrow, we'd see the watchers.

ASHES

"Can we talk?" Cady dropped down in the seat next to me at the watchers' table.

I looked up from my lunch. "Yeah. What's up?"

She stretched her arms across the table and leaned forward. "I spent some time with Rina last night. With Sin."

I blinked at her words. I hadn't been home when they'd gotten there. Stitches and I had gone for a ride on our motorcycles along the edge of the lake to burn off some steam. He was so quiet since coming home that I felt like he needed to get off campus.

He'd seemed happier once we were on the road, but he still hadn't been himself. I'd tried talking to him, but he was quiet and simply shook his head at me and smoked a joint.

I was surprised she hadn't told me sooner she'd been to see Sirena.

"OK. What's up?" I asked, hoping I didn't sound like I was a lost, eager puppy and she was someone with treats.

"I-I tried to take her." Cady gave me a worried look.

"Wait. What?"

She launched into her story, ending with Sirena screaming from Sin getting too close to her.

"You guys still don't have any leads on who helped Seth put her into that coffin?" She leaned in, her voice soft.

I shook my head. "No. No one is talking. I can see why. It's Asylum. He probably has dirt on them or threatened whoever it was. A guy who can pop out an eyeball with a fork and make you eat it probably isn't one anyone wants to betray."

She chewed her bottom lip for a moment before her words came pouring out of her mouth. "I think it was Sin."

I blinked rapidly at her words, not sure I'd heard them correctly.

"What?"

"I think it was Sin," she repeated. "Rina hasn't spoken in years. Not a single word. He got near her in the beginning, and she kept saying *Sinful*. Her reaction to him then was off, all things considered. Then, last night, she screamed and curled into a tight ball when he'd tried to help her. To add to it, Asylum told him he'd tell his secret if he didn't leave. Sin is a fighter. He didn't fight. He looked at Rina and left the room. I-I really think it was him. Or that he knows who did it."

I frowned at her words. They made sense, but Sin wouldn't have done that to hurt her. That was too far, even for him. I couldn't deny that I'd been suspicious of him lately though.

I shook my head, trying to clear it. "He wouldn't have done that to her."

"Come on, Asher! I know you're smart. Think about it, OK? I know he's your friend, but I'm telling you that something isn't right."

She was right. Sin had been acting oddly since Sirena's incident with Asylum. My guts churned with the implications of what it could mean. I didn't want it to be true.

I'd beat him to death if he had a hand in any of this because this shit had snowballed into Stitches trying to kill himself and Church and I nearly losing our minds over it all.

Breathing out, I flipped my lighter open and closed, my leg bouncing.

Five times.

Breathe.

Open. Close. Open. Close. Open. . .

"What's going on?" Church asked, sitting down beside me. "And why are you at our table?"

"Oh please." Cady rolled her eyes at him. "We live together. I'll sit here with you too, dick for brains."

Church scowled at her and focused on me. "What's wrong?"

I cleared my throat. I wasn't going to put a bug in his ear on this. Not yet. I needed to figure it out before I started shit. I shot Cady a warning look.

She slumped back in her seat and gave me a slight incline of her head.

Thank God, she got it.

"Nothing. Cady said Asylum let her see Sirena last night."

"Really?" Church sat forward. "And?"

"And nothing. She's really in there though. Lucid. She-She spoke," Cady muttered.

I leaned forward too. Cady had said she'd screamed. She hadn't said she'd spoken too.

"What did she say?" Church demanded, his hands fisted on the table.

"Only one word that matters. *Stay.* I said I wanted to leave. She said stay. So I guess that means I'm your problem now." She shot Church a forced smile.

He snorted. "The fuck you are. Get lost, Claws."

"Enough." I sighed.

Sin approached with Stitches at his side. I shot Cady another look, and she raised an eyebrow at me. She was as unpredictable as Church was when he was pissed.

The guys sat down, and Stitches pushed the piece of pizza around on his tray.

"How's today going?" I asked him.

"Fine." He shot me a quick smile that didn't quite reach his eyes.

"You know, I don't like the couch," Cady said. "You guys should bunk together." She looked at Sin. "Don't you think it would be nice of you to let Stitches bunk in your room so I can have a room?"

"No," Sin said immediately. "We were here first. Sleep outside if you don't like the couch."

She scowled at him. "You're such a prick."

"You can have the attic," Church said.

"Oh shit. I forgot about the attic." I looked to Sin who shrugged.

"The attic? Is it haunted or something?" Cady frowned.

"No, it's actually really nice up there. We store a few things for initiations and such up there, but that won't be hard to put into the basement. It's the locked doorway on the right side of the hall," I said. "It's finished. I mean, it's not a massive spot, but you'd have your own space."

"And bathroom? Do I get one of those?" She looked at each of us. "Or are you guys willing to share to give me one?"

"You could just get a dorm," Stitches murmured. "They have some with bathrooms if you're not a complete head case. Or if you suck Sully's dick good enough."

"Or room with Sirena," Sin added.

"She's rooming with Asylum." Cady looked at Sin. "Remember? We were there yesterday."

"Tell me about your visit." Church perked up.

"Yeah." Sin grunted, dropping his burger onto his plate. "She's fine since I know that's your next question."

Church nodded, a look of relief sweeping over him.

"Fine? Define fine," Stitches said thickly.

"I don't know. She rocked like she's been doing. She. . . was Sirena. Mostly. She seems coherent." Sin pushed his entire tray away.

"She screamed when Sin got too close to her," Cady whispered.

A muscle thrummed along Sin's jaw.

Damnit, Cady.

"I'm sure she just has a little PTSD," I said, hoping to soothe any doubts because I knew Dante Church. The look on his face and the way he was staring at Sin let me know the wheels were spinning in his head.

We needed proof that Sin fucked everything up.

The sickness washed over me again.

Please, God, don't let it be true.

"Praying so early in the day, Valentine?" Asylum's voice cut through my thoughts. I looked at him and dropped my fork as Sirena clutched his arm at his side.

I scrambled to my feet the same time Church did, both of us practically tripping over ourselves in the process.

"Easy. We're just passing through. Heard you praying to God and figured I'd make an appearance." Asylum flashed his smile at me.

At least I assumed we were dealing with Asylum.

The Seth version was much more normal than the Asylum version was.

Or at least he seemed to be.

But my heaven. . .

She kept her eyes trained on her shiny black patent shoes. She was perfect in her uniform. It took everything I had not to reach for her and haul her against my chest and never let her go.

"Hey, heaven," I said softly. "It's good to see you out."

Asylum looked at her and cocked his head. "She says it's good to see you too."

"What?" I looked from Sirena to Asylum.

"It's what she said." He shrugged. "Also, she's still upset and has questions."

"What questions?" Church demanded, stepping around the table. "We'll answer anything she wants to know." He hadn't even batted a lash at Asylum speaking for her like he was inside her head.

She kept her eyes downcast as Asylum tightened his hold on her.

"She's uncomfortable right now. We'll all chat later when there aren't so many watchers." Asylum took her hand in his and made to pull her away.

"Wait," Church called out.

Asylum stopped and turned back to Church, a smile on his face.

"She's not telling you who it was, Dante. She's decided to keep this secret for just a little bit longer. Isn't she sweet? She's loyal like that. She's kept my secrets for years. The good news is, I don't think you'll have long to wait. . . if you play your cards right."

"Son of a bitch," Cady said, getting to her feet and glaring at Asylum. He smiled back at her. I didn't have time to deal with this shit. I needed her. Shit. I needed her so bad it was choking me.

"Heaven," I said, taking a tentative step forward. "Please. We need to know who helped Seth that night."

"Asylum," he said tightly. "Stop calling me Seth. We don't like that."

"Fine. *Asylum,*" I corrected. "Who helped him, baby?"

I reached for her, wondering if Asylum would stop me. When he didn't, I twisted my fingers around hers and pulled her hand off Asylum's arm.

"Please," I whispered, noting Sin had stiffened at the table. The movement made that nausea twist tighter in my guts.

Tell me.

I traced the letters onto the palm of her hand, terrified of what her answer would be.

Her gaze snapped up and locked on mine, sending butterflies spiraling through my heart.

Her brows twitched for a moment before she squeezed my hand in hers and backed away into Asylum's waiting arms.

"I told you," Asylum murmured. "She's loyal."

I nodded tightly and backed away.

I needed to get her alone. That was my plan. If I got her alone, I'd get it from her.

"I like your fire, Ashes." Asylum winked at me. "See you on Halloween."

I watched as he led her away.

She'd needed him to guide her. She wasn't going willingly. At least that was what I told myself as he urged her forward.

She hadn't forgiven him for shit.

In fact, she was still scared of him.

He knew it.

But that bastard knew a hell of a lot more, and before the week was over, I'd have the answers too.

CHURCH

"For fuck's sake, Claws," I snapped, stomping over to her as she pinned a bat decoration to the top of the fence. "They're bats, not fucking cats. Bats fly. Cats sit." I tore down the decoration and pushed it into her chest. "Hang it. Don't pin it."

"OK, Susie fucking homemaker," she muttered, giving me a scowl.

I turned away from her but not before I saw her stick her tongue out at me.

She drove me to the edge of my fucking sanity.

This party had to be perfect. Asylum was bringing my specter. I had every intention of getting close to her tonight to. . . *fuck*. Anything? Everything? Beg her to fucking love me?

I shook away the thought. I wasn't that sort of guy, but with her? I could see myself falling to my knees and crawling wherever the hell she wanted to take me.

Completely out of character for me.

Fuck it.

She was worth it.

I watched as Cady hung the bat from a string from the tree in our backyard.

"Claws! Bats fucking hang!" I shouted at her as she hung it head up. "Haven't you ever seen a fucking bat before?"

She gave me the finger. "I'll hang your ass from this tree if you don't shut the hell up!"

"It's for Sirena," I snapped back. "Do it fucking right or don't do it all."

She sighed and pulled the bat down and hung it upside down. I let out a breath and nodded.

Finally.

I looked to Ashes who was setting up wood for a bonfire. He loved building this fire. It was the only time we really let him near flame on campus. Troubled thoughts masked his face. I'd been suspicious more than ever of what Sin had been up to, especially after hearing again that Sirena screamed when he was near her and the way his face twisted when the words were put out in the open.

I didn't want to think one of my best friends hurt the girl we all loved, but I was beginning to really consider it.

And it was pissing me off.

Add to it the fact he'd been MIA through a lot of this shit, and I'd say I was fed up with all of it. I'd do anything for him, even beat the fuck out of him to set him right.

I wasn't sure if I could forgive him if he'd had a hand in Sirena because when it boiled down to it, it affected all of us. I'd cut my brother out of his fucking closet because of this shit and begged him to come back to us.

I couldn't forgive this shit.

Someone would pay.

Maybe even with their life.

I really hoped Sin hadn't fucked up. It was all beginning to roll together though. His disappearance the night of. His withdrawn behavior. The way Sirena screamed when he was near. Asylum promising to take something from us and return Sirena.

Yeah. Shit wasn't looking good for him.

Tonight, I'd get my answers. I had a plan.

I walked to Ashes, and he straightened as I approached. Stitches rose from his chair on the patio as I gestured to him and came toward us.

"What's up?" Ashes asked.

Sin had disappeared again, but I looked around anyway to make sure we were alone. Cady caught my eye and approached. Typically, I'd tell her to piss off, but gave her a head nod to join us.

"Secret squirrel meeting?" she asked, stopping at Stitches's side.

He glanced at her. Stitches wasn't as familiar with her as we were. He'd been odd since he'd returned to us. I figured it was all the trauma from nearly dying and the fact he was somewhere inside his mind, fighting his bi-polar.

He never would have been this way though if someone hadn't fucked with my specter.

"I want to get Sirena alone at the party," I said. "I want to get her to tell me who helped Asylum that night."

Ashes widened his eyes at me. "Asylum won't let her out of his sight. You know that."

"That's why we need a plan to get her alone. Cady, I think you're perfect for the job," I continued.

She beamed at me. It was the first genuine smile she'd ever given me. "I'll do it."

I nodded at her. "Perfect. All you need to do is lure her away. Say you want to dance with her or just talk. If Asylum let you near her twice now, he'll do it again."

"And if he doesn't?" Ashes asked, glancing around at each of us in the circle we'd formed.

"I'll distract him," Stitches said quietly. "I need to talk to him anyway a-about some-some stuff."

I studied my brother for a moment. He looked sick to his stomach. He caught my eye and quickly looked to his feet.

Anger boiled inside of me. This wasn't him. Even at his worst, he'd always crack a smile and a joke. Stitches was deep in some internal turmoil, and I wasn't going to rest until someone was punished for it.

"I think it was Sin," I murmured, locking eyes with Ashes. "I think he's the one who helped Asylum."

"I think so too," Ashes agreed softly, wincing.

I looked to Cady. "Don't fail in getting her away tonight, OK? We need this. It's closure in a way. It would be nice to know the cunt who hurt her isn't walking around campus like nothing is wrong. And if it's Sin?" I breathed out, feeling sick.

"We'll punish him," Ashes finished. "No one goes unpunished. Not for this."

"Then why don't we punish Asylum too?" Cady asked.

"Who knows? Maybe we will," I said, catching a glimpse of Sin coming down the path to the house from the direction of the cemetery. "When you get specter, bring her to the cemetery. Got it? The old willow. I'll wait there for you."

Cady nodded.

"You'll leave her with me," I continued.

"With us," Ashes corrected. "Because I'll be there too."

I looked at Stitches. "Do you want to be there?"

He chewed his bottom lip for a moment. "Yes. . . but no. I think it's best if I keep Asylum distracted."

I nodded. I was agreeable to that.

"Just. . . tell her I'm sorry, OK?" he said, his big, dark eyes wavering. "She'll know what I'm talking about."

I wanted to get him to open up to me, but I knew he wouldn't until he was ready, so I agreed as Sin stepped onto the patio.

"Hey," he called out, eyeing us.

"Where were you?" I asked, breaking away from everyone.

"Out," he answered without missing a beat. "I went into town."

He sparked up a joint and smoked. He had a guy in town who hooked him up with weed whenever we needed it. It was good shit, so I wasn't going to bitch at him for it.

I'd save that for later if my suspicions were right.

"You know, once we get specter back, we still have two occurrences to give her," I said, leaning against the patio railing beside him. I took the joint from him and inhaled a hit, relishing the high. "What do you think? You going to give her the one you owe her?"

I was fishing. Hard.

He let out a soft huff. "No. I'm done with that shit."

"Why?"

"Because she's been through enough. Let Stitches do what he needs to do. I'm out."

I nodded. He wasn't going to break. That was fine. I'd try another way.

"You've been distant since she was hurt. Do you want to talk about it?"

He smoked some more as Stitches and Ashes helped Cady with decorations.

"Yes. I-I want to talk to you, but I can't. Not right now." He hung his head. "Fuck, man. Just... Fuck. It's hard for me."

"Well, we're here when you're ready." I pushed away from the railing. "It's better to admit your faults before someone finds them. That always ends badly."

He nodded tightly, his Adam's apple bobbing. "I know."

"Good. Don't forget it." I left him and went back to helping get shit ready for tonight. I adored this party every year. Halloween was my favorite, but tonight would be something different.

Tonight would be about truths and what fucking happens when you failed to tell them.

I sent out a silent prayer to whoever the hell was listening that it wasn't Sin.

But if it was, I was ready.

Punishment wasn't just for outsiders.

Sin would suffer if I got my suspicions confirmed. He could fucking bank on that.

STITCHES

I tied the noose around my neck and let it hang loosely down my bare, tatted chest as I stared at myself in the mirror. I didn't even need to wear makeup. The dark circles beneath my eyes already made me look like I was dead.

Sleep kept evading me. All I could think about was my sweet angel getting fucked in front of a roomful of twisted bastards and how I'd had a hand in it.

I'd never be able to forgive myself for being so fucking weak when she'd needed me most.

I hadn't protected her the way she deserved, and for that, I needed to repent.

A tear slid down my cheek, and I quickly wiped it away. The music was already pounding out around me. We had this party every year. They always let us. Like anyone was brave enough to tell us no.

Or at least that was what I'd always thought.

Now, I assumed Church just got us special privileges because of our father and no one wanting to tangle with Everett. Who knew. It was up in the air. It could all just be some elaborate fucking way for Everett to dig his claws deeper into Church. Like give him free rein to show him what power was like so he'd appreciate it and bow to Everett's will once everything was taken away.

I'd become paranoid lately.

It wasn't hard to see why when one becomes a player in a game of *who can fuck who* the worst.

All I knew was that once I was given the chance, I was going to tear Sully's head off his fucking shoulders and feed his dick to Everett. . . . after I'd made him watch me tear apart whoever was behind that mirror.

I wasn't going to let some sick assholes run around with the memory of my angel in their head like that. Not. Fucking. Happening.

I knew I couldn't stay holed up in my room all night. Figured I'd go as what should have been. Me with a noose around my neck and completely dead. I wasn't far off. I was definitely dead inside now.

The thought of being face to face with angel after the shit we'd been through made me sick. My biggest fear was that she hated me for all of it. I was the one to undress her. To hold her there. I was to blame. I hated myself. Fuck, I hated myself. The very real idea of lashing my noose back to the bar in my closet played on repeat in my head.

"Stitches? You coming?" Ashes stepped into my room in a fireman's uniform. Chest bare with a fireman jacket and pants on.

I let out a soft laugh. "You're going to drive the remaining sanity out of all the bitches coming tonight."

He offered me a sheepish grin. "The only girl I care about is Sirena. The rest can go to hell for all I give a shit."

"Well, you look good. She'll love it."

"I hope so. I feel sort of dumb though. Like I'm a thirst trap or some shit."

"Or like you're an extra for Magic Mike. Which isn't a bad thing." I tried to fix a smile onto my face.

He let out a chuckle before shaking his head. "You don't need to fake with me, Malachi. I know you're struggling."

I swallowed hard. "I am, but I'll get through it. I always do."

"You promise you're OK? I worry about you."

"I'm fine. Or I will be. I just need some time. That's all."

"Promise to talk to me when you need to though, OK?"

I nodded. "Promise."

"And this whole Sin thing?" He winced.

I licked my lips, the implications constricting my heart. "I really hope he didn't do this."

"He had all the motivation in the world," Ashes murmured.

He did. I knew he did. He'd been through hell with Isabella. I knew how he was. He'd shut down and decided he wasn't worth shit and refused to believe otherwise. That may have been all the motivation he'd needed.

Fuck, please. Please don't let it be Sin who did this.

"I know," I said. "But I really fucking hope he's innocent. . . it would crush me if he wasn't."

"Me too." Ashes sighed.

We were both quiet for a moment before Ashes spoke.

"Let's just try to have a decent time, OK? Fuck the rest for now. We deserve some relief."

"Do we?" My mind went back to my poor angel hurting before shooting off to what later tonight would bring if Sin had fucked up.

"We do, Malachi. You know we do."

"Church is going to hate my costume," I said, pointing to the noose around my neck.

"Good. It'll take his mind off other shit."

"I suppose that's a good thing, huh? I mean, this is where I *hang* out. He might laugh."

"You're killing me. Come on." He smiled again and nodded for me to follow him. I did, the music growing louder as we walked into the living room and out to the patio.

The backyard was packed with people in costumes, all dancing and having a good time. Ashes had the bonfire going. The flames reflected in his eyes as he smiled at it.

I clapped him on the shoulder, and he turned his head and grinned at me.

"The noose is a bit much," Church muttered sourly, stopping in front of me.

"Well, *Father Church*, I'd say you're not too far behind," I said, taking in the priest costume he wore.

"I figured it was a good outfit to deal with *sinners*." He looked out to the sea of students. Sin stood off to the side, his hands in his pockets. He wasn't dressed up. He never did for these parties. It always pissed Church off, but it wasn't something we'd ever get changed, so it was a moot point.

"Have you seen Sirena yet?" Cady asked, joining us in a black cat costume.

I didn't spend a lot of time with her or around her, but she was definitely the complete opposite of my angel. I didn't hate Cady though. She was annoying, but I knew she cared for our girl, so I'd tolerate her shit.

"No." Church looked out to the crowded backyard. "Not yet."

"I'm going to put more wood into the fire. Maybe a tire or Danny Linley. He's dressed in a dick costume. That counts as wood, right?" Ashes narrowed his eyes in Danny's direction as he bobbed around in a giant inflatable cock.

I let out a genuine laugh that lit up Ashes's eyes.

It felt good.

I didn't like it and knew I didn't deserve it after what I'd done to my angel.

Swallowing quickly, I went quiet, watching as Ashes went to the fire and began throwing more wood into it.

Church lit a joint and smoked for a minute before he offered it to Cady. She took it from him and inhaled a hit before holding it out to me. Hesitantly, I took it before taking a deep drag. I wanted to be lucid tonight in case shit got bad.

"They're here," Church said.

I followed his gaze and saw Asylum walk into the backyard dressed as a pirate with my angel on his arm and a tiara on her head.

She's a princess.

Her pink gown poofed out around her, the sparkles in it catching in the light from Ashes's flames and her black hair tumbled to her waist in wild waves.

I watched as Ashes stopped throwing wood into the fire and stared at her, his lips parted.

She was breathtaking.

"She looks beautiful," Cady murmured.

"She *is* beautiful," Church corrected her softly.

Cady tore her stare from Sirena and looked to Church and genuinely smiled.

Beat her clawing his face off, which I wouldn't put past her.

"Do you want me to go talk to Asylum?" I asked.

"No." Church shook his head. "Give them some time to settle in."

I nodded.

Good. It gave me time to settle in.

I needed it.

†

I WATCHED HER ALL NIGHT.

She stayed next to Asylum and never once stepped away. While she was near him, I could see she wasn't really there. Her eyes kept darting around as she took in her surroundings like she was looking for someone.

Church and Ashes were both watching her too.

And Sin. . . I caught him sneaking peeks at her from his spot against the patio railing.

"Hey," Melanie said, sidling up next to me in a sexy nurse costume. "I've been missing you."

I remained quiet as she reached for my hand.

I jerked away from her touch and took a step back.

"We can go upstairs. I wanted to give you a welcome back present," she said, closing the distance between us.

"Not interested."

"Why?" She jutted out her bottom lip. "You don't want your dick sucked? You know I'm good for it."

Before I could answer, Melanie was shoved roughly aside. She let out a cry as she stumbled in her high heels.

"Back off, bitch," Cady snarled. "He's taken."

I expected Melanie to bounce right back and attack. Instead, she sneered and gave Cady the finger before turning and marching away.

"How the hell. . .?" I murmured.

"I can pick a bitch out a mile away, and that girl is a raving one. I'm not going to have my sister deal with that. Next time, and let's hope there isn't one, you stop that shit before she touches you. Got it, pal?" She jabbed her finger into my bare chest. "Or I'll hang you with your necktie."

I nodded, having a shit ton of respect for her. I wasn't the type of guy to hold back when people fucked with me, but with Cady, I was cool with her.

That said a fuck of a lot.

"Now," Church said as he approached us. "Asylum smoked some weed and had a few drinks. Claws, you know what to do."

She nodded and strode away from us. I watched as she approached Asylum and Sirena at the bonfire and engaged Asylum.

He nodded at her as she spoke.

"Think he'll let her?" I murmured.

"Wait for it. . ." Church said.

Cady took Sirena by the hand and led her away from Asylum and up the patio stairs and into the house. She'd go out the front door and take the path to the cemetery from that angle.

"Your go," Church said. "Have fun. Be fucking safe, Malachi. No matter what. Got it?"

I nodded, staring into his eyes. "I will. No worries."

"Well, I am worried. Please," he whispered.

"Dante, I'll be OK. I promise. This noose is just for show."

He offered me a sad smirk before I couldn't handle the disappointment lurking in the depths of his green eyes.

All of this shit was fucked-up. I hated it.

Someone was going to pay dearly. Not that I could blame anyone for my own disorders, but it would sure be nice to nail someone's ass up for fucking with my angel and putting her through hell.

Angels should never go through hell. Hell was made for demons like us. Not pretty little angels.

I approached Asylum as he peered into the dark forest beyond the bonfire. Ashes had given me a tight nod before he'd left to join Church. Sin stood on the edge of the party talking to Bryce, which I found odd, but I didn't have time to dwell on it. Bryce was probably just asking for an update on angel since he'd not approached her since her release that I'd seen. It wasn't a surprise. With Asylum guarding her like a fucking hellhound, it was nearly impossible to get close to her.

"Hey," I said, stepping up beside Asylum.

He didn't look at me. "Welcome."

I cleared my throat. "Can we talk?"

"Need to kill some time?" He turned and raised a brow at me.

"I-I just wanted to talk about what happened at the facility—"

"She's fine. She's doing OK. She's scared of me a bit, but I expected that given our… history."

"The one where you hurt her? The shovel?" I wasn't sure why I needed to hear him say it, but I did.

"Bingo." He winked at me.

I steadied my breathing. He'd fucking hurt her. Tried to kill her.

"And yet, I'm all about her and want to save her. Strange world, isn't it, Malachi?"

"Get out of my head."

"How about I save us both some time. You think she hates you for what you did to her there. She doesn't. Sirena isn't that sort of soul. She cares for you assholes in much the same manner she cares about me. Or will care about me once I grovel hard enough for her."

"Don't fucking come into her life if you can't make it better, Seth," I said, my throat tight. "She doesn't need any more shit to deal with."

"I'm bringing what she needs," he answered. "And I'm Asylum. Not Seth. Stop calling me that. How can you not tell the difference by now? Do I fucking sound like him? I mean, come on. Even Sirena is able to tell us apart."

"Sorry, you fucking dick slap. What should I be looking for on you to tell the difference? You both have shitty personalities."

He let out a laugh. "You're right on that. We really do, don't we?"

I sighed. Conversations with him exhausted me.

"She's fine. Sirena. She's coping. I'm helping her. She's becoming more comfortable with me. That was part of the plan. I have her intrigued, and God knows she adores Seth, and she won't let him go now that she knows he wasn't the one who hurt her. So I feel confident about our relationship at this point. As for the watchers, she cares about you all too."

"You're still there. With Seth. Part of him or he's part of you," I said. "How will we know she's safe? That you won't do it again?"

He shrugged. "Guess you're going to have to have a little faith that things aren't always what they seem, huh, Malachi?"

Fuck, he was a nightmare to talk to. He spoke in riddles and circles. It made me want to dunk my head in cold water and scream.

He smiled knowingly at me. Add to it the fact he seemed to be up in my head... fuck.

"I want them dead. All of them. Everett, Sully, the men behind the mirror. The fucking orderlies and wards. The nurses. Anyone with a hand in that facility is going to die." He suddenly turned serious and cocked his head before looking to his left. He let out a snort and muttered something I couldn't hear.

"I want them dead too," I said, ignoring all the weird that came with interacting with him. "I feel responsible. When will we do it?"

He snapped his attention back to me, his head cocked. "I like your noose."

I swallowed thickly. "Thanks."

"We should hang at least one, don't you think?"

"I'll hang them all," I said.

He smiled at that. "We bide our time. Dante needs to be stronger. You need to be stronger. Sin needs to come back to you fully healed and Ashes... well, he's the only one who's ready. We can't go in half-cocked. All will come to be as it should be in time. During that time, I suggest you spend it doing what you desire most."

"What's that?"

"Loving my forever girl. She needs all the love in the world right now. She is damaged, and I'm sad to say I had a hand in it, but I don't regret it. It brought us to this very moment where everything is falling into place. As it should."

"How do you know everything?" I asked. "How can you be so sure?"

"Everyone in the world has a gift. Some are talkers. Some are doers. Us? We're seers. *Invaders.* The monsters they don't want you to know about. We slink through the shadows. We *listen.* We watch. We wait. We know. . . but it wasn't always so. It's something that slowly became us."

"And now you're going to save the world," I said, studying him.

He grinned at me. "Malachi. Who said anything about saving it? We're here to fucking destroy *their* world before we rule it. We don't need a kingdom of ash. We still need bodies beneath our feet to stand on. What's a kingdom without a few bodies? They won't see us coming. Imagine being one of the bodies they tread upon and then rising up to take over? It'll be glorious."

"Truly," I murmured as he threw his head back and cackled.

Something about destroying the monsters' world did something to me. I watched as Asylum danced in a circle, his head back and his eyes on the night sky.

Fuck it.

I danced with him.

SIRENA

"I've been so worried about you, Rina. I want you to come home," Cady said as we walked along the dark path. My pink dress swooshed around me. Seth had it delivered to me, and Asylum had placed the crown atop my head with a dark smile.

His touch made me shiver sometimes, especially when his blue eyes darkened and he spoke to the voices. He hadn't really hurt me though. I was beginning to relax a bit around him. He was forceful and rough, but his words tended to soothe those pains he brought, and he always pulled back before he did something bad.

Like push deep inside my body. He'd trembled when he'd touch me before breathing deeply and just holding me.

Each time scared me, but I was becoming used to his outbursts.

He'd bitten me before we'd left tonight.

On my shoulder as he'd rubbed his cock against my ass.

My shoulder was still sore and had bled, but he'd licked it away as he murmured I was his forever girl. His firefly.

And I'd taken it because I was just as broken and screwed in the head it seemed.

"But not our home. I don't think it's safe for us there. Mom and Jerry have been fighting since you left. Mom can hold her own and so can I, but you need help. The thought of that fuck touching you makes me want to set his car on fire all over again."

Asylum said she'd done that to Jerry.

I was proud of her, but I also wanted to scold her for being so reckless.

It had brought her to me though, so I couldn't be bothered to worry about it much.

Cady always fought her way out of everything and came out smiling. This was just another one of those things for her.

We reached the edge of the cemetery.

I shook, remembering what had happened to me the last time I'd been here with someone.

Cady took my hand in hers and pulled me forward through the stones as I tried to keep my breathing even.

"I love you, Rina. So much. I'd do anything for you," she whispered, stopping us beneath the willow. She squeezed my hand as two guys came from the darkness.

Church and Ashes.

"Hello, specter," Church said softly as he stopped in front of me, his green eyes drinking me in.

We stared at one another for a moment, my body acutely aware that Ashes had moved behind me as they sandwiched me between them.

"Leave us," Church murmured to Cady.

"No—" Cady started.

"Claws, do you want us to get an answer or not?" Church asked, not tearing his eyes from mine.

Cady released my hand. "If you hurt her—"

"She likes my brand of pain," Church whispered, his voice trembling as he reached out and thumbed my bottom lip. "Don't you, specter?"

I said nothing as my body tingled.

"Go back to the party and check on Stitches," Ashes said gently.

Cady backed away before disappearing into the darkness.

"Ah, now we're alone," Church said as Ashes pushed my hair over my shoulder, exposing the dip in my dress that displayed my bare back. His warm lips on my skin made me gasp.

"We want to talk to you," Church continued, cradling my face. "We want answers from you."

My bottom lip wobbled as he leaned in, his lips at my ear.

"We'll play dirty if we have to."

I swallowed, my breath hitching.

"I like your dress," Ashes said softly. "You look beautiful tonight, heaven."

I closed my eyes as his fingers pulled the zipper on the back of my dress down. The dress immediately loosened from my body as warm hands pushed it down to a puddle at my feet.

The cold air made goosebumps erupt along my skin. Warm lips met my shoulder. Strong hands held me at the waist.

Ashes.

I opened my eyes to find Church watching me as Ashes continued to kiss along my shoulder. He got to the mark Asylum had left on me and let out a growl before he pressed his lips to it and kissed it tenderly.

"You like when we touch you, don't you, specter?" Church ran his knuckles along my jaw before he wrapped his hand around the back of my neck. A soft gasp left my mouth as he crushed his lips against mine.

It was an old, dangerous dance I knew the steps to.

I parted my lips for him, the butterflies converging low in my guts as his tongue wrestled against mine, his kiss deep and soul-searing.

He pressed my body against Ashes, whose hands and lips continued to warm my skin.

Church bit me much like Asylum liked to. I rested my hands on Church's chest as the coppery taste of blood tainted my tastebuds.

A growl slipped past his lips as he tugged me closer to him, Ashes following behind.

My bra slipped down my arms as Ashes undid the clasp.

I didn't know what the hell I was doing.

So much turmoil raced through me. I had questions.

I needed to stop. I pushed against Church's chest, but he deepened the kiss.

Ashes reached up and took my hands in his and pinned them behind my back after tossing my bra aside, my bare breasts exposed as Church pulled away.

Church went to his knees and lifted each of my feet and pushed my dress aside before he fisted my silk panties and gave them a tug. My body jostled as he tore them from my body and let them fall to the ground, completely exposing me to them.

Ashes tightened his hold on my hands as Church lifted my legs onto his shoulders.

I swallowed hard, knowing what was coming next.

Me.

Church buried his face between my legs and ate, his hands tight around the tops of my thighs as Ashes held me against his chest, my arms painfully pinned.

Oh God. Oh my God.

The pleasure from Church's tongue made my eyes roll back in my head.

I knew I shouldn't be doing this before I had answers from them. Their confirmation they hadn't been involved in what Sin had done to me. That they weren't going to fuck me and leave me in the cemetery alone. That. . . I was safe with them. That they'd protect me from the monsters who wanted to hurt me.

Church's hand slipped from my thigh, his fingers probing my pussy. He pushed inside with one digit before adding another, his mouth making my clit throb with an impending release.

My breathing picked up as Ashes kissed along my neck.

"You're a good girl, heaven. So good. You like when Church does this?" he whispered in my ear, his breathing heavy. I could feel his hard dick against my pinned hands.

I rubbed my hand against his length, making him groan softly.

"You have a secret we want to know," Ashes continued in my ear.

Church nipped my clit, making me grind my teeth. He liked to make it hurt before he wrung the pleasure from my body.

"Can you tell me your secret, heaven? Please? We want to right the wrongs and bring you home to us." Ashes's warm breath tickled my ear as my chest heaved.

I was going to come so hard.

Church slowed his tongue and lazily licked up my heat, his fingers now gone.

No. No. Please. Don't stop. Please. I need it.

"Tell me," Ashes murmured, nipping at my earlobe. "Tell me what I want to know, and Church will let you come in his mouth, baby. You want that, don't you? To fill his mouth with your pleasure?"

I shook as the pleasure Church had nearly brought me slowly receded, making me ache with want.

I didn't know what had come over me, but I needed more of it.

I needed them.

Ashes released my hands and shifted so he was cradling my breasts, my back pressed to his chest and my legs on Church's shoulders as he languidly licked up my aching pussy.

I closed my eyes as Ashes rolled my nipples between his fingers.

"Tell me," he whispered. "I want to see you come for us."

This Ashes was feral. Demanding. Intoxicating.

I wasn't myself. I wasn't this girl.

I shifted, trying to push my pussy closer to Church's mouth as he stared up at me from between my legs, his slow pace never faltering.

Please. God, PLEASE!

"Whisper it into the night," Ashes said, kneading my breasts. "Write it on my palm. Come home to us, baby. Please. I miss you so fucking much."

I wiggled, a feeble attempt at getting more from Church. He bit the inside of my thigh, making my body tighten, before he went back to his languid licks.

Ashes rolled my nipples again, sending a shock of pleasure between my legs.

Church picked up his speed, making my chest heave as he ate me once more. My breathing grew ragged as my impending release teased me. As Ashes pinched and continued to roll my nipples and massage my breasts, his lips at my ear, whispering to me. Begging me to tell him.

I was ready to explode.

Then Church stopped again, making me wail silently in my mind.

"We can do this all night," Church said from between my legs.

I squeezed my eyelids closed, frustrated they were teasing my body like this. A tear worked its way onto my cheek.

"Don't cry. Don't cry. Don't cry," Ashes husked out, giving my breasts a squeeze. "You're such a good girl. You're doing so good, heaven. It'll feel so much better once you tell us. We'll make it feel so fucking good for you. Promise. Just give us a name."

I was on the cusp of screaming it.

God, I was.

Church ate me again, once more bringing the pleasure only to tear it away from me before I could crash around him.

They were torturing me.

I couldn't do this all night.

Again.

God, please.

Languid licks.

Kisses.

Whispers.

Praise.

Again.

Stop.

Again.

Stop.

Again.

Stop.

Again. . .

"Who helped Asylum?" Ashes demanded as Church pushed a digit into my backside, his tongue lashing at my clit, goosebumps rushing along my body as he brought me higher again.

"Tell me, pretty girl, so you can come in Church's mouth. So I can make you come next."

God, please. This was the sweetest torture.

Church slowed again.

I let out a frustrated whimper.

"Tell me, baby. Tell me who did it. I promise you can come as many times as you want once you tell me. The person will be dealt with. We won't kill anyone. Just hurt them a little."

Church flicked his tongue again against my swollen clit.

My body shook.

"You don't have to be such a good girl," Ashes murmured into my ear. "You can be our bad girl just for tonight. Tell me who helped Asylum. Once you do, we'll bury ourselves so deeply inside you, you'll see God, baby. I promise you that."

This Ashes was unhinged and so sexy and volatile.

It scared me, but it made me ache for him even more.

I wanted him.

I wanted them both.

Now.

God, please. What's happening to me?

Church went back to torturing my pussy with his expert tongue and fingers, the pleasure once more rising.

"He wants you to fill his mouth with your come, heaven. He can't until you tell me what I want to know," Ashes said, kissing along my jaw as my head rested on his shoulder, his hands working my breasts again.

My breath hitched as his hand slowly moved down my body and back up again.

"Tell me. Please, baby. I want to make you come too. With Church. Wouldn't you like that?"

I gasped at his words, desperate to experience him with Church.

"You belong to the watchers too. Not just Asylum and Seth. We can take you to God, baby. We can protect you from all the monsters in the world."

A tear snaked down my cheek.

I wanted protection.

"We can love you forever too if you let us," Ashes murmured, turning my head toward him as Church once again worked over my clit.

Ashes's lips crushed mine as Church fucked me with his tongue.

I couldn't do this.

I was a good girl, but I wanted to be bad just this once. I wanted to be free.

With Ashes's mouth still on mine, I grasped his hand and traced the letters onto his palm.

Sin.

He wrapped his hand around mine, a growl slipping past his lips.

Church didn't stop this time.

He flicked his tongue so fast I thought I was going to pass out from the pleasure. I came so hard in his mouth I saw stars as I dug my fingers into his hair and thrust against his face, Ashes's hand around my neck as my body arched.

"There you go. Keep coming, heaven. That's it. Good girl. So fucking good. Good girls get rewarded with us. Fill Church's mouth with it. I want to see it drip from his lips. I want him to never be thirsty again." Ashes's hand tightened on my throat as my body trembled.

I'd never come so hard in my entire life.

My body felt like a bowl of Jell-O as my release ended. Church licked up my pussy once more before putting me back onto my feet.

A moment passed between him and Ashes when Ashes nodded at him.

A hard look crossed Church's face before he turned his attention on me and cradled my cheek.

"You did good, specter. Now, we'll reward you further." He brushed his lips against mine before he stepped aside.

I'd been so caught up, I hadn't even considered we'd been standing on someone's grave the entire time.

Ashes pushed me forward against the tall tombstone, and Church's hand pressed the middle of my back, forcing me to bend over it.

They were going to fuck me here.

I breathed in, hating that I'd caved the way I had, but desperate to feel them inside me. I wanted to forget what happened to me in the facility. I wanted them to take that memory and help me shove it into a box I'd never unlock.

This wasn't who I was.

Or hadn't been.

Church pushed into my body, his hands gripping my hips in a painful hold as he let out a groan behind me.

"Fuck, so tight. So fucking good," he choked out, slamming into me.

Ashes tangled his fingers in my hair and ran his dick along my lips.

"Please?" he asked softly as Church jostled me against the tombstone.

I parted my lips, and he pushed between them, my name falling from his lips as he buried his cock deep into my throat, his fingers tangled in my hair.

And then they fucked me from both ends, neither of them taking an ounce of mercy on my body as they moved in and out of me.

I looked up at Ashes to see his lips parted, his abs tight as he railed into my mouth over and over.

"Fuck, baby. You're doing good. I missed your mouth," he rasped. "You going to swallow for me?"

Church slammed into me faster as I shattered around him, the pleasure so much that tears streamed down my cheeks.

"Fuck, that's beautiful," Ashes choked out. He tightened his hold on my hair and fucked into my mouth, each thrust hitting the back of my throat. I coughed and choked, but he kept at it, his moans filling the night.

Church unloaded inside me, his groan so feral it sent shivers down my spine. His hands on my hips were painful, and I knew I'd be bruised from it in the morning.

"Fuck. Fuck. Fuck," Ashes choked out. "Heaven. Fuck."

He came with a low moan, his cock twitching against my tongue. With each jump of his cock, his release jetted into my mouth.

"Swallow. Fuck. Let me see," he said, pulling his dick from my mouth.

I swallowed him down and opened my mouth to show him I'd done it. He captured my lips with his, his tongue sweeping inside as Church slapped my ass and thrust slowly in and out of me.

I came once more, Ashes eating my soft cry so it was silent.

Church pulled free of my body before he helped me to stand up straight. No one said a word as they carefully dressed me again and placed my tiara back atop my head.

"You're beautiful," Ashes whispered in my ear before he took my hand in his. Church twined my other hand through his, and they led me back to the trail.

It didn't take a genius to know they were angry, and Sin was going to pay.

I feared for all of them, and regretted telling them now.

We reached the edge of the forest, the party in sight, and Church stopped us and turned to me.

"You did good, specter," he murmured, fixing my hair again. "Go back to the party. Go back to Asylum. We'll see you soon, OK?"

I wrapped my hands around his as he made to lower them from my face.

"It'll be OK," he said, his eyes shining beneath the moonlight.

Tears.

He was hurting.

The regret washed over me in a tidal wave, making me gasp for air.

"No tears from you," he continued softly. "This wrong will be righted tonight. Do as you're told. I'll see you soon. Promise." He brushed his lips against mine and stepped away from me.

"It'll be OK," Ashes said as Church pulled his phone out and sent off a text.

I took his hand and wrote a word on his palm.

Scared.

"I am too," Ashes murmured. "But it's OK. It'll all be OK."

Don't hurt him.

I scrawled the words over his palm quickly.

Hurting Sin would hurt them. They were his family. I didn't want to tear them apart. God, I didn't. I'd faltered and regretted it.

"He will pay for his hand in this," Ashes said, pressing a kiss to my forehead. "No one goes unpunished, heaven. No one."

He pulled away from me as Cady came into view in her cat costume, Stitches at her side.

She stopped in front of us and Ashes handed me off to her.

"Make sure she makes it back to Asylum," Church said.

"He's waiting for her on the patio." Cady took my hand in hers.

I caught Stitches's eye. He'd stayed away from me since that day at the facility. Did he hate me for all that had happened? Did he blame me for it? Maybe I disgusted him now.

Cady pulled me away and beyond Stitches.

It was the briefest of moments, but he caught my pinky with his. I turned to look at him as his pinky slipped from mine.

And there it was.

The answer I needed.

Now, to go and pray for Sin's safety, even though he probably never prayed for mine.

ASHES

My heart was broken, my anger ignited.

Sin had shattered it and stomped on the pieces.

We sat in the cemetery after releasing Sirena to Cady. I'd had the time of my life with my heaven, but now reality was back in full swing.

"Did you text him?" Stitches asked.

"He said he's on his way," Church grunted, peering out into the darkness.

We'd spent the last hour out there next to a fallen wooden cross, digging a hole to put it back in.

The plan was simple.

Get Sin out here.

Give him a chance to confess.

Punish him accordingly.

I'd never been so angry in my life as I flipped my lighter opened and closed on repeat. Church paced the darkness.

Stitches fidgeted, rubbing his thighs. He leaned against a gravestone, his leg bouncing as he chewed his nails.

We were pent-up and pissed off. I wanted to know why the hell Sin had betrayed us the way he had.

I breathed out and looked to the night sky.

I knew why. Because he was scared.

But his fear had caused so much more damage than loving Sirena ever could have. And for that, he must be punished.

My hands twitched as I tried to steady my breathing. I let the flame dance on my lighter as I ran my fingers through it on repeat. I needed the calm. Fuck, I was going to lose it.

"Easy," Church said, his hand trembling as he rested it on my shoulder. "Easy, brother."

I closed my eyes and tried to steady my breathing.

Fucking Sin. Damn him for fucking up.

We sat in silence for what seemed like forever. I replayed in my head Sirena's kiss, hoping to calm myself, but it only angered me more because we'd missed time with her because of what Sin had done.

I was going to lose it on him.

I knew I was.

"Welcome," Church called out softly.

I snapped my eyes open to see Sin stop where we were. He wore nothing but a t-shirt, pair of jeans, and his shoes.

"I'm sorry," he whispered.

"How could you?" Church snarled, circling him as I pushed off the tombstone I'd been leaning against. Stitches moved forward with me, and we formed a circle around Sin.

The moon was full and bright tonight. The air was crisp and cool. It was a perfect night.

Except for this.

"I was afraid. I-I still am," Sin said thickly. "I didn't want her to ruin us—"

"*You* fucking ruined us," I snarled at him, kicking dirt at his feet. "What the fuck, Sinclair? Malachi tried to fucking kill himself over this shit. Sirena was trapped in the facility. We lost her to Asylum. Everything fell apart the moment you decided to not fucking listen."

"I know. I-I'm so sorry. Malachi—" Sin reached for him, but Stitches jerked away, glaring at him.

"I don't blame you for my lapse in judgment, but I do blame you for what we endured in that facility. You have no fucking idea what happened in there. *What I had to do.* What I had to fucking witness. For that, I blame you." Stitches spat at him.

It was the first time he'd said anything about his time in the medical wing. I glanced at Church to see the turmoil on his face.

When Stitches was ready, we'd talk it out with him.

For now, we had work to do.

I had a fucking fire to build and a girl to love.

And Sin. . . he was going to pay.

SIN

The pain of their boots was unbearable as I lay on the ground, taking each of their hard kicks to my body.

I'd gone to my knees willingly, ready to just fucking die.

I didn't deserve the next breath my body forced me to take.

I hoped they killed me and turned me to ash so I could join my demons in hell.

Ashes's boot caught my face, breaking my nose. The blood gushed out as Church cracked a rib.

Finally, the torment stopped, and Church fisted my hair and brought my head off the ground.

The beating I'd endured didn't even touch my sins.

I knew my brothers.

This wasn't the end.

I'd endure far more.

"You fucked up," Church said, his voice trembling. "I loved you, Sinclair. You were my brother. My best friend. I'd have done anything for you. You fucking knew that. *YOU KNEW IT! YOU SAW ME DO IT!*"

I wept softly as he shook my head. I could barely see through my swollen eyelids.

"All I wanted was a family. All of us. With the girl we loved. You just couldn't do that, could you? *She's not fucking Isabella!*" He slammed my head into the ground. "We could have had it all, but you fucked up." He slammed my head into the ground again.

I was going to throw up.

I was in so much pain.

"You did the one thing you feared," Church said softly. "You tore us apart. Well, guess what? Now you're fucking alone. I want you to fucking punish yourself for this after tonight. I want to see what we meant to you."

He released my head, and it banged back to the ground before he landed another kick to my guts.

I knew I could have fought back, but I didn't. I let them punish me, and I'd continue to let them do it.

I deserved it. I deserved all of it.

I didn't ask how they knew. I was scared to know.

I laid there as Stitches grabbed rope, praying for death.

A moment later, they were pulling me by my feet across the cold cemetery ground and placing me on something hard and painful. I'd lost my shirt long ago during the initial beating where they beat the shit out of my face with their fists. I'd taken it off to wipe the blood from my nose.

They stretched my arms out wide before lashing my wrists with the rope to the hard wood I was on. Before long, my feet were bound and tied.

Stitches came to my side and leaned down, his lips at my ear.

"She was raped. In the facility. Men watched as she was fucked, Sinclair. They made me hold her down. *They made me,*" his voice cracked. "Fuck you. Forever."

I wept softly as he backed away and left the night sky above me.

Crucified for my sins.

It seemed fitting.

Ashes kneeled beside me next as the sky spun above me.

"In case you're wondering how we found out, she told us tonight.

Sirena. She fucking told us. Guess you should have just killed her to keep your fucking secret, prick."

I wept harder.

I'd broken my own damn heart.

The stars swung above me as I was lifted on my cross from the ground. The guys quickly righted me into the hole they'd dug for the cross. Within minutes, I was hung as they stared up at me, pure loathing on each of their faces.

She'd been hurt. Raped. All because I couldn't deal. Agony tore through me just thinking about her trying to survive it. Trying to overcome it.

It hurt. It hurt so fucking much.

My siren.

I'm so sorry, baby. I'm sorry.

"You're dead to us," Church whispered.

My heart ached at his words, but I knew they were coming.

"May God have mercy on your soul," Ashes said, striking a match, the flame dancing in the night. "Because we fucking won't."

He dropped the match onto the pyre they'd placed in a wide circle around me. It ignited, the heat and smoke making me gasp.

I continued to sob softly as I hung from my cross.

Crucified for my own sins.

I'd lost everything because I was who I was.

I prayed I'd burn slowly.

It was less than what I deserved for what I'd done to siren. To my family. To myself.

I watched through swollen eyelids as the guys turned their backs on me and disappeared into the darkness, leaving me to suffer alone.

ASYLUM

Take her to them. Put her in his bed.

You better hurry.

Fuck off. This is me hurrying.

I'm serious.

Me too. Can't you fucking tell I'm running?

I shoved the voice out of my head and burst from the dark forest and into the cemetery. The fire was growing around the cross they stuck Sin on.

I raced forward and jumped through the flames.

His head hung, his body sagging forward.

Fucker could already be dead.

Better fucking hope not.

Shouldn't you be putting her in his bed?

Shouldn't you be cutting that prick off the cross?

Seth, seriously. Shut the fuck up. I'm working on it.

Work faster.

"Work faster," I mimicked, running to kick the fire out behind the cross so I could drop it to the ground.

Once I had that done, I kicked furiously at the cross until it tilted.

I hadn't banked on so much manual labor tonight. That was annoying.

The cross crashed to the ground, Sin's limp body bouncing against it.

Quickly, I went to him and cut the ropes from his wrists and ankles and heaved him away from the flames.

I got him.

Is he alive?

I checked his breathing.

He was beaten to fuck, but he was definitely alive. I slapped his face and his eyelashes fluttered.

"Hey, you pretty fuck. Welcome back," I said.

He let out a groan. "M-My feet."

"They're a little burned. Nothing that'll kill you," I said, falling to my ass to sit beside him. "I'd be more concerned with the rest of you."

He groaned again.

I admired the job the watchers had done on him. They were my kind of people. I'd probably have lashed him to the cross with his own entrails though. But really, potato, pah-ta-to.

He OK?

He's fine.

Thank fuck. I'll be there in a minute.

Silence descended in my head.

I inhaled deeply.

"It was me," I said. "They made me do it to her in the facility. I never would have. Probably, anyway. At least not like that. I know you keep rolling it around in your head on who touched her."

He stared up at the night sky, his breathing fast.

"It wasn't fun for me," I said, answering the thoughts in his head. He thought I'd enjoyed it. "That's not how it should have been, but it's how it was, so we deal with it and try to move on."

"You're a monster," he whispered.

"Agreed."

He licked his lips. "What now?"

"Well, a promise was made. I'd leave something with the watchers and take something with me. My currency is souls, Sinclair. And I have yours now." I got to my feet and held my hand out to him. "Come. I have someone I want you to meet."

He didn't take my hand for a moment. "I-I. . ."

"Do you want to be alone out here? I'll leave you if you wish it. But I'd really rather you get on your fucking knees and beg me to make it right."

He whimpered and took the hand I offered him. I pulled him to his knees and stared down at him. Waiting.

"Please," he wept softly. "Please. H-Help me."

I hefted him up, and he sagged against me.

"Making deals with a devil, Sinclair. How brave," I said softly into his ear.

He sobbed softly against my shoulder.

"Come." I led him away from the dying fire and to the tree line.

"Where are we going?" he mumbled, wiping at his eyes.

"I told you. I have someone I want you to meet. You've been wondering how I do what I do. We're friends now. I tell my friends my secrets."

He grunted. "You're nuts."

"Am I?" I laughed. "Or is that what we want everyone to believe? We're gifted, Sinclair. *Don't get the wires crossed.*"

We were quiet as I helped him to stand.

"I hurt," Sin said, his voice trembling. "I just want to sit."

"He's coming," I whispered, ignoring Sin's words.

I felt him nearby.

"He's almost here."

Sin let out a shaky sigh. He thought another personality was going to burst from me. I chuckled at that.

A twig snapped.

A pine tree's needles trembled.

And then. . .

He stepped out of the woods.

"What the fuck?" Sin choked out, shaking violently against me.

"Sinclair, I'd like you to meet Mirage."

Mirage stepped forward as Sin collapsed to his knees and stared up at him.

"I-I don't-don't understand," Sin rasped.

"I am me, he is he, we are we," I said softly as Mirage bent so he was eye level with Sin.

"And *we* have a lot of work to do," Mirage murmured, reaching out to cradle Sin's face. "Get ready. It's going to get rough."

Indeed it fucking was.

I couldn't wait.

ASHES

I stared down at Sirena in my bed, her black hair spilling around her. Her eyes were closed as she slept. I had no idea how she'd gotten here.

I looked to the bedside table and saw a small envelope.

I reached out and opened it and found a handwritten letter inside.

Ashes,

I'm truly sorry for the agony you're in and sorry it has to be this way. I've found that life gets better after the pain, as is the case with us and Sirena. I never thought I'd have her back in my life and now look. Here she is.

The same holds true for Sinclair.

We'll keep him safe.

You'll keep her safe.

And when the time is right, we'll burn this place to the ground and make love to her in the ash and rubble left behind.

Consider this a promise partially fulfilled. We have returned her to you as promised, and we have taken something in return.

We'll see you soon.

Seth

PS Tell Stitches it's OK to not be OK.

I folded the note up and placed it on my table and climbed into bed. I hauled Sirena gently into my arms and held her tightly, crying softly against her.

I must have woken her, because her warm hand took mine and traced words onto my palm.

It'll be OK.

"Promise?" I whispered into the darkness.

She turned and faced me in bed and brushed her lips against mine.

"Promise," she whispered against my lips.

That was all I needed to hear.

I closed my eyes and held her tightly, everything in the world a complete disaster, but I had her. *We* had her.

And right now, in this moment, she was all that mattered.

The rest of the world could burn for all I cared.

And who knew, maybe I'd set it on fire.

To Be Continued in Stitches: The Boys of Chapel Crest
Please consider leaving your review.

Need more from my world? Check out Black Falls High and Kings of Bolten. Both are dark reverse harem series. Black Falls High has a college series that directly crosses over into Kings of Bolten in a HUGE way.

ACKNOWLEDGMENTS

Thank you to my alpha readers. They're always on top of things and ready to rock and roll.

Thank you to my ARC readers, street team, TikTok team, and readers. You guys make it possible.

Thank you to Charlotte for all her hard work. She's really incredible.

Thanks to Mr KG for pretending he can't hear me when I say it's movie night just so I'll work on my book instead.

And...

I'm SUPER sorry about Riot's dad and what I'm about to do.

I just can't help myself.

ABOUT THE AUTHOR

Affectionately dubbed Queen of Cliffy, Suspense, Heartbreak, and Torture by her readers, USA Today bestselling author K.G. Reuss is known mostly for making readers ugly cry with her writing. A cemetery creeper and ghost enthusiast, K.G. spends most of her time toeing the line between imagination and forced adulthood.

After a stint in college in Iowa, K.G. moved back to her home in Michigan to work in emergency medicine. She's currently raising three small ghouls and is married to a vampire overlord (not really but maybe he could be someday).

K.G. is the author of The Everlasting Chronicles series, Emissary of the Devil series, The Chronicles of Winterset series, The Middle Road (with co-author CM Lally) Black Falls High series and Seven Minutes in Heaven with a ridiculous amount of other series set to be released.

Follow K.G. at the links below and on TikTok!

https://vm.tiktok.com/ZMexyRPcE

Sign up for her newsletter here:

https://tinyletter.com/authorkgreuss

Join her Facebook reader group for excerpts, teasers, and all sorts of goodies.

https://www.facebook.com/groups/streetteamkgreuss

ALSO BY K.G. REUSS

May We Rise

As We Fight

On The Edge

When We Fall

Double Dare You

Double Dare Me

Church: The Boys of Chapel Crest

Ashes: The Boys of Chapel Crest

Stitches: The Boys of Chapel Crest

Emissary of the Devil: Testimony of the Damned

Emissary of the Devil: Testimony of the Blessed

The Everlasting Chronicles: Dead Silence

The Everlasting Chronicles: Shadow Song

The Everlasting Chronicles: Grave Secrets

The Everlasting Chronicles: Soul Bound

The Chronicles of Winterset: Oracle

The Chronicles of Winterset: Tempest

Black Falls High: In Ruins

Black Falls High: In Silence

Black Falls High: In Chaos

Black Falls High: In Pieces, A Novella

Hard Pass

Kings of Bolten: Dirty Little Secrets

Kings of Bolten: Pretty Little Sins

Kings of Bolten: Deadly Little Promises

Kings of Bolten: Perfect Little Revenge

Kings of Bolten: Savage Little Queen

Barely Breathing

The Middle Road

Seven Minutes in Heaven

Printed in the USA
CPSIA information can be obtained
at www.ICGtesting.com
LVHW040058170624
783212LV00005B/472

9 798989 479450